D1248688

Chelynne

Chelynne

by Robyn Carr

LITTLE, BROWN AND COMPANY BOSTON TORONTO

FIRST EDITION

The author wishes to thank the members of the San Antonio Writers' Guild for their support and encouragement during the writing of this book.

Library of Congress Cataloging in Publication Data

Carr, Robyn.
Chelynne.

I. Title.
PZ4.C3126Ch [PS3553.A76334] 813'.5'4 79-23759
ISBN 0-316-12971-2

BP

Designed by D. Christine Benders

Published simultaneously in Canada by Little, Brown & Company (Canada) Limited

PRINTED IN THE UNITED STATES OF AMERICA

For Brian and Jamie,
with love

Chelynne

ONE

COACH AND EIGHT approached Welby Manor. Two grooms held on to the back with determination and several horsemen rode as escort. On the landing in front of the grand manor house the baron waited anxiously for this passenger's arrival. As the coach slowed to a stop, the footmen bounded from their station and rushed to have the door opened for the traveler.

At last the coach came to a complete stop and Lord Mondeloy sucked in his breath in anticipation. The door opened and a small gloved hand reached out to touch lightly upon the footman's as the woman within prepared to disembark. With the grace of a goddess and the regal affectations of a queen, her foot found the stool and then the ground.

Sheldon Mondeloy caught his breath as he beheld the beauty of the young woman before him. He had but an instant to light his eyes on her lovely face before she dropped into a deep curtsy.

"My lord," she greeted him with a voice soft as satin.

He broke into a broad grin and bowed. "My lady," he acknowledged.

She straightened and held her hands clasped in front of her while he appraised her beauty with a smile. Small and fragile in appearance, she greatly resembled her mother. The squareness of her jaw and the thinness of her lips were not part of her maternal heritage, but the soft brown hair streaked with blond and the finely arched brows were her mother's. It was as if the years had disappeared, as if Madelynne stood before him now. She was positively breathtaking.

Sheldon felt a strange catch in his throat and his vision began to blur as if he had tears in his eyes. He held open his arms to her and it was much like freeing a bird from its cage. She squealed with delight and flung herself on him, he lifting her clear of the ground in a hearty embrace and she clinging to his neck, wild with happiness. When she was on her feet again she giggled.

"Ravishing," he muttered. "You are ravishing! For a moment I thought you'd forgotten your uncle."

"I thought I'd never get here," she chattered. "I thought I'd die it took so long to get here! I've missed you so, Uncle Sheldon. Oh, it's so good to be home!"

He laughed at her enthusiasm. "Shall we stand out here all day or may we go inside now?"

"Carmel? Is Carmel still here?"

"In the stable," he replied, speaking of the mare he had gifted her with some years ago. "Not as frisky but still a fine mount. Surely you're not ready for a ride so soon after you've arrived."

"As soon as I might. I've been bound to the busk and the needle all winter, as you should know, since you bound me to them!" Her face formed a pretty little pout and then she smiled again as she stepped inside the entrance hall. Whirling around with childish abandon and flinging her plumed hat into the air, she lost all resemblance to a carefully groomed aristocratic dame. Sheldon caught her and stilled her some small bit. She was in a delirium of happiness in coming home.

"Chelynne," he ordered. "Calm down. Has all my effort in seeing you educated gone to naught? Must I send you away to yet another grande dame for training?"

Her expression grew intensely solemn. "My lord, I quite forgot myself. I humbly beg your indulgence in this simple maiden's brain of mine. It seems I've let myself forget all good breeding and social courtesies. I yield to your pleas and will find solace in my stitchery, penance for my misbehavior, if you'll be so kind." She fell into another curtsy and sank so low her nose nearly touched the shining floor. A broad smile covered Sheldon's face. Every inch of her cried woman, but there was still that child, that carefree immature little girl, and he loved her beyond his life.

He covered his smile as she rose, and held out a hand to her. She lightly rested her fingers in his and he brushed a kiss on her hand. "Very well, madam. If you will go to your rooms and freshen yourself for tea, there are some matters we must discuss."

"Of course, my lord," she simpered. "By your leave." She curtsied.

He gave a nod of his head and she practically swayed to the stair, her skirts swishing in a rhythmic pattern with the small steps she took away from him. Her hands lightly lifted the heavy folds of her skirt to just the top of her tiny slippered feet and she took two very careful steps upward. Then with a shriek of giggles she raised her skirts above her knees and dashed up the stairs two at a time.

Sheldon shook his head in happy exasperation. She might as well be clad in breeches for all the womanly grace she displayed. But he wouldn't change one inch of her. She was exquisite, elemental.

An older woman struggling through the door carrying a valise and two hatboxes caught his attention. She was grunting and frowning.

Lord Mondeloy bowed to the woman, but she did not curtsy. Another grunt escaped her. "How've you fared on your journey, Stella?"

"Not without a bump or two, I'll have ye know. I hope this marks the end of our everlastin' meanderin', but I know better. This tired old body can't take such movin' and toilin'. And that kiss o' fire you've saddled me with is 'bout to make this old heart stop."

"Your disposition is none the worse for it," he teased.

"I'll get her bathed and dressed, m'lord, and send her down for a space o' time with her kin."

"Is there not a groom to bring those things about for you, madam?"

"Aye, the bulk of it's in the cart and some brawny lad will drop it and strew it around a bit 'fore it gets to me." She grunted again, looked up the stairs to where she assumed her mistress had gone and then back to Lord Mondeloy. "She's grown up fine, m'lord."

"Aye, but not quite grown up, I think."

"What she's left to do she can't do alone, m'lord," the older woman advised.

He laughed, catching her meaning at once. "And is she ready?"

"More than you think to look at her, m'lord."

He raised one brow and peered at the woman suspiciously. "Would there be something you want to tell me, Stella?"

"Not I, m'lord. I won't be sayin' nothin' but that I think I know the reason we're home again, that's all."

"And does Chelynne guess?"

"If she does she hasn't let on." That said, she stamped up the stairs, leaving Sheldon to stare at her back. Stella had tended Madelynne from her birth to her death and took over with the only offspring: Chelynne. Stella would feel as if this child were her own, having had her since the day she was born. There had never been any doubt in Sheldon's mind when his brother and sister-in-law had both died that Stella would continue to care for Chelynne. He was the guardian and protector of the child, but Stella was the parent.

Sheldon went to his study and took a seat behind the huge desk. A maid brought a steaming pot of tea and cups a short time later and still he sat, impatient for Chelynne. He opened his desk and took out a gold ornament attached to a long, rather frayed ribbon. It was a bookmark, weighted down by the heavy gold disk that was almost as large as an egg. He kept it in the drawer of the desk when he was at home and carried it with him when he was out. He opened the disk into two halves and looked within to a tiny miniature portrait of Madelynne, the face so like Chelynne's, and sat in quiet musing.

He looked up to the study door and the portrait came to life. She stood there looking at him, that sweet seductive smile, the fine, delicate oval face surrounded by honey-colored curls. For a moment he was oblivious to reality. If he hadn't recovered himself he might have risen and kissed that lovely mouth. Instead he smiled. "Come in, my dear."

Chelynne took the chair in front of Sheldon's desk and perched on the edge. She poured for them both. "You got away from Stella quickly," he remarked, taking his tea from her.

"I tried. She said, 'If his lordship finds fault with ye, ye won't be puttin' the blame to me. It's like trying to brush down a horse while ridin' it.' " She finished with a giggle and covered her mouth guiltily, remembering he wished her to act like a lady now. "Where is Lady Eleanor?" she asked out of politeness.

"She'll be down later. She's resting. I'm pleased, Chelynne." He smiled. "You're looking fit. I've waited a long time to have this talk with you. You won't be going away again." She smiled happily. "But neither will you be staying here." Her mouth drooped abruptly. "If you had to decide, right now, what you would do with the rest of your life, what would you say?"

She thought for a moment, closing her eyes in concentration. She loved little games like this, guessing games, pretending games. "I would choose to be the Queen of England," she mused aloud.

"Will the countess of Bryant do?"

"Gracious Lord," she murmured, aghast. "You've gone and done it! You've married me off!"

He couldn't help his laughter. "It isn't done yet, Chelynne. Had you given any thought to your plans? If there's some other gentleman that's met your fancy, I'm willing to . . ."

She shook her head negatively but the dumbfounded expression remained on her face. She couldn't speak.

"Chelynne, are you concerned about my judgment?"

"Of course not," she whispered. "It's just that . . . well, I hadn't thought so soon. . . ."

"I'm not throwing you to the lions, my dear. A young bride is the best bride and you're more than ready to be making a match. I could have seen it done years ago, but once you're promised the wedding will follow soon."

The titled name stuck in her mind and she had a picture of an aging earl, wrinkled and thin, taking her away from home. She swallowed hard and shuddered.

"His father is coming here to negotiate the dowry and have a look at you. The earl ages and you will wed the heir to that family seat. There is a great deal of wealth there. We're most fortunate that he will even consider you."

"Why would he even consider me?" she asked stupidly.

Sheldon smiled proudly. "Because I boasted the land I offered as your dowry to be valuable and fertile and you to be the most beautiful woman in England. Neither is even slightly exaggerated."

"Did my father leave a dowry?"

"Your father left you only your uncle, love. I'm afraid there is nothing but that gold coin that your mother wore about her neck and this small portrait of your father."

Some of Chelynne's acquaintances had married even younger than this, going off to isolated manor houses in the country to bear brats for doddering old knights and barons. Even though her uncle had not described him, she could envision the groom. He would be a silly old man or imbecilic young gallant with skinny legs and a long nose. To a man like her uncle, a good match meant money and prestige. Title was all the mode.

"I imagine he is rich," she thought aloud.

"Rich? He is richer than his own father, whose title and money he will inherit. I met him a few years ago and I gather he's acquired much wealth since then."

"And thin," she guessed.

"He's a fine figure," Sheldon laughed. "I've had your best interest at heart, darling, and I don't mind telling you it's a great deal easier to get you wed than that fop of a son of mine. I'll be fortunate to find a woman who will have Harry."

Chelynne smiled at this open slander of her cousin. It was music to her ears for she had never liked him. Tolerating him was a chore she was obliged to do for Sheldon's sake. Harry was doted upon by his mother, and Sheldon's attentions toward Chelynne caused no small amount of chafing in this household. If she had to wed someone like Harry she would slit her throat.

She cringed unconsciously at the thought, a grimace growing on her pretty face. "Chelynne, does the thought of marriage truly distress you?"

"I fear it does," she said honestly. "I hadn't thought on it and now that it's here . . . it frightens me."

He frowned. "Then perhaps you are not ready, but your years will not allow us to wait. The earl is not a patient man when he's made his mind."

"But he hasn't made his mind yet, Uncle. Perhaps when he sees me he will —"

"Chelynne, when he sees you it will be all I can do to prevent him from taking you away on the spot. Now calm down, darling, there's nothing to fear. Your mother was married at your age and she did fine."

"Will . . ." The words seemed frozen in her throat but she pressed them out quickly. "Will he keep me with him from the wedding day?"

"Of course," Sheldon answered in astonishment. Then Chelynne's eyes went quickly to her lap and Sheldon knew what she had intended to ask. "There will be no delay in the consummation, sweetheart. I don't think you need fear it. As I said, I met the man and he appears to be a gentleman. It has to happen sometime, Chelynne."

She gulped and Sheldon laughed. "There will come a day, dear child, when you will laugh at yourself for this fear. I expect you'll be round with babe in no time and wonder what you shied at."

Oh, God, it was too much. She hadn't even settled herself on the act and he had her delivering a child. Her complexion lightened to a pale ivory, the pink gone from her cheeks. Sheldon noticed but disregarded her reaction.

"Your mother lived in a different age when her marriage was arranged. You've never been to court. I purposely had you reared away from it and the reason is this: I find most of their habits morally corrupt. It is the fault of arranging marriages in which no romance is possible. I did not interest myself solely in the title of the man or his wealth. My major concern was with his character and personal habits. I would have you wed a man you could love, hold faithful to, and cherish for all time. I see those possibilities in this match. I have selected a man you should find little fault with."

"How soon?"

"The earl will visit us within the next two months and no doubt the wedding will follow shortly. Accept this graciously, dear. You might be nervous but I trust you to conceal it well. My mind is made."

"Yes, sir," she murmured, feeling a little dejected now.

"You'll have a fine title and will be presented at court, darling. There are advantages to marriage."

Her face brightened some small bit. Yes, there were advantages, she thought. She had spent years visiting other noble families in and out of England. Grande dames filled her head with the glamorous stories of being in the company of the king and queen. As any child would, she began to turn her head to other thoughts, a handsome husband, a position at court, gowns, jewels, money . . . she smiled at Sheldon.

"That's better," he approved. "You'll get used to the idea."

It was a long while later that she left her uncle's study. They had talked of other things, theirs being a relationship closer than that of most fathers and daughters. He doted on her, but in respect to her dead parents, took the responsibility of seeing her brought into womanhood with the greatest of care. She had never doubted his devotion and, because of this gentle man's dauntless love, she had no longing for truer parents.

Welby Manor was nearly perfect for her. The only imperfection was the lack of love she had from her aunt Eleanor. And of course Harry. But Chelynne had Stella's love and did not crave any more maternal devotion than that. She had long ago accepted Eleanor's cool attitude toward her. The woman was always cross and insulting except when she came into contact with someone of a higher social station, and then she was unnaturally flattering and pretentious. Sheldon seemed to have a hard time controlling Eleanor's actions, but when it came to the treatment of Chelynne, Lord Mondeloy found the limit to his tolerance. Eleanor was not allowed to abuse this young niece, not even with a harsh word.

Harry was much worse. His hostility and jealousy were open. He and Chelynne had been squabbling for years whenever they were in the same house. In deference to her uncle, Chelynne avoided that contact, keeping herself as far from her cousin as she could.

On her way to her room she saw the tall straight back of a servant as he carried a tray toward the stairs. She stopped and cleared her throat. He turned, looked her over, and a slow smile spread across his face. "So good to have you home, my lady," he said with a slight bow.

"You're looking fit, Gordon," she replied.

"No longer a little girl," he commented. "A woman now. Was your journey pleasant?"

"Not nearly swift enough."

"Is that for my mother?" came a voice. The butler nodded to the young man just descending the stairs.

"Aye, sir. I'm taking it to her now."

"Then do it! What're you waiting for?"

Gordon, tall and broad with a bit of gray at his temples, nodded again. "Just a word of welcome to my lady Chelynne, sir."

"Ah yes, her royal highness." Harry bowed. "Come home for tidings of the match of the century."

Chelynne stiffened. Raising her chin, she passed Gordon and maneuvered her way past Harry on the stair. "Nice to see you again, Gordon."

"We've sorely missed your laughter here, my lady," the butler murmured as she passed.

"So the pauper princess shall wed a viscount. You certainly don't look like countess material to me," Harry sneered.

Chelynne turned slowly on the stair, looking down at her cousin with a malicious smile on her lips. "Have you wedding plans, Harry?"

He ground his teeth and his superior smile faded. "I haven't found the woman worthy," he baited her.

"Well," she said, looking over his pudgy frame with open contempt. "Should I chance to meet some fair damsel with as much to hang over her bodice as you pour over your belt, I shall bring her to you posthaste."

The young man stiffened with indignation. His paunchy gut was a sore spot Chelynne was aware of. She lifted her chin and walked up the stairs, struggling to keep in her laughter. Gordon was on her heels, delivering a snack to Lady Eleanor. As he passed her at the top of the stairs he murmured, "It'll be nice to have someone around to keep him in check."

"I shall do my best," she returned with a smile.

"Very good, madam," he said as he hastened to his task.

Chelynne spent the remainder of the afternoon in her bedroom. She had many thoughts on the subject of marriage. She had never thought not to marry, but her first experience with love had dawned only the summer before.

It had been Sheldon's decision to send her to other families for her training. Her education was primary and the summer before she was sent to Lord Stelanthope for his wife to take charge of some of her instruction in etiquette and court manners. In her free time, which was not much, she was allowed to ride. It didn't take her long to learn how to quickly lose the groom who attended her on her rides, and she had quite a reputation for her mischief. Before she left she had acquired a reputation for a few other indiscretions as well.

She met a young gardener who worked daily on the manor lawns. He was twenty years old and magnificently handsome. Her young body had barely bloomed with the first flushes of womanhood, physical maturity a thing still happening within her supple young form. Reuben coerced her into a kiss. Though reluctant, she found the joining of two mouths pleasing; the sensation of their lips meeting, touching, tasting, and blending brought the first blushing yearnings of womanhood to her. Soon they became very expert at handling this pleasure. It gave her shivers to think of it even now.

She gave up losing the groom on her rides for sport and started dodging him so she could meet Reuben and spend more time alone with him. She was reprimanded by Lady Stelanthope on this misbehavior and sought other means of meeting him. She slipped out at night to be with him, alone in the manor gardens.

Reuben had long since passed pubescent experimenting, but Chelynne was not aware of his emotional maturity. She was shockingly aware of his physical attractions in a way she couldn't understand. There was something about a simple man bent to physical chores that was so much more appealing than the mincing gallants. Reuben was muscled and lean, extremely handsome and masculine.

The pastime of kissing graduated to touching and his hands brought the most marvelous sensations when he sought out her breasts. Intoxicating delight spiraled through her at the first touch, left her weak and dizzy when they parted, and aching for their next encounter.

Neither of them was satisfied and the true trial came. Chelynne honestly never expected it and she was stunned by the possibility. He wanted her in a hungry way that was most difficult to refuse. He wanted to enter her and be a part of her. He became reckless with desire, begging to marry her and steal her away with him to any corner of the earth. She found it frighteningly impossible to accept and twice as impossible to refuse. It became torturous to be with him and torturous to be away from him.

She thought it a major crisis in her life when she returned to her bedroom one night, disheveled from her appointment with Reuben, to find Lady Stelanthope waiting for her. She was put through grueling examinations to confirm her virginity and sent home to Sheldon. The only saving grace was that the baroness did not give an unsavory explanation to Lord Mondeloy. She reported that they were due at Hampton Court to attend the king and queen and could not take Chelynne with them. Chelynne was simultaneously saved and destroyed.

Now at sixteen years she would be married to one of those mincing and delicate lords. Sheldon thought her distaste with the consummation was from fear. It was in truth repugnance. She couldn't stand the thought of long cold fingers trying to titillate her. She wondered if she could bear her own wedding night. As for being ready, she was never more ready for anything. The spark had been ignited and the flame hid in waiting.

"You're a moody one, miss," Stella remarked some time later.

"Aye, I've a lot on my mind," she sighed. "Uncle Sheldon will have me married!"

"Good, good. And when shall we know the groom?"

"Good Lord, Stella! I didn't say I was about to have dinner. I said I'm going to be married!"

"Aye, lass, and the time is ripe."

"Ripe? How can you say that. Just this morn you accused me of being the foulest-tempered infant you've ever tended."

Stella chuckled at the reminder. "For the most part you are that," she sighed. "It'll take a strong hand to calm you down."

"And that's what I have to look forward to?"

"That and a great deal more. Look at yourself, miss. You've a woman's body right enough and that's what interests his lordship now. He has to see ye wed 'fore ye spoil yourself."

"Oh! What a thing to say!"

" 'Tis truth." The old woman shrugged. "You've heard it before now."

Chelynne fingered the gold coin that hung around her neck. "Was she very much like me?" she asked.

"Who now?" Stella questioned without looking up from her chore of sorting through Chelynne's things and arranging the room.

"My mother."

"Ah, a great deal as I remember her. She was lovely and sweet."

"Undo this dress, Stella. I'll have to get ready for dinner. Was she in love with my father?"

"I guess only she could tell ye that. She was a good wife to him."

"But he was much older, wasn't he?"

"Aye, he was. But a powerful strong man. Much like your uncle, say ten, maybe twenty years ago. Had a fine handsome face for a man of fifty years. Never looked it, he seemed younger. Your uncle was but five and thirty then and they seemed the same in age."

"But was she happy?"

"Never did I know a brighter lass when you grew and swelled in her belly. Her eyes were brighter than the sky. Pale blue her eyes were, with golden bits of sunlight in 'em. Ah, she'd sparkle and shine."

"And this is all I have of her," Chelynne sighed wistfully, touching the gold coin.

" 'Twas a gift from the king. When the times were poor and the king himself had to beg a meal and borrow to eat, my Madelynne wouldn't have that gold used. Aye, all her jewels went to the king's cause, but that piece she saved. She'd have starved 'fore she'd part with it. She held that very piece while she birthed ye, believing it brought her luck. It's brought you luck enough," she finished with a sharp nod.

The days that followed were busy for Chelynne and allowed little time for worry about her upcoming marriage. She took Carmel for long rides. Tailors were brought to Welby Manor to sew for her and turned out a full wardrobe to be ready for her wedding. She dallied long hours in the gardens around the manor house and took refreshments with the servants she had known since childhood. She accompanied Sheldon when he went into Welbering to look at the records, visit the shops, and collect the tax.

Nervous tension mounted again for Chelynne when word came from the earl of Bryant informing Lord Mondeloy of his visit. He included in that message that his son would not accompany him but was due in London port sometime in June after making what should be his last voyage to the West Indies.

Lady Mondeloy made her presence felt in Welby Manor in a way that added considerably to Chelynne's anxiety. She hurried her huge form around the mansion with a perpetual scowl on her face. She worked the servants with no less cruelty than a slave driver and the gardeners labored long hours to meet with her approval. New items of clothing were sewn for herself and her son, though both were already exceedingly well garbed. Furniture was recovered, walls painted and covered with fresh draperies, and brass and silver shined to a high gloss. Every pane of glass was cleaned until it glistened on a daily basis, though the earl would not arrive for some time to come.

Chelynne moved through this madhouse in a daze. She had never known her aunt to display such energy. She sent out invitations to members of the ton she had scarcely met and had many an unused room readied for this grand visit. She intended to flaunt the occasion to the hilt, even though Sheldon had informed her that the earl was ailing and would not appreciate her efforts.

Three days before the expected time of arrival, a gilded barouche sped up the long drive to Welby Manor. Workmen were about the ballroom adding finishing touches to the floor and gardeners were manicuring the lawns. Painters were busy in many rooms and Eleanor was lying on her daybed indulging in a midmorning repast. Chelynne was using this time to ride about the grounds. Garbed in only a simple patterned skirt and linen bodice, she watched from the back of the mare as this retinue approached.

She held her breath as the man in the coach stepped out into the light of day. She almost gasped at the sight of him. He was small of stature and his legs bowed. He was done all in silk from his toes to the delicate froth of ruffles that seemed to choke him about the neck. Even from her distance she could see the jewels that adorned him, stuck in his cravat, just below his knees and on his fingers and shoes. He wore a monstrous wig and his hat sported a loud pink feather. He stood in indecision for a moment, there being no one there to greet him, and then he looked around.

When he turned in Chelynne's direction she could plainly see a long thin nose and high forehead. She swallowed hard. What more could she expect but that her groom be a younger version of his father. She knew at once what she would have for a lifetime mate. She could almost feel his long thin fingers as he pulled away at her clothing and his shrill voice as he commanded her . . . like Harry. Oh God, it would be like Harry!

Lord Mondeloy stepped out onto the landing and bowed, then extended his hand to the earl. Chelynne dug a determined heel into Carmel's side and with a strangled cry she sped away, never noticing that the earl shielded his eyes from the sun to watch her hurried flight. With brown hair flying wildly she floated atop the mare's back, her intention to find the most distant corner of her uncle's land and escape, for a while at least, the very idea of her predicament.

The earl of Bryant stepped into the house with his servants in tow toting his parcels and holding open doors.

"You've arrived early, my lord," Sheldon said once they were inside the huge manor. "I trust your journey was uneventful."

"It was. I'm sure our business can be concluded without much effort." He looked around to see the many servants and workmen and asked, "Have I set upon you at an inconvenient time?"

"Preparations for your arrival, sir," he replied.

"Have you a bed, a desk and a chair that are not being repaired?"

"At your disposal, my lord," Mondeloy replied with a smile. There broke upon the face of the older man a similar smile. There was communication. These two men happened to like each other and they agreed on many subjects.

"Good, that is all I have need of, my lord. When will the young woman be introduced?"

"She's riding and I bid you have patience until she joins us for tea. I would have her at her best appearance for you."

The earl thought for a moment of the young woman he had spied a few minutes ago. She was a lovely, fresh thing, full round breasts, thick flouncing hair, a face pleasant to look upon. "I rather liked her as I saw her earlier," he said thoughtfully.

"She's a willful sprite, my lord," Mondeloy smiled.

"Good," the man retorted, stamping his cane once for emphasis. "Then I'll see my rooms and have a rest before I meet her. Call me early so we have some time together before I make her acquaintance."

A long while later Chelynne sought out her bedroom from the back stairs. Perspiring as no woman of quality should, she gave away her hard ride to Stella at once. Stella waited for Chelynne with a tapping foot and a frown of discontent, glaring her down for her mischief. Stella did not speak, she merely pointed to the steaming tub and the gown laid out for her mistress. With a little pout Chelynne began stripping off the simple dress.

Much activity could be felt about the upstairs of the manor as Lady Eleanor, caught unaware by the earl's untimely arrival, hurriedly had herself prepared to meet him. For all the pains she took with her appearance and selection of jewels, one would suspect she was the intended bride.

Chelynne was pensive and quiet as she was groomed and dressed. A pleasant green was the color of her gown and the style was modest, as befitted a young virgin. The sleeves flared from her shoulders and tightened about her wrists. A bit of gold braid hugged her hips and slipped dreamily under her bodice. No other adornments or jewels were added. Chelynne was superbly figured for her small size, and heavy jewels would only draw the eyes away from her appealing youth and vitality. Stella, who had made the choice, showed a cunning in this that was rare for a woman never married.

Readied, perfumed and only lightly painted, Chelynne rose to posture before the mirror. She would have preferred to be homely. Perhaps then the earl would find the fault and refuse the contract. As if reading her thoughts, Stella lifted her chin with a finger and looked into her eyes. "Your uncle has been good and generous with you all your life and there was no one to order him so. Think hard on your manner, for should you shame him now, 'twould be his darkest hour. I pray you think too, his work is not done 'till he sees you wed, and a country squire can be as dangly and bumbling as any viscount. Take care you do not push him to those ends and give him another like Harry."

The words were full of meaning for Chelynne and she nodded her head in assent, only too aware of her situation. This was her uncle's choice and out of her hands. She loved him true and would not bring disgrace on him now.

As she tapped lightly on the drawing room doors she sucked in her breath and bolstered her resolve. The earl, Lord Mondeloy and Harry were seated and a young maid had only just begun to serve their tea. She curtsied and the earl and her uncle rose immediately to receive her. Harry rose, but he was a bit reluctant and slow. The earl was transfixed, his eyes glued to her in delighted appraisal. At last he shook his head and laughed lightly. "I found your appearance so striking astride I almost feared meeting you in person . . . in your finery. You have not disappointed me, my dear."

"You're overkind, my lord," she murmured, pinkening a little.

"Ah, blush is so desirable on a youth. I will pray that you do not lose it too soon."

He led her to a chair, one strategically lined up so he could look easily at her from his. She tried with her best effort to be relaxed and self-confident, but inside her nerves were wild and her stomach jumped. She sipped at her tea and thankfully the cup did not rattle and nothing spilled. She could not partake of the pastries being offered, for her stomach would never have tolerated food.

The men spoke lightly of politics and Harry appeared bored. He slumped slightly in his chair and huffed a few times. He answered his father with a frown or insolent sneer, but the earl was uninterested.

When Chelynne was beginning to wonder if she could endure much more of this chitchat, Lady Eleanor swirled into the room. The earl was taken aback by her size and heavy raiment. Jewels glittered under her double chin and loaded down her hands. Her bulky form and the heavy folds of fabric that fell gracelessly from her huge hips threatened to spill over furniture as she turned. She was much larger than the earl, larger than anyone in the room. Chelynne had never seen such a sight.

Eleanor extended her hand to the earl to be kissed without the benefit of an introduction. He took it reluctantly and Lord Mondeloy frowned his displeasure, embarrassed by this display. "A pleasure, madam," the earl greeted her, and released her quickly.

Eleanor smiled and batted her lashes worse than any virgin maid. "But the pleasure is mine, my lord," she simpered. She turned slightly and Chelynne had her first glimpse of Eleanor's full face. There were round pink splotches applied to an almost ivory white complexion. Red paint made her full lips even fatter and patches like those she had heard the ladies at court were wearing swirled about her bulging cheeks. She was a monstrosity. It would have been more pleasant to look on the face of an ass. Chelynne was a little afraid she would throw up her skirts and display a diamond garter.

"We've been most anxious about your visit, my lord," she went on. "And we've made some grand plans—"

"I'm here about business, madam. No airs were necessary."

"But I assure you, it was no trouble at all." Eleanor looked around. To her dismay there was only one place she could sit comfortably and still be close to the conversation, and the earl occupied that settee. She hesitated and he shifted before that piece restlessly, eager to be seated. Finally, in resignation, she chose a couch on the other side of the room. It was large enough to accommodate that generous frame, but the distance galled her. She released a little huff as she lowered herself into it and the earl sighed in relief, able to sit again.

Eleanor was given time to be served, to partake of the pastries, and then the earl started his business, without ceremony.

"Now that you are present, madam, we may begin with what I feel will be a very short business discussion between two families. Your husband's dowry offer pleases me, the appearance of this young woman is to my liking, and I have one question for you. Have you guarded the virtue of this maiden with care?"

Eleanor's mouth was full, stuffed with a sticky and chewy pastry. She couldn't chew it and swallow it in good time, so she pushed it to one side of her mouth and answered with slightly muffled speech, "But of course, my lord."

"But it has come to my attention that she has not been under your roof but for token visits. How can you attest to her status?"

Insulted at the insinuation that she was not an adequate guardian, Eleanor gasped and wheezed in a large part of her pastry, choking on her frustrated reply. Lord Mondeloy's voice was clear, relaxed and firm above his wife's choking fit. "I made all decisions concerning Chelynne's travels and lodgings. I entrusted her to the care of her own mother's childhood nurse and took full financial and moral responsibility. An inquiry would show that the nobles she has visited both here and abroad speak highly of her virtue. It is a matter of fact that you need not question again, but we will, of course, consent to an examination."

Chelynne smiled her satisfaction. The earl then turned to the maiden in question. "Do your uncle's marriage plans meet with your approval, Lady Chelynne?"

Though somewhat startled that her opinion would be sought, she did not show the surprise. "My uncle has always acted in my best interest, my lord. I would not question his choice for me."

The earl smiled and turned again to Lord Mondeloy. "What have you done to warrant the trust this youngster has in your judgment?"

"Quite simply, my lord," Sheldon answered easily, "I have never given her cause to doubt."

The earl was well pleased. He had viewed many a candidate for a bride for his sole heir and found the fondness in this family to be a pleasant change. The entire arrangement was favorable, the atmosphere to his liking. He humbled himself and spoke to the baron now as a friend and not a superior. "I would ask your indulgence in one more thing, my lord. Would you permit me the use of your study and a few moments alone with Lady Chelynne?"

"It's most irregular," Sheldon started, frowning slightly. He had no wish to make this more difficult for Chelynne than it already was. Though he admired and respected the earl, he was aware of a somewhat caustic nature and he wouldn't see Chelynne frightened or hurt in any way.

He had started to voice his disapproval when the earl held up a hand, cutting him off. "Let me assure you of my intention, my lord. I have come to the conclusion that this young woman would be a choice mate for my son. The dowry, the bride and all other things meet with my approval. There is but one question in my mind and it is a family matter. I would speak in confidence with the young woman seeking to be a member of our household. I would see her approval to the contract. I will take my son only a willing bride."

There was silence in the room as the men stared at each other in contemplation. "My lord," beckoned a soft voice. The earl turned to Chelynne and she spoke quietly. "If this be Lord Mondeloy's choice for me, you would find me willing."

The earl smiled in warm communication. "Chelynne, you stir the oldest blood with your gentle manner. My dear, I do not question your conduct. I believe you would do all in your power to bring only honor to my house. Would you spare an old man some moments of your time to talk of family affairs?"

Chelynne looked in indecision to her uncle, not knowing if she should answer or if it would be his place, his wish to answer for her. He nodded to her to give her reply and she looked back to the earl with a smile. "At your pleasure, my lord."

"Has the time come that we ask our young to decide on matters such as marriage?" Eleanor cried, aghast.

"In this instance, perhaps," the earl returned, unpiqued.

"In my day that was left up to the elders," she informed him. Then, turning to Sheldon she said, "Isn't that so, my lord?"

The earl looked to Lord Mondeloy and saw displeasure in his eyes. He smiled and said quietly, "Mayhaps they should have asked your pleasure." Lord Mondeloy nodded slightly and the earl extended his arm again for Chelynne. Eleanor was left to huff and grunt in disapproval as they left the drawing room.

Eleanor had long been entertained by deciding other people's lives. She was at her best when she thought she might improve herself in so doing. But this was the one place where Sheldon would not satisfy her whims. He disregarded her harping and meddling. She could do as she pleased with Harry, but Chelynne was always kept out of her reach. She was greatly chafed by this fact.

Chelynne found the earl more appealing as she got to know him better. He was polite and good natured. When they were seated in the study he did not cause her increased anxieties by delay. He broached his topic of concern straightaway. She listened quietly and with interest.

"My son has been most reluctant to marry. I've left him to find a wife of his own and he has failed to do so. Oh, he plays his charms among the ladies aplenty, but without the bonds of matrimony I cannot get an heir. There is hostility between my son and me, Chelynne. You'd be aware of it without my warning. I won't communicate the causes to you now for fear I would alienate you from the man who must have your loyalty without question. He may confide in you sometime. I hope so.

"The time has come at last that I have found an opportunity to quicken my son into marriage. He will oblige me because I have put myself in a position to offer him no alternative, but he will not aid my cause. He must heed my wishes or suffer unhappy consequences. Do you understand?"

It was with a bitter feeling that she understood perfectly. "He does not wish to marry and will not be happy with your choice of bride," she mumbled dully.

"Unfortunately that is the case. But then he has not seen my choice or had the opportunity to make it his choice as well. I am not a foolish man, Chelynne. You are beautiful and innocent. My son is a fine man, honorable and honest. He has a great deal of integrity and pride. You are a like match for a man like that. I think in time he will resign himself to this situation and relax to enjoy the benefits it can bring . . . happily."

"Why do you tell me this, my lord?"

"For the simple reason that should you find yourself beset with an ill-tempered and reluctant groom you would know that it is because of a conflict between father and son, and no fault of yours. I give my son credit, perhaps more than he is due, that he will not cause you pain to do me hurt. It is not his nature to be a clod."

"Is it possible he will still refuse?"

"No, he won't do that now. Had I the time, madam, I would wait upon a more solid reconciliation, but time is short for me. I have had a long productive life, I have slaved to hold that earldom through wars that sent every noble fleeing for his life. My only wish now is to place it in the hands of my heir and see him settled and happy.

"Your future is financially secure, Chelynne. I have acquired a modest fortune and my son has done extremely well for himself. Should you deliver him a round dozen children they will all have sound inheritances. He has property in Jamaica and America and a shipping business that is no small concern. But . . . your patience no doubt will be tested."

"But my lord, with all this talk of ill health, you seem to be more than fit."

"At this very moment I am that. I traveled to an inn not far from here and at the first hint of easing pain I came to see your uncle. I'm allowed some passing moments from my bed, a sudden energy now and then. I shall hasten to my home before I am beset again."

Chelynne felt a sympathy for the old man, thinking of what a burden and disappointment Harry was to his father. She knew no way to convey her feelings so she was silent.

"My lady, I await your consent."

"I . . . I . . ." she stammered, not knowing what to say, since in truth she greatly dreaded this union.

"I suppose I seem a cruel man not to allow you the counsel of your uncle. I know that you trust his wisdom, but this must be your decision alone. This is an age of deplorable habits, madam. Whenever there is marital strife a couple simply separates yet lives in the same house. I scarcely know a man who doesn't keep a whore, a mistress and another man's wife."

To her horrified expression he slammed his hand on the desk and went on, emphasizing every word. " 'Tis truth, by God, and the women have come to the like. I cannot name you one instance that is otherwise."

"My lord?"

"*I* would have it otherwise, Chelynne. I would bring my son a virtuous bride, fair of face and of gentle manner and breeding. I would not sew him into wedlock where there is no possibility of love, no chance of success. What is your decision?"

"You've not found another maiden who interests you?"

"I'm bound to find one with many qualities desirable in a wife. If there is beauty, they are hellish. If there is a kind nature, there is no blood in the name or they have a face no man can look upon. In those rare cases where I've found everything fitting, they've been promised straight from the cradle. No, Chelynne, I've not found one who could hold a candle to you."

"Then I would have a condition to my consent."

He was taken aback somewhat by this. He had not thought her so bold. He braced himself, hoping he had not been too far wrong in judging her to be compliant. "Which is, madam?"

"I would make your son's acquaintance before the contracts are drawn. I shan't judge him on reluctance or courtly manner. I would see only that he is not cruel or violent. I can condition myself to show patience to a reluctant groom, but I will not commit myself to a lifetime of harsh abuse. That is my condition."

She did not falter or stammer and the earl smiled when she had finished. She had a willful nature; this he liked. She was bright, and this, too, was admirable. He had nothing to fear of this condition, for his son was chivalrous where women were concerned. "Very well, Chelynne. We can tell your family that all is done. My son will charm you."

At dinner that night the earl took a seat beside Chelynne and left the rest of the family to shift for themselves. Eleanor kept up a stream of conversation, flaunting the many impressive names she claimed as friends and all the places she had visited. Harry was all but ignored. The earl and Lord Mondeloy simply nodded as they ate.

When dinner was done and an evening libation served the earl was once again bent on business. He related his plans to them as if he were holding court. Though small of stature he had a most commanding manner. "Chelynne and her retinue will come to Hawthorne House in one month's time. She may retain whatever servants she has a liking to and any other wants will be provided. There will be a generous household budget allotted to her for her needs. I have planned a ball, an occasion to celebrate the engagement. Two days later we will marry the couple in my chapel; however irregular, this is my son's most ardent wish . . . and the only request he has made."

"It seems fitting," Sheldon said, sensing the earl wanted his approval.

"Your family will of course be welcome in my home for all the festivities. We will sign the contracts at Hawthorne House when you have arrived. I will leave on the morrow and expect you to arrive as planned, in one month."

"Tomorrow!" Eleanor choked, her mouth again full of food, though dinner had long since been removed. "B-b-but Your Lordship, we've planned entertainment and have guests arriving for the pleasure of your visit."

"I'm here about business, madam. I thought I made that clear."

"But Your Lordship, we've gone to such —"

"Pity. I'd rather you had heeded my message. I said my stay would be short and I wouldn't have you troubled. My health is a scandalous affair and I would save it for the important events to come."

Eleanor almost gagged at the implication. She wasn't important?

"I had hoped to discuss other matters," she managed, still aghast at this breach of etiquette.

"And what other matters concern me?"

"Why . . . I thought . . . perhaps . . ." She stammered and shuffled her words not knowing how to broach the subject she had planned to lead up to with more grace. All eyes were on her, waiting. She raised her chin and spoke directly to the earl, matching his commanding voice. "The matter is my son. I should like to see him put in a position to improve his status. I hoped you would give us some advice."

The earl leaned back in his chair, amusement plain on his features. He stared at the woman in wonder, her gall the most incredible he had seen in some years and her tact virtually nonexistent. He laughed and shook his head, more in dismay than mirth. "Madam, for over thirty years my son has defied my every attempt at helping him. But he has built himself a veritable empire, taking advantage of neither my aid nor my approval. I am not grateful for his independence but I have a great deal of respect for his integrity. He used his head and his hands, madam. That is my advice."

"And sound advice," Lord Mondeloy interjected. "Harry has a future in this land. If it doesn't meet his fancy he has my blessing to set about making his own fortune."

The earl gave a nod and was about to leave the room. Eleanor caught him moments before his escape. "Perhaps you could suggest a suitable marriage partner," she attempted quickly, fearing she was losing ground.

"Certainly, madam," he said with a bow. He let his eyes go over Harry quickly and then turned back to Eleanor. "Before I leave in the morning I shall give you the list of those ladies I have interviewed and rejected."

Eleanor was cut to the quick and even Harry had the good grace to blush. Without further chat he bade them all good night and Harry and his mother were left stunned and helpless.

TWO

UNE IN ENGLAND is a glorious green, a majesty of rich tones spattered over hillsides, split by the shining blue of streams that quench the thirst of hungry crops. Setting the stage for the ceaseless labors of the hot months was a festival, a celebration for the people of Welbering to toast their planting. Spirits rose to a high pitch as all enthusiastically threw themselves into the work that lay ahead.

The lord of these lands attended every celebration, every fair and gathering with pride. He shook the hand of many a yeoman farmer, tousled the hair of the happy youth, and kissed the babies. These were his children in a sense. He could only prosper as they would. Every hand that turned the sod, every back that bent and every body that hauled crops in harvest, they were all his responsibility. In times of joy and sorrow.

Chelynne was innocently unaware of the real beauty of Welbering. She accompanied her uncle when he went into the village and took the happiness of his people for granted. She had visited many other manors, stayed for long months with other nobles both in

England and in France, and never took a very close look at the management of the lands. All that she was consciously aware of was that Welby Manor and the lands around it were heaven to her.

Here she could be a child again. Sheldon had tailors sew an elaborate trousseau for her. Heavy gowns were made from rich velvets undersewn with lustrous silks. Delicate lace adorned them and shimmering studs sparkled about them. Sheer and almost weightless chemises were sewn to her size and tremendous petticoats fashioned to hold out her gowns. Slippers were cut and joined to perfectly fit her small foot. But she found the heavy garments burdensome in the stifling heat and chose instead the simple linen dresses that were cool and light. However much this chafed her pretentious aunt, Sheldon would not have his niece chastened. She was allowed to do as she pleased.

Those whose positions were secure in the manor were a happy lot. The gardeners were content to show her the arts of manicuring the grounds and the pampering of a single rose. The women who groomed the huge home, keeping every speck of dust absent, every metal adornment shining, every crystal shimmering, smiled or hummed as they did their chores. Stella relaxed here as well, feeling reunited with old friends in this setting. When her own labors left her some time for leisure she sought out the other serving women in the huge Mondeloy kitchens and over a cool ale they laughed and exchanged gossip.

There are many pleasures in the life of a young woman gently born. There are also unpleasant things that must be endured gracefully. Chelynne had been taught the management of an aristocratic home, though she had never had the full responsibility yet. She had been cornered in libraries of the nobility and taught reading, bound to sitting rooms to practice stitchery and listen to the idle chatter of old dowagers. Most important, she had learned to appear content with such boring pastimes. Now she was faced with what seemed, in her short life, to be the epitome of unpleasantness. She would be given in marriage to the choice of her guardian.

It was a thing to be tolerated, taking one's finer pleasures in other diversions while minding dutifully the marital obligations.

She would perhaps be allowed to ride or even visit her uncle on occasion to reward her for good service. Since meeting the earl and learning of his son's probable reluctance she discounted any possibility of love in this union. And she reminded herself that love had little to do with marriage. It was the business agreement between two families, the matching of finances to hopefully increase the prosperity of both.

Her belongings were packed and lists made for the long journey to Bryant. Servants had readied every detail and several were chosen to accompany the retinue to Hawthorne House. Eleanor had again taken on the excitement that enveloped her previous to their visit from the earl. She set into motion a great rushing around the house. She was determined to see her son improve his circumstance and in that effort she was bound to play her part to the hilt. There would be visiting nobles attending the wedding and she hoped to win favor for Harry among that elite group since she had failed so miserably with the earl.

Chelynne escaped the bedlam in the house to find some solace in the gardens. She retreated to a space behind a row of rosebushes, taking a brief pleasure in the sweet fragrance that floated through the air. Her nerves calmed considerably, but her respite was short-lived, for a figure passed her way and she saw it was Harry.

"Hiding, Chelynne?"

"Not well enough, it seems," she snapped back.

"My, my, I do hope your disposition improves some before your fine wedding, princess. It wouldn't do to show the earl your horrid manners. He yet has time to refuse you."

"And wouldn't that please you," she said, turning away.

"More than you could ever know, my regal wench. That would be justice indeed."

"You're such a pestilent booby, Harry. Now run along."

"Who do you think you're giving orders to, my lady? I'm not one of your simple grooms —"

"Oh, Harry, leave me alone," she sighed, standing to leave.

"You're mighty full of yourself now, aren't you, Chelynne? Now that my father's got you a fine marriage, you really think yourself a queen. You no more deserve what you're getting than Monmouth deserves the crown!"

She stopped dead in her tracks and turned slowly to look at him. She knew well enough that Monmouth was the king's bastard son. "Does it pain you so much to see me prosper, Harry?"

"And why shouldn't it," he sneered. "My father dotes upon you and takes no notice of his own heir. One would wonder who means more to him."

"Perhaps if you would show your father some respect he would find the cause to work on your behalf. As it is, I imagine he can't see the need."

"The pox on you, you little witch. God, how I wait upon the day the wind goes out of your sails! It will come, dear, mark my words. It will come, and when you feel the full blow of it, you'll be doing dirty sheets for your living!"

"Harry, I'm in no mood for your trifling games. What lecherous scheme occupies you now?"

"Scheme? Why none, princess. I wouldn't play games with you. But someday the truth will out on who you are and whence you came. Then we'll see what grand favor you have."

"What the devil are you talking about?"

"Such sweet innocence, Chelynne. Don't you know what went on at the Hague when your parents were there?"

"I don't know what you're talking about."

"So, you've been protected from that as well. The truth is, sweet Chelynne, your mother was not so virtuous as you think. Rumor has it she kept most eminent company . . . favored by Charles, himself."

Chelynne shrugged, unperturbed. She was aware of that. Harry looked at her and began to laugh at her innocence. "Oh, Chelynne, you foolish little girl. You don't even suspect, do you?"

"What?" she asked dully.

"Don't you wear a coin of sorts about your neck? One that the king gave to Madelynne?"

"Yes," she replied, touching that piece unconsciously.

"Whatever do you suppose prompted him to give your mother that coin?"

She scowled angrily. "What slander do you lay to me now, you mangy goat?"

He laughed happily at her anger. "Slander? Slander is a lie, I speak only the truth. And the truth is, were my uncle not a fair and tolerant man, you would be called bastard."

She shrieked in anger, stamping her small feet in a furious rage. "You'd stoop to the very gutters to cause me pain with your lies! Abominations, all! Sheldon will have your head for this!"

"Tsk, tsk, princess. You should know by now there's little my father can do to hurt me. What could he do but free me from the millstone of this land? I want nothing to do with it anyway. But he'll not punish me for this. He cannot."

"My mother was a virtuous woman," Chelynne ground out. "How dare you slander her good name while she lies at rest in her grave. I promise you, Harry, for this I will see your nose slit!"

He shrugged, unafraid. "I doubt that, Chelynne. No matter, you shall have the doubt while I have the certainty of my true parentage."

"Of course you do," she simpered hatefully. "Who but her own husband would ever touch Lady Eleanor?"

Harry's face reddened and his jaw set. Chelynne stuck out her tongue at him, her childish insolence getting the best of her in this situation. She fled from the garden.

As her temper cooled she began to wonder where he would have heard such lies. Servants? There wasn't one in this house who didn't speak admiringly of her mother. She knew Stella would give her life before bringing doubt to Madelynne's virtue. Eleanor was a good possibility, but to have Sheldon's wrath for such an action would likely keep her quiet.

Chelynne sought out her uncle's study, empty now while duty took him elsewhere, and curled up in a chair. There was a small portrait of her father, a miniature painted over twenty years before. She studied the face, so like Sheldon's face now. She had been told she favored her mother, but there was no portrait of her. She looked for one of her own recognizable features and saw nothing.

Realizing what she was doing, she damned her vulgar cousin for bringing her to this. He had achieved his purpose, for she was filled with doubt. And she was afraid. What if it were true? What if she were nothing more than the illegitimate whelp of the king? She would have no right to her name, to this marriage, to anything. . . .

She was oblivious to time, still curled up in the chair and pondering her father's face when Sheldon entered. "Has my study become your newest hiding place, Chelynne?"

"This house is a flurry," she said absently. "There's not a corner here that's peaceful."

"My study is yours whenever I have no use for it," he said with a shrug.

"I'll leave you to your work, Uncle," she muttered, starting to leave.

Lord Mondeloy went to his desk, pulled out the papers he needed, and went about his business. Chelynne paused at the door and watched him for a moment. When he looked up again she was still standing there in some kind of indecision.

"Does something disturb you, miss?"

"Oh, a petty problem. I shouldn't trouble you with it."

"Soon enough you will be another man's trouble. Come, sit."

"Have I caused you much strain, Uncle? Truly, you have been most generous and never have I heard your complaints, but have I been a terrible burden?"

He smiled warmly and folded his hands in front of him. "You've been one of the few pleasures in this tired life, darling."

"But it must have lightened your purse sorely to send me abroad so much of the time."

"It was worth every farthing, dear. This house was not the place I would have you raised."

"But why? Why did you keep sending me away again and again? Surely I could have learned as much here."

Sheldon frowned. "I think you can see my reasons if you will, Chelynne. Eleanor has always been jealous of the attention I gave you. She was jealous of your mother and her higher station before you were born. The only one she finds favor with here is her son, and that one treats her with constant disrespect. I sought to keep you out of Eleanor's influence and have you learn of life. Court life is not the most important on this earth, sweetheart. All styles of living can teach you. I can see the maiden before me has not suffered ill from her many travels."

"You were not ashamed of me?"

"Of course not, darling. I'm proud of you. I always have been."

"Did you know my mother well?"

"You know that I did. Haven't I told you time and again how lovely she was, how sweet? She married my brother when she was as young as you. She was every inch a lady, one of the most beautiful women I've ever known."

"Were you with her at the Hague?"

Sheldon nearly blanched, but answered smoothly. "For a time."

"Was she virtuous?"

"Chelynne, what troubles you? Have it out now and be done with it."

"Harry claims she was not. He says I'm not my father's own."

Sheldon's scowl was black and vicious. "That insolent pup! What would he know of your mother? He was an infant then."

"Gossip perhaps," she offered.

"Perhaps," Sheldon fairly snarled.

"What do you know, Uncle Sheldon? Did my mother have lovers?"

"Chelynne, I did not stand guard over your mother day and night. Your parents were married years before your birth. Their marriage is recorded and you were accepted by your father beyond doubt. I stood as godfather at your christening just days after your mother was laid in her grave. Any man who questions your right of birth now takes a chance with his head."

"But I doubt," she said softly.

"Put it from your mind. Harry only seeks to distress you."

"Uncle Sheldon, I must know. Is there any possibility it is truth?"

"Darling, Charles Stuart's reputation was set long before he returned to England. Any woman he showed kindness to would be the topic of gossip for a time. Your parents lived through frightening wars in which all their worldly possessions were lost. Nobles in exile were hard pressed to find enough coin to eat. If your mother's reputation is to be questioned because she took refuge in his court, then there is nothing you can do. Gossip is only as damaging as you allow it to be."

"Then you're saying there is a possibility?"

"Only God knows every exact set of circumstances, sweetheart. But I knew your mother and she was good and gentle. I doubt she had it in her to play your father false."

Chelynne shook her head dejectedly. "I will wonder long."

"Why must you wonder? No one but Harry would dare raise such a question and I vow I will close his mouth. Your name is Mondeloy and you will wed soon, granting you escape from your cousin's cruel tongue. You are aware that your name and station only sealed the contracts. It was your manner and beauty that persuaded the earl, and that no man can ever take from you."

"How gentle is a king's bastard?" she asked softly. Sheldon's face reddened. "You implied it yourself, Uncle. I never mentioned that Harry said I was got of the king . . . but you explained that away carefully. I imagine my question is answered."

He sighed wearily. "It was rumored."

"How many others know?" she asked hesitantly.

"Chelynne, gossip is like illness. When it's covered all the ground it can, it dies away. That was many years ago. It's over now."

"And what am I to do if it springs forth again?"

"Lift your chin, darling, and dare anyone to spill such foul trash about you. It has long since been over."

"Oh, Sheldon, this would greatly shame the Hawthornes. How could my mother allow—"

"Chelynne! Never decry your mother again! I say this to you, and take my words to your heart. A child has no say in his coming to this world. It is only as beautiful and gentle as the love that got it. I knew your mother and she was an honorable woman. Any affection she had, whether for her husband or another, you were born to the name you carry and she would never have had you but for a strong and honest love. That will have to be enough for you to know . . ." And then with a strange tightening in his throat, he added, "For she can never tell us more."

"I didn't mean to anger you, Uncle," Chelynne murmured.

"I'm not angry with you, sweetheart," he sighed. "It hurts me to see this distress brought upon you and the question to your good mother's name makes me burn. All for a foolish youth who drivels garbage! Chelynne, don't let this get the best of you. It will be your ruin if you do."

"I have little choice but to live with it," she said softly.

"Darling, I wish this weren't so, but if that's the worst thing you ever have to live with, yours will be a nearly perfect life."

She looked into his warm eyes and smiled. This gentle man had eased her through this much of her life with love and understanding. She could not leave him now with bitter feelings. She rose, placed a fleeting kiss on his cheek, and wandered out of the room.

Sheldon was frozen in his place, his mind drifting helplessly, the heavy black line between reality and fantasy growing thinner and thinner. He went back momentarily, years before Chelynne was born, to when Madelynne first came to Welby Manor as his brother's wife. There was such a brief time of happiness for her here.

Sheldon, being the second son, didn't stand to inherit the Mondeloy title and lands. He had counted himself fortunate to have Eleanor, who brought money and more land to the marriage.

Not long after Sheldon's marriage, perhaps even because of it, Sylvester took Madelynne to wife. Madelynne's father was a simple knight whose marriage hopes for his daughter had never been that high, so high as a baron. Sylvester was as old as Madelynne's father, but that had little to do with it. He was still a fine figure of a man and had a most commanding manner. Sheldon watched with envy this fine-looking couple. Something seemed missing from their union. Sylvester did not dote upon his beautiful wife and at times seemed to scorn her. But Sheldon fell in love with her the first moment he laid eyes on her.

Then they put their lots with the Royalist cause and ended up fleeing England, grateful for their lives. They sold everything for the king's cause and were left to meander about Europe with other exiled nobles. Both men were hard pressed to care for their families.

Those times were more difficult than he could ever hope to make Chelynne understand. Charles's restoration seemed an impossible dream to them then. Everyone was forced to live for the moment, breathe as if every breath might be the last. It was at the Hague, where Sylvester and Lady Madelynne found refuge, where Sheldon confessed to her that he loved her. She was moved by his declaration, he could see it in her eyes. But she fearfully warned him to put those feelings aside. "Sylvester is a very possessive man, Sheldon. You would see the lash for thinking of it."

"What are you to him, Madelynne? Really, what value does he place on you?"

She laughed a bit ruefully, for she had often wondered that herself. "A prize to look upon, Sheldon," she had replied.

"You've given him no heir," Sheldon ventured.

"There's not much to leave an heir. It is a blessing perhaps that there have been none."

"I think the reason has little to do with blessing," Sheldon accused.

Madelynne's reaction to that was almost angry. She turned away from him and presented her back.

"Come, darling," Sheldon urged. "I know you feel nothing for him, nor have you ever. I see the way you look at me. Don't fight me now . . . now when there's so little time left."

"You take the part of an impetuous youth, sir. I am not a maiden free to be courted."

"Impetuous youth!" He laughed heartily. "At five and thirty years? Madelynne," he said, turning her around to face him. "I am a man and you are a woman. I love you. I want you."

"It cannot be," she murmured. "Never say this to me again, Sheldon. I will not see you lose everything, including your brother's love, for this foolish notion. It is done!"

It was far from done, especially in Sheldon's mind. What he felt for Madelynne then, what he felt even now so many years after her death, was no infatuation. Duties prevented him from being near her often, but that did not cool his affection.

Two years from the time he had first admitted his love, Madelynne delivered Lord Mondeloy a child. Sylvester summoned his brother and bade him act as godfather. No one wondered particularly at Sylvester's mood or Sheldon's melancholy, for Madelynne had died in childbirth. Sylvester's brooding silence was not born of grief, however. Sheldon learned the reasons when he saw the peculiar name given to this child. Sylvester showed his brother the document for the christening as he had had it drawn up. The name was Shelynne.

"I thought it the perfect combination of her parents' names," Sylvester said dryly.

Sheldon frowned his puzzlement. "I don't see," he said.

"Don't you? My vengeance may come late, brother, but it will come."

Sheldon couldn't do anything to stay his brother's wishes or argue the point. Sylvester would not hear his excuses and was determined. Before his daughter passed through babyhood Sylvester died and Sheldon was her guardian. A slight mark on the parchment changed the *S* to a *C*. This new name would not bring implication to Sheldon. And if Charles was implied no one would dare ask. Idle gossip was the very worst result, and even that was quiet and short-lived.

For Sheldon, the part of him that had been destroyed with Madelynne's death was restored when he had total custody of Chelynne. He contented himself with that much of a lost love. Looking at her now brought a heavy sadness to his heart, for she was so very much like the woman he had loved.

"I had hoped it was not so, Madelynne," he said to the emptiness in his study. "But for me it is true. Love comes but once."

The Mondeloy party set out for Hawthorne House as planned. Three coaches, carts carrying belongings and several horsemen made up the long retinue. With every inch put behind them Chelynne dreaded her fate the more. But she was true to her gentle rearing and all doubts and anxieties were covered with poise. She was stunned out of her melancholy at the first sight of Hawthorne House.

The rich ancestral home stood back from the courtyard in majesty. It was fronted by an elaborate water spout and the trees and shrubs lining the drive were carved into intriguing little shapes. Ivy covered the walls and beautiful flowers bloomed before the carefully laid stones. A cherub riding high above a large pond seemed to watch over the ducks and swans that played there. Being married to the devil himself could not have made this an ugly place. It was the most magnificent home she had ever seen.

As their party approached, neatly garbed servants stepped out onto the landing to ease the ladies down and carry in the many trunks and parcels. The earl was there to greet them, bowing to Chelynne in particular and taking custody of her hand for the grand tour. He gave no time for pause but proudly led her through what would be her home. Every room took her breath away, the many fine trappings of this mansion filling her with awe.

With her excitement mounting, he showed her to the wing of the house she would occupy after her wedding. He threw open the door to her suite and she gasped audibly at its immensity. The entire room was done in red and royal blue. A monstrous canopy topped the bed and a stool was placed before it to ease her entry to the resting place. A fireplace large enough to walk into took up the major portion of one wall. The other furnishings — a desk, cupboards, dressing screens, couches and settees — were all done in the French style and shined with a high gloss.

From this room there were many doors. A large set of glass doors opened onto a terrace from which she could view the gardens. Another opened into a private closet and yet another led into an anteroom that could be occupied by her women or later adjusted to keep a child close at hand. And finally the door, the location of which she memorized immediately, that would lead to her husband's room.

A sitting room separated them and oblivious to custom the earl led her through it to her intended groom's bedchamber. This was all done in gold and brown, all the pieces large and heavy and of a design she did not know. There was a cabinet for liquor and a desk and other functional pieces, again the huge hearth and monstrous sleeping place. She noted that there was no footstool to aid him on entering and she had an instant vision of a little man, the size and stature of the earl, making a long running leap into the bed on their wedding night. Hesitantly she asked the whereabouts of his son.

"He seldom confides in me, but he's a man to find duty wherever he is. You could make his acquaintance tonight, if you're so inclined, but your aunt seems to favor having you publicly presented to him at the ball tomorrow night." He shook his head as if exasperated and muttered, "God, but she's a pompous creature."

Chelynne giggled lightly. Eleanor was playing this part out as far as it would take her. This time the excitement of it was getting the better of Chelynne, or starting to. She had never been treated with such importance. The entire Mondeloy party was led to the opposite wing in the tower apartments reserved for guests of special importance. The earl bade them seek out their pleasures as they desired, his home and staff at their complete disposal. But Eleanor was adamant. They would keep privately to the tower and have their meals there until the ball. He argued that the diversions were there for the asking, but Eleanor thought a rest from their traveling more the order of the day.

However womanly her charms, Chelynne was a child at heart. Her young body was restless with excitement and apprehension. Resting was a favored pastime for overweight ladies like her aunt. For a maid in the sixteenth summer of her life, adventure and intrigue were preferred.

Stella settled Chelynne on the bed with a firm hand, insisting that rest was the most important thing now. It was not very long before the aging serving woman filled the room with her snores. Chelynne crept carefully from the bed and rummaged through her trunk for something unobtrusive to wear. Clothed in a less pretentious linen bodice and skirt, she slipped down the tower stairs and went swiftly away from the house.

The stables were not hard to find, but again the grandeur was stifling. They did not appear to be shelter for simple beasts, but yet they were. She had never seen anything so fine, nor so much activity within. Many grooms were hard at work and she approached one as he tended a most attractive mare. She touched the horse fondly and remarked on its beauty and fine lineage.

"One of 'Is Lordship's finest," he told her.

"Might I take her out?"

The boy seemed uncertain. "She's new to us, madam," he stammered. "She's broken but still a bit 'igh strung." He had noticed at once how lovely this maid was and didn't know the way to refuse her without hurting his case with her.

"But the earl assured me I could have the mount of my choice." It was only a slight distortion. He had almost said that. "I am a guest in his household, you see."

"You are one of the bride's party?"

She laughed a little, considering the way she was dressed. She would resemble one of her own servants. And she noted the boy's open admiration. She would probably not get nearly so much attention if she confided that, in spite of appearances, she was in fact the bride. "I am."

The groom was filled with sudden hope. "And will you be staying with your mistress?"

"I shall," she replied with a giggle.

She thought his a fine game, while he thought her a flirtatious maid. He seemed very near saddling the mount for her, but he paused and asked, " 'Ave you the permission of your lady?"

"Of course I do."

"I don't know if I should let 'er out. She's a special mare and 'er spirit is light."

"I assure you I can handle any mount in this stable." It was no lie. She was indeed a fine horsewoman.

The groom bowed gravely. "I offer myself as escort, madam."

"I should better like to go alone."

"It is the rule of this stable. I cannot saddle a 'orse for any woman from 'Is Lordship's 'ouse'old without attendants."

"Very well," she said. She worried with her time away. "But do hurry. It's getting late."

The mare was golden, a mount of fine quality. She wore on her forehead a star and white stockings graced her forelegs. Chelynne loved the horse at once and murmured to her in light, comforting tones. She was called Summer and she had come only a short time before to their stables.

"Summer," she tested. "For your bright and youthful look," she said to her horse. The mare bobbed her head as if in agreement and it set them both to laughing. Chelynne stroked her lovingly, giving her a firm hand and gentle touch, and before very long the horse and rider seemed inseparable friends.

Her young escort thought himself to be well in control of the situation, leading Chelynne down a road that put Hawthorne House farther and farther behind them. His horse was not nearly so young and fine, but he was little concerned with that. His thoughts all revolved around what secluded place he could find and whether or not she would let him have a kiss.

Chelynne eased the mare along carefully, learning her temperament with unhurried grace. Summer pranced a bit, but Chelynne showed her firmly who was mistress of the reins and she quieted again. Her escort praised her control and ability, but Chelynne had almost forgotten he was there. She was completely absorbed in the horse.

The trees that bordered their path grew thicker as they moved farther into the countryside. Mischief sparked her. She saw her chance and took the reins in a determined grip, much to Summer's confusion. A well-placed heel sent the mare bounding off the road and through the trees, leaving a much-bemused groom shouting at her back and trying in vain to follow. She rode in lighthearted abandon, finding this sport of losing an escort even more to her liking in this alien place. It wasn't long before there was no sound behind her and she was shed of him.

Chelynne had an uncanny sense of direction in the out-of-doors. In a mansion like the one she would occupy she could become lost and disoriented in no time, but where there was a sky above and trees all about her, she was at home. The maze of rooms in the manor house was still confusing to her; she was a little afraid to venture through Hawthorne House alone. But that didn't worry her as she rode. She could sense her way.

The countryside was beautiful and the ride refreshing. She found the familiar road and eased Summer into a trot. She wondered if she would find an angry groom waiting or if a party of searchers would have to be sent out to find him. She thought briefly about going after him but a fierce pounding of horse hooves behind her quickly changed her mind.

She turned to see a great black stallion with a rider astride who seemed as large and fearsome as the beast. Instantly afraid of this assailant, she squealed and urged her horse into a faster gait. Summer was tired from her ride and could not best the stallion given any advantage. Chelynne took the only chance open to her and turned Summer into the trees, hoping for escape in the wood. He was close at her back.

Her plan turned to folly as she came through that small copse into a clearing that seemed to stretch for miles ahead. She would surely become swift prey, but not without a fight. When he grabbed her reins, she threw herself to the ground and started away on foot. Ten steps, perhaps twelve, were taken when she felt his arm go about her waist and she was hurled to the ground.

Chelynne was stunned by the impact of her fall. The first sound reviving her was that of hooves beating the ground as her frightened mare fled the scene. He held his stallion in tow, preventing his chase of the mare. The face above her cleared and she looked into angry gray eyes.

"What the hell are you about?" he demanded.

She couldn't manage a reply and found she didn't have to. He walked away from her to a nearby bush and tethered his horse. As he accomplished the task he looked in her direction, his brows drawn together in a black scowl. She trembled at the sight of him.

"Where did you come by that horse?"

"The Hawthorne stables, sir," she fairly chattered.

"And how did you gain permission to use her?"

"The groom saddled the one I selected," she responded dully.

"His name?"

"Sir?"

"His name! The one who saddled the horse!"

"I . . . I didn't ask."

"So, one of my grooms just gave you the horse of your choice, just like that?"

"Your groom?"

"My groom! My horse, in fact! I would know your intention. Were you planning to steal the mare?"

"No, sir!"

"The men tending the stables are given strict orders not to lend out any horse but on my approval or the earl's. I cannot believe that one of them would give you a horse, much less that one."

"I didn't take the horse without permission! The earl said I might have the mount of my choice. I am his guest."

"A member of the Mondeloy party?" he asked with a raised eyebrow.

"The same," she replied coolly, standing to brush the dirt off her skirt.

"My father," he muttered, as if vexed. "By not letting me handle my own affairs he ruins virtually every project I set my mind to. That horse was to be a gift to my bride. It was brought to my knowledge that she enjoys a ride. Now we must hope that the mare knows the way home. It's not a beast I should like to part with."

Chelynne watched him with wide, disbelieving eyes. This was to be her husband? Nothing about him resembled the earl. He was tall of stature, his chest broad and muscled, and he was fiercely dark, perhaps the mark of some Bourbon ancestry. Lean and handsome, he had jet-black hair, and his jaw was set in a firm, square line. His clothing would never give him away as nobility, for he was garbed in breeches and a tunic of animal hide, and at his waist was fastened a crude knife and not a sword. The boots were well worn and his hat, which he now struck with vicious intent against one thigh, gave evidence of a long and dusty ride.

"And what part of the bride's party are you? Cousin to my betrothed, serving girl, perhaps?"

"I serve my lady closer than any, my lord," she said softly.

"She's lenient with her servants, then," he snorted. "Sit, we'll take a rest and let the horse blow before going back." He dropped to the ground without giving her any further consideration. A blade of grass was pulled from its stalk and stuck between his teeth as he looked off into the distance.

Chelynne dropped down to the ground as well, carefully tucking her dress in around her knees. A quick survey told her they were secluded, and she was left to stare at his back, wondering at this strange, beautiful man. She had never dared hope for this. He was magnificent.

When he turned to look at her, she jumped in surprise. He chuckled, running his eyes slowly over her. When they met eyes again his were sparked with mischief. "Well, tell me then, is my intended going to give me a bony ride or will I be lost in mounds of fat?"

"My lord?"

"Is she too fat or too thin?"

"Why . . . neither, my lord."

"Come now, I know you're loyal, most servant girls are. But I would know my fate. Is she terribly ugly?"

Chelynne lifted her chin a notch. "I've heard some say she is beautiful."

"Oh, I'm sure," he said as if doubting it heartily. "Whatever young gallant is seeking her dowry would find her a handsome pet. But what do you think of her? The truth now. Is she at least bearable to look upon?"

"My lord, I know of no gallant to speak of my lady and I think her fair of face."

"And her figure?"

Chelynne blushed. Her whole being seemed to burn with embarrassment. But she could see that what the earl said was true. He was not eager for his bride. "Much as my own. In truth we are the same size."

"That I cannot believe," he huffed. "If she has a body like yours, she must have the face of a mule."

"My lord!"

"My lord, my lord. . . . My name is Chadwick Hawthorne and while we are alone in the country and forced to ride one horse home, you may call me Chad. Your name?"

"Che . . . Charla." She looked away nervously.

"Does something trouble you, my dear?" She lowered her eyes and pinkened a little bit more. "Well, you're the finest thing that's come of this wedding thus far. Will you be staying with your lady?"

"Until she dies, my lord," she murmured.

"She must have a great deal of confidence to dangle you before my eyes." He reclined on the earth, his head braced on his hand,

and studied her leisurely. His gray eyes smoked over with a warm and liquid darkness. She looked into them then and saw a tenderness that she loved at once. It was at that moment that her head began to swell with dreams of what would come to pass between them. She had already fallen in love with him.

"You are not eager for your bride?" she asked softly.

"Hell, why should I be?"

"She brings a dowry . . ."

"That I could have bargained for without the promise of marriage. I would gladly have changed gold for the land and left her more fixed for other proposals. How many nobles want property in Jamaica? Many want gold."

"You do not wish to marry?"

"Not under the circumstances," he muttered.

"Whatever could be as serious as that?" she asked innocently.

"Oh no, my little lamb," he laughed. "You'll not wheedle my life's story out of me. Your lady would hear about it straightaway." He reached out and crushed the silky softness of her hair in one hand. "I would much prefer a wife of my own choice, that is all."

"Mayhaps when you meet her you will find she is your choice."

"Life is never so kind as that, sweetheart," he said hoarsely. "Yet I think for once fate has dealt me a gift in lieu of the usual blow. I had not hoped she would bring such a lovely maiden with her."

"You flatter —"

"I don't flatter . . . ever. I'm sure you've been told often enough how beautiful you are. It is a simple fact. I'll not mind looking at you too much."

"You would be a bold husband for any woman," she whispered.

"I'm afraid, darling, that I wouldn't be much of a husband for any woman at this time in my life. Just the same, a satisfactory lover."

"My lord, you take too much liberty . . ."

She lowered her eyes, for his stare seemed to penetrate her very soul. When she dared to look at him again he was watching her still, his eyes dark, smoky and filled with lust. She couldn't seem to escape them and she was falling, helplessly. She realized with some surprise that he had slipped a hand around her neck and was pulling her to him, slowly and steadily. She could summon no resistance. Their lips met and a wave of excitement spiraled through her, causing her stomach to jump involuntarily. She could concentrate on nothing but the bold urgency of his mouth and the warmth of his breath.

With a quick movement she was pulled down beside him and he rose over her to kiss her again, obviously experienced in his passion. She put her hands to his chest with the intention of pushing him away, but the signal her brain gave her limbs was lost and instead her arms went around him to hold him to her. One large hand found the small of her back and pulled her hard against him while another found her breast. A low moan escaped her as her desire mounted. She was lost in this wild and beautiful madness. Her breath came in shallow panting gasps. She had never lived before now. He covered her with his long lean body and she felt his masculine desire hard against her thigh. A vision of them tumbling naked on the grass before they had even been introduced came to her mind and with a cry of panic she wiggled away from him, pulling her clothing around her.

At some distance now and perched on her knees, she trembled from ardor stirred and her own fierce abandon. He stared at her with like shock, with equal parts of frustration.

"What is it?" he asked gently.

"F-forgive me, my lord," she stammered, brightening in color. "I can't say what came over me."

"Come, sweetheart," he urged. "I won't hurt you."

"No, my lord," she murmured. "I cannot."

"There's no need to fear my touch. I'll be gentle with you."

"Please," she said with a half sob. "Don't . . ."

"Are you afraid?"

She nodded her head pathetically, tears threatening to spill. He studied her for a moment and took some deep breaths. He was resentful of her sudden reluctance in a way only a man can understand, but he was not oblivious to her youth. He reached out a hand to caress her cheek and she turned pleading eyes to him. "Are you a virgin?"

Again she nodded and looked away, totally ashamed of her passionate display, yet stirred no small bit by the sensuality of her intended groom.

"Well," he said, getting to his feet. "Never let it be said that I forced a young virgin." He ran his eyes over her again, appreciatively. "Let me offer you some advice, maiden. Never toy with me again unless it is your intention to finish what you start. You may find your maidenhead stolen before you can offer it next time."

"You're kind, my lord."

"Kind? Not I," he laughed. "Patient, sweetheart, but not kind." He bowed slightly so that his face would be closer to hers and said softly, "I think the best tactic now is to keep only good feelings between us."

"But you're to be married!"

He laughed again and his smile was bright and wild. "I think my poor wife will have a hard time keeping me from you. You're a tempting parcel."

"I'm glad you find me so," she said softly, her eyes bright with love and longing.

"Then let's be off, Charla. I would have you home and see to the mare."

"My lord, there's something I must explain . . ."

"Speak no more of it," he said, waving her off with a hand. "I understand your reluctance. Think better on it next time."

"But my lord, it's —"

"Never mind. I hope you'll consider your motives more carefully and in time come to me willingly."

"Of that you can be sure," she murmured.

He cocked a questioning brow and his eyes sparkled as if he pondered the possibility of continuing this tryst. She moved away from him quickly. He chuckled, more than a little fond of this maid. He gave her a push in front of him toward his horse and a swat on the rump put a jump in her step. His laughter was amused at her back.

He left her off at the tower stair, the ride much too short to please her. Without looking back in his direction, she flew to her rooms to meet with Stella's frown and tapping foot. But Chelynne disregarded her woman and went to the window. While Stella murmured behind her, Chelynne watched Chad as he went to the stable and after a brief moment came toward the house. The distance was great but there was no mistaking him, his tall lean body, his self-assured gait.

Behind her Stella fretted impatiently, lecturing on such escapades and worrying with her young ward's mischief. Finding her concentration sorely interrupted, Chelynne turned on her maid with a curse and hushed her. "Come here," she bade Stella.

Stella went to where her mistress stood, and though quite bemused, she looked to where Chelynne pointed. Chad was walking toward the house, striking his riding crop against his thigh. So bold and determined were his steps, so quick was the beat of her heart.

"That's him," she whispered to Stella. "That is to be my husband." As the words broke from her lips the reality of it sent shivers through her. Stella for once was speechless, for even she had not expected him to be so fine looking. He paused and looked up to where Chelynne stood in the tower window and she lifted a hand to him. He doffed his hat briefly and strode on. Chelynne let out her breath and nearly collapsed from delight. Her mind rumbled a silent prayer of thanks and her heart ached with a yearning she had never before known.

THREE

HADWICK HAWTHORNE rose with the sun, as was his custom. Whether he was toiling in the management of a plantation, commanding a ship, or hunting, it was always a full day. Since he first began his rigorous and adventurous businesses, he found it more profitable and efficient to sleep less. So it sits with a man then, that even when there are no toils or adventures, he cannot sleep past the first dawning.

Sensing his waking, his manservant, Bestel, entered bearing a tray holding the strong black brew that Chad preferred to the English favorite of tea — another small custom too important to his daily regimen to change. There were no ledgers to examine, no cargo to inspect, no fields to survey . . . no work.

It was not the first time he had had leisure. He made it a point to set aside holidays for himself. He was methodical, a slave to his own efficiency. It was waking in Hawthorne House that put a nervous edge on this idle time. Instead of feeling a sense of coming home, he felt displacement. The worst of it was that this coming home would almost certainly be permanent. He would assume the responsibilities of the earldom and in time become the third earl of Bryant.

When Bestel returned again he brought a silver tray with a white parchment bearing the earl's seal lying upon it. Chad picked up the thing, read the note, and placed it again on the tray. "Is his business so pressing that he must make an appointment to see me?"

"No, m'lord. He complains it is you whose business bears no time for trifling."

"So it is," Chad laughed. "Bring my breakfast and tell his lordship I am at his disposal."

Chad curbed the urge to pour himself a stiff drink. It was, after all, only daybreak. He knew what discussion lay ahead and there was little he could do to bolster his temperament against the topic. The thought of his coming marriage threatened to turn his stomach against his breakfast. After the way of life he had enjoyed for the past several years, it didn't sit well with him that he could be so easily coerced into doing something that went against his nature.

He had been born with a bit too much determination, his mother had told him. And too much like his father for them to survive their lives without conflict. Each was so stubborn and strong willed that there was little room for bending. He was just a lad when his mother died, but with her passing went the only buffer that kept earl and heir from constantly clashing. Chad had not yet begun to shave his face when the time was upon him to either stand up to his father or lie forever under his thumb.

It was the matter of a neighboring burgh that brought about their first dreadful fight. The closest friend that Chad had known since babyhood was the son of Lord Bollering, the baron of a nearby shire and the humble acreage surrounding it.

The Bollering family, estate and all, fell upon hard luck. They suffered through attacks from thieves and ruffians, large stores of food and supplies were destroyed, and the people who served them were robbed and ofttimes killed, along with what livestock there was to tend and to transport the goods. Warehouses burned and the town lay ravaged. Bollering could do little to defend himself and bought no aid from the Parliamentarians, since his allegiance was to the crown. Raiders struck other towns, but not as harshly. The final blow came when a charge of treason was levied against Bollering and he could do nothing to stay it.

During the worst of his plight, Bollering was given aid from a squire who resided in London. The man, Cyrus Shayburn, lent him money and support to help him try to pull himself out. When the final blow was struck and Bollering was removed from his holdings, it was that good squire who replaced him, gaining not just lordship there, but later, when England was in the hands of Cromwell, full title to that land. The impoverished people of Bratonshire found themselves abused by the same men who had robbed and plundered them before, by the privy orders of their lord . . . Shayburn.

It was obvious to everyone, even to Chad in his youth, that the plot had been well thought through. Shayburn straddled political alliances for as long as possible and when finally he was forced to choose, by luck he chose profitably, with the Parliamentarians.

Chad urged his father to fight this injustice, but the earl was reluctant. He, too, was postponing his declaration. He had little concern for the monarchy and the whole of England. His thoughts were only of this portion of England that was his, that his father had first secured. He was bound to keep it and hold it for his son at any cost. He kept silent about the injustice done to his friend and neighbor and in time pledged fealty to the Roundheads. The earl watched then as noble after noble fled into exile, every man and his family that declared for the crown. And Lord Bollering, though charged with treason by his king, died in defense of the Royalist cause, his family left to manage as they could in Cromwell's England.

Chad had no regard for the fact that what his father had done might be for the interest of his son. He had no concern for the earldom. Chad was filled with a sense of justice. His father thought it was the altruism of youth, but indeed it drove him even as a man. So Chad fled too, but from his past. He left the earl, Bryant and the whole of England.

He sought out the exiled court of Charles II and gladly took up his cause. With little training and less reward he met his first battle in the same season he was meeting puberty. They were badly defeated, but by luck and some obscure twist of fate, Chad came out of it with his life.

He smiled to himself now as he remembered the stories after the battle of Worcester. Charles was the greatest teller of stories, his narrow escape and careful journey out of the country to be recounted many times. But other stories of heroics in battle were recalled, Chad's among them. Chad lacked the gall to sing his own praises, for in truth the memory most vivid in his mind was the meager fare that left his stomach and joined the blood on the battlefield and the stains on his breeches from the urine that flowed uncontrollably down his legs out of utter fear. He trailed in the tracks of an aging but talented mercenary who later told the tale of Chad: roaring across the field of battle in a rage, swinging a mighty sword that was almost as large as one of his own legs, cutting down men in his path and running them through viciously.

The tale was true enough as far as it went. Chad did just that, so certain was he that he would die. But later, when with the aid of the companion he followed, he escaped, he sobbed in the older knight's arms. He was racked with vomiting spasms and unable even to lift his sore arms over his head. He owed his life to the man who made him sound the hero. In the next battle his companion died and the rage that drove Chad was born of a different emotion. After that he was knighted, one of the youngest ever.

Chad was not surprised to find that his friend, John Bollering, followed him. They fought together from then, two angry youths. They became strong and hearty and independent, growing their first beards together on battlefields and the backs of warring vessels. Charles's forces were seldom victorious and more often bored, but Chad and John found adventure and challenge in many different places, their loyalty first to the exiled king who gave them the first opportunity. They were with that number that moved to London, where Charles was received for his restoration by a joyful throng of English. All were glad to have their sovereign return.

The years had matured Chad and lent him the tolerance to make amends with his father. The earl held Bryant still and because of Chad was able to keep it after the restoration. He encouraged Chad to take up the workings of that estate to ready him for his inheritance, but there was a restlessness in the young man and he fled again. But this time there was no anger in his leaving, only the excitement of seeking his fortune and adding prosperity to the earldom to compensate for what was lost in the wars.

Again it was with John that he did his adventuring. The two were inseparable comrades. They took up a privateering venture, increased their holdings, fought for the king, and saw the world. They sailed to the West Indies, fought the Dutch in New Amsterdam, and traveled to Tangier. When they returned to London they found the entire city seized with the Plague and retreated to Hawthorne House in the country.

The quiet brought a certain peace to Chad, something he had never before sensed. John was still as restless. Being so close to his boyhood home sent his spirits soaring, and he spent his energy making plans for his revenge. Chad's was another course.

It began so innocently. He had taken a favored mount to the village to be shod. So many nobles were fleeing to the country that their own smith and other stable hands had moved into the village to give aid. Chad found mania within the usually quiet village. Many were waiting for service from the smith, the inns and taverns were crowded to their capacity, and the street was flooded with grand coaches and elite personages.

Among this confused throng the daughter of the village smith scurried about to find a place for a noble dame to sit and sup or a cool drink for a traveling lord. Her bare feet padded anxiously from one to another and her hair loosened from its braids to fly about her face. Chad watched her with some interest, for she was lovely, and then took himself to a grassy spot behind the business conglomeration to wait and rest. It was the first time in years he had enjoyed the peace of quiet and ease.

Not long after he had settled himself the girl fled there as well, taking no notice of him. She sought out a single tree and, leaning against it in total exhaustion, sank to the ground. Even after this many years when he thought of her as he first saw her then, his heart had an ache for her he could not subdue. In even his dreams he envisioned her escaping that bedlam for a brief rest with the wind blowing her hair and the flush high on her cheeks.

He looked for her constantly and then started seeking her out purposefully and finally persuaded her into meeting him secretly. Chad courted her, though he hadn't intended that in the beginning, but she was young and virginal and hesitant. He began to fall in love with her, being away from her causing him agony and being near her making the agony worse. He could not speak of her to anyone, not even John.

Chad's feelings were so new to him that he never suspected he loved her as he did. Just the same his pursuit was heated. In his impatient youth he pressed her until she could deny him no longer. He had told himself that when it finally happened he would be able to forget her, finding in her the substance of every other wench he had lain with. But in this, too, he was wrong. There was a richness to their passion that he had never before tasted and never since matched. Had he known then how totally it would bind him, how eventually it would destroy her, he never would have touched her.

She came with child soon after that. He found he couldn't live without her happily and neither could he be content to let her wed another or bear him a bastard. He expected his father's wrath, but her family played against them as well. Her father served the earl loyally and was ashamed of his daughter's recklessness. He put Anne on a coach to be delivered to a country squire, an aging man who would be content to have the lass in any condition. It was with a great deal of difficulty that Chad managed to find her, free her, and marry her.

When he took her to Hawthorne House the earl turned them away angrily. Never had such a disgrace marred their good name. Not only was the lass common, but the simple daughter of one of his own churls, well known by all who served him. She couldn't even write her own name. And this to not one of many sons, but his sole heir.

Anne suffered miserably, convinced she had sinned against all worlds. She was turned from her family, outcast by her husband's, and possibly turned away from eternal life because of her weak will and her sins. Chad took her to London, found a humble home and one servant to aid her, and joined his companions to support her by the only means available to him: warring.

He was called to the battle of St. James's day when Anne was near her time. It was as if she had a premonition of her fate, for though she urged him to go she made him swear that his child would never be called bastard. "Let him always have his father's love," she begged. "We both know the misery of being without it."

Chad returned from the battle with John and three other comrades, the sons of an acquaintance, Lord Sutherland. They witnessed what Chad found. His son thrived at the breast of a wet nurse while his beloved lay cold and dead from bringing him forth. His grief was almost overpowering, but he took it in tow, finding some strength in this newborn life. He wrote his father and asked permission to bring himself and his son to reside at Hawthorne House. The earl's reply was fast in coming. "The devil take me when I acknowledge your bastard!"

Hatred bred in Chad and gave him ambition and energy he had never before known. His goal was no longer simple adventure, but money at any risk. A pair of years later he was able to bring his son and servants to Jamaica to live on his own plantation. With shrewd business tactics and courage, ethical and otherwise, he bettered himself. It was a ship and then a fleet. A servant and then a staff and slaves to tend the cane. His son was dutifully tended by Mistress Connolly while her husband served Chad in other areas of his estate. He kept his hand in the court activities when business brought him to England. He was nobleman, warrior, businessman and merchant. He never burned a bridge and worked tirelessly to aspire in every circle.

When his son was four years old he returned to England. The earl learned of his presence through some unknown means and sent him a message asking him to come to Hawthorne House. Curiosity drove him, but he was very suspicious. He found that his father had aged considerably since he had last seen him.

"Can you guess why I've sent for you, Chadwick?"

"No, my lord."

"To ask your forgiveness first. I greatly regret that I did not open your own home to you in your time of need."

"You're a long time in considering this, my lord. My wife is dead now four years. Are you ready to bless our union?"

"You're bitter," the earl started.

"Bitter?" Chad laughed cruelly. "Bitter is a pretty word for what I feel."

"Are you not prepared to make amends? Say so now, for I will not beg you."

"What are your terms, my lord?"

"You are my heir. I'm growing old. Shall the house and lands fall to the current cuckold of the king's favorite mistress or will you step forward and receive?"

"I don't need —"

"No, you don't, son. But there are many who would play the game for it and snatch up this holding. It is not meager." Then he added shrewdly, "Shayburn has many friends at court now."

"Is he a threat? Might he find a way to —"

"I honestly don't know. I haven't been able to make many appearances for some time now. In truth, I think you're seen more about the court than I."

"It is the family seat you wish to protect?"

"It's rightfully yours, regardless of our differences."

"And in turn, my son's," Chad taunted.

"You will not make this easy," the earl sighed.

"What have you done to make my life easy, Father? You'll forgive me if I'm skeptical?"

Taking a breath, the earl bolstered himself for an unpleasant scene, one he had hoped he wouldn't have to play. "I've asked some of your friends your status. It would seem that you've attained some substantial wealth and that you are not yet married. They don't seem to know you were ever married. Do you hide the boy?"

"Indeed not. He resides in my home and under my protection."

"And he is your heir? Your legitimate heir?"

"I thought that was quite clear to you," Chad fairly snarled.

"It is clear to me, but there are some who would speculate."

"My lord, I married the mother of my son and the marriage and the birth were in like recorded."

"I'm aware of that," he said slowly. "I have the record." Chad stiffened visibly, his glare full of venom. "A small abbey in Browne, was it not?" the earl asked.

"What is your intention, my lord?" Chad ground out through clenched teeth.

"I have no wish to cause you or my grandson injury, Chadwick. All I want is to have you come home and settle here, marry respectably, and see about the business of this estate and Bryant. I can no longer manage and I want my personal affairs in order before I die."

"Or perhaps I should marry some blooded dame, fill your rooms with blooded brats, and the only proof of my son's legitimacy will meet with some unfortunate accident."

"Not by my hand, I give you my word."

"And who is to be the bride?"

"If I left that to you, would you bring me one with a name?"

Chad smiled at his father, that lazy, self-confident smile that could make any opponent feel inferior when locking eyes with him. It told of a secret, even if there were none. "We shall, both of us, have a hard time seeing this done, since there is no bride."

The earl held up his chin. He was much shorter than his son and therefore never met him for a confrontation unless they were both seated. It made him feel a great deal better, if not more equal. "Don't hold your hopes on the possibility that I can't find one, Chadwick. I'll look long and hard."

"No fat widows or skinny spinsters, Father, if you truly want my kinship."

"There are women of desirability to be found with good names and fair looks, Chadwick. Think what you will of me, I couldn't alter that now. I would no more accept a common bride well known to every peasant in the countryside now, than I would when in anger I denied you and your bride your rightful home. I will accept the boy, however, as a means to have you home, my only heir."

"Kevin is my chosen heir, whether or not I can ever prove it," Chad said threateningly.

"So be it. I cannot accept this alienation between us and so I accept your chosen heir. I have humbled myself that much, son. Can you not meet me halfway?"

"If you truly accept this as you say, then turn the record over to me now and have the matter done. Show me that you trust me now, my lord."

The earl chuckled softly. "That is something I would dearly love to do. But would you flee from England with this one paper that you care about? Would you leave me and all of this to fall into a stranger's lap? Nay, I'll not take any chance. I've given my life to this. First you'll meet the bargain."

"And that is the last word?"

"This or nothing," the earl said resolutely.

Chad knew the battle was fought more on principle than importance. A war of prides, not issues. Chad had been denied what it was his right to possess and he believed that had Anne been received with compassion and love into his father's home she would not have died, afraid and alone. He could keep Kevin out of England, establish him in a number of ways, but without the record his father held there would always be doubt. That was not a great problem for a noble whose birth was witnessed and whose parents were well known, but Chad had had few confidants during his marriage to Anne. There was left only one Sutherland and John Bollering. It was not enough. And this was rightfully Kevin's. He would not let it slip away easily.

He finally met his father's determined stare and said very slowly, "You can force me home and force me to marry, but you will have little success in deciding what I feel. Never forget that, my lord."

That was one year ago, almost exactly. He had returned to Jamaica, tied together some loose ends, seen that his land and home were in good, competent hands, and then returned to England. He settled his son with Mistress Connolly and her husband in a fashionable though modest house in London in a section apart from his own home there. Kevin was kept carefully quiet about his true parentage; Chad believed it wisest to anticipate his father's actions to be the cruelest. He had never thought the earl would go this far, and therefore special care was taken to secure the boy's safety.

Beyond a few words of greeting, Chad had not spoken to his father for a year. Now he prepared himself mentally as well as he could to meet the earl and suffer through another conversation about the marriage he had committed himself to. Donning jacket, periwig and courage, he strode the distance to his lordship's rooms.

Servants bustled around the huge home, passing him with smiling faces and giggles as he walked through the galleries. A great deal of polishing and shining was going on all about him and he turned full circle more than once to view this wild preparation for his wedding. Voices could be heard within rooms as he passed and he knew that many of their guests had arrived for the festivities.

The earl was up and dressed, a project rarely accomplished in his days of ill health. "There you are," he greeted Chad. "The house is full of guests and my sorry health has eased somewhat. Tell me, are you anxious to meet the young woman?"

"Should I be?" he returned with a raised eyebrow.

"Indeed you should! You can't possibly find fault with her looks. She is lovely. Lovely!" Then the earl sat heavily and his exuberance quieted somewhat. "She's young, Chadwick. She has accepted this graciously."

"I'm certain she has," he laughed. "What woman would not accept an earldom graciously?"

"I pray you treat her kindly," the earl sighed.

"My intention was never otherwise."

"Dare I hope you've reconciled yourself to this marriage?"

"I'll see the bargain met."

The earl was skeptical, but he could read nothing in Chad's expression. "Gwendolen has already made her presence felt, Chad. Treat that matter with care also."

Chad smiled at his father, the memory stirring some humor in his mind. He and Gwen went a long way back, back to a time before Chad first left Hawthorne House. He had spent many a pleasurable afternoon bending that fair maid against the dew. The fact of the matter was that he had learned loving on her well-endowed frame. His most recent encounter with her was just the year before, partially to ease his masculine need, and partially to pique his father.

Gwen was now married to a neighboring baron, a slim monkey of a man who allowed her the same freedom with her affections that she had enjoyed previous to her carefully arranged marriage. As the thought came to mind, Chad smiled more broadly than ever. Gwen had always thought herself to be in love with Chad, but his long absences discouraged her and finally, at the insistence of her family, she wed her father's next choice for her. Her marriage mattered little to her the last time he was with her; it wouldn't likely matter now. No need to confide in his father that he felt nothing above tolerance for this brazen creature.

"Do you give me lessons in manners, Father?"

"While your bride's family is in this house you'll not disgrace me and that innocent! This would be a poor time to see me angry!"

"Then it is until I make the payment double, as I expected. Now it is not enough that I wed the woman of your choice, but I must act in a manner that suits you as well."

The earl's face reddened somewhat. "Will you make this more difficult than it need be?"

"No, Father, but you will make this more difficult than it need be. You have held your advantage well and I cede you this victory. If you insist on baiting me into anger by demands over and above the stipulations in our agreement it is not too late for me to leave. I still have another place to go."

"Then you will wed the maid without quarrel?"

Chad nodded. The earl relaxed somewhat, though he never for a moment believed his son would give up this easily. Still, he could find no cause to create more strife between them now. "There are some things I would have you know of your bride. I believe her uncle actually sought the match ahead of me, though he won't admit to that. He dangled a lovely dowry, would you agree?" Chad said nothing; not even the slightest change in his expression registered. The earl cleared his throat and went on, annoyed with his son's lack of enthusiasm. "You'll have the deed on your wedding day. She is young and innocent. She is a virgin, so examined by my physicians, and comes to you willingly. I will trust you to your word that you will not abuse her."

"Have you ever known me to be abusive to women, Father?"

"Only in the reverse does your reputation lie. I've known you to be far too generous and quick to fall in love where women are concerned."

Chad's face darkened and his jaw twitched, though that was the only outward sign of his anger. When he spoke it was most smoothly. "Only once have I been in love, Father, and that was with my wife. She died in a fever at night only hours after birthing my son. She lay on a mat of straw with only one servant to tend her and little money to see to them. I didn't think you needed reminding."

"I knew the maid Anne!" the earl cried angrily. "She was not a stranger to me! She was fine and sweet and it pains me to know how she suffered! I say this to you, son, one time only. The young woman I bring to you now, though gently born and of some substantial wealth, is as young and fair as your dear Anne. To treat her unkindly would be just as wrong regardless of her station."

"Have no fear, Father," he said easily. "All will be well."

The earl let out his breath slowly, his color returning. "Give this a chance, Chadwick. If not for me, for yourself."

"Father, you've done your part in setting the stage and writing the words for this play. I think when it comes to my marriage you would only create more trouble for my bride by interfering. Next I shall have to prop you on the bed and let you consummate my marriage for me."

"Don't be vulgar! It is my sole intention to —"

"My lord!" Chad shouted, cutting his father off. "Have you any idea how vulgar it is to have your life prearranged and your words read from a manuscript? You already hold my firstborn's birthright from me. Pray let me spill my own seed for the start of a new!"

"I want nothing more," the earl said earnestly.

"Then let me breathe," Chad pleaded, emphasizing each word singularly.

The earl looked away from his son. It was another attempt at conversation that had fallen down the slide, the antagonism between them seeming never to ease. "There are many guests about the house you should take the time to see. Some are old friends and some new acquaintances. I shall rest so I might be fit for the ball tonight. Seek me out for any matter that needs my attention."

"Very well," Chad said on rising. "Do not wait upon me."

The earl gave his son a nod. Chad saw that the old man's eyes were strained, deep lines of age seeming more prominent to him now than ever before. He looked at a certain sadness with remorse of his own. Both wanted to speak, smooth over harsh words, close old wounds. Neither did.

Chad took long strides away from his father's room. He thought his anger well in check until he realized with some surprise that he had walked unheeded for a great distance, ending up in the earl's gardens with no remembrance of how he'd come.

He pondered his bride, but he could feel no warmth, no curiosity, nothing he could even compare to desire. He saw dread. His heart would always ache for Anne. There were times the longing was nearly overpowering, lessening only long enough for the pain and anger to seep through.

A female voice summoned him and he turned to see Gwendolen walking toward him. The earl was right to have so little respect for this woman. Gwen was nothing more than a very nicely garbed whore. But even with the knowledge that his father despised this woman, as she walked toward him now he had a vision of his future bride, and she resembled Gwen.

"You've been a long time away, my lord," she greeted him, her eyes alive with mischief.

"Don't call me that. I have no lordship here."

"Of course you do, darling. And soon you will have a great deal more than that," she simpered.

Chad smiled and eyed the woman coolly. There was no question that she was one of the most beautiful in England. She could rival many with her blond hair and lively green eyes. She was full figured and well tuned to a man's desires, her voluptuous body being pleasing to ride. She was desired by many and could not be considered niggardly with her affections. She neared thirty years now and her age did not show; rather, maturity did her justice. Looking very closely he could detect a harshness to the eyes that bespoke many trials, most of which revolved around her love affairs.

"You've always found my inheritance my most desirable characteristic," he laughed.

"You know that's not entirely true," she murmured, sidling closer. "And even if it were, what would you have a woman admire about you?"

"Certainly not that!"

"Well, then. Show me if there's something more . . ."

"For the love of Christ, Gwen! Have you no shame? Is Lord Graystone watching your play from some distant window?"

She threw him a rather shocked look and muttered, "You had not heard?"

"What?"

"Lord Graystone met with his end, a miserable affair. I dread that you must hear about it at all, but best I suppose that you learn it first from me. He lost his life in a duel of the swords."

Chad frowned blackly. He had no taste for a woman who allowed her mischief to cost a life. His feeling for her dropped one notch lower, his level of tolerance being strained even now. "Who, then, challenged your husband? Who was the victor?"

"An unworthy chap, poor fellow. And he did not issue the challenge, of course. 'Twas my lord Graystone. He believed the man had abused me sorely, finding us in a . . . rather precarious position. He was an actor in the Duke's Theater."

"An actor," he guffawed. "Good God, Gwen, I thought you only lay with lords and princes!"

Her face reddened slightly. She raised her chin a notch at the suggestion. "I did not say I was in bed with the fellow, my lord. Just the same, my husband did not wish to see my reputation damaged."

"I daresay that is already too far gone to be saved by a sword. Where is your hero now?"

"Transported. It was not meet that he should murder a baron."

"Murder? I thought you said it was a duel."

"I'm sorry to say the courts did not see it in that light. I grieve at the man's poor judgment, truly."

"No doubt he's grieving at that himself," Chad muttered. "You don't wear black. Have you already remarried?"

"Oh, of course not, darling. I simply put aside the black for this morning. I couldn't meet you in that drab, you having been so long away and all. I hope you don't think too unkindly of me . . . meaning no disrespect to my departed husband . . ."

"Stop it, Gwen. Was it in your mind to take him in his victory?"

"An actor? Of course not!"

"What was his name?"

"Why on earth would that interest you?"

"I'm curious. Who was the poor skunk you set up to rid you of your pestilent husband?"

"You make unkind inferences where there are none, Chad, and you do me injury. Do I assume you no longer have any affection for me?"

"You've come for my wedding, Gwen. Take care with your advances. Mayhaps my bride will see you clawed."

"That helpless little twit?" she laughed. "I doubt she could injure me in any way."

"You've seen her?"

"I breakfasted with her this morn. Frightfully homely little creature, don't you think?"

"I've not met her."

"You haven't? You would choose a bride you've never met?"

" 'Twas my father's choice. So, what does she look like?"

Gwen laughed. "Like a frightened rabbit! Truly, I couldn't believe it was she. She's a stringy little thing, far too thin, much like a newborn calf. She's no face whatever, her lips tight and pinched and a look of total bewilderment . . . mayhaps slightly daft."

Chad smiled. It was the first derogatory remark he had heard about his intended. "Then you don't find much about her to admire?"

"Certainly not! I daresay you might refuse her on sight."

"I think not, Gwen. I wouldn't want to disappoint the maid."

"I would question that as well. She doesn't carry herself as a maiden would. My guess is she's been mounted aplenty."

"She's only sixteen years old, Gwen."

"That means nothing," Gwen replied with a shrug. Chad ran his eyes over her slowly, meeting her gaze again with a mocking in his eyes. Gwen felt the gibe, for it had meant little in her youth, as Chad would know.

"Well, I shall put your suspicions to rest, madam," Chad told her with a slight bow. "My intended bride has been examined by the physicians and is a virgin."

"I suppose it's possible," she said contritely. "After all, I did say she was an ugly little thing."

"I thank you for your honest opinion, madam, and I will offer you some advice. Do not decry my lady again, here or outside my home. She will be my wife, and in time, a countess."

"Why," she said, taken somewhat aback. "Certainly."

Chad turned his gaze away from her for a moment, as surprised as she was at his own words. He had acquired, if anything, a hatred for this one who would sew him into bondage. How strange that acting the gallant husband came so naturally, unconsciously. And defending a maiden he didn't know and already didn't like to his previous mistress was even more shocking. He tried to shrug it off, but he faced Gwen a little dumbly.

"About that other matter. The name of this actor?"

"His name is Allen Potter Shaw, but I can't see —"

"Do you know where he was sent?"

"I didn't pursue the matter that far and I fail to see how it could interest you."

He smiled. "Nothing could interest me more, Gwen. If I ever see the opportunity I shall lend the man some advice about women. One in particular."

"I have no doubt he now regrets his impetuous interest in me," she said smugly. "Poor fellow."

"I have no doubts either, my dear." He reached out and touched one of her diamond earrings.

She laughed softly, thinking his play to be an affectionate gesture. "But men are all such creatures of bondage. Slaves to their own lust. They can't seem to control their actions even when the price far exceeds their purse. Do you find it so, my love?"

"Not at all, Gwen."

"You are fortunate," she murmured, her eyes rich with passion.

"Neither that, Gwen. Wise perhaps, but never fortunate. There are women who use men and men who use women. We are each one of one. But when we two are wont to meet, *you* might wish to hope for fortunate circumstances. I am not so kind as your Lord Graystone . . . nor so foolish as Mr. Shaw."

He gave her earring a slight tug, his eyes laughing at her, and then turned on his heel and left the garden, never once looking back in her direction.

FOUR

HEN CHELYNNE WOKE she found that her body was no longer her own. She was rousted and handled by maids and tiring women the moment her eyes opened. Like a lifeless doll she was dressed, coiffed, painted, and led to a place where she was to breakfast with her aunt and other female houseguests of the earl.

Her mind was certainly not on the food or the conversation. She was still off somewhere on a grassy field, luxuriating in the warmth of a lover's embrace. Several times she missed an attempt made at conversation with her and more often she answered dully, sounding foolish to these older women. But they derived much pleasure from her mood. A young bride, especially the bride of Chadwick Hawthorne, was expected to be off on some romantic cloud.

Chelynne recalled later that her aunt had bullied her way into the conversation, trying to monopolize it with trifles about her son. There were many planned activities before and after the wedding and Eleanor made several lame pleas to these other women, hoping that she would find either a wealthy maid to marry to her son or a noble to take him in tow and become interested in him.

"Will his lordship be riding to the hounds?" Eleanor had asked one of the visiting countesses.

"I suppose," was her idle reply.

"I don't know if Harry will participate," Eleanor sighed. "But perhaps his lordship could . . . that is, if his lordship invited him it would be a good time for them to become better acquainted."

The countess sighed. "Can he stay astride, madam?"

"Of course!"

"When my lord husband rides to the hounds he hunts. Conversation is for idle times, of which there are far too few." The countess then turned her attention to the other ladies and Eleanor's bumbling attempt was lost, but not forgotten. In just two short days she was well known for her passionate interest in her son, whom nobody seemed to like, and her lack of interest in her niece's wedding.

Chelynne's room was a conglomeration of servants, scattered clothing and countless articles to be used in preparing her for the ball. The confused atmosphere did little to give her nerves a sense of ease. She once stole away from the bedlam for a moment of peace at the window. As she looked below into the gardens she caught sight of Chad. He paused there, raising one leg and resting his foot on a marble bench and pulling aside his coat with a hand on his hip. He made a different picture now, garbed in the rich dress of the elite. His tight-fitting breeches and waistcoat were brightly colored and an abundance of lace could be seen at his neck and wrists. Buckled shoes and periwig did not seem to suit him as boots and windblown hair did, but there was no mistaking him. He was a fine figure of a man. Even in this attire there was nothing foppish about him. He wore even lace and wig with a strong masculine flavor.

Chelynne was not allowed the peaceful daydreams brought by the sight of him. She was pulled away from the window and the ministrations of grooming were applied to her again. Many years of training had gone into the making of a gentlewoman who would aptly fit into the class of nobility. Chelynne had been served, pampered, and waited on by her own women since birth. Being bathed was nothing new to her. Having her body clothed and her hair fashioned by hands other than her own was routine. But what she went through that day stripped away the last vestige of her pride. Not one portion of her body was overlooked. A large pumice was rubbed along her arms and legs until every last trace of body hair was removed. She was bathed and oiled and massaged, and then the same procedure was repeated. Her hair was washed, dried, and shined with a long piece of silk, and a hot iron was used to make tight ringlets around her face.

When at last it was time to complete her hairdressing for the ball there was a great deal of commotion, everyone attending her seeming to have a different opinion. But this once Chelynne was insistent. She wished to have the long heavy masses pulled tightly away from her face and crowning the top of her head with thick curls. She was small beside Chad and would have the elaborate style give her height.

A gown of pale blue was chosen for this first affair. It was sewn with many tiny silver studs, twinkling and shimmering. One blue sapphire in the center of a silver blossom adorned her throat while two tiny sapphire buds touched her ears. A blue ribbon was woven through her curls and, to catch the candlelight and delicately glitter, little silver stones were buried beneath the locks. The gown hugged her youthful figure, letting her full breasts rise and her small waist tempt any man to touch.

She eyed her own appearance with satisfaction, slightly agog at her own striking beauty. She had dressed formally before but never had there been this lift in her heart, this eagerness to please a lover. It was in fact the first time she had ever dressed for a man . . . and the difference delighted her.

Slightly breathless, she turned and murmured to Stella softly. "Do you think he will find me attractive?"

"Unless he is blind, dear heart," Stella answered proudly.

Outside her window she could see the torches in the garden being lit. The moon was full and round and the night was beautiful. With pages holding up her train, she took slow careful steps down the stairs. The servants she passed bowed and smiled, their eyes lighting up in appreciation. The moment she had lived for was here. All the poise and charm that had been bred into her would be put to the true test. She was afraid it would all be useless to her now. She had never wanted to please more, but she was frightened half to death. She paused as she reached the ballroom doors and sucked in her breath. She gave a tiny nod of determination to the butler and the doors swung open to admit her.

She had seen this room before, but never had it filled her with fairylike wonder. The elegantly garbed ladies and gentlemen who lingered along the walls, becoming reacquainted with friends, looked her way. There were great tables of food ready to be tasted; impressively uniformed servants picked their way among the guests to replace empty glasses with full ones. In the middle of this tumult stood Chad and his father, waiting for her arrival. They were chatting with one of the women she had met at breakfast, a recent widow of admirable beauty. The woman between them saw her first and stopped her conversation to stare. Then, as if by magic, a hush fell over the room as the earl and Chad looked in her direction. Her eyes were fixed on her betrothed and he stared at her in dumb wonder.

His shocked expression sent her thoughts sailing. He recognized her at once, that much was obvious. Was he pleased? Angry? She smiled at him, an intimate smile she had practiced, but he was barely shaken out of his dismay. The earl made a move to receive her and take her to Chad, but Chad caught the movement and held up an arm across his father and pressed on ahead of him. Breaths were held as he approached her, and when he neared she lifted warm brown eyes to him for the merest instant and then dropped into a deep curtsy, holding her gown back with her hands.

When she rose his hand was extended to her and she placed hers trustingly in it. After placing a kiss on its back he held it high above their heads and led her into the ballroom, presenting her to the guests. He raised the other hand to the orchestra that stood ready; the first note was struck, and Chelynne and Chad led the dance. They touched with only fingertips and eyes, yet her entire being was filled with his presence. She glided as he would have her, dipped when she should, every movement unconscious, spontaneous. She was aware of nothing but him.

With another wave of his arm, those who stood and watched joined the dance and she was swept away in a dream, his light touch burning her. She paid no heed to his direction and would not have argued if she had been more aware. They came to pause near the glass and iron door leading from this grand ballroom to the gardens. A handy and almost invisible footman opened the doors automatically, closing them softly behind the young couple.

The brisk night air brought Chelynne out of her state and into full awareness. She took a deep breath and turned to face him. "Did I keep you waiting long?"

"It was worth the wait." He ran his eyes over her slowly. "You played me false, madam."

"It was not my intention, my lord. I tried to explain but you would not hear."

"You didn't try very soon," he admonished.

"It was your reluctance for your bride," she confessed. "I couldn't resist. . . . Was I so wrong?"

He laughed a little awkwardly, never taking his eyes off her. "So, you've managed to learn a little of me without my knowing. Beware, madam, from now you will know only what I choose to tell you."

"Then you are angry," she said softly. "I was afraid you would be."

He lifted her chin with a finger so he might study again the face. Tight-lipped indeed! Gwendolen had so badly slandered her beauty that the act could only have been wrought from jealousy. He saw in the moonlight a pale oval face with a slight flush on high cheekbones. The lips were thin but well shaped and parted now in a half smile that begged to be covered and tasted. Though small of stature she was hardly thin. Her breasts rose and fell temptingly with her breath and her waist was tiny. As he immediately judged, it was the perfect size for his hands. As if performing a special test, he touched his thumbs and forefingers together around her waist. Then sliding them lower, he found firm and tender hips and felt there the promise of a wonderful ride. This would be no easy battle. He wanted her at once.

"You'll find, love, that I am angry in the best of times. I give you fair warning."

"Will you be a difficult man to live with?" she asked coquettishly, her little head tilted up.

"Of a certain, my lady."

His expression was cold, that smoky quality gone now from his eyes as they became again that hard, impassive flint. Worried, she turned from him and took a few steps into the garden. She had not thought to bear witness to his reluctance so soon. From his earliest actions she had been filled with hope.

"See here, Chelynne. I've no wish to spoil your fun."

"But you discourage me so," she murmured. "You did not seem to be a hateful man when first we met."

He laughed huskily. "Have a care, love. You do me no honor when you pout. I am not as hateful as that."

"And you are no callow youth," she said in confusion. She turned to him again, her brown eyes twinkling with the light of the torches. "Indeed, you are much older than I. Old enough to be my —"

"Hold!" he said laughing. "Not quite so old as that, my dear. I am now three and thirty and not yet tottering about with a cane. I can assure you of a few more good years before I wither away."

"Why then have you never married? Is it not meet that you should give thought to a family?"

He looked directly over the top of her head and she noticed that his jaw set firmly and his temple pulsated. "It's a matter I should have liked to pursue on my own."

"Then you will not give this a chance," she said softly.

"Don't worry yourself needlessly, my lady," he said matter-of-factly, with a slight formal bow to keep it distant. She was looking up at him with earnest brown eyes, loving and soft, but he would not meet her gaze. "The contracts are made and I shall not prove too difficult."

"Yes," she murmured, though she knew well enough that there was still time to refuse this commitment. She was afraid to tell him that, however. What if he grabbed at the chance to be free of her? She couldn't bear even to think about that; a young heart is too hopeful. "But if they were not prepared?"

"It would make little difference." He shrugged. "The earl would bring yet another to replace you."

"He is that determined to see you wed?"

"It is the very breath in him," Chad sighed.

"Why then have you not brought a woman of your choice for his approval? Why do you not give him aid and seek to please him?"

"You quibble too much for a woman having naught to say of what I do or why. I think you'll have the difficult nature in this marriage."

She laughed softly and he looked down at her. "Of a certain, my lord." His eyes were glued to her face. She could see them cloud over, taking on that warm and moist quality that meant victory to her, however small. "Is there something you find fault with, my lord?"

That beguiling smile in the darkness did strange things to him. He had such a mixture of emotions, the simultaneous urge to strike her and take her into his arms and kiss her lovingly. But her loveliness eliminated the urge to mark her. Still, bred into him was an instinct for danger, and faced with this gentle beauty he felt as trapped as a cornered animal. "I am too old, Chelynne, to appreciate youth as your husband should." His smile was mocking, almost cruel. "Your patience will be sorely tested." He noticed the emotion that swiftly passed across her features. He was pleased to see it was very close to fear. "And what of me?" he asked sarcastically. "Does the manor have fault? Is there enough wealth here to suit you? Have I some unsightly twitch I must curb?"

It was as if she hadn't even noticed the harsh sneering of his voice. She laughed softly. "And would you change one thing to suit me better?"

"Never!"

" 'Tis well," she sighed. "I found no flaws but for the stubborn streak. It should prove most burdensome."

He stepped nearer, wondering how she could stand so calmly, speak so softly when faced with his hostility. She should want to claw at his face or slap him, but there she stood, her lips parted in that delicious half smile and her eyes shining with adoration. He could not gather his good sense, so overpowering was the urge to taste that sweet mouth again. He crushed her to him suddenly, roughly, insistent enough to hurt her. He wished she would be less tractable, strain against him at least and not allow his advances, but she did not. Rather, she complied, molding to him, seemingly pleased with the harshness. Yet she responded and encouraged him softly, her small arms slipping around him gently to hold him ever nearer. She turned the cruelty of his touch to tenderness so easily that he was barely aware of the transition.

"Here now, son. There's time enough for that."

The couple broke apart reluctantly to catch the earl on the garden path. "I thought perhaps you would need some persuasion to join us again," he chuckled. He turned and was gone, thinking that brief interruption would prompt them to cool their ardor and return to the party.

" 'Tis not your kiss I find fault with," Chelynne said warmly.

"Be assured, madam. You will find my faults soon enough." He reached into his sleeve and pulled out a handkerchief for her. "I might have smudged your paint. Pray put yourself together so that we can join our guests."

She looked up at him and laughed softly. It was for this very reason that she had not allowed her attendants to apply the lip paint. "I wear no paint, my lord."

He looked at her again, taking a moment to digest this. Her appearance and, indeed, her taste, were simply and naturally hers. One short tussle with Gwen usually left them both marked. He shrugged, looked her over again, and presented his arm.

Inside the ballroom the earl accepted another drink though he knew he should be careful of the amount he consumed. His spirits were too high to resist the urge to celebrate. He felt success sailing through his veins just as a ship rides the waves. Chad could pretend discontent but his actions spoke loudly for him. The earl greatly envied his son. He was not so old as to have forgotten the force of desire that belonged to the young.

Across the room he could see Gwendolen. She was chatting with Lady Mondeloy and casting frequent anxious glances at the garden doors. When the earl approached that pair she turned on him with some malice. "Shouldn't you go see about them? It wouldn't do to have the girl's reputation sullied so soon before she is wed."

"I wouldn't think a few moments alone is out of the question, my lady."

"Your guests will wonder what holds his interest for so long."

"I doubt that," he replied. "Everyone who saw her will know what holds him." He smiled lazily as Gwen simmered. "And who better to protect her virtue than the man she will marry?"

She snorted and huffed. "I've known your son for a good many years, my lord, and protecting a woman's virtue was never among his more noble gestures."

"Truly," he mocked. "Maybe he was lacking a woman whose virtue was worth protecting."

He turned and walked away, thinking, "There. That felt a great deal better than anything I've done in years." He went then to the terrace doors and as if the whole scene was planned they opened to admit Chad and Chelynne. He bowed over the young woman's hand with much pomp as Gwen glowered at them from under lowered lids.

The earl's guests had begun to gather to be introduced and a small line was formed, the earl presenting his guests to his son, Chad in turn passing them along to Chelynne, who found her uncle Sheldon next in line to receive them.

Chad stood relaxed at her side, nodding and accepting congratulations graciously while her beauty was praised. He smiled courteously when it was expected and bowed over old dowagers' hands with courtly grace. He did not think himself closely observed, but Chelynne watched her fiancé's every move. There was a manner most suave about this man to whom she would be given. His words flowed effortlessly from his tongue in complimentary grace and he smiled easily into the eyes of giggly maids and well-rounded, middle-aged ladies. He carried off this affair as if nothing could fit closer to his own plans. She decided then that his difficult nature was an intended thing meant only for her, but she had no idea why.

When a stout man of perhaps fifty years approached, Chelynne felt Chad stiffen beside her. It was a movement barely discernible but to one who would so closely analyze his every action. Outwardly he maintained the same self-confident appearance, not even an uncertain frown touching his brow. She simply sensed his tension. "My dear," he said smoothly, "I should like to present my lord Shayburn."

She nodded her head as she had done a hundred times that

night and then raised her eyes to look at the man being introduced. "Your fair beauty shall add much to the desirability of this wonderful land."

"Lord Shayburn is baron to the lands lying east of us," Chad explained. "He possesses the shire of Braton within his boundaries and has served Bryant and the crown for many years." Chelynne thought his voice was slightly brittle and carefully stole a look at him, but still, no outward sign.

"A pleasure to meet you, my lord," she said sweetly. "And I look forward to visiting your fair Bratonshire."

"As we look forward to your visit, fairest lady." He took her hand and brushed a kiss on it. She was hesitant for the first time this night, for she found the man oddly repulsive. His elaborate style gave her unease, and though he was not unhandsome, there was a look about the eyes and mouth that she found insincere, almost wicked. As if he caught her slight reluctance, Chad pulled her hand away from the baron's as soon as he straightened. He tucked Chelynne's hand in the crook of his arm securely, giving her cause to think she had the right to be wary.

"You're to be envied, my lord. She is every measure of a man's desires."

"I must agree," Chad said stiffly.

"And such a pleasure to see you again, my lord. I was in fear you wouldn't be returning to us. I've heard of your interest in Jamaica. And you've been away a long time."

A sardonic smile twisted Chad's mouth. "You worried needlessly, my lord. It has always been my intention to return. The wedding is but a timely surprise."

"And tell me," Shayburn went on. "Has young Bollering crossed your path? I've a concern for the lad you might well understand, the unfortunate circumstances of his father and all . . ."

"Sir John has had occasion to be in contact with me. He does well."

"*Sir* John?"

"Aye. He was knighted some years ago and serves His Majesty well. He was not hampered by lack of coin in making his way, my lord, so you need not fear."

"And where does he make his home?"

Chad glanced at his father, who was at this moment frowning his displeasure over this conversation, hoping Chad would exercise care with his temper. "He has not claimed any port as home to my knowledge. I know the man had an interest in the Americas some years back."

"Then he is sailing. I had heard . . . ah, well, never mind what I heard. Gossip is plentiful here." Chad smiled wickedly at that, trying to conceal his delight.

"That and other ventures," Chad confirmed.

"Well, then, you must notify me if you hear from him again. I was never able to offer my condolences when his father died. How does his family?"

It was going a bit farther than Chad would have it. "I wouldn't know, my lord. And his father has been a long time gone; I doubt if condolences would be necessary or appreciated at this late date."

"Perhaps you're right," Shayburn said thoughtfully. "Just the same, should you see the boy . . . I would greatly like to see him. Ummmm . . . have him come for a talk. I could perhaps . . . that is, I'll take it up with him if he ever comes to call."

Chad's father hurried Shayburn along, fearing what this conversation might be leading to. He had no desire to see Chadwick lose his temper on this night.

Chad relaxed beside Chelynne once again. Of course Shayburn would want to know if John were to come home. It would be imperative that he know, Chad thought hatefully. But Shayburn would know nothing, not so long as Chad had breath in his body.

There was dancing after the introductions were made and Chelynne was set upon by every eager young man present. As any young maid would, she responded coyly to the compliments and never grew tired of the flattery. There was but one who had not openly praised her since she entered the ballroom, and that was Chad. This ball being in his honor as well, the ladies were bid to ask him for the dance.

Chelynne was not left much to her own ends, there always being someone to see her hand busy and her glass filled, but Chad was not among them. Later, then, it was with a great deal of happiness that she saw him coming toward her. She looked at him uncertainly, for she noticed a scowl on his handsome face and his eyes fixed across the room.

"It seems my cousin has found a friend in Lord Shayburn," she said, indicating that twosome Chad seemed interested in.

"It would seem," he grunted. "I wonder what they could have in common."

"From my short acquaintance with the baron I couldn't say for certain, but Harry has a most insolent nature in the best of times."

"Then that is it," he said, looking down at her with an amused grin. "Shall we join our guests in a dance?"

With a smile she gave her assent and they went again onto the dance floor. Many admired the couple from afar for they were a fetching pair. His bold and masculine frame and hard good looks were accentuated by her slight albeit womanly form and delicate beauty. The contrast in their coloring added flavor to their attractiveness. He was dark of skin and hair, his eyes the shade of ashes, while she had a soft brightness to her fair complexion and light brown hair streaked with a honey glow. There was many an old dame who silently mused on what manner of heir these two might make, but none thought other than that it would be the best of both. The match seemed too good to be true.

And while they danced, each studying the other, they seemed in love. In the age of arranged marriages, though manners were rigid and etiquette closely observed, it was not uncommon for the groom to give a sour face at the first sight of his plump bride, or the bride to grimace while looking on the stature of her homely groom. In this fine pair neither could complain of the other's handsomeness.

When the dance ended Chelynne had no time for tender words to her betrothed, for she was led away again. Chad watched as she went and the earl sidled up closer to his son.

"Can I assume that you are not displeased with my choice, Chadwick?"

"She is lovely," he relented, raising a suspicious eyebrow and looking down at his father. "I congratulate you, your lordship."

"I congratulate you, my son. She is yours."

"Not yet."

"But soon. Soon. You are anxious?"

Chad simply smiled down at his father, declining any further answer. The earl just laughed in good cheer, for nothing could dampen his spirits now. A man would have to be blind not to notice the desirability of this young woman. He hated being of smaller stature than his son, especially at a time like this, for as Chad watched Chelynne dance, the earl could not judge his expression accurately.

But Gwen was taller than his lordship so as she approached she chafed slightly at what seemed to be open desire in Chad's eyes as he watched Chelynne dance. She cleared her throat but he was not drawn away from that sight. With a smothered chuckle the earl walked away from them and Chad finally noticed her.

"It would appear that you're pleased with your intended bride, Chad."

"What? Oh yes, of course."

"What is it you find so attractive about her?"

Chad looked into her eyes and saw jealousy sparking there. "What is it you find so unattractive, Gwen?"

"I didn't think you would have to ask," she bristled.

"But I am asking."

"To taunt me? Then you shall have an answer! Were we so little to each other that when it finally met your mood to marry you would throw me down for another?"

"What were we to each other? Illicit lovers! Would you have me bind that in an abbey on the church's blessed parchment? My God, Gwen, you were married."

"I was not always and I have no husband now," she argued. "Oh, the lovely phrases that floated from your tongue while you took me . . ."

"Took you? I took nothing. It was freely given."

"You are not married yet!"

"What the hell are you proposing, Gwen? You couldn't have the gall to suggest that I —"

"Of course I suggest it!" she ground out bitterly.

"Easy, Gwen," he said slowly. He looked into those angry green eyes and smiled. "Everyone is watching us. I don't think it would do to give them anything more to talk about, do you?"

"What do I care?" She pouted.

"You should care, love. I'll tell you why. I said I would never marry you and you should have taken me at my word. Whatever we had together was by mutual consent and you were not injured. Now you have laid away one husband in his grave. Unless you intend to live out your days devoid of a protector, alone in that manor house, you will do well to act the lady. You'll attract more prospects that way."

"You're only afraid that that willow switch you plan to wed will learn of our affair and be —"

He laughed, cutting her off. "She'll learn of it in due time, of that I have no doubts. It seems a man isn't allowed the meagerest secrets these days. I will tell you this once, Gwen. My father has brought a virtuous bride to his house for me to wed and I approved his choice. If she is hurt over my past sins she will no doubt live in misery all her life, for they are many."

"You talk as if virtue is the most precious pearl. What of love?"

"Why Gwen," he mocked. "Methinks they oft go hand in hand."

"Ooooo! You are insufferable! To think of all I have given you to be treated this way! What could she possibly mean to you?"

His expression grew cloudy, cold. "She will be my wife, Gwen," he said very slowly. "She will have my support and protection. Take care with your words."

She looked up at him in wonder. Never in her life had she allowed a man to treat her as this one did. Always she was in control, manipulating the man. And she wanted him still, though this was the epitome of humiliation to her, letting a man have the upper hand. "And what will I be to you?"

"What you have always been to me," he replied. She was totally unsure of his meaning. Something in his eyes told her he held her in some contempt, but then his steely gaze moved over her body and she warmed. Unconsciously her eyes moved to where Chelynne danced. She was pretty enough, but she was a child. Gwen knew Chad's habits well. He could not possibly find entertainment enough with this youngster.

She made up her mind. She might have to set her sights on something other than marriage, but not less important. All she would have to do to wield her power was to get this handsome man in her bed again. He wouldn't leave her to seek out that infant.

When the dance was at an end Chad took Gwen to where Chelynne danced with young Philip Snow. "I envy you sir," the young man said. "You have the most beautiful woman in England as your own."

Gwen stiffened, remembering times when that same compliment had been paid to her.

"I thank you, sir, and I must agree." Chelynne flushed delicately, happier in her heart than she had ever dreamed she could be. "I told her she was beautiful when first we met."

"I didn't notice you speaking," Gwen snapped.

"I didn't mean tonight, my lady," Chad returned with a smile. "I told her so yesterday."

Gwen gasped, believing he had played her for a fool, extracting all those unkind comments about his intended bride when he knew perfectly well what she was like. "I thought you said you had not met."

"I thought we had not. I took her to be one of her own servants, taking a mare from my stables for sport. She led me a merry chase and my intention was a sound thrashing for her, until I had a look at her."

Gwen whirled away and was gone instantly, but Chelynne did not wonder at her strange behavior. She was so lost in the ashes of his eyes that the house could have crumbled around her and she wouldn't have noticed. Philip Snow slipped away as well, unobserved.

"Is the mare safe?" she asked.

"She is. Did the beast please you?"

"She's beautiful. Is she truly mine?"

"On one condition, Chelynne. You will not be allowed to ride alone, and that is an order. Were your uncle's lands so subdued that you never had to worry with thieves and ruffians?"

She shrugged. "There was little trouble in Welbering."

He snorted. "I'm sorry to say 'tis not so here. You'll have to conduct yourself with a care for safety. These lands are far too wide for patrols to cover every inch and we have had our share of thievery and destruction. You'll go with escorts or not at all."

"Is your state a dangerous one, my lord?"

"At times it has proven to be. Should you play that folly again you will not be allowed to ride. And now that you know me, never try to outrun me again. Is that understood?"

"Why sir, do you act the husband?"

He started a little at the accusation and then realized he sounded more like that than anything else. "Intended only for your safety, nothing more," he said stiffly.

"Yes, sir," she said softly, but inwardly she smiled.

Chelynne was tucked away in bed to suffer through an incredibly long night filled with delicious daydreams. Two days passed so slowly she thought she might die of waiting, and then at last it came, the morning of her wedding. The dew was shining when she rose from her bed. This day, in the second week of July, was her answer to a dream. It would be long remembered by those who were close to her, but she had no idea that for some it would bring disappointment and despair; to yet another, entrapment; to still another, fury. For her it was heaven. Her wedding: marriage to the most magnificent man alive.

In the early hours of the morning the women went to work, dressing Chelynne in a gown of the palest pink. An elaborate veil studded with diamonds adorned her head and a lace train trailed down from this headpiece to the floor. Her hair was brushed to a high sheen and fell gloriously down her back.

Before the July sun could swelter and steam the guests waiting in the small Hawthorne chapel, she fell to her knees beside her groom and spoke the vows of marriage. Her voice was soft but steady and his was strong and firm. The priest bade them rise and seal their promises, and Chad lifted the veil to kiss her. It was soft as a whisper, this kiss on her wedding day, his hands gently and steadily holding her at her waist.

When he released her she smiled, a soft and tender smile. He did as well, and that much caught in the hearts of many observers. He took his bride's hand and turned her, presenting her to the gathering, and with that the long day of celebrating began.

There was a wedding breakfast first and all who attended the bride and groom were in good cheer. Toast upon toast was offered and drunk, the hour still early but the merrymaking getting a good start on its fast pace.

People from the village and neighboring burghs brought gifts and presented them to the bride and groom. The earl put out large quantities of food and drink for these well-wishers and scattered monies to those in need, as was the custom.

All through the afternoon there were more arrivals. The men engaged in games and sports and the women gathered in little groups to gossip and reminisce. Chelynne was led away for a brief rest but no matter how Stella prodded and crooned she could not sleep. She rose again, for there was a banquet and dancing and yet more champagne to while away the evening. They were toasted again and again and again. Chelynne's head began to spin and her legs throbbed from the abusive standing. Were Chad not most often at her side she would have collapsed from overimbibing and standing too long. Finally she was taken to their bedchamber by the women to be prepared for her wedding night.

They made her ready for her husband, pulling off the elaborate gown and dressing her in a sheer and seductive cover of light pastels. Her hair was brushed, and when they came at her again with fragrances she shooed them away emphatically. She couldn't be sure if it was the consumption of too much wine or nervous anticipation of the event soon to come, but she was nauseated and the perfumes were an unearthly thought just then.

She had a brief look at herself in the mirror and was shocked to see that she was, for all practical purposes, naked. She had never been so naked. The women didn't leave her until her husband arrived, and then there was a great deal of snickering and giggling. Chelynne was mortified. She could be grateful for one thing. Chad had defied custom to the extent of demanding they not be publicly bedded. He came to her alone.

She was sitting in the bed, the covers drawn to her lap and her hair spread across the pillow. He recoiled slightly at the pomp involved in even going to bed. He approached the bed and she flushed so red he was concerned for a moment she might faint.

"Are you afraid?"

"No, my lord," she replied, but her voice was just a quivering spasm.

"Take heart, Chelynne. I'm not going to ravish you. Would you like some wine?" She blanched at the thought. Her stomach was churning now. She shook her head vigorously and pursed her lips. He chuckled a little. "Well, do you mind if I have a brandy?" Again she shook her head, unable to speak to him.

He took off his coat and threw it across a chair. After pouring a drink he looked at her again. "Relax," he ordered impatiently. Unable to bear the sight of her sitting there stiff as stone as if waiting for her death, he went to sit before the hearth and enjoy his drink.

The thought sat ill with him, that she would be prepared like this. He pitied her circumstance. Better he should woo her in a country field than that there should be this much anxiety all around her. He damned the old crones who had prepared her; no doubt they emphasized the pain and humiliation of the consummation. He looked over his shoulder in her direction. The curtains were drawn around the bed but for the side he would enter. He could only see her form, devoid of detail, sitting still as stone just as he had left her. She must be terrified.

Then the thought of her alluring little body came to mind and he hoped he would not do her too much injury in his haste. He had been a long time without a woman and his need was growing strong within him. He forced himself to wait and then finally, sensing that enough time had passed to give her some ease, he began to undress.

He cast furtive glances in her direction and still she sat, just as before, awaiting her fate. With a sigh of exasperation he pulled off his breeches and blew out all but one candle. He climbed into the bed beside her and moved near. He slid one arm under her and she gave a sleepy sigh and moved a little closer. His face came up over hers to look into her eyes and he almost laughed out loud. She was sound asleep. Too much wine for his little bride.

FIVE

HERE WAS A SOFT LIGHT aglow in the large bedchamber when Chad first came awake. The day was already warm and he noticed that he and his young bride had recklessly thrown off their covers in their sleep to keep cool. Chelynne's lovely young body lay bare to his gaze now, covered only with the thin wisp of her nightdress. He studied her now with naked adoration.

She was a woman barely blooming. Her skin was soft and pale, the pink of her nipples faint and blushing. Her hair wove a seductive web over the satin pillow on which her head lay. There was a pure and simple beauty about a virgin lass that brought him closer to worship than lust.

He remembered when his wife was like this, so chaste and untouched. He had had less patience then and at her merest sigh that she would yield, he had forged ahead and robbed her of her maidenhood, putting his mark on her. It was the sweetest moment, yet once it passed he watched her bloom ever the more as she came alive with his love.

He recognized the emotion with such an impact it nearly shook him. The strange feeling he had now was much like what he had had for Anne. In his callow youth he had thought it to be simple desire, but in the years since, he had tasted much desire and fulfillment there, in that simple and uncomplicated joining of two bodies. Once desire was sated, the feeling passed, but with love there was everlasting thirst. One taste of physical possession would not quiet the wanting but tempt him to more.

That is a man's curse, he told himself sharply. To find that special thing, live for it, love it, have it change the course of your whole life, and then lose it. It was worse than a curse, it was a living hell. Once gone, it could never be replaced. If a man could not be stronger than the emotional desires that moved him, he would never survive his life with his sanity. Chad was determined. He would never depend on anyone again, especially not a woman.

But his hand moved over her with a will of its own. He touched the young breasts and her eyes lazily opened. She blinked away the sleep and smiled at him. There was no look of question in her eyes, no dismay at the way he fondled her. She seemed secure and at ease.

He smiled. "You've slept away the wedding night, my love," he whispered.

She stretched lazily, but with feline grace. The sight was much appreciated. She was rubbing her eyes when suddenly they flew open and she looked at him in awe. "Have I . . . was I . . . goodness! Did I miss it entirely?"

He laughed heartily, drawing her near. "Would I have taken you in your slumber and never even stirred you into wakefulness? It's not so dull as that! Nay, love, you've missed nothing. I'm not so inadequate that you could sleep through my lovemaking!"

She flushed scarlet and closed her eyes. "You must be entirely disappointed in me."

"There's time enough, Chelynne. Sometimes, I've heard, it's a hateful thing for a woman. Especially one so young."

"It wouldn't be a hateful thing, my lord. I'm not afraid."

"My lord . . . my lord, Chelynne! We're in bed, naked! I have a name!"

She stared directly into his eyes, her cheeks growing pink, pinker, and deepening into a flush that was so incredibly red that she burned with it. She blinked her eyes closed hard. "Chelynne," he urged. "What is it?"

She covered her burning face with her hands, shaking her head, unable to speak. He pulled her hands away but she wouldn't open her eyes. "Come, sweet," he said gently. "Tell me what's wrong." Still she could neither speak nor look at him. Her face flamed. "Are you embarrassed? Do you want me to fetch your gown?"

She shook her head negatively; that was the least of her worries now. She was so afraid she would faint or be sick and there was no graceful way out of this now. "Please," she murmured. "It's yourself."

"Well, you're going to have to get used to the sight of me," he chuckled.

"Oh, I can't," she wailed miserably. "Not in the light!"

Chad laughed and pulled her near again. She could feel the strong-muscled legs against hers but thankfully she was so close she didn't have to look down at him. She opened her eyes and looked into his. One long arm reached down and pulled the coverlet over them both. "Is that better?" he asked, the chuckle in his voice.

"Thank you," she whispered.

"I can hardly believe you're real, love."

"It's just that . . . well, I hardly know you at all and here we are . . . so close . . ." Her voice was nervous, some of the pink returning to her cheeks.

"It's not as if there isn't time to get to know one another, Chelynne. But I think perhaps we should start with breakfast. I don't think you're ready for anything more intimate than that."

"You might be right, my . . . er, Chad."

He laughed with amusement and rolled over to fling his long legs over the bed. He threw a look over his shoulder and saw that her eyelids were clamped tightly shut. He dressed swiftly and when his breeches were donned he turned to her. "You can open your eyes now."

She saw him then partially clothed and the relief was obvious on her features. Chad had a very difficult time not melting into laughter at her predicament. It was unreal. He brought her wrapper to the bed and gave it to her.

"I suppose I should be dressed," she muttered, starting to rise. "There are so many guests . . ."

"No, love. Much would be thought amiss if we were seen among our guests today. You will have to be content with this garment if only for the sake of appearance. They won't force our company."

"I suppose you're right," she agreed.

"Do this," he explained. "Call your women to help you freshen yourself and the room and have our breakfast brought. I will see my father about some business and join you shortly."

"Very well," she consented. He held her wrapper for her so she could slip into it. When she was pulling the ties she turned her fresh little face to his with deep earnest showing in her eyes. "I am most grateful that you know how to go about getting married," she sighed.

Chad laughed again, gaining more entertainment from this little sprite than he had ever hoped to. Even though he felt more like a nurse than a groom, the change was delightful. "You'll soon learn, Chelynne. Never fear."

He placed a light kiss on her brow and left her to seek out his father's rooms. It was a fair distance to the earl, but he did not notice it this morn. He was most anxious to have everything settled and over, anxious to give a little time to a young bride since the thought of marriage was no longer so appalling.

All the bedchambers he passed on his way had the doors tightly closed. The celebrating had gone far into the night and all guests would be taking advantage of their beds for many hours to come. His father, however, had seldom enjoyed a night's sleep since his days of ill health, and Chad had no fear of disturbing him.

He knocked and was admitted by his father's manservant, Sebastian, to find the earl up and dressed and seated before his own breakfast. "About so early," the earl scoffed. "What of your wife? Is she still abed?"

"No, Father. She calls for our breakfast while I've come to speak to you." Chad smiled, allowing his father that amount of comfort, and accepted the offered dish of tea.

"I think you know why I've come. It's about the paper you hold, and now the bargain's met, I would see no more delay to this matter. I would gladly count it done."

"The paper," he sighed. "Even now it is so important to you? You couldn't even relax the morning without it?"

"Never question the importance to me, my lord," Chad advised, adding some sternness to his voice. "It has been and always will be my first concern to see to the welfare of my son. I'll not loll abed and play the lusty groom while his future is in jeopardy."

"But tell me true, son. Are you totally displeased with the bargain? Can you not see a good side to it?"

"I yield you that, Father. The lady Chelynne seems to be as kind as she is fair, yet I don't love her well. That takes time."

"Ah, but time is what you have so much of! So much time! How I envy you your youth, your young wife! A trip, perhaps. An opportunity to have some enjoyable seclusion with Chelynne . . ."

"My lord, as you say there is much time ahead, but no longer do I coddle your whim without the paper you hold from me." Chad's voice had risen slightly and the earl felt his impatience.

"I do not have it, nor have I ever. I located it and that is all. It is still in the rectory of the small church in Browne where you and Anne were wed."

"Then it was all a lie?" Chad scowled.

"I did breach the truth to see you home and wed, but never did I touch and thus defile church records. I only asked for confirmation from the priest. Had you gone and investigated one year ago you would have found there was no threat to your son. Mayhaps you would have refused to placate me. I took that chance, but I would sink no further, certainly not to stealing from a lowly parish to see my own ends met."

"And how do I know you tell the truth now?"

"I expect you'll go at once and see. There's hunting near there, a fine inn and horseracing. Why not take the lady Chelynne and rest for a time? You could use the trip as an excuse to relax and enjoy your wife . . ."

Chad's face darkened, anger glowering in those gray eyes that bespoke fury so intense the earl's speech dwindled off. "You have used me badly, my lord. I wonder what I have done in my lifetime to warrant such deceit from my own father."

"Our friendship has weathered many a storm, son. I know the ground on which I tread is thin and worn. I did this because I believed my meager apology would gain me nothing. I thought of your future, your happiness with a fine woman like Chelynne, and our family reunited."

"You have so little faith in my charity that you thought to lie would be better? To lie and hold my son's future around my neck like a noose? Do you find me totally incapable of seeing to my own future and selecting my own wife? My God, Father, why?"

"Chadwick! I thought not to anger you with this confession, but relieve you! Go, see the record is intact, and bring your son home. Enjoy your life again. I thought you might understand. I am a father, too. A father seeing to his son's best interests. It was only good intentions that urged me on. No other fault was mine!"

Chad was silent. When he spoke it was slowly, carefully. "No, my lord. This all is for your faults, your greed. You would take possession of my very soul, living your entire life through me. You would select the bride, breed us like common stock, and hold our very life's breath from us when we would balk from your desires. I am disgusted."

"Son, I swear, I used my knowledge as a tool to initiate a truce between us, that is all. I sought out Chelynne with only one thought, to see you settled and happy with a woman who would do you honor."

"A truce would have been a simple matter. It would have been afforded at your meagerest request. This time you have gone too far."

Chad rose to leave and turned when he reached the door. "I go to Browne, but I go alone. The record will be moved, so you need search for it no more. I bid you see to the maiden you've brought to this house. The rest of your eager ambitions for truces and happinesses will be discussed at another time."

"Chad," the earl pleaded. "Chelynne is innocent of this. Do not hurt her, I beg you."

"Innocent? It seems so, but I have been much fooled in my life by appearances, my lord. There was a time I thought you to be my father, wise and true. I was wrong, many times over." He opened the door and turned once more to the old man. "I wonder . . . do you remember youth? Do you remember love? Do you remember being your own man, possessing your own will, or was your life planned by your elder?"

"You know I was left with this estate at a very early age. I much grieved that I was without the advice of an elder!"

"And I am much grieved that my elder never sees fit to leave me alone!"

Chad's pace to his chamber was fast and hard, his heels hitting the floors with anger and rage. He was so intent on his wrath that he never noticed the figure quietly concealed behind the curtain in the gallery as he fled his father's room. An eavesdropper, still completely undetected, trailed along behind Chad as he made his way to Chelynne.

Chelynne was seated at the breakfast table, her expression bright and happy, awaiting his presence before starting the meal. Stella worked at a furious pace putting Chelynne's things in order so she could leave the room.

Chad's anger increased as he looked on this scene. His father had trapped him. He was married now and had even come to like the situation, just as the earl would have it. With Kevin's birthright as the pawn Chad had yielded first with his acquiescence, then with his free will and finally with open desire for his bride. He would be damned if he'd play the game any longer.

He was unsure of his plan until he noticed the two maids busily pulling the covers over the bed and fluffing the pillows with a great deal of whispering and murmuring. Chelynne seemed oblivious to their business but Chad knew what they were about. They sensed there had been no consummation, for it was well known his wife was a virgin. He smiled to himself as he saw his way clear. No longer would he play into their hands. His father and his "innocent" bride would learn that Chad still held the highest card. He sent all the servants from the room impatiently.

Chelynne was far from sensing his mood so it was not necessary for Chad to work at concealing his feelings. She looked at him across that short distance with simple adoration, not seeking to see beneath the surface. He took up his knife and casually addressed his plate, not speaking until he had washed down the first mouthful with coffee, hot and black.

"Tell me, when your uncle broached the subject of marriage, were you pleased?"

"I was surprised," she replied.

"You were anxious to be wed?"

"I knew that it would happen someday. I thought it a bit soon, but no matter. He felt it was time."

"Then you were ready?"

"I thought not. I was frightened," she said with a light laugh. "I was much afraid you would be ugly and mean."

Chad chewed his food thoughtfully, watching her out of the corner of his eye. "But you accepted the proposition."

" 'Twas Lord Mondeloy's choice for me and out of my hands." She shrugged. "I am not displeased."

Her conversation came so easily, her mood so compliant and trusting that it softened him somewhat. Not for an instant did it change his mind, but nonetheless, the rest came a little more gently. "Shall you like being a countess?"

"I think I shall," she returned, not greatly upset with the question.

"And this, of course, was your reason for accepting so quickly?"

"Not mine. Perhaps my uncle's reason. He recalled making your acquaintance some years ago and vouched for your good character. He was most pleased that your father would consider me."

"Does he seek compensation from you for arranging this?"

"Of course not," she gasped. "How could you think it?"

"Chelynne, it is not uncommon," he said. "Know you so little of politics?"

"My lord," she said earnestly. "He never suggested that. It was only my future that concerned him. God's truth."

Chad went on with his breakfast. Chelynne slowed down with hers, wondering at this topic of conversation. She watched him as he ate, noticing only now that some of his movements were tense and strained, his brow creased with thought lines. When he looked up from his plate, she was staring at him.

"Have you ever been in love?" he asked.

"No. I think not."

"Not even a little, perhaps?"

"Nay, never love," she said softly. Not before this man, she could see that now.

"Had we met, things would have gone quite differently, I think. I might have courted you for a while, but more likely I would have had little time for that. What did my father tell you of me?"

"Very little," she confessed, growing nervous.

"Did he warn you of my attitude toward this marriage?"

"He . . . he said you would likely be reluctant."

"Did he think to tell you that he used force of a most distasteful sort to bring me to the altar?"

"No," she whispered, growing more alarmed.

"It is so. He could have brought me a fat old widow or a bony pox-faced spinster, but he chose a young woman of rare beauty. Do you know why?"

She hardly knew what answer he could expect her to give. Her eyes were frightened and when she looked at him he could almost feel her shudder. "For your pleasure, I assume," she replied, lowering her eyes and folding her trembling hands in her lap.

"I suppose," he muttered. "Primarily it is because he wants heirs, fine looking and well bred. You've done well for yourself, it's true, for you've gained a fair amount of wealth and a fine title. You're pleased, are you not?"

"I thought only of the manner of man I would wed. The title means nothing to me and I was content with my family's wealth." She was near tears, her eyes moist and troubled. She couldn't fathom the reason for this discussion since it was done and they were wed.

"But you are willing to give me heirs, though a little naive?"

"I didn't think on it heavily, my lord."

"Ah, then you hadn't considered pregnancy?"

"I . . . ah . . . well, I never . . . I don't know," she mumbled, distraught. She hadn't thought of anything past kissing him and being near him. Thoughts of the consummation fled her mind but for that brief fear. Touching, loving, she had thought of that. Pregnancy? She hadn't really thought that far.

"I will say this as gently as possible, Chelynne. I am simply not ready to be married. I have a great many matters of business that require my close attention and will take me away frequently, sometimes for long periods of time. Sharing this house with you is no great burden and there is no one else I seek to wed. The contract is signed and I will not break it. I was not well keened to the idea of marriage and the earl would not consider a delay."

"But 'tis done," she murmured, the shock obvious in her voice.

"Not entirely done, Chelynne. The vows were said and that is all."

"Before a man of God," she gasped, awed at this blasphemy.

"The problem is this," he said easily. "I have made myself responsible for a great many things. There are business and personal matters that I will not explain to you because they are complex and private. Had the matter of marrying been left up to me, I would have waited to see these things done first. Had I met you, fallen in love with you, and desired you for my wife without the earl's interfering, I would have asked you to wait to see these problems of mine solved. Do you understand?"

"I don't think so."

Chad sighed. "It is not very complicated, Chelynne. You are welcome to remain here as my wife, live in this house as its mistress and have everything you are due. I simply cannot tie myself down to the burdens of a family now and it will have to wait. I will not betray the personal terms of our marriage to outsiders. Enjoy the comforts of this home as my wife —"

"But I am your wife," she cried, tears springing to her eyes.

"Partially," he returned, taking another drink of his coffee and raising one brow at her.

"But if I do not live here as your wife, how could I stay? And I said the vows, and in truth I meant them, so how may I go?"

"The blossom of youth," he muttered scornfully. "There are years ahead of you, my dear. There's no need to despair a few weeks or months. The time will come one day when I can settle myself to family matters. To use you as a wife would be deceitful, for I don't want one now. I have no time for fussing with garters and petticoats. There are important matters that need my attention and cosseting a youthful bride is not very high on my list of obligations. If this is going to send you into a fit, then go to your uncle and tell him there was no consummation and you wish to go home."

"But . . . but he would be humiliated . . . your father would . . ."

"My father could stand some humbling. He will be my concern. What of you?"

"Sheldon would be . . ." Tears rolled down her cheeks pathetically. "You feel nothing for me?"

"Come now, Chelynne. We have only just met! You're lovely and desirable but so is half of London. This is your choice: stay here and act the part of wife with patience or do as you please elsewhere. There's no need to weep, it's a simple matter of giving me the time I need to finish business."

"I don't understand," she whimpered.

Chad was becoming more agitated with this upset every moment. "Had you married a knight who was called to war the morning after you were wed, what would you do?"

"Wait," she replied softly.

"*Now* do you understand?"

"I suppose." In her lap her hands twisted nervously, her fingers slipping on and off the ring she wore that bore his crest. This proposition was not frightening, only disappointing. That the groom was reluctant, she expected. That he would use her was something she had not expected. He was asking her to win him, deserve him, sit in patient exile while he made his decision. He could obtain an annulment whenever it suited him, cast her away and be done with it.

But she was not one to give up so easily something she wanted. She would stay rather than shame Sheldon by being returned as an unsatisfactory bride. She would stay rather than embarrass the earl by leaving and thus proving his failure. And she would stay because the dreams of a young heart that had never known total defeat could not be easily erased.

"Of business problems I know nothing and of personal ones I have had few," she murmured. "And as you say, there is time ahead . . ."

"That's fine," he said casually. "Now let's not have a great deal of fuss over this, my dear. There's no reason for airs between us, no reason for hostilities. You'll be fine as long as you remember that I set you aside temporarily to see my work accomplished. If I thought I could explain it to you and make it simpler to understand, I would do so. As I said, it is a private business as well as a complicated one. One such matter will take me away two days hence for a while."

"For very long?" she asked hesitantly.

"I hope not."

"I'll keep busy," she murmured, totally dejected now. He saw the disappointment on her face and felt horrible for having to use her at this rate. The poor child could never have known what a miserable affair she had been sold into.

"You're a child," he said softly. "A few years from now you won't even think about this. I promise you."

Her eyes rose to meet his and there was a new depth to the clear brown that he hadn't noticed before now. It was a kind of maturity, cynicism perhaps, that told of thoughts much more complicated and introspective than he had believed her capable of. "I hope so, Chad."

That was one of the first steps Chelynne took toward womanhood and a worldly education. There were a great many to follow, and none of them very easy.

In the next two days Chelynne was busy and Chad was much in her company, though she strongly suspected it was for appearance' sake. They rode, took their meals together, played card games or simply sat, she taking up some needlework and he reading or writing letters.

She accustomed herself to this much of a rote, becoming comfortable in the presence of a man. He played his part very well, as though he knew the details expertly. He routinely allowed her some short time alone to prepare for bed and strode into her rooms like a well-acquainted groom and hurried the servants away impatiently. He would pour a brandy from her stock, kept there and replenished by the servants for his pleasure, and visit with her while she sat propped in the bed. Then a light and somewhat affectionate kiss would be dropped on her brow and he would go quietly through the sitting room to his own bed.

When she woke in the morning, at the first sound of her stirring he would stride in, refreshed and well rested, and take the breakfast meal with her. He paid her strained courtesy as if they had only just met. If he took tobacco, it was only with her permission. When fixing his drink he would offer her wine. It was not at all as if they had lain naked together in the same bed, but rather as if they had been formally introduced at a recent ball. She would be a long time in understanding him.

On the third morning, when she rose and he did not come, she wondered aloud about his absence to a serving maid. She was informed, secondhand, that he had gone about business in some faraway shire and that his time of return was not known.

Most of the guests had either left or were preparing to leave within the week. Since the earl was suffering again and confined to his bed, Sheldon persuaded Eleanor that they should be going as well. To Chelynne's disappointment they allowed Harry to stay. She wondered at her uncle's wisdom in this, but it was fairly certain that in his room the earl would not be disturbed with the younger Mondeloy's presence. As for Chelynne, she sorely desired to stay as far from him as she could. But Harry was invisible, unpopular enough to go completely unnoticed. Even his father did not see him for days following the wedding.

Chad had been gone from Hawthorne House for over a week when early in the morning there came a persistent knocking at Chelynne's door. Stella admitted the intruder and Harry smiled across the room at his cousin.

"Good morning, cousin. I've come to bid you farewell."

"You're going this morning, Harry?" she asked, trying not to sound too eager.

"Speak not of how you'll miss me, dear. I'll be nearby."

"Truth is that I've not seen you since the day of the wedding, yet your things were all there in your room. What's busied you here?"

"Your new lands, Chelynne. Many pleasant diversions for a man who knows what he's about. I've been quite busy." There was a sly smile twisting his mouth and Chelynne assumed he had been occupying himself wenching in the villages around them. She hoped Chad would not learn of it.

"Have a safe journey," she said without much feeling, turning away from him.

"I shall. I left you a gift, Chelynne. A surprise."

"A gift?" she asked, startled enough to look up expectantly. "You needn't have, Harry. That . . . was very thoughtful of you. What is it?"

"A surprise, my lady. It's hidden, but you'll soon come upon it. You'll know it when you see it and I pray you remember, it is your gift."

"Why . . . that's very kind of you, Harry." And out of character, she thought.

He laughed, that impish laugh that she despised. It was rather shrill and feminine sounding, not unlike a cat in the night screaming at the moon. "Yes, it was kind. I can be kind, my dear, but if I were you I wouldn't expect kindness again."

"Harry." She pouted. "You spoil everything in the end, don't you? You might have left the gift and said no more."

"Good-bye, cousin. You'll hear from me." And he was gone.

Chelynne didn't have to wonder long about her surprise. She found it readily enough and when she did she blushed. It was a letter, aged and worn, and the signature at the bottom was simply "M." It was not the fact that he had left her a letter that her own mother had most obviously written that embarrassed her; rather, it was the fact that she found it in the jewel coffer near her bed. The only way he could have managed was to put it there while she slept. Her loathing for him was so intense that to think he might have caught a glimpse of her scantily clothed left her livid and shamed.

Her anger faded quickly in her eagerness to read the letter at hand. She sent Stella from her room so that she could have complete privacy for the enjoyment of this brief link with the past. It was a long letter, it being hard to find couriers during those times. Many pages were held together mostly by age and the writing in some places was smeared and indiscernible. She read of what the exiled nobles were doing while hoping to gain England again for their home. Her mother thought the cause hopeless by now, believing they were bound to travel like poverty-stricken gypsies forever. They were already bereft of the finer things they had known before the wars. Madelynne professed she was proud, in any case, to be serving Charles. She praised him openly in her letter. She would be glad to live by whatever means for the royal cause.

There came, very suddenly, another mention of the king, and Chelynne was not quite prepared, though she thought later that she should have been. It was not so frank as she would have hoped, but the message to her uncle Sheldon was this:

> The child is expected some three months hence, Sheldon. My husband is convinced, beyond doubt, that there is a conspiracy against his name, but he seems not to hold me in any contempt for my indiscretion. He has long been beset with an ugly problem in getting an heir to his name, and now, after many years, there shall be one. He will accept it, as of course he must, because he cannot and will not challenge the man he suspects. Were there any need to confirm the possibility, it would easily be done. You know now who that man must be.
>
> I ask this of you, Sheldon. Should anything happen to either Sylvester or myself, see to this child of ours. You have known me well and for many years. I need not explain that anything I would do would be for a strong and passionate love. I am left now with only brief memories of moments past, and love to me, especially now, is as rare as moon dust. But do my child this, if I cannot. Teach him that love is just. It is more merciful than war, more nourishing than bread and more soothing than wine. And I have decided that it is the only logical reason for living.

There was a great deal more to the letter, but Chelynne only skimmed it. Nothing further was mentioned of the child. There was no doubt now that her mother had fallen in love with Charles Stuart and that Chelynne was the product of that love. Her name was Mondeloy because her father had no choice, his service being to his king. She felt the sharp sting of pity for Lord Mondeloy, being cast aside by his wife for another lover. But strangely, she felt no shame or anger toward Madelynne. The letter had touched her deeply. She respected her mother's honesty and sensitivity. It was much as Sheldon had told her, that a child was only as gentle and worthy as the love that got it. Could it be more right to bear a child to a man you loathed, even if the bonds of wedlock bound you to him?

And she held the evidence in her hand. Sheldon had told her there was nothing of her parents. He must have either treasured the letter or hidden it for her protection. But then would Madelynne have made the crude mistake of explaining this circumstance more than once in a letter? It was highly unlikely, for the risk of doing so once was foolish. Chelynne determined, logically, that this must be the only written proof. She would see Sheldon in a few months and must ask him then if there could be something more. With this letter in her possession, he would not dare mislead her another time.

She read it again and again and again, memorizing every word carefully. Then, with a smile on her lovely little face, she walked to the fireplace and set it upon the hot coals. It was gone from human eyes and sealed in her heart. She laughed guiltily and then covered her mouth, though no one was there to see her. Harry was a fool. No longer could he taunt her with it. Could he?

Another strong urge possessed her. To see this king she had heard so much about. To judge for herself whether her mother had been sane or half crazed to allow this illicit love. Whatever her determination would be after meeting him, one thing kept pounding into her brain. He was the king! The greatest man on earth!

Chelynne whiled away the days, riding as she could, bored with being bound to escorts. Chad had left orders as to the routes she was allowed to take, never even allowing her to explore these lands at will. Finally she went to see the earl, more out of boredom than goodwill.

"Shoo, girl, begone from here. This illness is no sight for a young maid."

"I've seen illness, my lord," she replied from her place just inside the door. "Would you favor company?"

"Ah, you're a lovely sight for this ailing heart, but don't be troubled. It's a hideous thing, this."

She came a little closer, pitying the man who had been so lively at her wedding. She couldn't understand this illness that came and went so abruptly. He had been bright and cheerful and now was obviously low in his health. He had a stale gray pallor; a mere shriveled hump in the bedclothes was the earl of Bryant.

"Perhaps I could read to you. That should not tire you terribly."

"Ah, you've a tender heart, Chelynne. Mayhaps a little . . ." He wheezed abruptly and she withdrew. Then sensing that she might have appeared repulsed, she went near again and sat close to the bed.

"I'll fetch a book if you recommend one," she offered.

Instead of replying he wheezed the more, turning near purple from loss of breath. "My lord?" she questioned. "Shall I call —" All at once he sat straight up, choking and coughing and trying to talk.

"My . . . breath . . . my . . ."

The gasping and choking terrified her and she made a frantic rush to ring the bell that sounded for servants. Feeling totally helpless and confused, she aided him in sitting up, for that seemed to be his desire at the moment.

"I'll die this time," he gasped. "This time . . ."

"Nay, m'lord, ye'll not dee so soon," came a deep voice from behind them. The huge manservant drew in on them. Chelynne had seldom seen this man. His large frame was hard to miss but he was so rarely about that she had wondered at his duties. She guessed now that he was most oft needed here, tending his lordship in his illness. "It wouldna do to leave the lass 'fore the first wee bairn comes."

The earl's tight expression seemed to ease in the presence of the manservant. His breath came more easily and he settled back into the pillows. The servant spoke softly and with much confidence to the earl, and from over his bent shoulder Chelynne could see as he applied a poultice to the aging man's chest. He turned when he was done and faced Chelynne.

"It wasna a bad one, lass. Ye needna fear. He'll rest now."

"What is this illness?"

"It shrivels his gullet and the chest. I'll see to him now."

"Could I stay for a while? Could I help in some way?"

"I'll be makin' a brew to have him take when he comes 'round again. There's naught else to be doin'."

"You tend him very well. What is your name?"

"I be Sebastian, lass. I've been with the mon o'er twenty year now."

"What's in the brew?"

Sebastian laughed. "Yer a curious one, now. It's a thing I've been makin' since me days a'home. Scotland, that is. Me grandfather first taught me healin' ways and here they've found use again. Watch."

He moved to a table in the room and she watched as he took tiny portions of herbs from many little bowls and blended them together in a cup. When he added milk and wine to the cup and warmed it, the smell was pungent, causing her to wrinkle her nose. Sebastian laughed heartily at her reaction. He put the posset down to await the earl's waking.

"How long has His Lordship been ill like this?"

"Ah, some years now. He's old, though not so in years. More in the way of life. He could as well dee now, but willna go until he wishes to."

"What?" she gasped.

"Because even in his weakness he's strong. His will. He willna dee 'till he's tired of fightin'. Now he fights for his heir, the good Chadwick."

"He watches over Chad quite carefully."

"Aye, when the lad'll have it. He's gone from his pa o'er and o'er again and he'll go yet another time, t'be sure. They're too much the same, those two, and neither would lean nor bend."

"But why?"

"I wouldna know, nor would I be sayin' if I did. I am bound to His Lordship fer healing, not fer speakin' of the family battles."

"I see," she muttered. No help there. "Will he be all right now?"

"Aye, lass. Fer now."

"Shall I come again?"

"Bring the book *The Willow* from the library. That's one he likes."

Her eyes grew round with dismay. "Were you here all the time?"

"I'm never far away, lass. I know where my place is and that's where I'm found."

She brought the book the next time, though her visit was cut short by another attack. She knew without a doubt that the earl's passing was not far away. She had never felt death before as she felt it now. It was thick and foul in that room. And it was not frightening, for the earl seemed to long for that haven. But when she would have thought him well on his way, he began to improve. She found him a few days later sitting up and waiting for her to come. Sebastian warned her not to take heart in it. His illness was as unpredictable as nature.

She had had no word from Chad. He was in her thoughts always but she had no idea when he would return. She saw him from the garden as he rode toward Hawthorne House. She struggled for patience. When he had given his tired horse to the groom she rushed toward him with a glad smile on her lips.

Chelynne couldn't have known how anger had welled up inside of Chad for many days, for countless miles. When he was faced with the untimely sight of his young wife it brought him near the breaking point. She froze in her tracks at the sight of his fierce scowl.

"Welcome home," she said uncertainly.

His jaw twitched nervously and his fists were clenched at his sides. "Were there problems in my absence?" he asked coolly.

"Your father is ill. Nothing else."

"He is in bed . . . again?"

"Aye. Was your trip a hard one?"

"It was the hardest trip I've made in a lifetime," he ground out. Brushing past her he strode into the house, leaving Chelynne to stare after him in much confusion. She sank to the garden bench in bitter helplessness.

Chad did not delay in going to his father, daring illness or any other excuse to slow his rage. He threw the door to his lordship's rooms open angrily; no inclination toward any courtesy did he show. His father was propped in the bed. Sebastian quickly disappeared.

"Greetings, Chadwick. You're a long time in getting home. How did you find Browne?"

Chad's face was twisted with wrath. "Browne is the same but there is much amiss in their burgh. Would you know the cause?"

"I've not seen the place in two years, son. How would I know what disturbs the town?"

"Perhaps you had some men sent there for some purpose —"

"What purpose? Get to the point."

"I found the church in which I wed my Anne has burned!" he cried. "The priest was murdered and the church destroyed. Nothing remains of the records and no one saw the bandits!"

"And you suspect it was my doing," the earl said wearily.

"And who would have cause besides you?" Chad growled.

"I had nothing to do with this thing, Chadwick. On my honor, son, I would never have had such a thing done in my stead."

"Damn! It is gone!" Chad cried, almost sobbing like an ailing child. "Gone!"

"Adopt the boy, then! See the courts and have him named heir!"

"He is my son! Adopt my own son? My lady Anne should not be laid to rest with a question to her virtue! My son will not be called bastard! This is too much!"

"What were the thieves about? Were there other robberies? Abuse?"

Chad laughed harshly. "Do you think me the simple fool to leave that town before I learned all I could? What do you imagine I've been about these many days past with Browne only a day's ride west? Did you think I was riding to the hounds? Watching the cockfights?" He sobered slightly. "There was nothing else amiss there. 'Twas only the church played havoc on. The only murder was that of the priest as he sought to protect that humble shed. There was not even a chalice of much value there."

"And that is why you accuse me?"

Chad shook his head, his anger deflated somewhat from the

mere force of anxiety he had held for many days. "Why?" he asked pleadingly.

"Keep your head," the old man snapped. "Think of your son, if you must, but keep your head and don't turn now to boyish whimpering. This thing could have happened without any hostility between us. Do what you would in that case. Find the course and claim your son again. No one will stand in your way and I would even stand witness to it! Don't let your emotions rule your life, Chadwick! No one here plotted against you!"

Chad stood stone faced. "The matter will not be done until I find some cause. Good day, my lord."

Chad turned on his heel and was gone, leaving the earl to stare at the open door. He thought for a moment.

"Sebastian," he shouted. "Sebast—"

"Aye, m'lord."

"Where the devil do you hide yourself in here? No matter, did you hear Chadwick?"

"Aye."

"Call a party of men to go to Browne. Set them to the task of finding what intent was for that town. He, of course, assumes I had something to do with it. Promise a reward . . . a good one."

"The number of men?"

"Make it twelve to twenty, whatever we can spare. And set them out immediately!"

"Crime is bad, m'lord. The lad does you wrong. The same happens oft about the smaller shires."

"The devil it does! Not like this!"

Downstairs Chelynne waited patiently, just now finding the courage to face her husband again. He was just descending when she approached him meekly. He stopped, glared at her with nothing less than hatred, and brushed past her to leave the house again.

Stunned, she paused there, then followed him again only to find his fast pace left her well behind. She managed to see him as he took a fresh mount and fled her further pursuit with a great deal of speed.

Wearily she returned to her bedroom and groomed herself for

his return. She dared not leave the house lest he should return and want something of her. Since she feared his angry display she went to a great deal of trouble to please him.

She had a meal prepared that she thought would be appreciated, but when the hour was past ten she yielded to Stella's pleas and took a tray in her room. Finding little sense in having the household go without sleep, she bade those waiting servants seek their pallets and she donned her own nightclothes.

She paced about for a time, wondering what would stir him into such a rage. Impulsively she walked through the sitting room and entered Chad's chambers. Bestel had prepared a fire, giving the indication he at least expected his master's return.

She pulled a chair near the hearth and curled up in it; the time dragged clumsily by. She knew little of the more personal wifely duties, but feared being remiss. If he wished a meal or bath she would be ready to aid him. As the hours passed Chelynne drifted off to sleep.

A chill in the dark room caused her to stir into wakefulness, and she found the fire low but a quilt covering her. She smiled to think Bestel would be so thoughtful. She came awake slowly, unaware of another presence in the room, and found the tinder. She lit the candle and the glow showed Chad's bed to be empty still. With a disappointed sigh she turned to go and seek out her own bed.

"Good night."

Chelynne started and nearly dropped the candle. Spinning about and squinting into the darkness she attempted to make out the owner of that voice. "Chad?"

"Aye. You needn't wait up for me unless it is specifically asked of you."

"Very well," she returned softly. "Since I am here, is there anything I can get you?"

"Nothing." He came out of the darkness. Still garbed in his riding outfit he looked worn and tired. His hair was blown and paths parting the dust on his face from where perspiration had streaked added to the grimness of his features. The odor of leather and horses filled her nostrils as he neared. Flecks in his eyes glittered in the light of the candle and she was a little afraid of him.

"I'll see you to bed," he said, taking her arm.

"There's no need," she argued, uselessly. He took her arm and led the way to her room a bit roughly. Once there he stood and waited while she crawled into the bed. She settled herself back and without thinking she held out her hand to him, offering more than a touch, offering peace to aid him in his strife if he would take it from her. She was immediately afraid that he would push it away.

But he did not. He touched the hand gently in indecision and then took it in both of his and sat down on the bed beside her, absently turning his ring on her finger.

"Is there anything I can do?"

"Do?" he returned dully.

"You're troubled, Chad. Can I help?"

"Yes, Chelynne. You can find a way to live in this house quietly. Carefully. Find a way to be my wife without posing any more difficulties for me." And then with a voice sounding tired and hopeless, he added, "I've had enough."

SIX

THE END OF AUGUST grew near and the fields of Bryant and the surrounding areas ripened with the summer's plentiful crops. Another month or even less would see the harvest. Every farmer and his family labored hard and late into the night to have the work done well.

But for Chelynne the days were the same, one just like the next, all spent within the great walls of Hawthorne House or riding on the privileged roads near the mansion. It was a surprise to her when one morning Chad came to her rooms just as she had seated herself before her breakfast.

"I'm about business today, madam," he started. "I've matters in Bratonshire that need my attention. Is there something I can get for you there?"

"I can think of no needs," she thoughtfully replied.

"Should you like to accompany me? I was going to ride, but I'm willing to take the carriage if you want to go."

He had hardly finished his sentence and she was on her feet. "I'd love to go. Have they shops? Might I perhaps make purchases while you see to business?"

"They're simple folk, madam, but there are some small shops there. Nothing that would suit . . ." But she was already calling Stella to find her dress and had slipped behind her screen.

"I've not been about the towns," she was chattering. "Can you give me the time to dress?"

"If it's done quickly," he started.

Looking around he noticed that before he had even settled any details with her Stella had gone into a mad rush and Chelynne's dressing gown was already hanging over the screen. He caught a glimpse of that lovely young body just as she was pulling her dress on and rushing to her dressing table. So unlike the aristocratic dames, Chelynne was pulling the heavy masses of her hair up herself, holding it firmly while Stella pinned it into place, tying it with a bright ribbon. He watched the scurrying around with some wonder. Chelynne quickly applied powder to her nose and cheeks and red to her lips. Stella bustled away to fetch her wrap and gloves and Chelynne whirled around to present her back to Chad, silently requesting his aid in the fastenings.

His knuckles brushed against the silken flesh and he sorely felt the bite. He cursed under his breath, damned his father for choosing so carefully for him. She had a way of promising, so innocently with those slim, firm thighs and tender little rump, long passionate nights. He wanted her again. Always, if she was this near, he wanted her.

Unconsciously his hand crept within the folds of her gown and tested more carefully her soft, tempting skin. She coyly turned her eyes around to him and braved a smile. "You were in a hurry to go, my lord."

He grunted, pulled his hand away, and gave her a little shove in the direction of Stella. Chelynne, smiling inside, bade Stella hurry to fasten her.

She was ready, almost too quickly to be true, and her appearance was flawless. It was unheard of that a woman would go so quickly to please a man. Even the simplest whore seemed to think it enticing to drag out the process. Dressing was overdone in its importance as far as Chad was concerned. But Chelynne, simple maid in her heart, had not thought to be wily and scheming. He had asked her to hurry, so she did. It left him slightly dazed.

"Take along your woman to carry your parcels if there be any," he instructed, preceding her out of the room.

Chelynne found that the carriage was waiting, as if he had anticipated that she would want to join him. She felt a small victory in this.

The ride was a silent one, but thankfully Chad did not seem angry this once. His mood was quiet as it often was, but she did not ponder this too deeply. She hoped they would have something to talk about on the return trip. That was as complicated as her thoughts about her silent husband ran, thus far.

Their carriage was slowed as they approached a broken-down cart blocking most of the road. Two men labored hard to line up a wheel deeply embedded in mud, and a woman paced about the cart nervously, muttering and twisting her hands. Chad, chafed at the delay, jumped out and went to assess the situation for himself.

He talked to the men for a moment, gave some unasked-for advice, and was about to get back into the carriage. The swirl of a deep green dress caught his eye and he looked to see Chelynne near the cart talking to the woman and attracted to something within.

"Come, Chelynne," he called. "Let's be on our way."

"Chad," she called back. "Will you see? The child is ill and still there is no certainty they can move the cart." She pointed to the deep groove where the cart had swerved. "It's deeply caught."

"Come along," he said crossly. "Leave these men to free their cart."

She turned away, ignoring him, and touched the child's brow. He lay shivering beneath the blankets. "How long has the boy been ill?" she asked the woman.

"Days now, madam," she said fearfully. "We could summon no doctor and must take him now to the shire of Braton to see one there." As if to reassure the stately dame, she dug into the folds of her dress and produced coin. "I can meet the cost," she said, almost apologetically.

Chelynne looked up to find her husband standing beside her, his impatience building and his good humor stretched. The small blond head of the boy was hot to the touch and his breathing labored.

"He's so ill," Chelynne told Chad. "Could we take him with us to Bratonshire?"

"Come along, Chelynne. It might be plague."

"Nay, not plague," the woman argued.

"Chad," Chelynne bit through. "We cannot leave them thus."

"Get in the carriage," he said sternly. "Now."

She bit her lip and did as he ordered, shamed at having no more influence over this man than she did. He settled himself beside her and noticed that as the men continued to labor with the cart she watched them with pained eyes.

"Damn," he swore, taking up his gloves and clambering out of the carriage with a quick angry hop. He shouted to the driver for aid and removed his coat, tossing it carelessly into the carriage. He moved to the scene again, positioned his own driver to lead the horse, and pushed from behind with the two other men. There was no yielding.

Mud, thick from the summer rain, caked his boots and splattered on his once spotless stockings. He walked to the edge of the road and found a split log. Placing that under the front of the deeply sunk wheel, he pushed again. Still there was no progress.

Cursing loudly, in English and in French, he removed his shirt and threw it in the carriage with his coat. He bent to the task again, straining his arms and back against the unmovable cart. Chelynne watched with something akin to worship as his muscles played across his broad back while he strained with the chore. She imagined her fingertips would not touch if she had the chance to encircle him with her own arms. Loud grunts escaped him as he pushed with amazing power and the thing began to ease. With one last command and a vigorous jolt, as he threw his entire body into the action, the wheel found solid ground and eased out of the impacted hold.

He stood and watched for a moment as the men and woman scrambled aboard the moving cart and rode with the child toward Bratonshire. He pulled on his shirt, turning his back to the women to stuff it into his breeches, and replaced his coat. As he climbed back into the carriage he glowered at Chelynne, but she smiled sweetly.

"I'm sure they're grateful for your aid, my lord."

"They'd have found a way out soon enough," he grumbled.

"But you're responsible for them, Chad," she argued carefully.

"Not their every breath," he snorted.

"Aye," she murmured. "This once, their very breath."

He looked away, not wishing to discuss the matter further, and kicked his muddy boots at the floor to chip away what had dried. He cursed again, under his breath this time so as not to bruise delicate ears, seemingly annoyed. But in his heart there came a strange softening. He made no sign of it but he was beginning to feel this gentleness move in on him and change the course of his thinking. Even though the feeling was good, he feared rather than savored it.

In the little town they visited there was much hubbub. Chad went immediately to the sheriff to see about some business and Chelynne was left to her own ends. Before he left, he told her where he would be, which was a great deal more than he usually did.

She hurried along with Stella to see what this village had to offer. Though the great majority of citizens were set to the task of tending the fields, there was a great deal of activity on the main street. Sensing the harvest and celebrations, traveling merchants headed their carts in the direction of the farming villages, ready to accept hard-earned coin and barter with farmer's wives for trinkets. There was a booth set up displaying glassware, one for jewelry, and the usual tavern and inn. Chelynne noticed a humble dressmaker's shop and a bakery.

It was not long before Chelynne was recognized. The fineness of the Hawthorne carriage alerted some and others remembered her from the day they traveled to Hawthorne House to take advantage of the earl's generosity on his son's wedding day. She was surrounded by villagers almost immediately. While one woman was eager to display her yard of cloth, another was tempting her with a fine pastry. There was still another anxious to brag about the newest addition to the family. In the midst of this confusion someone called out to show the lady to a coffeehouse where she might sit and take her ease and another bellowed about the newest cart of trinkets arrived with a gypsy to tell the fortunes of patrons.

Chelynne was enthralled with their hospitality. It was much like

Welbering and touched a place in her heart. She begged to hold the tiny babe, a red-faced little creature nuzzling at his mother's bosom and squeaking in discontent. She took a bite of a sweet tart and fondly caressed a length of velvet.

Suddenly the babe was pulled from her arms and the crowd dispersed to allow someone through. She looked in the direction of the approaching personage and saw that it was Lord Shayburn, with much the look of an overstuffed bear, heavily laden with lace and jewels.

"Welcome, my lady."

"Thank you, my lord." She curtsied. They moved together and the people moved farther away.

"I was unaware you planned a visit, madam. I would have gladly seen to your comfort."

"Not necessary, I assure you," she was quick to say. "I decided to come at the very last moment and I hope to enjoy the shops."

"Allow me to take you to my home and serve you tea. You can't possibly be comfortable here."

Chelynne stiffened. She so disliked this man's manner that she had a hard time keeping her feelings concealed. "I assure you, sir, this is what I do enjoy. And I haven't had the opportunity in a long while. I'll see some glassware before joining my husband."

"I'm sorry to say we've nothing here of much quality, madam, but if you're insistent, I shall escort you."

"My lord, if my husband thought an escort necessary he would not have left me to go alone. By your leave." She started away. She was annoyed with his pursuit, and more so when she found her arm seized.

"Never mind, madam, I'll take you myself. I consider your welfare as my obligation."

She snatched her arm away. "I assure you, I'm quite capable of walking!"

"I would consider it an unpardonable breach to leave you without proper escort, my lady," he said with a bow.

"Oh, very well," she sighed. "But I have no need of your support. I've two good legs, as you can see."

He grunted disapprovingly and gave a jerk of his head, bidding

Stella to fall in behind them. Stella's gasp alerted Chelynne and she turned to see a young girl dressed in rags struggling to keep up with the baron. She stopped and looked over the pitiful creature.

"My lord, who is this child?" she questioned.

"Nothing to concern yourself about, madam. She is indentured to me for her father's debts. That is all."

Chelynne coldly eyed the leg irons. They chafed the child's ankles as she hobbled along. "And bound so?"

"A scraggly little animal." He coughed, digging a perfumed kerchief out of his sleeve. "I'll have her minding her manners soon enough, I warrant."

Chelynne went immediately to the young girl. She had a battered face, her eyes hollowed and bones threatening to burst through the young flesh she was so thin and frail. Her hair was a tangled mass of matted filth and the stench as Chelynne neared her was almost overpowering. Her torn dress, baring her legs to her knees, displayed the many bruises on her shins and the dried blood caking and scabbing around her ankles. Chelynne put an arm around the child to question the baron further, but she winced away with a pained yelp. Shayburn's hand came up as if to silence her with a blow but Chelynne's arm deftly crossed his at the wrist. Eyes usually soft and brown held Shayburn in his place with a golden sheen so cold it chilled the air around them.

With the baron stopped in his tracks, Chelynne turned her attention again to the girl, lifting her dress away to peer down at her abused back. Stella's eyes went there as well, the older woman gasping audibly at the marks of many thrashings, festering and weeping.

"Why was this child beaten, my lord?"

The people of that humble village had begun to draw near to this scene once again.

"She's a most difficult nature, madam," he said easily. "She'll not work as she's told to."

"Perhaps she has not the strength. Do you feed her?"

"Madam?"

"She's thin and weak. Is this how you treat your servants?"

"Madam, you misunderstand. She is not in my employ at all.

She is indentured to me. Bond servant, nothing more." His tone was most courteous, carefully hiding the displeasure he felt at being cross-examined by this wisp of a girl. "She gets only as she's due."

Chelynne had never felt disgust this strongly. She would have impulsively slapped the man's face had she not caught herself. Anger welled up inside of her until she seethed, but the close presence of the townspeople cautioned her to mark her words carefully and take care with her privy authority. "She's not even ten years old, my lord. Must one so young be impounded for the debts of another?"

"Nay, madam. She is four and ten. Already she bleeds."

Chelynne knew the habits of some lords and their dealings with their churls, but Sheldon's fairness and decency had spoiled her. She had come to think of some of the things she heard about as severe fabrications, or at least as happening only on the farthest corners of the earth, never so close to her own home. With considerable distaste she pressed the point, the words souring in her mouth. "And has she been used?"

"Of course, madam," he said easily, not an ounce of shame in his voice.

Chelynne's lips formed a tight, furious line. She was mortified beyond anything she had ever known. Her mind was set and she gave no thought to consequences. "What are her father's debts?"

"Madam?"

"The amount. I wish to know."

He bristled no small bit at having to answer to this young woman, but remembered painfully well that she was a young sprite of special importance to the earl of Bryant and that he was without choice. The amount was thirty pounds and he answered smoothly, "Five hundred pounds."

Her response was a sharp, cruel laugh. "Five hundred pound!" she cried. "You must think me an addled fool. Surely, my lord, you don't expect me to believe that your generosity would extend itself to those limits for a member of this simple burgh. Here now, try me again with a figure, and make it at least more believable."

The man reddened and clenched his fists at his sides. "Two hundred, in that case."

Again Chelynne laughed and started to walk away, a light hand pulling the child along with her. "I shall have sent to you one hundred fifty pound, my lord. In return I would like her father's papers. It should see the matter done well enough, but let me tell you, I know it's a gift I give you."

"Madam," he shouted. She turned and eyed him with cold contempt.

"Sir?"

"I do not wish to sell the girl."

"That is unfortunate, sir, for I wish to have her. Shall I speak to His Lordship and have him bargain for me?"

Shayburn huffed and snorted, drawing the lace kerchief again to his nostrils and breathing deeply. He would not be pleased to have this battered child in the earl's own household to remind him again of matters often and wearily discussed: the management of this village. But he was trapped.

"I, being your most humble servant, madam, will gift you with this parcel, if she be to your liking."

"Nay, my lord, it will be a purchase fair and good. I would have it no other way. Expect a courier in a few days. Does the child have a name?"

"Aye, Tanya, but she'll not answer to it. You've got yourself a problem with this baggage, madam, and you'll see it soon enough. No doubt you'll be begging me to take her back soon."

"I doubt that, sir. I'm sure the child will respond to some kindness and do me honor in my home."

"You would use this mangy beast in your home?" he choked. "Why, she's not fit to empty slops."

"My wife will use her where she will," came a slow and steady voice.

Chelynne had been completely unaware of her husband's presence. She had no idea how long he had been there or how much he might have heard.

"And now, my lord, what was that sum?" Chad asked slowly and confidently. "I believe this is the correct amount," he went on without benefit of an answer, placing coins in the baron's hand. "I'll expect the papers delivered posthaste. See it done. Good day."

Shayburn had not the gall to count the coin, for the argument was so pathetically lost. Chelynne went quickly ahead to the carriage, Stella plodding along behind with the young girl.

It wasn't until they were on their way that Chelynne began to tremble. She had never spoken so to anybody, especially not a man of importance in a town of this size. It was as if she were seized by a spirit taking the part of her tongue. The plight of the girl left her without reason. Anger led her where her senses had failed.

Stella fussed over the trembling girl beside her, soothing and crooning to her as one would a babe. Chelynne hoped to get home quickly, avoiding discussion of this incident. But Chad was not so inclined.

"What possessed you to do this thing?"

"He's used her so badly, Chad," she said softly, her voice quivering from the upset. "She's just a child and already he's used her. He's bedded her."

"And if she's with child?"

Chelynne gasped at the thought. "It might kill her to bear a child. She's only a child herself." She shuddered.

"The baron might be right. You might have bought more trouble than you know."

"What would you have me do?"

"You could have brought the matter to my attention. I am capable of handling some situations without a presumptuous wife to act in my stead. As it was, you've brought the question of the man's integrity to the entire town. The treatment of his serv— um, people, does not concern you."

"But this is scandalous," she argued boldly. "I wouldn't be able to sleep had I left her with that beast, knowing how he abuses her."

"Then the proper course would be to bring the matter to me and let me attend to it."

"But you took my part," she said pleadingly.

"The immediate situation warranted that I take a part and my choice left me to take the part of my wife or a neighboring baron. I hope not to meet that fork in the road another time. Do you understand?"

Chelynne frowned openly. This marriage and her new position had turned into a confusing game, heavily laden with rules she did not understand. "In the name of charity —"

"In the name of charity I shall find myself penniless from your sympathy and my back broken from doing yeoman chores. Your position is not that of patron saint to these people. School yourself in the behavior of the part you play here and do not cause me much undue hardship as you do battle for fairness to poor unfortunates."

She looked away, much upset with his reprimand. He sat across from her, his arms folded over his broad chest, trying not to smile. She had surprised him once again with something he hadn't expected. This sense of justice and quick action amazed him. But women, he reminded himself, were impractical beyond good sense, ever seeking to lick available wounds. He grunted.

"How did you propose to pay the baron?"

"I was allotted a household budget for myself and my women," she replied quietly.

"Then you will debit from the balance one hundred and fifty pound. Examine your ledgers carefully before seeing to any other unnecessary purchases."

"Yes, sir," she said meekly.

Chad's eyes fell to the young girl in Stella's protective embrace. The poor little thing stared blankly ahead, her eyes holding only a small bit of the light of sanity. His contempt for the baron doubled, if that were possible. But to have Shayburn sense his ill will would do him no good. He needed to be on reasonable terms with the man. He set his mind to the distasteful task of writing a note of some apology for Chelynne's impetuous behavior, hoping to stay the man's temper a bit.

"I'm sorry I've angered you," she said quietly.

"The baron is the law of that shire, Chelynne," he carefully explained. "He treats the people there harshly, but backs his justice with much coin and influence. He has successfully concealed any injustice while adding to his wealth with illicit business. And there are those of wealth and title who do likewise and would vouch for him. There is no band thicker than thieves. For the sake of those people who serve him, do not make the man look like a fool. He would likely rear up in anger and abuse ten for every one you save."

"How can he do this?"

"Because," he said simply, "there seems to be no way to stop him."

"At least one is safe," she murmured, glancing at Tanya.

"I do not wish to have every reprobate housed with me, Chelynne. Stifle your tender heart some small bit or you will find yourself devoid of funds."

"Yes, sir," came the meek reply.

The nights of late summer were clear and cool, the only hint that the heat would give way to a biting chill. A heavy wool coat against a man's back would bring comfort now, but in a month's time it would barely be enough to keep out the damp, cold wind.

John Robert Bollering rode slowly, though the moon was bright enough to light his way easily across the countryside. The horse was a fine mount from the Hawthorne stables and John had been his master long enough to be assured of a good performance from the beast. He would make his journey to Bratonshire from his hidden dwelling on Hawthorne land many times in the coming months, and always at night.

He paused at the top of a rounded knoll to view this village lying so peacefully against the beautiful English countryside. This was his father's land. These were his father's people. John had seen his father lose his lands and then his life as he fought for the king's cause. The king was beheaded and England was at war with itself. John had fled England to fight with the Royalists while still a youth.

When Charles II was restored to the throne John felt England calling him home. He found that his mother had died during the sovereign's long exile and the Bollering children still living had settled themselves in marriages and businesses. The safest and surest thing to do was to ask King Charles for a grant of land in Virginia and begin to rebuild his dream. But instead he went to Bratonshire.

There he found the burgh mismanaged and the people afraid

and abused. What he had known to be a fruitful and happy place was a mere shadow of its former worth. The villagers were poorly fit while the baron's purse grew heavy and the fields and keeps flourished with crops and livestock. He knew then that vengeance was his goal and that he must find a way to right that old wrong.

John spent the next five years building his wealth and hoarding his gold with a miser's zeal. A year before Chad would return home permanently these two longtime friends staged a falling out that convinced all associated with them that the friendship was over and they could not be reconciled. Chad was helpful in seeing that those rumors reached Bratonshire. And while John served His Majesty faithfully and well within the confines of the law, another convenient lie was circulated: John had turned pirate and thief and would not dare set foot on English soil again.

John's presence in the country now was secret, for the time was ripe. He planned to strip Shayburn of that land in the same ruthless way his father had been beaten. This time, however, he would gain the confidence of some courageous villagers who would aid him with his work.

With a few men from his ship and a few of Chad's men-at-arms, John was setting out to cripple Bratonshire. There would be murder, destruction, thievery and rape. But it would be a play for the baron. Those robbed would have their possessions returned, those thought dead would actually be spirited away, and whatever was destroyed John would promise to rebuild when the land was his.

Shayburn had a mean troop of men he called guards to do his bidding and deal out his punishments, but for himself he was a coward. It would not be long before he requested aid in protecting his lands. The most likely one to be asked was the earl of Bryant. If all went as planned, Shayburn wouldn't know until it was too late who had attacked him. He would lose his battle before he could fight it.

Tonight John would visit a man whose help he needed to see his ends met. As did every village, Bratonshire had one humble citizen who was held in the highest esteem by his fellow villagers. This man was Talbot Rath, a large man, not awesome or powerful looking, but still larger in size than most of the men in this town.

He had a good sense of reason and justice; many times with finesse and diplomacy he softened Shayburn's blows against the people. John had known him for years. The people in this shire would follow Rath.

It was Rath that John was on his way to see. Night after night they met in Rath's house and John heard stories of the baron's abuses and injustices. Gossip of the lord's illegal business interests and tales of the company he kept filtered down into this little hut. Rath knew every guard, every guard's house and every inch of this community. He knew the amounts collected for rents, taxes and tithes, all more than they should be.

The first attack against the baron would be easy, if Rath had obtained the confidence of his friends. Carts would be overturned and burned, houses would flame, many precious things would be stolen, and at least one badly bruised woman would scream that she had been brutally raped. The entire village would be in chaos. There would even be murder done if it could be contrived without actual loss of life.

Soon after his arrival, John anxiously asked Rath, "Have you talked to your neighbors?"

"Aye. Tess!" he called. "Bring our friend a drink." Turning back to John he spoke low. "There are those who remember your father, but now they age. It's best to go with the young men and hope they believe that times will be better for their cooperation. For most the promise of lower taxes and rents would be enough."

John's eyes wavered away from the conversation to watch as a young maid brought him a cold drink. She kept her eyes cast down until reaching in front of him to offer it. In taking it he briefly touched her hand. She let the touch linger as she dared, meeting his eyes for the merest second, then lowering hers again and hurrying away. John quietly thanked her as she fled.

"I've not told them yet who comes to us with this promise of salvation, but neither do they ask. They know well enough it could be twisted out of the strongest man. But don't doubt they're bound to find out, John. Your face is not unlike your father's and in time you'll be recognized."

"To keep it from Shayburn is the only thing," John returned.

"To keep it from him until he's weakened some small bit . . . then . . . then I'll war with him openly and not feel the bite."

John's eyes roved from Rath to the young maid as she busied herself around the room so that she could be near enough to hear part of the plotting. Rath looked between the young swain and his daughter and sighed. "Draw up a stool, child, so John can concentrate on my words."

Happily, the girl took her seat. John gave a smile and, remarkably, a slight blush at having been so obvious in admiring her. "She grows beautiful, Rath," he remarked earnestly.

"Aye, as her mother was. I've gained now ten families in my confidence and I would trust any one of them with my life. It could start there and more would be drawn in with us. When they learn it's a play and no real threat, aye, they'll be glad to follow the plan then."

"Never that, Rath. It's a play right enough, but never let these poor bastards think there's no real danger. When Shayburn's anger is stirred he'll be a hard man to abide."

"I'll not lull them with talk of ease, lad. But if they look to the light at the end of the darkness they'll have more cause to stand hard."

"They've got to know the truth from the start, that it could all come to naught! There can be no other thinking or they'll crack when they're afraid. Tell them from the first, Rath. There could well be deaths before this is out. I can't lead a troop of fancied bandits looking for a play or sure they'll —"

"Not with Papa to give them a strong arm," Tess broke in. It brought a quick smile to John's lips to hear her strong defense of her father.

"She is your best friend," John teased.

"Not always, lad. Do you think it's a simple blessing to have one such as this prancing about? Aye, if she were a lad, 'twould be a simple matter to see her will to lead them when I've gone, but a lass? Bah! I've naught but trouble keeping the besotted boys off the stoop. She spins their heads so it's all I can do to see them lift a hoe or shoe a horse."

"Then see her wed," John offered.

"Aye, it's done now. She's promised."

John saw the sad droop of her eyes and knew at once it was not her choice, but her father's.

"But, lad, the vile and crude habits of the man on the hill would set your blood to boil. It's come to the time when no man would have a wedding in this godforsaken shire. With the aid of an ale or two the devil will take the maid of his choice to his bed and let her walk the distance home when he's through with her. Was not so long ago he stood in a young groom's stead for the wedding night. My Tess will wait with the wedding for a time and if it must be sooner it will be secret. I'll not let that scoundrel plunder my own flesh. By God, I'd kill him myself first and at least lie happy in my grave."

John was silent as he digested this. It was not one of the worst things about Shayburn he had heard. It was not even very uncommon. It happened in other shires, the law of the master being so absolute. And who would dare question? Their tongues would be cut out for the protest.

"We cannot live with his ways, but neither can we flee or stay him. He holds us in a bondage we cannot fight. Aye, you'll have support here, John, as much as you need. They fear him, but not one is loyal to him."

"Are you sure, then, that the time has come?"

"Aye, whenever you say."

"If not the first snowfall, then the second. Whenever it's thick enough on the ground to slow a horse and chill a guard through to his bones. The first attack will be as we planned. I'll need only a fast horse and a strong hand. The men in your confidence will do the rest. Lend your faith to your friends, Rath. If they show their true colors to the baron, we fail."

"Aye, lad. Shayburn will see us suffering our hurts as we never have before. You can depend on these people, John. They know the way of suffering well."

"Good, then. The place?"

"When the heaviest clouds are above, the stable will be loosed of horses and they'll be moved to other sheds. It won't be sorely missed and God willing, spring will bring us a newer, finer one."

"God willing," John confirmed. He clutched the man's hand. "My thanks, friend."

Rath's eyes clouded with an uncertain emotion. "Never thank me again, lad. I could not accept thanks from a man who offers us the only hope we've seen in over twenty years."

John's eyes flicked over Tess and then went back to Rath, the question bright and burning in them.

"Nay," Rath said with some assurance. "He's vulgar and he's mean, but he's not slow witted. I don't think he'd dare touch what is mine. I'm his only friend here. I caution the farmers to work and spare their backs the lash. With me gone there'd be no one left to urge them on. They would either lie down and die or risk life and limb to get away. They're broken bad enough as it is."

"I wish I could promise you this end we seek will be met and the land mine. It could be willed otherwise. It could go to some other man, a favorite of Charles's petitioning for lands. We'll get one thing done, Rath. We'll get the devil out and hope for the best. Let's pray while we work."

Rath laughed heartily. "Aye, I'll pray, lad, but I think I haven't much of a voice for that either. The Lord don't look too kindly on a man with as many sins as mine."

"Tread carefully, Rath. I've need of a good man here."

"I'll see you start the planting, John. Have no fear."

John left the Rath house and walked out into the clear night. He paused and listened to the quiet sounds, comfort coming to his breast at the thought of this being a happy place once again. Anticipation of the events to come gave him energy as he walked behind the houses to the shadows where his horse stood. He glanced briefly at the stable and pondered the night he would raid his own village.

He whirled instinctively at a sound behind him and frightened a yelp out of the creeping shadow with his quick movement. They were two in the dark and neither could see the other's face clearly, but they listened to each other's breath in cold contemplation.

"John?" said a small female voice.

"Tess! I wish to Christ you'd stop this foolery! You could've been anyone. I might test you with the blade the next time!"

She laughed a little. "Oh, monstrous beast! You would have me believe you would slay a man whose identity you don't even know? You may wish me to believe you are that ruthless, but I know otherwise."

"Was something forgotten?"

"Nay," came the answer he expected.

"Did your father send you after me?"

Again the expected response. "Nay."

"Then you've come as the other times. He thinks you abed?"

A small giggle came from her. He knew that she held a fondness for him. It was in the eyes of the maid, and it was unmistakable. And even here in the darkness he was acutely aware of the fair beauty of her face and the ripeness of her young body. "You shouldn't follow me like this," he lightly admonished.

"Of course I should not."

"But then why do you come?"

"To be with you once again."

"What of your betrothed?"

"I do not love him." She shrugged. "And I do not think you'll spoil me against my will."

"And risk your father's anger? But what do you expect of me?"

"As always. A lecture on the evils of toying with strange men and then you will send me away."

He laughed in spite of himself. "Your husband will have a hard time handling you."

"Oh, those ties will bind me soon enough. I'll not cause him undue trouble. Now, while there are no ties, I should like to see where my frolics lead me. Tonight they lead me again to you."

"Tess, you need a thrashing badly. How many men have you chased down in the night?"

"You are the first," she said with a shiver.

He pulled her wrap a little tighter around her and as he did so she moved closer, nuzzling against him in the process. The freshness of her hair rose to his nostrils and aroused his senses. He embraced her lightly. "You've made a mistake in coming here, Tess. You're not a little girl anymore. You're a woman now, and you tempt a man."

"Your troubles are many, sir. You must ever deal with temptations."

He pushed her away from him to see her face in the moonlight. "You little minx! What game do you play with me?"

"No game," she whispered breathlessly.

He covered her mouth with his and warmed to the response on her part. Releasing her, he muttered, "That was not your first kiss."

"I confess it was not." She shrugged. "But the finest ever, I vow."

He laughed softly. "You outrageous little witch. You posture here before me like an anxious little harlot. What is it you would have me do?"

"Please," she whispered, lowering her eyes. "I dare much, but do not think me a whore. Truly, I am not that."

"I know that," he began.

"It's the whole of my life to be lived out here, living till I die in the same house that saw my birth. The farmer I am to wed is good and kind, but I feel no great stirring for him. What harm is there in one small taste of dreams before I settle myself to my fate?"

"One small taste?" he laughed. "Do you lust after me, Tess?"

"I had not thought so brazenly on what I've done. But I've wondered after you long, and many of my musings would be cursed by my father. For too long I've wondered at the greatest distance. Am I truly so foolish, John? Am I so shameless for coming this far at the first stirring I —"

She was pulled swiftly into his embrace and he moved over her mouth with searing hunger, her body crushed against his. There was a glow within her that mounted and grew and she knew a wanting never before felt within her young body. Her arms could not meet against the broad expanse of his back and her legs were not long enough to reach her to him, so he held her easily off the ground. She felt as though they would blend together permanently from the molten contact, never to be separated again.

She groaned in misery as he set her again on her feet. With a startling weakness her head dropped against his chest and he held her there, stroking her hair, tenderly embracing her. She heard the quickened breathing within his chest . . . it matched hers.

"A taste?" he said hoarsely. He lifted her chin with a finger and placed a light kiss on her lips. "There now. Will that taste make your life so much easier to bear? Ah, Tess, I am not a foundling youth to play at passion. If I hold you a moment longer I will find us a bed of hay and make love to you."

She trembled slightly, from fear or anticipation she did not know. He kissed her again, quickly and lightly. "Go home, Tess. Good night."

The cold air struck her with a crushing blow as he whirled away and was gone. She ached for the strength and warmth of him, but instead she heard the steady footfalls as they sounded farther and farther away. With another shiver she turned and made her way back to her house, back to that other life she led: daughter to simple Talbot Rath, betrothed to Stephen Kilmore, yeoman farmer.

SEVEN

UMMER WAS BECOMING a memory as England faded from its green into the promise of cold rain and snow. Fires had to be stoked through the day as well as at night and the halls and galleries of Hawthorne House were damp, dark and cold. A cloak hung on a ready peg to be donned before passing from room to room.

Tanya healed, her face taking on a bright appearance in lieu of the cuts and bruises she had previously worn. Time brought the blessing of proof that she would not bear the child of her crude lord, but the mental scars were deeply embedded in the child still. There was a pain in her eyes that bespoke maltreatment and depravity. And she would not, or could not, speak.

Chelynne, with a patience almost saintly, kept the girl strictly to her rooms. Always either Stella or Chelynne was near her, not allowing the slightest misfortune to befall her. Tanya thrived on the love of these two and eventually began to smile her pleasure over small things. She took great care with her grooming and clothed herself neatly with the money Chelynne allowed her. Now she looked like any neat and trim little maid reared to take her place serving in a stately home. She was industrious and courteous, though silent.

Tending Tanya was more than an act of charity for Chelynne. Tanya was a project that gave her rest from her other worries. But the time came when Tanya no longer needed Chelynne's constant guidance and Chelynne returned to her mirror, trying desperately to mold her face into a womanly one, hating the childish features she felt so self-conscious about. She studied Chad from a distance, for he was never very near, and she had come to believe that her youth was the cause of his indifference to her. He was such a man of the world, so knowledgeable and determined, even in his walk and his manner of stance.

Chelynne watched him often from her window as he stalked to the stable and rode out at a hurried pace. There was always some business calling him off, drawing him to his study or the desk in his own bedroom. Since she had come to Hawthorne House his visits with her had been dutiful, obligatory ones, courteously asking her if she had any needs or complaints. When he noticed that she had been supervising all the household help, inspecting the cooking, cleaning and serving, he told her it was not necessary. That was his reason for keeping the steward. Of course that meant to her that it was not only unnecessary, but unappreciated.

In the midst of her monotony a note came from Lady Graystone informing them she would be paying a visit. Chelynne was elated, hoping that a friendship with this woman would perhaps show her the way to become more experienced, more learned in the ways of women of her station. She was determined to make the effort to call Lady Graystone into her camp, and failing that would at least watch every movement and gesture and later learn to apply them for her own use.

In spite of the efficient steward Chelynne made ready the guest apartments, tasked herself with menu preparations, and set every servant alert to the needs of the baroness. It did not distress her that Chad seemed uninterested in this visitor. He seldom showed much interest in anything that was not business. Recalling the divine manner with which he greeted guests at the ball before their wedding, she assumed he could act the part of a congenial host without any coaching.

At last the good lady arrived. Chelynne had gone to great pains with her appearance, hoping to put forth her best. She was in awe of the woman's regal nature, her coach drawn by eight white horses, footmen, driver and horsemen neatly attired in the red livery of her house. She descended with the flair of any queen and her hair and throat sparkled with jewels. Her velvet gown draped her well-endowed form handsomely, cut low to expose the most beautiful bosom Chelynne thought she had ever seen. Chelynne sighed her appreciation quietly, so intent on this sophisticated creature that she completely missed Chad's black scowl.

Totally ignoring Chelynne, Lady Graystone extended her hand to Chad. He bowed somewhat stiffly. "Greetings, Gwendolen. Good of you to visit."

"The ride was a dusty one, my lord," she said with a laugh. Her eyes went briefly over Chelynne and she gave a little nod. Chelynne wore her admiration openly, her smile warm and her greeting sincere. Gwen almost laughed. Chelynne was grateful for the visit! "Might I have some time to freshen myself before tea?" Gwen asked her hostess.

"Of course. We're at your disposal. Chad?"

Her husband's next actions confused her. Lady Graystone was in like afflicted. Chad took his wife's arm and allowed Gwen to enter ahead of them but without escort. Once inside he beckoned a servant to show Lady Graystone to her rooms, a breach of etiquette digested with some difficulty by both women.

Gwen had little choice but to go with the servant, but the minute she was out of sight Chelynne turned to Chad with a curious frown. "Surely you could act better the host to Lady Graystone, Chad. I hope you haven't insulted her."

He grunted. "You worry too much over her, Chelynne. It's obvious you don't know her very well."

"And how could I? We've only met once."

"Well, I've known her for a good many years. Let's see about tea."

When Gwendolen joined them in the drawing room some time

later she was dripping with gossip fresh from the court. Chelynne listened with half an ear. The Duke of Buckingham had killed his mistress's husband in a duel. Barbara Palmer, the king's favorite mistress for many years, had fallen far from her post and the most recent slander was that she was paying her lovers. As the news went on Chelynne felt her cheeks pinken more than once, for all the information concerned the various adulteries, aborted plots and questionable births. And she was not accustomed to such descriptive detail.

Chelynne was bemused by two things during the conversation. The first was the fact that Lady Graystone, recently widowed, did not wear black for her husband. The other, that every snippet of conversation was directed completely toward Chad. Chelynne might as well have been invisible.

"And will you be going to London, Chad?" Gwen asked.

"We will. Though I can't say when. My father is not well."

"Oh, pity. Where will you be staying?"

Chelynne pricked up her ears, for the trip had not been mentioned to her and she thought perhaps he meant to leave her in the country. "I have a house there, Gwen."

Gwen stiffened slightly. Now both women were listening attentively.

"When did this come about?" Gwen asked.

Chad smiled a little and answered with ease. "Two years past."

If he was aware that he had insulted one woman and hurt another, he didn't show it. The fact of the matter was that Chelynne had been told nothing of a residence in London. Indeed, she was informed of nothing about him but what little bits of information he let fall her way. And Gwen had been his favored mistress in London less than two years ago when he had pleaded no place to take her but a scurvy room atop a tavern in a not very pleasant part of the city. They were both more than anxious to see this house.

Chelynne sat quietly watching her folded hands in her lap, but Gwen seethed. She wanted to hurl herself at the arrogant varlet and scratch that smile off his handsome face. That he should use her like a common harlot! Her words caught in her throat and then suddenly her eyes took on a mischievous gleam as Tanya entered bearing a tray of sweet cakes.

"Why, Chelynne, is this the little wench you've taken away from Lord Shayburn?"

From across the room Chelynne could feel Tanya's shudder at the sound of that man's name. With a reassuring hand gesture she bade the girl set down her tray. A light pat on the hand and a gentle smile smoothed out the fear and Tanya was sent about her duties.

"Your pardon, my lady," Chelynne said. "We don't speak of that around Tanya. The girl was distraught enough with her treatment there."

"But you've done wonders with her, darling. And I was told you lifted her right off the street!" she laughed. "I believe you'll manage very well for yourself if you can get the best of that man. He's not an easy one to outwit."

"I never thought to outwit him, madam. I simply couldn't leave the girl there in good conscience. She had been abused."

"She seems to be doing well enough here," Gwen observed.

"Indeed," Chad confirmed. "Chelynne has taken a great many pains to help her recover."

Chelynne wondered where he would even learn of her efforts, being so often absent from the house. But without worrying over that she turned to Gwen. "When did you hear of it?"

She laughed her best embarrassed laugh. "Why, Chad, didn't you tell your wife that you visited me? Surely she'll think the worst now."

"I don't imagine she'll think any worse than you intended her to, Gwen," he muttered.

"Chelynne, your husband and I have known each other for a long time. The truth is we were playmates as children." With that statement her eyes glittered toward Chad knowingly, advertising to Chelynne that they had not been engaged in children's games. Then with sincerity so obviously mocked, she continued. "Since my husband's death there have been some problems with my estate. I do hope you don't hold it against me, but there was no one I trusted more that I could call upon."

"Certainly not," Chelynne returned graciously. "Call upon us whenever there is need."

Through the rest of the conversation Chelynne longed to be

away. Her hands were clammy and she kept them folded in her lap to prevent them from trembling obviously. She smoothed her hair nervously a few times, realizing only after she had done it that the woman opposite her watched her reactions with some amusement. She felt an ache creep through her. She was so far removed from Gwen's stately airs and the same distance at least from Chad's affection. She was an alien here, in her own home, and it simply could not be denied.

Finally, able to withstand no more, she begged to be excused to freshen herself for dinner. Chad rose to see her out of the room and she went quickly, never acknowledging him for his courtesy.

Chelynne escaped to her room for quiet, not grooming. So that was how it was, as the earl had explained it to her. That was how noble lords played at their leisure, with whores and mistresses and other men's wives. By repeating the court gossip Gwen had made it obvious that a man who found no contentment with his wife could be easily taken care of. And her husband, who did not need her, not even for base relief, found his vigor and satisfaction in other beds. Chelynne felt lacking when faced with Gwen. There was nothing she could claim that Gwen did not have more of.

She rested with a closed book in her lap, her eyes shut. To her surprise she heard Chad call to her from the door.

"Madam?" She opened her eyes to look at him. "I thought you were asleep."

"No, come in."

"I've come to explain —"

"There's no need," she replied, looking away from him.

"There is a need or I wouldn't have come." That sure, that matter-of-fact voice again. He came not out of guilt or sympathy but to finish business. "There is little I can do to shut that woman's mouth and I've found another course to dealing with her more advantageous. Now, listen to me carefully. Gwen has been about a long time and plays this game well where you do not. She was in fact a mistress of mine and is not now."

"Her manner with you is most familiar —"

"Of course it is, and she would have you think it is intimate as well. She has had a keen eye on this estate for a long time and seeks favor here as more than a mistress. Even if that position were open to her I would not see fit to let her have it. Deal with her as you might, Chelynne, but don't let yourself be driven into a state of distress with her crudeness for there is no real cause."

"She doesn't like me," Chelynne murmured.

Chad laughed heartily. "She doesn't like anyone better than herself, my dear. You may be assured that when you are a countess she'll treat you with more care, if not more kindness. Perhaps this visit was a good idea. You'll have to learn to cope with others like her when we go to London."

"I had so longed to see London," she sighed. "And now . . . I don't know . . ."

"Well, London these days is not a pleasant party. It's a mess, and you'll be faced with those who would prefer to spit at you than to treat you with courtesy. But they will be masked, madam."

"I'm quite willing to stay here," she offered.

"I'm afraid that's out of the question. I have business there and much would be thought amiss if you did not accompany me."

"I thought wives often stayed —"

"I'm afraid I wouldn't consider it. And neither will I be able to coddle you through every tea you attend. Rest now, if you wish, and I'll see you downstairs for dinner."

Gwen was the first downstairs. She handed a young maidservant a few coins and thanked her with a sly smile. Her assets were running low but she had no compulsion to be frugal.

She made her way to the drawing room to await the others, and when Chad entered alone she was pleased. He offered her wine and she accepted, taking the glass from his hand with a lingering touch and a sweet smile.

"There's a great deal of whispering about your halls, Chad," she said after a long silence.

"Is there now? I don't doubt it."

"There are those who say there isn't much affection between the bride and groom."

He laughed and took a sip of his drink, cocking an amused brow at her over the top of his glass. "Music to your ears, Gwen?"

"Then it is so? You don't care for her?"

"Don't get your hopes up, Gwen. I care for my wife a great deal."

"But it's said you don't darken her door often and when you do you don't stay long."

He laughed again, seeming to gain mirth from her comment. "Surely you, of all people, would not doubt my inventiveness."

Gwen felt as though she had been stuck with a pin. He had certainly changed. Now he was condemning the very thing he once loved about her. There was a time when her sensuality seemed an addicting brew to this man, and now he treated it more as a curse, a joke. She stabbed for a deeper wound. "Some say they doubt the marriage was even consummated."

He smiled, but eyed her coldly. "That is amusing, Gwen. I, for one, have no doubts whatever about that."

Gwen was pushed too far. "What farce do you fob off on me? I've known you too long to believe that little chit to be the manner of woman to keep you occupied on long winter nights! I could teach the child —"

"I beg to differ," he broke in. "She is exactly as I would have her."

"Playing the gallant husband does not suit you, darling," she sneered.

"Indeed? Playing the harlot suits you perfectly."

"How dare you!"

"How dare I? By right of conquest, in which I am far from alone."

"You monster," she breathed.

"Then you do not desire me any longer? Pity." Since the day of his wedding he had been called to Gwen's manor several times. Matters of business were her excuse, but he had barely warmed a chair in her sitting room when her unabashed proposals came. He was not surprised, for he had fully expected that to be her game. What did surprise him was the repugnance he felt. It had been his intention to take advantage of her willingness, if only for convenience' sake. But her enticing body did not arouse him. He found himself increasingly preoccupied with other thoughts, something of a smaller stature, full and fresh, the untouched maiden that he housed.

"Chad," Gwen sighed. "I've not come to quarrel with you. After all we've been to each other —"

"The thing between us is over, Gwen. And every word that leaves your mouth takes you farther from friendship here. That wheedle won't pass with me. I am nothing to you that a dozen other men haven't been and troubling my wife with your improper insinuations is taking a grave chance. I think you understand me."

"You will never understand —"

"You're wrong about that, my dear. I understand you perfectly."

Gwen rose, and swayed about the room uneasily, feeling she was knuckling under to this child who played at being a woman. Nearly thirty years now, at a time when youth was by far the most admirable feature a woman could claim, she was forced to compete with this little girl. She figured quickly in her mind. She remembered many years ago to a time when she was but a child on her father's lands. She had sought out the pleasures of a man's body so early in her youth that she could almost have borne a child who would now be the age of her lover's wife! A shudder of fear and revulsion shot through her and she turned on Chad with green eyes flashing.

"It is her youth!"

Chad smiled lazily, knowing that jealousy smarted sharply in Gwen's heart. His answer came in a warm, sensual breath. "Yes, there is precious little of that around."

"You seem to have a taste for children," she sneered. "Mayhaps when she's aged you'll throw her down and seek out the cradle for yet another."

"What the hell are you talking about?"

She laughed wickedly. "You've gone to such pains to keep your affairs secret, but do you really believe it has been so? I've heard tales of your wenching. The stories go a long way back. I even know about the smithy's brat you eased yourself on. Some say there was a child —"

"Shut your mouth," he snapped, "lest you spill something you regret."

Her laughter was loud and vicious. So finally she had hit a raw nerve! He *was* smitten with the wench; she hadn't thought it possible. "Aha! Do tales of your bastards bring you pain, my lord?" she simpered. "We've had a mighty hard time finding out what's yours, you play the ladies so sparingly, in this country at least. But tell your dear friend, darling, how many little bastards of yours are running around the —"

She was caught up in arms with an iron grip. His face was so close to hers that she could feel his breath in her half-open mouth. She had never been so afraid of him as she was at this moment.

"I have no bastards, Gwen. And since I've had done with you I have no whore. Take care that I don't hear absurdities from you or I promise you . . . you'll regret it."

The drawing room doors stood open and there in their frame was a small figure in swirling skirts. Chelynne hesitated, arms out and palms turned up as if in embarrassed apology, watching their close embrace. "I . . . I'm sorry," she stammered. Chad released Gwen so abruptly she almost fell to the floor. He started toward his wife, but with a strangled cry she fled up the stairs.

All the way up the stairs Chelynne thought wildly: apologizing to my husband for seeing him in another woman's arms in my own house. Heaven above! She found her room and with a shriek she slammed the door. Stella came running to see what so upset her mistress and found Chelynne pacing angrily to and fro about the room.

Here I play the well-trained wife, she silently raged. Watching my husband from the greatest distance, seeing to his comfort as he would allow it, playing the perfect hostess to his friends, even his mistress, begging the slightest kiss as reward while he beds that whore beneath my nose! And loving him! Wanting him! Willing to wait for his good favors to turn to me! Ha! How could he ever need me when the wenches are groveling at his feet and displaying their treasures? How could he desire me when every noble dame seeks to bring him ease? Fool of fools, playing the game and biding my time!

The door to her bedroom opened and Chad strode in, an angry frown on his handsome face. He pointed a finger to Stella, who shifted from foot to foot, uneasy with this fury that seemed to have gripped them both. "Out!" he commanded. The old woman fled, twisting her hands nervously.

Chelynne faced him boldly. "Have you come to explain once again, my lord?"

"I need not explain myself to you. Calm down and listen to me. Gwen seeks only to shake your confidence. Do not judge me on what you perchance see, for you do not know the circumstances."

"Pray tell me what I need to know of circumstances that find you clutching her body so closely. Did she perhaps faint?"

" 'Twas in anger I held her, not passion!"

"Tell me then what I must do to anger you to that point! Tell me what hateful sin I must commit to find myself in my husband's arms! You must think me a shallow-witted fool!"

"Not shallow-witted, but narrow-minded for certain."

"Get out!"

His face was a stony surface of utter rage. "You do not order me here," he said slowly. "Now freshen yourself and cool your temper so you might play the hostess."

"On my word, you expect me to play hostess to your whore?"

"Chelynne," he warned.

"Nay! I'll not coddle that bitch and welcome her into my home to sit and watch as she fondles my husband! Seek out another fool to play your games!"

"You will do as I say!"

"I will not let you shame me to that end!" Angry tears streaked down her cheeks. "You may play your affections on any ready slut while I sit in patient exile and wait for you to come to me in all good time, but I'll not help your cause! Tell me, my lord, is my lady Graystone one of your little problems on which my exile is bent?"

"She is nothing to me! Cease your accusations! I'll not answer to them!"

She clenched her fists in utter rage, her eyes clamped shut and her mouth forming a straight, tight line. "What am I to you, my lord?" she asked evenly. "Am I servant? Housekeeper? Ornament to add to your collection? Am I even friend?"

"You are my wife!"

"Am I? Upon God's own Word, am I even that? Nay! I am guest in this house and one of little importance. I've seen you treat the animals in your stable with more consideration than you do me!" She walked closer to him and looked up into those brooding gray eyes bravely, heedless of her own tears. "Nay, Chad. I'll warm your meals and wait upon your pleasure, I'll see your rooms in order and keep the staff at your disposal. I'll play the mistress for you if you will it, but I'll not grovel before your whore. You may use me, my lord, but not to that end. I said my vows before God and will heed them true, but I think this is too much to ask of any wife, however unimportant."

He looked down at her in wonder, this being the first time her temper was turned to him. He had watched her with Shayburn but hadn't put much stock in it. He wouldn't have expected his mild-mannered wife to behave this boldly.

"A proud vixen," he muttered.

"Aye," she said. "Your purse allows me treasures aplenty and comforts I might never have known, but all I have to soothe my injury is my pride and whatever dignity I will fight for. When you have stripped me of even that . . . I will be gone."

"I would not have guessed that under your gentle cover there was such courage and conviction. Tell me," he said, lifting a curl from her shoulder. "What is it you're fighting for here?"

"My feelings are not secret to you. I'll not ply you now with words of love. In truth, I am beginning to wonder myself what I am fighting for."

"Then find your cause lest you know no reason for victory or defeat. Come now, we dine soon."

"No, lord. I'll not play the hostess."

"It is within my right by law to beat you."

She gnashed her teeth and turned from him, walking to her cupboard in which her riding crop was stored. She returned to him and offered that as a weapon. "Shall I bare my back, my lord?" she ground out, her eyes glistening with determination.

"You do not do battle in any small way, my lady," he said softly, taking strange pleasure in her action. "Would you truly be driven to lashings to prove a point?"

"Aye, my lord, even that. It is the part of the servant to take thrashings and I am not more than that in your eyes. Yet even a servant, I think, must maintain a measure of self-worth."

"More countess than servant, I think." He reached out and touched her cheek but she stepped back and would not allow his gentleness. He laughed softly. "And though it is not that yet, in time my lady Graystone will have to learn to wait upon your pleasure. 'Twould be a good lesson for her. You have my leave to stay in your rooms. I will see to her comfort."

"I'm certain that you will," she bit out icily.

Again he laughed, amused and no longer angry. "Jealousy does you well, Chelynne. I hadn't thought I was that important to you."

Hatred welled up in her at the sound of his mocking tone and she lifted a small statue from her table to hurl at him. He ducked the piece easily and his laughter filled the room. "I think I should warn Lady Graystone as well, that you are not so gentle natured as she thinks. Indeed, I think the good lady is in mortal danger."

With a last laugh he was gone and she threw herself on her bed and had a most fitting tantrum. It suited her age far better than the words spoken earlier.

Stella was accustomed to spoiling her young ward, giving in to her rages and seeking to please her with any conceivable means. But now, in this situation, Stella could do nothing. The tantrum blended into tears and sobs that shook her young body until she slept.

In all good time she awoke and regained a bit of her composure. She allowed Stella to help her out of her dress to don a more comfortable dressing gown. A small draught of something was brought to settle her nerves and she consented to receive a meal. She stood at her window and stared out over the Hawthorne lands as a serving maid prepared her table. With a deep sigh she turned to attend her lonely meal and saw that the table had been appointed for two. A tear came to her eye and traced its way slowly down her cheek.

"Take the other dishes away," she pleaded softly. "I dine alone."

"But my lady," the girl argued. "My lord bade me attend you and call him when you're ready."

"Where is he?" she asked in surprise.

The girl simply pointed to the sitting room door and Chelynne stared at it, disbelieving, and then opened it. Chad sat at a table in that room and appeared to be writing, but at the sound of the opening door he stopped, looked in her direction, and smiled.

"Are you ready to sup, my love?"

She nodded dumbly and he rose to come to her. He, too, was comfortably attired in a dressing gown, black velvet breeches underneath.

"Where is Lady Graystone?" she asked in confusion.

"She dines alone." He shrugged. "She has a hellish nature. It will do her good."

She smothered a giggle. "The word will be out that we're not fit company."

"I don't think so, Chelynne. Gwen wouldn't let it get out that I dined with my wife and left her to eat alone. The word will be very different, so prepare yourself."

"She would lie?"

Chad laughed. "Chelynne, you're going to be miserable if you carry on with this blind trust you have in everyone you meet. Of course she would lie. She would lie, cheat, steal, do whatever she has to do to see things her way."

"What excuse did you give?"

"I gave her none. She deserved none."

"You're most gallant, my lord, to help me pass away this lonely time when one so eager awaits your pleasure."

Chad frowned, not knowing if this was her naiveté speaking or if under that simple cover there was a sharp and quick cynicism. "Not gallant, my dear. You are mine by law and I am responsible for you. I told you well and honestly that you would not find handsome husbandly qualities in me, but I promised you your due."

"You're overkind," she murmured somberly, thinking she had never been told more plainly that she was an obligation neither loved nor desired.

As he held her chair for her he spoke matter-of-factly. "Because I take my obligations seriously makes me neither kind nor cruel, Chelynne. And never will I allow such a temper in my presence again. Were it not for the fact that your anger was justified and you were within rights to assume the worst of Gwen and me, I would never have allowed your rage. You might wish to remember that."

"Husband mine," she sighed. "You go to such trouble to make me wary of my life with you. I wonder why."

He seated himself across from her and raised his glass. "I wonder myself, Chelynne."

He would have expected to see those brown eyes fill with tears again but when he looked at her he saw a faint smile. "Methinks to find that servant's garb and steal a fine horse. I might yet find the merits to being a mistress instead of a wife."

He raised an eyebrow in question. Good God, she was reaching a point inside him where he actually wondered about her, wondered what she thought and felt. Women didn't usually affect him in that way. And their emotions were a burden to him, not a curiosity.

"The house in London, Chad," she began. "What is it like?"

"It's nothing so large as this, nor so fine as the earl's home in the city, but it is mine and it will do. Functional for my purposes at least. If the earl is able to travel to London he will occupy his own lodgings and we will stay at my home."

"Two fine homes in one family? Isn't that odd?"

"My major concern before my father called me home was shipping. It brought me to London regularly and I finally decided to buy the house a friend was selling. It is closer to the merchant populace than noble, but in every way a fine aristocratic home. I happen to prefer it."

"When do you suppose we'll go?"

"That depends on the weather and the earl. A month, maybe more; I can't say. I've a great deal that needs my attention there and I can't wait very much longer to go. Playing the country gentleman is not my rote, Chelynne. I am a businessman and have several ships to my credit. It started with privateering and is a great deal more than that now. It is a legitimate merchanting operation. However bound I am to the court and Bryant, my businesses will be my major concern. That, you see, is something I made for myself . . . without anyone's help."

"And will you sail?" she asked hesitantly.

"Not in the immediate future, but that may become necessary. I have a plantation in Jamaica and land in Virginia. I plan to operate from here for as long as I can, but I may have to go to Jamaica . . . time will tell. It would suit me fine to have no ties here."

She had placed her elbows on the table and leaned forward, listening to his every word. It was in fact the first time he had told her anything about himself. "Virginia," she mused aloud. "In the Americas . . ."

"The most magnificent wilderness ever to behold. A noble that I met nearly twenty years ago moved his family there. I planned a visit and a cargo or two of tobacco, but I stayed for a few months, and it was never tiresome for a moment."

"Years ago?" He seemed ageless to her. He was seventeen years older than she, but he had done so much living. In the last twenty years he had lived more than many men did in an entire lifetime.

"That was only four years ago. I met Lord Sutherland at the Hague and he chose a plantation in Virginia for his family rather than begging back his lands from the king.

"The plantations there are sophisticated in some areas, yet not far beyond every man's boundary there are hundreds of miles of untouched wilderness. Tribes of savages inhabit most of the country. I swear that a man could wander to his death." He laughed softly. "Perhaps it's a blessing I'm bound to this. It could be extremely dangerous."

"What is the danger?"

"Primarily the Indians. They run naked through the wood, quiet as air. It is said there are as many different tribes as there are trees in the forest. And their customs vary as well. Some pray to the sun and eat only grass and leaves while there are others who cut the flesh off a man before he's even dead and have him for dinner."

The excitement mounted and rose in his voice until he stopped to see Chelynne leaning back in her chair, swallowing hard and taking on a rather odd pallor. "Madam," he laughed. "Methinks England more your style."

"I'm a coward," she confessed. "But it sounds grand."

"They haven't the advantages we have with sale and barter. There are many things that must be brought from England and the wait is a long one. They live in some mighty meager shelters while their homes are being built. But once you've known the thrill of seeing something made with your own wit and devices it's hard to think of living any other way. Why, any man —"

He stopped as he noticed a faint smile on her lips and a twinkle in her eye. He looked at her empty dish and his nearly full plate. She had listened attentively, genuinely interested in every word. But he had been led into a conversation on a topic he had been pleased to discuss. The mood had been passable if not unpleasant and she had changed it without his even realizing it until now.

"I think I would love it there," she said thoughtfully. "So fresh and new. I think it would be better to start your own traditions, rather than to live your life for ancestors dead a thousand years."

"Oh, they've a fondness for their heritage, perhaps more so than we, but they're far enough removed from it all to give them some peace. Here we're constantly bound to it, afflicted with it. The court, the state . . ."

"But you're so often at business, so determined . . . I would have thought you loved that part of it."

"Love it? Hardly. I'd leave it in an instant, but I cannot. There is no other in the family to take the earldom and if I did not it could fall to some meager-witted bumpkin or a devil the likes of Shayburn. No, I don't love it, but it must be preserved. For the Hawthornes and for England."

She watched him adoringly as he talked. It was the first time he had really talked to her. And it did not stop. He told her about his plantation, about his land and ships, about the overseer who was managing things for him and about all the servants he had left there. Then came the ports he had visited and the battles fought. He was candid about his feelings toward the court, disliking intensely the inane games they called diversion. He could be coerced into throwing the dice now and then, but he found little pleasure in going to the theater every day and drinking himself into oblivion. For him there was more contentment in business dealings and men's games that involved skill and vigor, such as hunting and yachting.

She was seeing here a depth of character she wondered if he

would ever let her probe, touch. And his strength and confidence could be the pillar she could lean on if they ever reached a point where they could share and build together. But everything he had acquired now was being maintained. His habits and way of life were set. There was only the possibility that she could slip into his world, fit into his pattern; but he could never fit hers.

When she smothered yet another yawn at the end of a long and happy evening, he suggested it was time she prepare for bed. She hated to see it end, but called Tanya and Stella to prepare her anyway. It was not unusual to have him stay while she made ready, but when he lingered long after she had slipped into bed it struck her as odd. When he started to remove his coat as if he would slide in beside her she almost gasped with astonishment. As if remembering something, he halted himself, blew out the candles, and continued undressing.

He chuckled lightly, almost apologetically, as he climbed into bed. "That loose-lipped servant who reports my every move to Gwen will inform her that I slept the night with my wife."

"What servant is this?" she asked, sitting up in surprise.

"Would that I knew," he muttered, settling himself deeper in the bed. "The fact is that whoever, the story is startlingly accurate. I prefer my private life to be my own and not the issue of some wagging tongue."

Chad seemed at ease in the same bed with her. His breathing, smooth and even, indicated that he found sleep easily. For Chelynne it was not so simple. His totally, alarmingly naked state brought a combination of excitement and unease. She was a long time in falling asleep.

Sometime deep in the night a slow smile grew on Chad's lips. He felt Anne as she pressed close to him. His soul was flooded with contentment, peace. He pulled her nearer, covered her sweet body with kisses, whispered love words and gently titillated her with caresses. His brow beaded with sweat as he noticed a deep and gaping hole somewhere behind them. It beckoned her, called her name. He held her to him, trying to love her, but she was being pulled away. He pleaded with her, told her how much he needed her, how he loved her beyond his own life, how their son needed her. But she shook her head sadly and withdrew slowly from him. He clutched at her frantically but his usually strong hands were limp and lifeless. He urged his whole body, hold her, he commanded himself, but he was useless. She moved into the open ground and the dirt slammed together over her like a door, sealing her off from him.

A scream formed in his subconscious and his eyes popped open. The canopy of the bed was above him, the breeze billowing out the draperies in the large bedchamber. Only a dream, a foolish dream, but the body of his wife was too real. His eyes moved to Chelynne, sighing in her slumber and moving trustingly close to share the warmth of his body. His hands were on her hips, drawing her near, and her soft limbs were thrown casually over his. His first reaction was to throw her away from him, so bitter was his resentment that she would even dare occupy this place beside him, this place that rightfully belonged to Anne.

But he was aware of the security of her sleep, the innocence of her presence in this bed, and he moaned softly as he drew her near to warm her. A slow unconscious tear traced its way down his cheek and dropped unheeded onto her hair. The ache in his heart slowly and haltingly gave way to slumber.

Three days after her arrival, Chelynne was informed that Lady Graystone was preparing to leave. Chelynne had avoided contact with her. While she wondered painfully if Chad was seeing Gwen, she never asked. For herself, she had some pride and would not stand witness to the woman's seduction of her husband. She had no hope of changing either of them or preventing them from doing what they would, but she would not encourage the affair by being complacent about it. She was angry and hurt and did nothing to hide it.

But there was a social responsibility bred into Chelynne that would not cease nagging her conscience, and she finally made her way to the landing when the coach was ready to take Gwen away. Gwen flounced down the stairs, making her way quickly to the door, but stopped short when she saw Chelynne. Her green eyes sparkled with hatred as she looked over the young bride Chad had claimed.

"Have a safe journey, my lady," Chelynne said softly.

"My thanks for your warm hospitality," Gwen bit out icily.

"I'm sorry it couldn't have been more pleasant for all of us, my lady," Chelynne replied with calm dignity. "If you would pay us a visit again perhaps we can share our common interests."

Gwen laughed. "It seems to me we have only one common interest, my dear. I strongly doubt the day will ever come when we can share that."

Chelynne lowered her eyes. She refused to give in to anger in front of this woman and could think of no polite response to this brazen statement.

"You're young, Chelynne," Gwen was saying. "You've a great deal to learn of this world. Whitehall will surely be your doom if you react to every innocent indiscretion with such candor."

Chelynne looked into Gwen's twinkling eyes with disbelieving ones of her own. She had never expected this much frankness.

"I'll give you some advice, Chelynne, though I shouldn't. It would be much more fun to watch them eat you alive at Whitehall. But since you're Chad's and he seems to have a penchant for protecting you, I'll give him aid. The way of a wife now is to accept a man's habits graciously, without fuss. Even the queen manages herself thus. She befriends and acknowledges His Majesty's mistresses with ease, never attempting to manage the king's affairs to suit herself. Chad has been about a long time. He'll do as he pleases with or without your approval. To create hostilities where there is no cause will be your ruin. If you don't accept him as he is you'll lose him." Gwen's teeth flashed in a bright, wicked smile. "I think you've probably begun to lose him already."

Chelynne's eyes took on a dullness as she studied the woman before her. Gwen couldn't read the expression. Was it pity? "If what you say is true, my lady, I won't begin to lose him." She shook her head lightly and then went on very softly. "But he may begin to lose me."

When Gwen was gone the days were as before. Chad was seldom about and Chelynne used her time in riding and in visiting the earl. The old man was deteriorating. There was no hope that he would go to London unless some miracle quickly restored his health.

Every afternoon Chelynne brought a book from the library to his bedside. She didn't know when she went to him this day that it would be the last time she would visit with him.

"When the smell of death is so strong as to drive any other away, still you come to me, Chelynne. You're an angel. I'm grateful."

"No angel," she laughed. "You fill my days, too."

"There are some things I cannot take to the ground with me, Chelynne. Tell me truly, have I failed? Has he not yet reconciled himself to the marriage?"

"He is very good to me, my lord."

"Of course he is good to you. He is tolerant and fair. Is he in love with you?"

She looked down into her lap and folded her hands over the closed book. "In his own way," she murmured. "Yes, in his own way I think maybe he loves me. He is kind."

"But there is no child . . ."

"Not yet, but there is time, my lord."

"Time is a tender thing, Chelynne. Time can be a healer in some ways and in other ways it is a curse . . . a tomb."

Chelynne looked at the old man and saw energy in his eyes while his body lay wasted, the aura of death almost strong enough to touch.

"Every time I've thought for my son, planned for him with his best interests in my heart, I have failed us both. I won't fail you, too. Give him time, then. Give him ease and offer him love, but when he has cast the last part of you away, as he has me, do what you must. Don't let him destroy you, too."

"Why do you tell me this? Why do you encourage me to flee him?"

"Because, dear heart, 'twas my hand that brought him his misery and I thought to find peace from my conscience before my death. It will not be so, but this is no fault of yours or Chad's. I do not deserve his hate so heartily as he believes." Then he groaned, and whispered, "He hates me with every fiber of his being."

"He'll come to you in time and with but a small urging will —"

"No! I'll not grovel and beg my son to forgive my actions! I was quite taken with my position, doing only what I was forced to do under the circumstances. Chad is a man now, he should better understand obligations and what a father's love means. I have crawled like any aging fool and begged him to see that he accuses me unjustly in many things. I will not again. If there can be no dignity in my death, what purpose has there been to my life?"

Chelynne hung her head sadly. She was the last person able to answer a dying man. She looked at him with tears in her eyes and reached out to touch an old and withered hand. "Rest easy, my lord. If there is any way I can bring Chad ease in his life, I will do so. There is always tomorrow."

"And for you there will be many. But one day you will be old, like this. I hope you do not ask yourself then what has become of your life."

She rose and placed a kiss on his cheek, patting his hand, forcing a reassuring smile. " 'Twill not be so. All will be well."

She sought out the drawing room in quiet determination. She sent Bestel to find Chad, he being the only servant in the house to know where his master could be found. The afternoon was aging when he finally returned.

"I was told it was urgent," he said, as if piqued at being summoned home.

"It's your father. He seems to be . . . dying."

"I for one am surprised he lasted this long. I thought it hopeless a year ago."

"It's different this time, Chad. Now he wishes to die."

"Good," he muttered under his breath. Her eyes shot to his face in stunned disbelief. "He's suffered much, Chelynne. It pains me to see him go on like this. I wish him only rest."

"Chad, go to him . . ."

"Aye, I'll go."

"This time let it be different, Chad. He dies heavy of heart. Make your peace . . . if not for him, for yourself."

He stared at her, his eyes cutting through her. She had been cautious not to dig into any open wounds. She had never mentioned or questioned the battle between father and son. Now she lost her voice. As he started away from her she timidly touched his arm. "Chad, I have never known the love of a mother and father. I was left as the burden to a relative shortly after my birth. I would give anything to have one small chance, one short moment with either of those who brought me to life."

Without response he turned and walked away from her. She was drained of emotion now, had said all she would dare. There was nothing left to do but hope that Chad would do the honorable thing.

Quiet gloom settled over the house. Servants spoke in hushed tones and there were days of strained tension, the smell of death heavy in the air. There was no peace in it, only the restless waiting for it to be over. The earl lay in a coma with his son most often at his side. Chelynne did not go to that room.

When it finally happened Chad came to her rooms, his features hard and stony. He stood for a moment without speaking, looking at her. There was a wall behind the moody clouds of his eyes. "He is gone."

Chelynne donned black. The earl was laid to rest without fuss, Chad seeing to the arrangements swiftly and quietly. The body lay in state for only one afternoon. Chad defied all custom and tradition. He would not have his father's wasted form viewed by the curious. He gave a meager contribution to the poor but refused to put out barrels of ale and pounds of roasted boar for the multitudes. He was a huge, dark statue of granite, his back straight, his jaw set. He accepted condolences with a nod. He knelt with the others but offered no prayers.

The entire thing was done in two days' time. The earl was buried on his own land, in his own graveyard beside his wife. Chad closed the door to his bedroom and sought the seclusion for his own private mourning.

The hours ticked slowly away that night, Chelynne left completely helpless. She knew no way to give comfort, to offer her support. In the middle of the night, still restless though exhausted from rushing through the preparations and the funeral, she pulled on her wrapper. Her hair was loosened and her slippered feet took her without pause through the sitting room and into her husband's bedchamber. She walked in quietly, almost expecting to see what she did when she entered. Chad sat, fully dressed still, in front of the fire. He stared blankly into the flames, never acknowledging her presence. She stood directly in front of him and his eyes slowly found her face. Those gray, concealing eyes told her nothing. They looked like clouds heavy with rain, begging to spill out their emotion in plentiful drops.

With an ache in her heart she opened her arms to him. There was no hesitation. He rose, pulled her to him, and she buried her face in his chest. He lifted her in his arms and bore her gratefully to his bed, resting his head on her breast. She stroked his hair, feeling a faint moisture on her bosom that she suspected were his tears. Finally she knew that he slept. They clung to each other through the night, their bodies giving and receiving each other's comfort.

In the morning she reached for him and found herself alone in the bed, Chad already gone. She sat up and looked around the room to find him sitting at his desk, busily inking through another letter. She watched him silently. Always he worked. He started early, kept on until late at night. He spared no time for rest, for pleasure, for grief.

As if her eyes on him were long, caressing fingers, he turned to look at her. He came directly to the bed then and sat on the edge.

"I'm going to London today. I've given the steward instructions to close up the house. Have your women pack, select the servants you wish to have with you there, and follow us as soon as you can. I can't delay my own departure any longer."

"Very well," was her simple reply.

He looked at her long and hard, gave her hand a light squeeze, and kissed her brow. "Thank you," he said, but he never said for what.

EIGHT

THE WEATHER IN ENGLAND had cooled considerably but the business about the wharves was such a flurry of activity the very air seemed warmer. Tall masts towered to the sky while smaller craft buzzed around the huge vessels. There was a ship for every purpose, for trade, for pleasure and for warring. Every hand was hauling, lifting or pushing. Heavy loads were carried on and off these destriers of the sea, taking soldiers and goods to far-off lands and bringing back victories and treasures.

There were merchants and nobles, richly garbed ladies and gentlemen scattered about the sailors, strumpets, beggars and thieves. Ornate and jeweled coaches moved around rickety, well-worn carts. Noble steeds tiptoed between ragamuffins and jackasses. Fine dames lifted their skirts lightly while their pages carried their trains to keep them from dragging in the filth and garbage that lay unattended in the streets. There was subdued haggling over the price of cargo and shrill cries from someone accosted and relieved of his purse. It was every facet of life: wealth and poverty, beauty and filth; a fascinating combination of every aspect of humanity.

For a newcomer to London there are a great many sights to see. A grand cathedral was being built to replace the one burned in the Great Fire. One could waste away hours of the day in the many interesting shops and meeting places of the Royal Exchange. The vast structure of Whitehall stood in all its magnificence to take the breath away. But for the young countess of Bryant the most incredible feature in London was the grand and horrible wharf.

So this was what enthralled and bewitched her husband. This was what he had built his life around before he was tied to the duties of an earldom. He had called it trade, very simply. Or privateering, plainly sounding like a small business to take up the time. To see it now from her coach brought his blasé description to incredible heights in her mind. And, for once, she understood a part of him. She was filled with a sense of adventure and excitement as she looked on this wild scene.

Now that his most demanding duties revolved around Bryant and the court, he held fiercely to this part of his life, working tirelessly to keep the lines of his trade open and contact with his life so far away on his plantation. To do both kept him constantly busy and away from their London home, sometimes for days at a time.

Chelynne watched the business at the wharves with a keen interest, trying to fully understand in her mind how this could shape a man, what he might become because of it. This industry had built his wealth, or at least a goodly portion of it, and the love of it flowed through his veins with the binding potion that kept him here, pursuing it still, though he had not the need or obligation to do so.

As she sat she caught sight of Chad twice. Once she saw him standing with his back to all the commotion, looking away as if he looked beyond England. His hands were braced behind his back and he seemed alone, oblivious to the hundreds of people all about him. Another time she saw him fiercely arguing with a merchant, pausing to shout orders to a sailor or laborer, and finally striding away to be lost in the throng of people.

A woman, however young, does not watch a man so, ponder his thoughts and his businesses this thoroughly, unless she is truly plagued with the essence of him. Chelynne had not seen enough summers to give off the impression of a woman well advised, but she had lived long enough with a man to know desire, to yearn for some reward, if not acknowledgment of her love.

She had expected the invitation to court to come so she was not surprised. She had carefully scrutinized the dress of every grande dame she saw strutting through the Exchange or entering the theater, so that she might aptly garb herself. Her excitement mounted as she readied herself for the grand occasion of being presented at court.

The earl had not taken many pains to see to her comfort or acclimation in her new home. He left word with servants that he would call for her to take her to Whitehall and she had to be content with that. Their rooms were close enough so that if she were quiet she could hear sometimes as he moved around, took a meal, dressed to leave again. They had not so much as supped together since her arrival almost a fortnight past.

Now it was more than the court appearance that excited her. It was that she would go on the arm of a man she worshiped and loved from a great distance.

A young mind is impatient, and Chelynne reminded herself constantly that impatience now would do her no good. If she must wait, she would, for she had a frightening longing to share his life with him. She studied his mood and manner constantly to see if she thought the will to love even existed within that carefully covered heart of his. If any members of their household suspected the great physical and emotional distance that existed between them, they never let on. Chad occasionally made visits to her bedroom as she was preparing to retire. He would stroll in with a brandy in his hand, remove his coat, and his mere appearance and casual manner would drive Stella into a fit to finish her duties and leave the two alone. Servants were hushed and doors swiftly closed and there the two would be, the entire staff aware that the earl had paid a visit to his wife's chambers. No one would dare touch that portal until Chelynne opened the door in the morning. Chelynne alone seemed to be aware that only a few brief words were exchanged before her husband went quietly to his own bed.

Tonight, when he called for her to deliver her to Whitehall, his manner with her was strangely different. His mood seemed light, and that alone sent Chelynne into a flurry of excitement. She lost all desire to be dignified and whirled around before him to show off her gown.

"Will it be suitable?" she worried.

"You'll be the loveliest there, I promise you."

"And you shall be the most handsome," she assured him with a giggle. She swept into a low curtsy and rose to meet his warm eyes with hers twinkling.

"If you're ready, madam . . ."

"I don't know if I'll make it through this," she chattered. "I don't know if I'm more afraid or nervous or —"

He stopped suddenly and looked over her carefully, his eyes moving from her head to her toes and back again, very slowly, a frown wrinkling his brow. "There is something wrong!" she cried. "Oh, is it the dress? I chose it carefully! There isn't time for my hair to be done again . . ." A finger touched her lips to hush her.

"Wait here just a moment, madam. I won't be a minute." She turned a worried look to Stella as he walked from the room. Stella was nearly as frantic herself, worrying all day long over her mistress's appearance for this occasion. They both looked her over again, Chelynne turning around in front of the mirror and Stella making long, perfect circles around her. Neither could see what was amiss.

When Chad returned he held a box, which he opened to expose a diamond necklace. She gasped as she saw it and looked up at him with confusion in her eyes.

"I simply didn't remember it, madam. Forgive me."

"Is it for me?" she asked timidly.

"In a manner. It is for you to use. It belonged to my mother and it was with a great deal of care that it was hidden away and saved. These jewels have belonged to the Hawthornes for generations and will for many years to come. I gladly give you leave to wear it when you will, with care."

He placed the jewels around her throat, glistening, and adorning that beautiful neckline exquisitely. Tiny droplets of diamonds fell to just above her gown, accentuating the full bosom. She had never worn anything so beautiful. It gave her an odd sense of belonging, that he should have her wear these family jewels.

"I'll guard it with my life."

"I'll make it easier for you than that, my dear. Return it to me so that I can put it safely away when you've removed it. Anytime you would wear it, it is yours. I keep it only for safety."

"Of course," she assured him, nodding her head. He smiled at her seriousness and traced a finger around the necklace.

"You wear it divinely."

"I wear it proudly," she murmured, quite taken with this gesture.

He chuckled and took her arm, leading her out of the room. "Well, that's fine, but wear it carefully as well. It will belong to my son one day."

She stopped, looking up at him with wide eyes. "Do you hope for a son one day, my lord?" she asked innocently.

Chad stiffened, unsure of her. "Every man hopes for a son, madam. I am not so very different from other men."

"In some ways you are," she reminded him.

"My ways, however strange to you, have good purpose."

She looked up into those hard, unreadable eyes, never understanding him, never able to have him answer her questions. She sighed and touched the lovely necklace again as if to reassure herself that she actually wore it. How generous he could be, and then so suddenly distant and angry.

Chad saw the discontentment and was sorry for nearly ruining her evening. He condescended to smile and she returned the gesture, a silent agreement to remain temporarily companionable.

She walked through the great cold galleries in nervous anticipation. Chad knew the direction, nodding to people he also knew, and moved them quickly toward the queen's presence chamber. The galleries were packed with onlookers, the throng of spectators so thick Chelynne could not see the walls. But she was so awestruck with her own purpose here that she didn't notice when the group separated, allowing the earl and his lady to pass through.

When Chad stopped walking and waited, Chelynne waited too,

never even thinking of what they were waiting for. Then very suddenly the doors that admitted them seemed to scream their names. "The earl of Bryant. The countess of Bryant."

Chelynne had to forcibly shut her mouth. She was aware of the title, but it was new to her and had never been used in such a manner. A countess. She had never considered it before now. She was still that little unpretentious Chelynne, basically a country girl. Birth and marriage put her here but she instantly decided she couldn't possibly belong.

Chelynne was aware of eyes, hundreds of them, looking at her, or them, mutterings, whisperings. She could not countenance the possibility that they would be appreciative mumblings. She worried about her appearance and manner. She tried desperately to smile and nod at those she passed but it was impossible. She held her chin as high as she could and attempted small, graceful steps. She was pleased, for the first time, with those great folds of cloth that covered her. At least her trembling knees were her secret.

The tall, strong presence beside her led the way and soon she could see the dais at the end of the long length of carpet. Everything else left her mind. The murmurings of the onlookers were silent to her ears and the fear of being at some fault disappeared. She was completely absorbed in the regal majesty of the royal couple: King Charles of Great Britain, France and Ireland, and his queen. He might as well have been God.

Charles sat relaxed, at ease in this glory, one slippered foot outstretched as he leaned back in his throne, viewing the approaching couple passively. Lazy dark eyes with lids that lay half closed in either shrewd comprehension or boredom went over the earl and countess. A grand wig of dark curls added to the grimness of his features and there was a smile, faint and enchanting, his full lips curved only slightly for the sensual and alluring effect.

The queen, Catherine, banked by her husband's huge and commanding frame, was the fragile vision of a flower. Her eyes, lips and small face were all soft, sweet and pure in appearance. A small white hand was stretched out, and Chelynne fell before it to kiss it reverently.

Had Chad not been there to lead her around she would never

have been able to function at all. They joined that great number that stood back to view the rest of the presentations, and soon she could see nothing more of the royal couple. That was what she thought she would have to hold forever in her heart, that brief glimpse of the king and queen.

She had the odd sense of being placed among aliens. All these nobles in their laces and jewels were in her mind the finest the world had to offer. She never for a moment wondered about their worth or thought of each as having an individual personality. She considered them as a whole, a single glittering, majestic entity. And she was proud to be let in the door.

As the mystic moment faded into reality the presence beside her was obvious once again. She looked up at the man towering over her and she found his eyes on her.

"He's magnificent," she breathed.

Chad chuckled. "There's not a woman in England doesn't think so."

"And the queen . . . lovely . . . so lovely . . ."

"There are many more beautiful," he whispered, as if sharing a great secret. "But she is good, and that is rare here."

She frowned a little, wondering how he could decry this amazing exhibition. What could possibly be wrong? What could be amiss when the beauty so stung the eye?

Chad pointed out the duke of Monmouth, not far from the dais where his father sat, the duke and duchess of York, the duke of Buckingham and other awesome and important people. Chelynne asked, with slight guilt, to be shown some of the women she had heard so much about. With a grunt he obliged, showing her where the most recently favored mistress stood. Louise de Keroualle far outshone the queen with her beauty. There seemed to be none to compare in Chelynne's eyes. She was surrounded by her own private party of admirers and Chelynne was quick to see the importance of that position.

Chelynne found Frances Stewart, the duchess of Richmond. She cleaved very closely to the ladies-in-waiting. Looking at her now, Chelynne found it hard to believe that she was once considered one of the most beautiful women in England. Though she was elegantly garbed and had a mien of courtly grace, her face was disfigured from the smallpox and her eyes seemed dull and distant as if her despair reached her soul.

Barbara Palmer was lost among the crowd, though Chelynne had heard of the time when she could well have been considered the most important woman in England. When she occupied that position as the king's mistress she flaunted her importance with a great deal of cruelty. Nonetheless, the hold she had over Charles was a long-lasting one and might have gone on longer had she practiced some discretion and kindness. Still lovely at more than thirty years, she looked like a fixture here, with not so much pomp and glory as Louise had, and lacking the crowd of supporters as well. But even as a fixture, she was not an inconspicuous one. She looked as if she at least considered herself important.

Suddenly there came to Chelynne a certain confusion. Her eyes darted from one to the other of these women and then on tiptoes she looked again at the fragile and lovely queen. Then her large brown eyes drifted to Chad, the question in them obvious. He bent low and whispered. "I suppose if there's a man on earth can do as he pleases without reprisal, it is he."

Her question vanished, her eyes clearing as she nodded. Yes, if he chose to have a thousand mistresses, who was to question? If he chose it so, he was the King by the Grace of God, the most powerful man under the sun. Therefore, it must be just. Noting her acceptance and approval just because of the power of the decision maker, Chad sighed and slipped an arm about her waist. What a lot she had to learn.

Dancing began and she watched that too in fascination. She stood proudly beside her husband and not a muscle twitched. The duke of Monmouth caught her attention and gained most of her stares because he was so like his father. She decided he must be a replica of Charles in his youth. It was possible that her mother had loved the image of the young duke over seventeen years ago.

She hadn't noticed that they had been approached and that Chad stood speaking to someone. When she looked up she was introduced to the earl of Rochester, a handsome man about her husband's age. She curtsied and before she knew it, she was led to the dance on his arm. He guided her about, postured before her, and when they came together closely he whispered in her ear.

"I am, for one, most appreciative of beauty. I thank you most humbly for getting yourself an earl."

Her eyes snapped to his face; she was quite awed by his words. When she realized he meant to compliment her, she flushed attractively and lowered her eyes demurely. "You're most kind, my lord."

He continued to pay her compliments throughout the dance and she was forlornly out of practice at having so many come to her at once. When the dance was over she was grateful, for they had begun to seem foolish and insincere.

She was not returned to her husband as she expected to be, but surrounded by young gallants wishing an introduction. As Rochester obliged them, she looked around for Chad and found him a long distance away in the firm grasp of Lady Graystone. Chelynne found she had no control over her temper where that woman was concerned. She frowned immediately. When Gwen rubbed one practically naked breast along his arm in a very intimate fashion, Chelynne blanched and nearly fainted. But Chad was not concerned. He talked to another pretty young woman over his shoulder and his casual manner told Chelynne he was accustomed to such brazen gestures.

"Why does Bryant toy with those when he has one such as you?" Rochester whispered. Chelynne's eyes misted. What answer could she give? When she looked at him she found she didn't need one. He was chuckling. "A man can't be happy until he's spread the skirts of every . . . ah, but darling, you're not distressed? There now, do you know so little of your own husband?"

She bit her lip and looked away. "By God, you love him!" he laughed. "Now, it's not so bad as that. There's love aplenty in these walls and you'll have more than you're due in no time. I, for one, am at your call." He bowed.

"What've you found?"

They both turned to find young Monmouth watching them with amused interest. She could see mischief in his eyes but it seemed a happy sort and she could not believe that he was actually guilty of all the crimes she had heard the king had to pardon his son for. When she rose from her curtsy she noticed the merriment all around her had increased substantially. There was a minstrel occupying the king in one corner and the laughter of his gentlemen drowned out the song. The orchestra continued for dancing and different diversions took place in far-off corners of the great room. It was much like a fair to her. And she could see no sign of Chad.

"Where might I find his lordship?" she began nervously.

"What, darling? You've a taste for your husband still? Could it be we've an honest woman in our midst? Well, never mind. I'll see if I can find him if that's what you're after." He turned to Monmouth and bowed briefly. "Your Grace was planning to steal her away from me anyway."

Chelynne danced with Monmouth, wondering if his young wife was somewhere in this crowd. She found him most enchanting, his lazy eyes dark and soft like his father's. His manner was very gallant but so flirtatious. And still she could not see Chad. Neither could she imagine who was married to whom anymore. No one in the room seemed interested in remaining with his spouse.

Chelynne couldn't help thinking of the duke as a boy, though he was older than she. Being married to a man a healthy ten years older than Monmouth made a great deal of difference. She enjoyed keeping his company that much more because she wondered at the possible kinship that they might share. At one point she noticed that the king paused and watched them as they danced. She thought it touching that Charles held such interest in his bastard.

They all stopped to pay respect as the queen and her women left the room, Charles giving escort. Soon the king was back and the tempo of the party became even more vigorous. Now the day was catching up with her. It had been a long one in preparing for this evening, and she had danced several dances with the duke and was simply bereft of any more conversational niceties. And there was no sign of either Chad or Rochester.

"What have you seen of the palace?" Monmouth asked her.

"Only this, Your Grace," she replied. Her feet hurt and she was growing more alarmed by her husband's desertion. If Monmouth walked away from her now she would have nowhere to go, nothing to do. She saw herself standing alone in the middle of this room looking like a ninny.

"Would you like me to show you something of Whitehall?" he asked.

She was greatly relieved. She had an interest in seeing more of it and she could free herself of burdensome time in a tour. "That would be delightful, Your Grace," she said, beaming.

With a twinkle in his eye he led her through a door, not the one she had entered by, and they were out of sight of those in the presence chamber. She entered a narrow dark hall with him, which was not what she expected but she lacked the nerve to question him. He led her along silently and swiftly and soon there was another door, a short stair, nothing very well lit, and yet another door. She felt as though he were leading her through Whitehall's secret passages that would eventually put her in the river. She was not very far wrong.

Monmouth closed the third door after them, and they were alone in a dark little room that was smaller than her own closet. One flickering candle was dancing its light off the walls. It had only just occurred to her to ask where they were, and when she turned to do so he came down swiftly on her mouth.

Her gasp of surprise was stifled by his searing mouth. What of the duchess? What of Chad? What possessed him to think he could force himself on her like this? She didn't know where she was, how to get out or, worse, if there was any way she could. His body held her pinioned against the wall and his hands began to rove. Even through the heavy layers of her gown she could feel the lusty desire of her aggressor. He was firm and exquisitely strong and she could see herself as the helpless victim of his rape.

She panicked at the thought and began to beat against him, a frightened whimper leaving her, but his lips only slid to her neck, completely undaunted by her protests. "My God, you're the most beautiful woman I've seen! Don't fight me, darling."

Pure terror gripped her. This could in fact be her brother. Hopeless, she was held against the wall, her pursuer passionately intent. Less than three hours ago she had come to the most wondrous experience of her life, the dream of any young maid gently reared, to be presented at court. Now her husband had vanished and she was the victim of a nightmarish encounter with a noble she had admired. What madness struck this dream away? The merriment of the court seemed a sham, a disaster.

A low rumble of laughter from within the room seemed to startle Monmouth enough to release her. He let go of her completely, rearranged his slightly off-balance periwig, and took a deep breath. He bowed to the stranger in the room and muttered, "Your Majesty."

"Scamp," the man scolded with a chuckle in his voice. He came into the light and revealed himself to be the king. Chelynne shook too severely to curtsy. She leaned against the wall as if she would crumple without its support. "Go along," the king told James. He took Chelynne's hand to feel its coldness as evidence of her fright. "I'm mightily glad to see the lad has good taste. He'd not have hurt you, I think."

"I beg your forgiveness, sire," Chelynne stammered, her voice breaking. She couldn't meet eyes with her rescuer but she felt his presence as if he were a great archangel who had swooped down to save her. He tucked her hand in the crook of his arm and started to lead her away.

"There's nothing to forgive, unless of course young James should beg it of you. Did he offend you badly, my lady?"

"No, sire," she murmured. She looked up into his brooding brown eyes and smiled gratefully, but still she lacked the courage to tell him his son had been well out of line.

"Good, then. I've told the boy never to attempt to usurp what is mine, and in this I mean my ladies as well."

They traveled down a hallway different from the one she had come through, and she was convinced one had to be a magician to get around this maze. She halted before the door he meant to open and looked at him with worry. "Your Majesty . . ." she started.

The king hushed her with his eyes and reached around her to open the door. Inside she saw a dressing room, with several maids and tiring women present and a few noble dames sitting to fix a curl or just relax. She had had no idea such a room had been prepared or she would have sought it out long ago. There was a slight murmur from within as the king made his presence felt. Two young women rushed to do his bidding and he spoke quietly. "Help Her Ladyship freshen herself and see that she has an escort back to the drawing room."

She turned her grateful gaze back to him. "Thank you," she murmured.

He chuckled. "It's not the first time I've had to set aright what the duke has wrought havoc on."

"You know a woman's very mind," she whispered.

He bowed over her hand and she was faint as a result of his charm. "In that, madam, I've had a great deal of practice."

Chelynne was not eager to go to the drawing room. She had no idea what awaited her there, but she could postpone it only so long. She was no longer frightened, for she thought herself to be well out of danger thanks to the king's charming concern. But she was disappointed, almost heartbroken. She had nurtured a dream, to be a fine lady to an earl, to venture into the court and be a part of its elegance. Could it truly be a lie? Could it be that there was nothing here for her? No place for the young woman who had for all her life been reared to stand in royal company? What of the long years of learning poise and grace? Were they to be put to use in fighting off lusty nobles?

The drawing room was filled with gaming tables surrounded by the richly garbed ladies and gentlemen. She saw Chad straightaway but her relief faded into dread as she saw that he was talking to the king and had a very obvious scowl on his face. She approached that twosome reluctantly. Chad did not mince words. "By your leave, Your Majesty."

Charles bowed. "I thank you for sharing your wife's loveliness with us, my lord. I hope to see you both often."

Chad's scowl deepened. There was no mistaking a royal command.

They departed Whitehall swiftly. Her husband's hand on her arm was tight and unyielding. The party they left had not begun to dwindle, and there was still much gaiety. They were going, the affair over for her all because of her foolish mistake.

When they were inside the coach she could feel Chad's cold,

unrelenting stare. The ride was silent and disconcerting. Finally, after a very long quiet pause, he let out an exasperated sigh and spoke. "I cannot believe you are as naive as you pretend, Chelynne. What in God's name were you thinking of?"

"I was left much to my own ends, my lord," she argued proudly. "I had no idea His Grace's intentions were so dishonorable."

"Good Christ," he muttered. "Were you sold into this marriage without any education? Do you know nothing of men?"

"And how would I know?" she asked.

"I thought you were at least schooled in the facts of life! Could you not see what the duke intended? Had you not heard something of this man you so willingly left the room with? He is a rake, madam, in the best situations. I doubt he would have been repentant had he raped you!"

"I know nothing of him," she said softly. "Only that he is the king's bastard."

"Fortunately you achieved some very influential protection on your first visit to Whitehall. Imagine being dragged out of a lovers' tryst by the king himself. I wonder that he didn't try to take Monmouth's place!"

Her eyes shot up to his face, though she could not see him clearly. He sat opposite her and his anger was heavy in the air. It seemed unfair to her, that he should blame her so totally when he never offered protection or advice. How could it be entirely her fault? How could she be expected to guess a thing like that?

"You might've warned me, my lord," she whispered.

"Chelynne, for Christ's sake, I've more important matters on my mind than raising a little girl into womanhood! As it stands it appears I'll be kept quite busy beating the men out from under your skirts." He laughed a harsh and bitter laugh. "It's going to be mighty hard if you insist on lifting your hem to them!"

"My lord! I promise you it was never my intention to play such a game with His Grace! I simply didn't —"

"How can you not know something as painfully simple as that? What did you suppose is the most attractive thing about a woman? Her stitchery? Don't you have any idea what a man wants when he invites a woman into a dark room away from other eyes?"

She looked into the blackness across from her and said very softly, "I repeat, sir: how would I know?"

Chad's anger mounted. He wanted to shake her. This pretense of innocence and chastity was his undoing. Her young firm breasts were constantly billowing out of her gowns, her tiny waist turning and aiding the delicious swing of her hips, her moist lips always parted as if eager to be kissed. How could any woman possess such an aura of sensuality and be totally unaware of it? It simply couldn't be. It was impossible for her not to know how she appealed to a man.

"Chelynne, I'm warning you, I don't want to be bothered with a lot of nonsense over the way my wife displays herself in public. If you've a notion to play lovers' games then do so discreetly. I am not anxious to be dueling over your precious little rump. You will learn to take better care of your virtue or let it fall where it may!"

Chelynne raged inside. "You've a mighty gallant way of seeing to your wife, my lord. For a man who can't even be bothered with the smallest niceties in his own home you surely do embarrass easily!"

"What happens in my home is no one's business but mine!" he shouted. "And it has nothing whatever to do with the way you behave in public. You are the countess of Bryant and should conduct yourself in a manner that befits your title. Do not test my patience any further!"

"Your patience! You wouldn't know the meaning of the word! Who sits and patiently waits —"

He leaned over to her and caught her in a powerful grip, his hands biting into the flesh of her arms. "Chelynne," he said sternly. "Whether or not you are entirely pleased with your circumstance is of no matter to me. If you insist on swinging your delightful little backside into trouble I will not stand and bear the humiliation of your actions. Don't be looking for me to give gallant defense of your ill-planned adventures. Is that clear?"

She nodded piteously and he released her. She sat back, slow tears streaking down her cheeks. Finally little sobs came from her side of the coach. Chad tried not to hear it. He looked away and sought to pretend himself alone but a vision of her fighting for her virtue at the hands of the lusty young duke crept into his mind.

The fact that the king thought ill of him for leaving his young wife unescorted on her first visit to the palace did not lessen his chagrin. He would have thought her sensible enough to stay out of mischief for that short time at least. His anger began to fade away under the onslaught of her persistent weeping. There she sat, dejected and afraid, simply ignorant of the ways of the court, and he knew it. Of course then he was more the beast for not taking closer care to educate her. With a frustrated sigh he transferred himself to her side of the coach and took her into his arms.

"Chelynne, calm yourself. I realize I was harsh and you're not completely at fault. Come now, you'll spoil your pretty face."

She sniffed away her tears and looked up at him with that vulnerable innocence while not far below those tempting round breasts rose up from her tight bodice. God, what a package this was.

"I'm sorry if I embarrassed you, my lord."

"It was a sorry way to learn, but perhaps you'll take greater care next time someone offers you a pleasant stroll." She bobbed her head obediently and brushed the wetness from her cheeks.

"I was mighty scared," she admitted with a sniff.

"I don't doubt it," he said with a faint chuckle in his voice.

"Truly . . . I didn't know . . ."

"Chelynne, don't you know that you're lovely? Desirable? I imagine that there are plenty of men at court who would love to have a taste. Do you think they will care that you're a little reluctant?"

She shrugged her shoulders, innocent. Always pure and chaste. Chad groaned. His arm slipped around her waist and with a finger he lifted her chin so their eyes would meet. "Take greater care, sweet. The wolves love fresh game."

Those wide brown eyes full of confusion stared at him blankly. All his wrath disappeared. She was a child, an infant in this world. He held her head against his chest, wishing that he could protect her from it all and knowing he could not. There was simply no way to conceal all the cruel realities she would find here, no way to shield her from them. He could only hope that she could sift out the more censorable portion of her upcoming education and hold onto some of that moral conviction, some of that goodness and innocence that was all of her now.

"Come love, we're home." He helped her out of the coach and took her to her rooms. Stella had been waiting by the fire for Chelynne's return and jumped to her feet to help her disrobe. But Chad lingered for a moment, thinking of all the things he should say to her. He should have a little talk with her, tell her candidly what actually went on at court, what those elegantly dressed ladies and gentlemen did with their leisure time, with almost all of their time. Not finding the right way to begin he helped her out of her cloak and handed it to Stella. And there he was, faced with the young fresh beauty of her again. Unaffected and ravishing. He drew her into his arms and kissed her brow.

Instinctively her arms went to his chest and moved around his neck to draw his lips down to hers. This was as much as she had ever dared. He moved over her mouth tenderly, and her lips parted for him deliciously. Her small body molded to his and neither of them noticed Stella blanch and retreat into the shadows. Chad battled need against good sense. His mind called out a warning again, a familiar one. No attachments now. No bonds, no commitments. The pain grew and grew and he ached with longing. He needed something he didn't want, couldn't have. He had had years of needing, wanting, and he had learned to curb that desire. It hurt so violently to become dependent on another for love, for ease. He pulled away from her. He didn't want her. She was thrust on him and he didn't want her.

Chelynne puzzled at his change of mood. She looked up at him searchingly and he thought that if he didn't get a reprieve from that blind devotion and trust in her eyes he would die. He placed another light peck on her brow and quickly left the room.

Disappointment was one thing, but this little encouragement was enough to bolster her. She had dared much in brazenly offering herself as she had, but she had felt his need and desire. It couldn't have been her imagination. He wanted her. He lectured her angrily against tempting men. That must mean that he found her tempting, since she had never tried to do so.

She let Stella brush out her hair but she wouldn't be undressed. She waited some moments, and thinking enough time had lapsed, she took the diamond necklace as her excuse to go to her husband's bedroom. Perhaps if they talked for a few minutes and if she saw the opportunity she could be close to him again. He could not brush her aside forever.

She heard voices in his room and assumed that it must be his manservant he spoke to. She tapped lightly on the door and Bestel admitted her. Surprise stunned her for a moment, for Chad had changed clothes. He was not dressed gaily now but done up in poor attire and devoid of his wig. He stood quietly, waiting for her to speak, and she realized that she had scrutinized him carefully, remaining silent for too long. "The jewels, I . . . ah, thought you wanted to keep them."

"Of course," he said brusquely. "Thank you."

She started to leave and then turned back to him impulsively.

"Are you going out?"

He nodded curtly. "I have some business."

"At this hour?"

"It's not uncommon. I'm meeting merchants in the Gold Frog on Prior Street. That is the reason for this fashion. It's a poor place and one nobles do not frequent."

Her mouth formed a silent "oh" though she didn't understand at all. She lingered for a moment and seeing that he was anxious to leave, she went back to her room. How often did he leave in the night without her knowing? Why would a man do business at this hour? What kind of business?

The thought struck her with sudden clarity. He was going to see a woman. She was as sure of it as she was of her own name. He wasn't pretending desire; it was real enough, but not for her. Who then? Gwen? She had to know. As if her life depended on it, she had to know who he loved and wanted.

Chad was not in good humor when he entered the Gold Frog. He was angry, impatient and curious. He didn't ponder his young wife much now. More he wondered what John could have called him here for. That other problem, his long-starved desires, he meant to take care of later, routinely.

He had not been in the tavern long when John found him and then went to an out-of-the-way table. The decent places had private rooms, but their business was not for such places, where other acquaintances might linger. This was a particularly scurvy ordinary stocked with unscrupulous patrons. Neither Chad nor John was dressed to look the part of those with incomes, and they confined their conversation to hushed tones within the packed hall.

"Well?"'Chad inquired.

"When did the message come to you?"

"A page at Whitehall. Christ, John, you've got to be more careful than that!"

"I hadn't intended that," John muttered.

"I've a night full of good intentions, friend. Take better care. Now, what's your business?"

"It's not my business this time, but yours. I was able to uncover something in Browne that I thought you should know.

"I sent someone out there. There was an injury, it seems, that went purposely unnoticed. There was a girl raped and taken poorly. She was badly beaten and abused. Her family kept her quiet and hid her well. She was the lass tending the chapel, the laundry and cleaning. She saw the man who killed the priest. Chad, it was . . . it was that young Mondeloy . . . Harry, with the help of Shayburn's man, Captain Alex."

Chad's face turned to stone. Fury flowed in him; the blood of the priest cried out for revenge. Alex was a character with a vile reputation. Shayburn had long ago surrounded himself with protectors, men who had previously earned their bread by robbing others. Alex was the worst of a bad lot. The title of captain was his own idea, for he took charge of the men who served as Shayburn's guards. And the combination, Mondeloy and Alex . . . it was beyond his comprehension.

"What does this mean?"

"I'm not altogether sure, Chad. I found that there were others gone to Browne to have a look about. Sent by your father. They learned nothing, of course, just as you learned nothing. I'm nobody." He smiled, indicating his pauper's garb. "Simple folk don't fear talking to me as they do to an earl's henchman." John sobered.

"I'm sorry about the other news. It comes to you a bit late. Were you aware your father investigated the crime?"

"No."

"Proof enough he had no hand in it, Chad."

Chad looked away and nodded. The earl was gone. Chad was relieved to know his father was cleared, but wise enough to know it would have made little difference in the way he left the world. "No matter," Chad said shortly. "I'm only concerned with what happened and why."

"Well, the girl was sneaking away when she saw the priest being held. Her parents confided that it was the noble who hurt the girl, though they didn't know his name. I found that out much later from witnesses and descriptions. It seems Harry amused himself while Alex finished off the priest and the church. I'm not sure that it was Mondeloy's intention to have so much damage done there, but Alex is the kind of man who can't stop until he's done all the damage he can.

"As it is, the girl won't confess another time and it's certain she'll never act as witness against Mondeloy or Alex. The people are sore afraid. The girl was left for dead. It was no simple mischief."

"What could his intention have been?" Chad asked dully.

"I have no earthly idea. That's as much as I could find out. I'm going to have to get back to the country but Mondeloy is in London. The rest of his family hasn't arrived. You'll see him with the other fops."

Nothing more needed to be said for Chad to know exactly what to look for. The young gallants roved the streets in droves, done up in lace and ribbons, speaking in the latest French euphemisms, looking more feminine than masculine. "I can't imagine what he would hope to gain with this," Chad growled. But he knew about the young gallants. Most of them were small children when Charles was restored and had not lived through revolution and exile. They were bored and spoiled and sometimes for amusement they played havoc on the innocent peasants, doing vandalism and even murder. But did that explain it?

John was reluctant to ask but knew he must, if for no other

reason than friendship. "Could this have anything to do with your wife?"

"There is not much goodwill between Chelynne and her cousin."

"Does she know of your marriage?"

"My father insisted she was innocent of his scheme to see me wed and she acts as if she does not know of Anne or Kevin. She's never made mention."

"If she knows, Chad, she would profit by having that record destroyed. Her children would inherit and Kevin would be regarded as a bastard."

Chad's eyes were icy slivers of silver and he spoke through clenched teeth. "Only if I were of a mind to allow that. Kevin will be getting his due no matter how I have to assure it."

"Well," John sighed. "I think it more likely to expect Mondeloy to seek compensation for his knowledge. Chelynne is terribly young . . ."

Chad was not listening. He was thinking, deeply. He was not only unsure of Chelynne, he was unsure of himself. He didn't know what he felt for his young bride. If ever there was a reason to see his marriage to Anne disregarded . . .

There was a hand on his arm. "Patience, Chad. There's time enough to learn the truth to this. Don't fly into a fit. The girl is young —"

"If I could only believe — She alone would have cause —"

"Your memory stirs too much hate in you, Bryant. You've got to be objective. You can imagine how Mondeloy abused the girl, you know the type of man we're seeking. It could be he's after another prize. It could be the marriage record is for sale. Think about it."

"I'll find his cause. I'll learn his price . . ."

"There's another matter. I've got to find a way to get word to you better than this. I'll be back and forth bringing people here and taking some back. I can't sit still . . . too much risk in that. Are you still in this with me?"

"Didn't I give you my word?"

"It's not your burden."

"It's my burden because I make it so. I'll see Bess. She would be a willing courier between us."

"I have two sisters in London and I've seen them both. I don't want any more of my family involved in this. The people of Bratonshire await my attack. Anxiously so. I've a feeling that if the baron has a brain he'll seek out my kin to be assured of my whereabouts. He shouldn't be expecting anything but it won't take him long before his suspicion is aroused. If there's any way to get into his house we've got to find it."

Chad raised a brow. "How well known was the animosity between my father and myself?"

"It was the talk of the shire before a prettier matter came along."

Chelynne. Again. "Shayburn was aware of it but my question is, does he believe it was severe? Since I came home he might assume that there were amends between us. Do you know what I'm thinking?"

"I believe so. One of the earl's old servants out of work?"

"Exactly. Someone faithful to my father that cannot serve me because of old wounds. I'll see what I can do."

The conversation was short and sweet. It wouldn't do for them to leave together even though the possibility of their being recognized was slim, especially in this area of the city. Chad set out, bound to see a young woman of simple means who he knew he could trust.

Chad had hired an unobtrusive hell cart that left him at the door of fashionable new lodgings in the city. He rapped impatiently on the door and the landlady was a long time in coming. He knew her from other visits here. When she opened the door a crack and recognized him, she stammered and stuttered. It wasn't often that people of quality visited her house.

"Cap'n Daniels is not about, m'lord."

Chad smiled leisurely. "I've not come to see Daniels. Is my Bess here?"

"Aye, m'lord. To 'er rooms, she is."

"Is she . . ." He cleared his throat and started again, more determined. "Is she occupied?"

"No, m'lord. She sleeps. I seen to 'er beddin' meself, sir. The lass is done in from the day, she is."

"It's not as if I would disturb her slumber," he chuckled. "Would you mind asking her if she's up to company?"

"Come in then, m'lord. I'll go up."

Chad stood inside the door. He knew Bess kept apartments on the second floor but he was not inclined to go barging in on her. They had a strange relationship that he did not ponder very deeply, but he had an unpledged respect for her privacy.

It was a few years ago that he first met Bess. She was a youngster then and mistress to a hired sea captain he employed. Daniels was no lad, he was a swarthy old dog, but generous and good-hearted. He had a wife and a brood of children in London. Daniels was paid fairly and got his share of the plunder if they took a Spanish ship, but he was hardly rich. Chad was surprised to learn he had a wench in keeping and doubly so to learn how well kept and lovely she was.

Chad had never intended to abuse a friendship and had only gently pursued Bess when he was invited in. That was when he learned the most desirable things about this lass. She had no eye on power or fortune, never troubled him with questions or requests. He never darkened her door if Daniels was in port and rewarded her handsomely for his brief and infrequent visits. He had taken her out to dinner in a tavern a couple of years before and she had charmed both him and John with her simple gaiety.

He had learned since that time that she was one of the few women he could trust. She was closemouthed and had no traffic with the nobility. She befriended Chad only because she wanted to, not because of his generosity with her. She was in love with him and had no ambitions beyond having him occasionally come to her. And now, he was eager to enlist her aid. Second, he relished the fact that Daniels was conveniently out of port.

The landlady returned and said nothing, simply handing Chad a candle to light his way up to Bess. When he entered the room he saw that she had risen and was brushing out her long blond hair. She was wearing a sheer dressing gown and was the best sight he had seen in a long time. He threw his hat into a chair and moved toward her. She rose and met him halfway, their mouths coming together hungrily. The need within him ached so violently he didn't know if he could spare the time to woo her at all. His hands found the buttons and roved over her eagerly. Then suddenly he broke away and placed a hand over the slightly rounded stomach, chuckling softly. Their eyes met and she nodded.

"Again," she confirmed to the unasked question.

"This will be the third child," he commented. "Does he do nothing to prevent it?"

"He intends but forgets. He's good to the children and I've no cause to complain."

"You're not far along?"

"Not to my discomfort."

"I've come to talk. I wouldn't press you."

"I know that. It's all right."

"Bess," he groaned, pulling her into his arms again. "I've needed my Bess."

"I know, love. I know." She took him by the hand and led him to her bed. It would be swift and silent from then; she knew the routine well. She loved him in a way she could never admit to him or anyone else. It was less painful to be his convenience than to have him know how she truly felt. He was gentle and kind with her, thoughtful and a marvelous lover.

But he came to her only like this. Like a man long at sea, starved for the ease of this need. They never talked beforehand, and talked afterward only because he was conscious of the need to treat her humanly. It was the same, rushing in, throwing his clothes aside, and having it done. Then he would relax with his head at her breast and sometimes talk to her. Yet in his eyes she had always seen the reflection of another woman, one he had truly loved, and one he seemed to search for in her. To have even this much of him was enough for her.

She stroked his hair affectionately, just as she often did with her babes when they had satisfied their hunger at her breast. He handled this as he would any call from nature, accomplishing it because he had to. Once done he was grateful, thankful, and he turned to her to love her again, this time not so urgently.

He whispered sweet lover's words as if she were the only person alive, the only woman he had ever longed for. He took care with his caresses, moving against her gently and sensing her moment perfectly. Then he let it end again, falling against her in happy exhaustion. Beautiful. The ease. The wondrous softness of having the burden partly gone. A great weight had been lifted. At last, at last . . . he felt a certain peace.

"My lord," she beckoned softly. He turned to look at her. "An earl now, I'm told. But why, my lord? Why? Does she bring you no pleasure?"

Chad turned away from her. Bess was often in the 'Change and tiring rooms. She would have learned of his new status and marriage. He couldn't answer her. Bess knew men well, especially those who had been without a woman for a long period of time.

"I have seen her," Bess said softly. "I was out about shopping and John pointed her out to me. She is lovely and kind. She spoke to me over the ribbons . . ." She sighed wistfully. "She made me feel old. I hardly remember when I was that young." Her voice took on a sudden, purposefully happy note. "I was so happy for you, that you should be gifted with one so lovely and kind, but you still —"

"She is beautiful," he relented, not much appreciating the memory at a time like this. It brought to mind the fact that Bess was far less so. She was older, fuller, and her golden hair was beautiful only when he was in need. Sated, he saw it had a dullness he didn't find attractive. And being with her when she was full with another man's child was not particularly appetizing, but at least he did not worry about leaving her with one of his own.

"But still you have a woman you cannot love? After so long?"

"I could love her," he said, rolling over onto his back.

"And still seek your sport from Bess? Is a simple woman so much better? No pride to shorten your pleasure?"

"Bess," he groaned.

"I don't ask for jewels and gowns, though you leave the coin for more than that. But you are starved! Always, like a man long at sea! And you are strong and handsome and the finest lover . . . why do you not use the countess?"

Though the room was dimly lit she could see the bright, piercing silver of his eyes as he looked at her with anger. "Must I leave lest I answer you?"

Bess was not afraid. She knew he would not hurt her. She ran a hand along his arm and whispered to him. "Don't leave me. I won't ask you again. But I have seen this one and I know you don't think of her when you are with me. I could never be the countess to you."

The lass had no more schooling than any other peasant in London. She could not write her own name or read from a book, but in some things there was absolutely nothing she did not know. Chad sighed. "I don't think of her now. I think only of you."

NINE

OHN BOLLERING had a great many matters on his mind, enough so that another tall tankard of ale was conducive to dreaming, to planning his actions and pondering his life over and over again. Tonight there was no business demanding and tomorrow those men he had gathered up would be ready to leave for Bratonshire. Ordinarily there wasn't much time for leisure, but tonight he allowed himself.

The men around him drank heartily and teased the wenches. He faced the crowd for his own diversion and had it been any other night he might have joined in, grabbing a wench to warm his lap and falling headlong into drink. Traveling vagabonds, merchants, sailors and strumpets — the clientele was about average for this type of ordinary and this was not a particularly dangerous place. But then there were very few taverns in London that wouldn't have a brawl or two for sport every night.

A squeal rose from within the crowded room — a woman's obvious indignation at being carelessly handled. On the other side of the room there was a quick shuffling as the men moved back for two ruffians as they engaged in a serious arm-wrestling contest. It was not so odd that this would relax a man; in this company John was completely unnoticed. At a time in his life when the sight of his face might well bring him a love affair with a noose, it was awfully nice to be ignored.

He hadn't noticed her come in, but she stood out so sorely that he wondered where his brain must have been to miss her for even a moment. She spoke quietly to the proprietor, her cloak swinging open to expose the expensive fur of its lining and her vizard pulled down to show her lovely little face to all the world. She was not well known enough in London to be immediately recognized as the countess of Bryant, but the obvious wealth stung the eye in a place like this. She turned to go, as she must have come, without escort.

John looked about quickly, seeing exactly what he expected and feared. Three men, their clothing advertising that they earned their livings unscrupulously, their physiques crying out that they could fight well and would do so eagerly, conferred together for an instant and were on their feet. Forgetting his hat in his anxiety, John darted out the closest exit and made his way swiftly around the building to where he guessed her coach must wait. He felt the handle of his knife in his hand.

When he rounded the building he spotted the coach that had carried her ladyship and he groaned out loud. The little fool! She had come with only a driver and two grooms. The protection was almost nonexistent and she wore no disguise. She was an easy mark. The footman was just helping her into the coach and the driver, thankfully, was still atop and holding the reins.

John saw a shadow on the opposite side of the coach and knew his move would have to be fast. He ran to where Chelynne was still half out of the coach and gave her a hearty shove, bouncing her into the seat. Swiftly vaulting up the side, he managed his maneuver just in time to prevent a murder. By getting rid of the driver first the thieves could make away with coach, parcel and all . . . more for their trouble. He managed only to throw that man to the ground and jump from the coach himself. There was no time for fighting, no time to do anything but find flesh with the point of his knife and move along to the next aggressor before it was too late.

A scream from the coach alerted him and he found a man struggling to get inside. The countess was preventing his entry with wildly kicking feet. Bollering threw that man to the ground, noticing that his companion made fast work of one groom while the other stood watching, frozen with horror. John felt the knife in his arm before he realized his opponent was up again. A struggle ensued but lasted only a moment before John pinned the man down with his knees and stabbed him efficiently. He jumped up, grabbed onto the open door, and shouted, "Drive, man!"

The horses were startled out of their melancholy; and with a last kick in the direction of the sole uninjured thief they were away. With some effort John pulled himself inside.

He could see the little figure huddled in the corner opposite him, her eyes round and terrified, shaking uncontrollably. "What the hell were you about?" No response came from her side of the coach. He grabbed his arm and moaned. "What were you doing in that place?"

The smallest little voice, plainly reeking with fear, responded. "Who are you?"

"Your friendly tavern gallant," he sneered. He let out an exasperated sigh. "You're safe now. What were you doing?"

"I . . . I was looking for someone. I didn't know it would be so dangerous."

He laughed cruelly. "Had you thought to disguise the fact that you're mighty rich it could've been all right. Even so dressed, you might have been left unaccosted had you thought to bring proper protection!" His voice boomed in the small space. "The instant those men saw your coach you were like sleeping prey! Good Christ, they were only one for one! Where do you come from that you think to go tinkering around London in the middle of the night?"

"I'm not . . . I don't know the city very well."

"That was obvious on first sight. Who were you looking for?"

"A man . . . it's not important. I knew he wouldn't be there."

"What man meets you in such a place?" he roared, clearly

forgetting his place. "You've quality clothes and coach and my guess is there's ample protection to be got as well. Who uses you at this rate?"

"Please —"

"Madam, I have received, on your behalf, a most painful wound," he ground out with carefully restrained rage. "Now what man?" he exploded.

Chelynne shook in her corner, terrified of her rescuer. But his anger made it impossible not to answer. "My husband," she said, very softly, tears collecting in her eyes.

John was slightly embarrassed. "Why didn't you send someone from your household to do your spying? Do you have any idea what those men would have done to you? Noting your wealth, they would likely have held you for ransom, but not before they used you themselves. And that, madam, would have been the kindest thing that could have been done you!"

A harsh, bitter laugh, verging on hysteria, answered him. "I'm most fortunate then," she said, her voice taking on a caustic edge. "For I'm certain they would have had to kill me. There would have been no payment."

"A few gold coins will buy a better spy. Next time you would do well to send some member of your house."

Again came the laughter, mixed with choking tears. "There is no one in my house to do my bidding, except maybe my woman and she has seen over fifty years. I have not one ally in my husband's home."

Something in the sound of her voice caused him to look in her direction and forget the almost insane rage he felt at being forced to act in her defense. He could see that she was crying and it was hurt, angry weeping, not frightened tears.

"Why do you look for him?"

"To see what wench pleases him so that he cannot even come to his wife in need!" More tears followed that, quieter and sorely strained. Her voice, though youthful and soft, had a bitter quality. She had been badly hurt. John watched the display in wonder. How guileless she was to so brazenly admit her jealousy and disappointment. At first he had thought her suspicious of Chad's meeting, that perhaps she was plotting something, spying for a more practical purpose. Now he could see she was just a hurt little lass, her heart breaking because her husband was a-wenching. It was almost humorous. This little slip of a girl, no more than a child actually, was thus undone at the thought that her husband would seek out another and not love her and her alone. Where in the world did this creature come from?

The pain in his arm turned his thoughts and he leaned his head back, growing more pale and drawn by the moment. His hand clutched his arm and a river of blood ran down to his fingertips.

He hadn't noticed that she moved until he saw her face in front of him, studying that injury through tear-filled eyes. "Oh . . . you are hurt. Let me look at it."

"No, leave off. I'll borrow your coach if you'll be so kind, and let your driver take me home when he's left you off."

"Here, you're bleeding badly," she said, wiggling onto the seat beside him. "Have you a knife?"

"Aye, in my boot." She reached her small hand down and dug around until she felt the handle. She never gave thought to what she was doing as she wiped the old blood off on her velvet gown and slit his shirt to expose the gash. Her lips formed a round "oh" and she lifted her hem to take a strip of cloth from her petticoat.

"Aye, they cut you badly," she muttered, never looking at him but working industriously. She wrapped the wound tightly, tearing two more strips to tie the first into place. He winced as she pulled the final knot tight, the thing paining him a great deal more than he would admit.

"There's a man at my home who is talented with healing. You'll have a warm bed and . . . and a reward for your gallantry. What name do you go by?"

"John is enough, my lady. And I'd much prefer my own room."

"I must insist, John. You've paid me a grand compliment in coming to my rescue. I can't have you on my conscience." She smiled sweetly at him but her eyes were still red and weary.

"Your husband will consider much amiss to find me in one of his beds."

"I doubt he would care much if he found you in mine," she muttered. She brightened her face as if on cue and gave his hand a pat. "Now I'll count the matter done. I owe you at least that much."

John looked at her as if he would look through her. There was a faint smile on her lips but in her eyes there was the glimmer of sadness. "What excuse will you give your husband for tending me?"

"I'll give none." She shrugged. Then with a light laugh she added, "He seems to notice me only when he's angry. Mayhaps I'll gain some attention."

"And mayhaps he'll call me out."

"Oh, I think not," she laughed. "I can assure you, he's warned me not to expect that from him. He is a good man, truly, it's just that —" She lowered her eyes again, biting her lip against the urge to cry. A gentle hand, still stained with blood, brushed her cheek.

"What manner of man goes wenching when one so lovely as you awaits his pleasure?"

She raised her eyes and shook her head in confusion. "I had hoped to see what his preference be. I've no idea what he would have in my place."

"I should like to meet this beast," John said, trying to hide the amusement in his voice.

"I imagine you'll have that chance. It seems a grand fault of mine is saying things I'm later sorry for. I hope you'll not make mention of this talk we've had."

"You fear him?"

"Yes, I suppose I do, but it's not for that. I'm a little more afraid of looking like a fool to him."

"You must love him very much."

She raised her chin and took on a look of duty and tolerance. "Sir, I am his wife. Regardless of how I feel I am left without the right to decry him in any way when I speak of him. I was much too candid. I beg your discretion."

She looked back at him and read his expression accurately. He was amused. There was no way for her to conceal the fact that her love was a most agonizing thing. It was so painfully obvious that it almost sent John into a fit of laughter. She had nothing of the courtly dames' ability to play games. He patted her hand as a fond older brother would. "I wouldn't give you away for the world, sweetheart. I'll never let the monster know how you love him."

Chelynne knew she was being laughed at. She looked away again, coming close to tears yet another time though she fought them gallantly. "I suppose you can see why he feels as he does," she murmured, feeling absolutely infantile. How unattractive and juvenile she must appear.

"I certainly can," John said with a chuckle in his voice. He turned her face back toward his and wiped away a tear. "And I envy him more than I've ever envied a man."

There was no time to wonder at his words or reply, for the coach stopped. She virtually bounded out, not waiting for any aid from the driver. John followed, and momentarily blacked out. He was weakened more than he realized from the loss of blood and found he couldn't reach the house without assist. Chelynne had already thrown open the door and was calling for servants within. John, stumbling in on the arm of the driver, overheard the last command from her ladyship: "Fetch Sebastian to me, Stella. Don't stand there gawking now, this man is hurt."

The old woman shook off her surprise and went quickly to do her mistress's bidding. Chelynne shouted at her back. "And make ready a bed. Quickly now!"

The driver eased John into a chair in the front hall, where young maids were busy lighting candles for her ladyship. "Me thanks, gov'ner," the driver said. "We was bound fer trouble, I told me mistress so. Mighty lucky yer 'appened along. Me thanks."

Chelynne muttered something under her breath that had much the sound of a curse and with lips pursed in a tight little pout she glared at the driver as he left the hall.

She sighed, throwing off her cloak and letting it fall to the floor as she bent again over John's arm. John blanched and his eyes widened. It was not her preoccupation with his makeshift bandage that brought this reaction. He had seen Chad's wife before now, but only at a distance. While he knew her to be lovely the space between them had always been great or, as in the coach, the lighting inadequate. Now, with the lighting bright and her face this close he could see at least one good reason for Chad's poor humor.

There was a flush on her cheeks from the excitement and her

hair had begun to tumble out of its pins to fall in taffy-colored ringlets to her shoulders. Two finely arched brows were raised as she turned her sparkling brown eyes to him. He was caught by that sight, the deep pools floating between sooty black lashes. Her skin was flawless and pale but for the pinkness of her cheeks and her lips that were moist and red and luscious. She was absolutely beautiful.

His eyes traveled reluctantly lower, a little afraid of what he might find. He almost gasped, for as she leaned over him her bodice threatened to split and spill out full, round breasts. She inhaled deeply as she took note that the wound was still bleeding, and that action brought John's hands up as if he would catch those lovely mounds as they escaped. She looked at him again, that bright little face carefully judging his expression for a hint of pain. "Does it pain you overmuch, sir?"

John shook himself out of his stupor and smiled her fears away. "With one so lovely to tend me I think aught of pain." He looked around himself and commented, "Someone of great wealth lives here."

"Aye," she replied, straightening and relieving him greatly. "The earl of Bryant."

"The earl!" he cried, acting out the necessary surprise. He gave a long low whistle. "God's blood, he'll have my head!"

"John," she sighed, smiling at his fear. "He'll express his thanks if anything. Now, do be still. You've lost blood enough."

Footsteps sounded and he watched as Stella approached with a huge manservant in her wake. John knew who that would be. Sebastian stopped short as he sighted the wounded man slumped in the chair. Though it had been a good many years since they had seen each other, Sebastian was aware of his identity at once. John made a quick sign with his lips to be silent.

Sebastian looked at Chelynne and raised a suspicious brow. "Who be this lad, mum?"

"His name is John, Sebastian. He has an injury I would like you to tend at once. I fear he's lost a great deal of blood." She looked down at her stained gown and mumbled, "A great deal . . ."

"What be he doin' here, mum?"

"He lent me aid. Now let's get him up to a warm bed."

Sebastian still stood, confused, almost angry, if a servant were allowed such feelings. "What be ye doin' about at this hour, mum? I wouldna let ye go out. What did the lad do?"

"Oh, later," she snapped. She turned on her heel, and lifting her skirts, started swiftly up the stairs. John looked up at Sebastian with the glitter of mischief in his eyes. Sebastian didn't budge. He frowned down at the younger man. "What be ye doin' with me mistress, ye bloody scamp?"

"And she said she had no allies here," John mumbled.

"Sebastian!" came a stern command from the top of the stairs. Sebastian gave a grunt and dragged John's good arm around his neck, aiding the man to his feet. "If ye've hurt the lass I'll be seein' ye burn, John. By God!"

"I wouldna be hurtin' Chad's own wife, mon," John teased with the Scottish brogue. He looked at Sebastian more seriously then and added, "Be quiet about it, Sebastian. She doesn't know who I am."

John was weakened — not badly so, but he allowed the servant's aid to get him to the bedroom, and there he saw Chelynne and Stella pulling back the coverlet together. He was gaining a fair amount of pleasure from this pampering. His boots were pulled off and his shirt removed. He lay back in the soft down and sighed appreciatively at the luxury. He had been far too long without these comforts. Well-worn stockings were yanked off next, and when Sebastian touched the belt that held his breeches in place his relaxation came to an abrupt halt.

"Here, man! I can do with these on."

Chelynne stood at the foot of the bed with a finger on her lips as if in thought. The breeches were blood soaked and had to go. "I think I can manage to find you something clean to wear in the morning," she said hesitantly. "You look to be close to his lordship's size."

"Aye, the same," Sebastian muttered without looking up. He went after the belt again and John gave up the fight. Chelynne turned delicately away to find another chore. She returned when the covers were pulled to his waist, but not without the light blush that deepened her color.

"I'll see to him now, mum," Sebastian told her.

"I'll see you in the morning, John. Rest well." There was such a look of relief on her face, the smile a truly happy smile. She was no longer afraid and it was easy to tell she found pleasure in being able to offer comfort to a friend. He watched her as she left, the rhythmic swing of her skirts keeping time with the small, graceful steps. He leaned back into the pillows and a slow smile spread across his face. So this was the little witch who had trapped Chad into marriage? This was the wench Chad suspected of plotting with her cousin to destroy the proof of birth that made Kevin his heir? This was Chad's most carefully kept secret. Poor Chad. John made his mind. He would offer Chad his deepest sympathy at their next meeting.

A sharp pain in his arm brought his eyes open and darting to the manservant. Sebastian was intent on his chore and John relaxed again. Another pain startled him out of his complacency and John bolted upright. This man had mended scrapes for John and Chad in their early youth and his touch had always been marvelously gentle. Now it seemed rough and quick. John eyed him carefully. There was a glint in Sebastian's eyes that warned John of suspicions. Sebastian tied the new bandage into place and did so with a harsh jerk.

"Sebastian! For the love of —"

"A touch of brandy will aid ye to yer sleep," the old man suggested, going to a cabinet to fetch a bottle and a glass. "And while ye're havin' it, I'll be hearin' how ye come to be savin' me mistress in the dead o' night."

John had a gulp of the brew. He smiled. So nice of his lordship to provide such luxuries. "It was the merest accident, Sebastian. I was just about to leave a pub and found her ladyship in the hands of thieves. That's all."

"Aye, and if that be all I'm the king himself. Ye knew the lass, did ye not?"

"Aye, and the Hawthorne coach. Could you doubt it?"

"Then ye've seen the lad?"

"I have."

The servant's face softened considerably. It had been for Sebastian a long time since he had had the pleasure of seeing Chad and John together. When they were youngsters he had taken them fishing and hunting, mended their scratches, told them old stories. They were a pair in their younger days, these two. "Then ye'll tell his lordship that I tended ye and did so gladly. And I'll be keepin' a better eye to the lass from now."

"I think he already knows that, Sebastian. Any ill will between Chad and his father does not apply to you."

"I couldna take up those battles, lad. Never could I come between them and never could I serve the pair." Sebastian looked into his lap and then with soft old eyes looked to John as if he would explain away all his doubts. "The word hadna made ye friends with himself, did ye know that?"

"That's the best news I've had all day, Sebastian."

Sebastian nodded and smiled. "Aye, I was thinkin' it might be that. I'll be sayin' this to ye once, lad. It couldna make a heart more glad to see ye've come home."

"Why, Sebastian," John teased. "You've gone soft. You missed me!"

Sebastian growled and filled John's glass again, his complexion darkening from the sentimental kindness. It was his habit to keep himself from such emotional expressions. "I'll be leavin' ye t'sleep. Ye won't take much tendin'. I'd say ye play a fair game with the lass."

"Now, Sebastian," John playfully admonished. "Are you saying my wound isn't serious? Far be it from me to deny the lady the pleasure of a good deed."

"Argh," Sebastian scoffed. "T'sleep with ye now." He blew out the candles and closed the door behind him.

John closed his eyes, resting a little uneasily in the almost forgotten comfort of the earl's fine bed. At morning's light a maid brought him water for washing, and strong hot coffee and bread with honey to eat. He propped himself in the rich bed and enjoyed the meal lazily. Something for him to read was delivered and a bundle of clothes came later. Sebastian must have chosen the garb, for it was Chad's but not the rich attire he usually wore. It wouldn't do for John to go about looking like a prosperous lord.

In the past there had been offered gifts of lands. Charles offered him a land grant in Virginia, which he accepted as Chad had his, and neither had so much as measured their boundaries. He was a knight of the realm without lands, for all that he wanted and had ever wanted was Bratonshire. The mere thought of it was enough to send him bounding out of bed and on his way. Just as he would have done that, the door to his room slowly opened.

Chad entered, leaned against the closed door with his arms folded casually across his broad chest, and raised one eyebrow in question. John leaned back into the pillows and smiled.

"Are you quite comfortable?" Chad asked with belated concern.

"My thanks, your lordship. The pleasures are as swiftly delivered here as ever they were."

Chad chuckled a little and then went to a chair near the bed. He was a bit reluctant to get into any deep conversation with John. Every servant had a price and theirs were among the most alert ears in London. Quietly he asked his question: "What's this fob of saving my wife?"

"I think I at least saved you the price of a ransom. The little minx followed you to the tavern to catch a glimpse of your wench."

"My what?"

"She thought to see what woman you preferred over her. That's her story." He shrugged. "She was without disguise or protection and of course it was only moments before her coach was struck. I am amazed that she made it so far as the Gold Frog."

"What the hell gave her the idea I was with a woman? I told her I was going to the Frog on business."

"You *told* her?"

"Aye, she came to my room to give me the —" He stopped short and gave the matter some thought, more clearly now. The passionate display in her chamber and the subsequent visit to his. So, the necklace was only an excuse. She intended to seduce him. "It seems my wife had other plans for the evening," he mumbled.

John simply smiled. "It isn't like you to leave a lady in distress, Chad." His voice teased and Chad chafed slightly with the aggravation.

"To my knowledge the lady was suffering no distress. I'll speak to her about her reckless behavior."

"Why not just send her home to her family where she'll be out of your way?"

"That is worth considering," Chad muttered. "Does she suspect your identity?"

"No, but Sebastian isn't fooled. He's hot to the entire thing as far as I can tell. Ah . . . but she's a lovely vixen, Chadwick. And to think you never made mention of all that she is!" John laughed outright at his friend's discomfort. "She indicated she's not entirely pleased with the lack of attention she gets from you. It's my guess you don't frequent her bed as you should."

Chad winced involuntarily. More and more of his idle thoughts drifted in that direction. Even Bess had failed to remove one very persistent fantasy. He thought it brought him near lunacy. "Her Ladyship is well enough cared for."

John laughed again and threw his legs over the edge of the bed and started to dress. "You'll be sorry if you keep her in London and continue to ignore her. She'll find a lover and soothe her injured pride. Hell, if she weren't yours —"

He was stopped short by an icy stare piercing him from the depths of steely eyes. Another man might have frozen in fear, but not John Bollering. He shrugged, chuckled, and went on with dressing.

"You don't fool me any more than she does," he laughed, attempting to pull on his breeches with one hand. He stumbled, fell back onto the bed, and repeated the act again. Finally he looked up at Chad and winked. "Lend me a hand here, will you friend?"

"Not a chance. You've earned your struggle."

"You're not the least bit grateful, are you?"

Chad bowed. "For your chivalry, you'll be rewarded. For your jesting, you can be all day getting into your drawers for all I care. You'll never be above pirate, John."

John took on a more serious expression and sat in exasperated failure on the bed, his breeches around his ankles. Chad laughed loudly. With determination and finesse John carefully maneuvered them into their proper position and sat down again, a sly victorious smile on his lips. "One good thing's come of this. You can be damned sure she has nothing to do with her cousin's mischief."

"What makes you so sure?"

"God's blood, Chad! It's plain the lass isn't wily enough to go unattended to the 'Change! You can't make me believe you're fool enough to suspect her of conspiring in something as dishonest as that! She simply isn't experienced enough. She's simple and candid and young . . . oh, so young. And I would have to be totally blind not to see that love you she does . . . and deeply."

"She hasn't seen seventeen summers, John. What would she know of love?"

"Ahhh," John recalled with a smile. "I knew love in my seventeenth year that burned in my loins so strong I fairly lost my mind! A washwoman's daughter, that —"

Chad laughed uproariously. "And even that was not the first love. Your reputation has preceded you."

"No, but as good as the first." He looked down at his lap and then turned serious eyes to Chad. "I knew a maid as young as Her Ladyship. She ached with love for a man she was denied. She could stay him no longer and took her to him, nurturing his seed and bringing it to life. Young and simple she was, but no one could doubt her love. I saw it there myself, lighting in her eyes. Of course she was round and clumsy when I first laid eyes on her. I've always regretted that I couldn't behold her in all her radiance, when love first touched her, before she was swollen with babe." He paused and then said meaningfully, "Never did you doubt the possibility that she could love . . . totally."

Chad's expression turned hard and impassive. Even after this long it was a memory he couldn't bear easily. Many were the nights he tossed and turned and felt the burning ache in his throat. Tears stung his eyes and he turned his back on his friend. He couldn't think again of what he had so briefly possessed and so quickly lost.

"So, you've had your troubles, friend. Well, that is the one, and probably the only, difference between us. I manage my problems and your problems manage you."

Chad whirled around and faced John. "What would you know of it, John?"

John raised a brow. "Losing something one loves?" He shrugged. "You know everything of me, Chad. Do you honestly have to ask?"

"It's a matter I will handle on my own and without your advice," Chad returned angrily.

"That is a fact I have been aware of for a very long time. Your hate is a most awesome thing, my lord. I hope to God it isn't your ruin."

"You act as if hate is alien to you!"

John smiled. "Your point. You've turned me around appropriately. And as to business, it's been grand, my lord. One day I'll be glad to give you a warm bed. Maybe one as fine as this." John stretched and rubbed his back with his good hand, muttering, "I don't know if I'll ever be able to bear the luxury again."

"Will that slow you up much?" Chad asked, indicating the injured arm.

"It's nothing much."

The quarrel was forgotten. John was the only person alive who could speak honestly to Chad and not pay for it. The friendship was so secure that neither had doubt of the other's loyalty.

"We'll find the means, John. I'll do my part."

"Did you see Bess?"

"Aye, that's done. She'll act as go-between and hire couriers when it's necessary. How long will you be gone?"

"I have no idea," he said wearily. "This first turn against the devil should be the easiest one, but I'll accept your good wishes just the same."

"Go with God. I'll be waiting to hear."

"Chad, go to your countess. I think she's needing some comfort. She was really in trouble."

"Aye, and not the first. I'm of the mind she needs her skirts thrown up and her backside warmed. The little minx. God, but she's a package of mischief."

"Your burdens are many, my lord," John laughed.

"You don't know the half of it," Chad muttered as he started away.

"Guard your back," John called after him. "And remember, Your Lordship. There's no enemy more difficult to best than one so eager to submit."

Chad walked the distance to his wife's rooms. He opened the

door without knocking and entered. There she sat, immersed to the shoulders in her tub, her women fluttering around the room.

Chelynne threw a look over her shoulder to take note of his entry and then, totally disregarding him, went back to her washing. She hoped she looked angry. She didn't have to be very well known to him for that much to be obvious. She refused the slightest embarrassment at being put-upon during her bath and there was certainly no light greeting for her husband.

Chad smiled lazily and went to sit on the stool by the tub. "Good morning, madam," he greeted her, splashing his fingers lightly in the water. "Did you sleep well?"

Hesitantly she looked at him. Smiling. That damned lopsided smile he used when he wished to intimidate her. "As well as you did, my lord."

He gestured to Stella and waved her away with his hand. She hesitated, flushed, and under his determined stare, left the room. Tanya simply turned white and fled, still unable to give the slightest consideration to what intimacies might exist between man and wife.

Chad turned his attention back to Chelynne, and saw agitation showing vividly on her little face. "So, we have a guest."

"We do. Have you seen him?"

"I have."

It was bound for a staring contest, neither giving in to the other. He was chafed by her courage and she was more than irritated by his nonchalance. Finally she took up her cloth to lather. "Well, I do hope you've extended your gratitude. He did me a gallant service."

"He dragged you out of the hands of thieves, I'm told. In the middle of the night on Prior Street."

"It seems you have the story, my lord."

Chad ground his teeth. "Would you mind telling me what the hell you were doing there?"

She looked up at him with open defiance in her eyes. "Have we reached a point in our marriage where we exchange secrets, my lord?"

"Chelynne, I've no desire to go around with you. Now what were you doing at the Gold Frog?"

She pursed her lips. "Why, it was business, my lord."

"Business of what nature?"

She laughed insolently. "Oh, just small matters that trouble me. I'm afraid I must see them done before I can go about the business of enjoying my family." She dipped low into the water to rinse her shoulders. She looked up at him innocently, noticing his anger was steadily building. She smiled sweetly. "Would you hand me my towel, my lord?"

Chad kept his seat, determined to browbeat her with that icy stare. She simply rose from the tub. "Very well, I'll get it myself."

Chad's eyes widened in surprise. There she stood, not a foot from him, naked and in spellbinding beauty. Her ivory skin glistened with the moisture and her stance was relaxed. His eyes roved over the whole of her, over a shapely breast, down the smooth flat belly, his gaze gently caressing a delicately shaped thigh. She stepped from the tub and pulled her towel around her, shielding her nakedness from any further scrutiny. She seemed perfectly confident but the display was a rather shattering experience for both of them.

He cleared his throat. "I am responsible for you, madam. You are making matters most difficult for me with your reckless behavior. I don't want to have to suffer any more discomfort from your antics. Is that clearly understood?"

A soft ripple of laughter came from behind him. He turned to see one shapely leg outstretched from the slit in her dressing gown as she pulled on her stocking. She tied the garter, crossed her legs, and leaned back on the bed. "Discomfort? Why, my lord, I am scarcely worth your discomfort. There is no duel for my honor and you have not been chastised for your lack of escort. Indeed, I carefully considered all your warnings and have violated nothing."

"Chelynne, you're pushing me —"

"Why, were you worried for my welfare, perhaps?" she asked with mocking smile and teasing tone.

"You could have been killed!" he boomed.

Her smile faded and she took on a serious expression. "But as you can see," she said very softly, "I am quite well."

"Madam, you must use better sense than you have. Was it simple curiosity that took you to the Gold Frog? What were your intentions?"

With honest dignity she spoke, not flinching or trembling at all. "I was curious, my lord. I was interested in your meeting. That is truly what it was."

"It was business and I was gone by the time you had arrived. Now, are your curiosities stilled?"

She laughed a little and replied, "Oh yes, my lord. As much as they can be."

"What the hell do you mean by that?"

"I know you were with a woman, Chadwick. I waited for you after our guest was cared for and sleeping. I waited the night through in your room. Whatever business you had took a very long night. You are only now returning from it."

"And so you have decided my circumstance."

"Oh, why do you pretend with me? Why don't you just tell me truly that you cannot be bothered with me? If you have another preference, why not just free yourself now and spare us both any more trouble?"

"Do you wish to leave?"

"I wish to know what part I am to play in your life! Am I to go on like this, acting out the part of a proper wife . . . void of escort? Am I to sit in blessed eternal exile while you amuse yourself with your whore? Well, my lord, what?"

"I have business, madam. When that business is stable, I can give consideration to coddling your whims. As to now, just keep yourself out of trouble or I shall be forced to take action."

She flounced back down on the bed and took up her other stocking, drawing it on with haste, jerking and tugging at it. "Good," she returned saucily. "I'm most eager to see you in action."

"You pestilent little wench," he said with a laugh. "You're mighty full of yourself this morning. You lead me to think I should keep you under lock and key to save London from your antics."

She tied the garter with a jerk, muttering, "Oh, go to hell." Her head snapped up in surprise at her own wicked tongue and she stole a hasty look at Chad only to see him striding toward her with quick, even steps. He reached for her and she gave a gasp, trying to skitter away from him. His size, speed and strength were no match for hers. She was lifted off her feet and found herself lying across his lap. Her dressing gown was yanked up and her little rump bared. "No, no, I'm sorry! No, please!"

It was not heard. What was heard was the loud resounding *thwack* that came from his hand making contact with her flesh. She shrieked in pain. "If I have to beat the part of countess into you, you will learn," he cried. Another loud smack and shriek sounded. "If you can't use sense above a child's, then you shall be treated like a child!" Another loud smack and shrill cry. He stopped momentarily and listened to her panting apologies and smiled. He released her, and she stumbled to her feet and hurried across the room.

From the opposite wall she faced him, a look of surprised anger on her face as she rubbed the feeling back into her abused posterior. "I warn you, my lord. My endurance has a limit and that limit draws near. I will not be used at this rate!"

"Very well, madam. I have no use for a woman without endurance and for a weak-willed one even less. Good day."

He turned and left the room. Closing the door behind him, he leaned against it, paused, and reflected with a smile. Then a crashing of glass against that portal startled him out of his complacency. But still he smiled broadly, shaking his head with amusement. Soft, low laughter came from somewhere down the long dark hall. Chad heard a couple of steps and then the hidden man came into sight. John Bollering smiled.

"I had no idea you were serious," he teased.

Chad raised a hand and studied it. It was red and still throbbed from the blistering spanking he had just delivered. "I wasn't."

"It's a piece of business should've been done last night."

Another screech and the crashing of glass rended the silence. Both men shook with silent laughter. What hellfire she was.

"The countess is not happy," John whispered.

"Nor am I," Chad returned. He listened as the temper tantrum melted into sobs within his wife's bedroom. "But I feel a damn sight better than I did." He shook his head wearily. "I've come to think it's easier to break a horse than temper such a spitfire."

"Indeed?" John asked. "If you're thinking to try to break her, you're a bigger fool than I took you for."

TEN

FILTH IN LONDON was as constant as nature. The heavy rains that came in the late of the year ran with muck and slime into the gutters and streets, producing a stench that was almost more than the nose could bear. Those who were forced out pressed pomanders close to their faces to protect their senses from the insult. Those same ones emptied their slops from second-story windows with the rest of London.

There was one man in the city who walked briskly every day regardless of weather or smell. Charles Stuart was a man of great energy, thriving on little sleep, great amounts of exercise, and more ribald diversion than most human bodies could bear. Whether his fast pace was a necessity in avoiding petitioners, fleeing the nauseous odors or making haste to an appointment was always a mystery, but his courtiers hurried along to keep up while silently cursing their sovereign's enthusiastic gait.

King Charles had ruled for eleven years. He had long ago come to the conclusion that it was not a divine right, but the right of whoever would take it. He was not a born skeptic, though it was often said that even as an infant his brow had wrinkled into that same cynical and skeptical frown. He had seen his country seized and his father murdered, forcing him into exile at an early age. For eleven years he warred, negotiated, plotted and schemed to regain his kingdom. With the death of Cromwell, Charles victoriously reentered London to be greeted by multitudes of joyous subjects. They were wild with pleasure, for the return of their sovereign had rescued them from the harsh and swift disciplinary hand of the Lord Protector.

Charles was moved by their enthusiasm, but not fooled. He observed their displays and heard the shouts celebrating his return and bore it all gracefully. When it was done and he was allowed to relax and unwind, a brooding cynicism settled over him.

It would have pleased Charles to see England flourish, his people thriving and happy. Instead he saw a great many unpleasant things. Since his restoration a plague had killed hundreds of thousands in the city. The Great Fire had swept through miles of London, and though it killed off the plague, so it killed off people and destroyed homes and public places. His country warred against the Dutch, and while victorious, lost a fortune in ships and arms; many of the sailors starved because they could not be paid. There was no child he could name as heir and England would likely go to York, a weak-willed Catholic.

The people of England, in their tradition, grumbled loudly about their king. Charles was not perturbed. It would be thus until the end of time. Until they had a king who could make every peasant wealthy, every disease curable and every mishap easily remedied, the people would complain. It was the favorite English sport.

Charles had no illusions about himself. He was a man first and then a king. He knew that to do all that was humanly possible for his country and himself would never satisfy the multitudes; therefore, he never brought to bed the nagging feeling that he was solely responsible for every unhappiness around him. There were plenty of others willing to believe that.

He was a man of sound reason and a great deal of tolerance. He wished only that everyone would do as it suited him best while taking care not to injure his fellow. That was the standard by which he lived. Eleven years had not changed him much. He was still the same man with the same values.

Charles was one of the greatest lovers of his time and he knew it well. He loved the romantic game, the great chase, and pursued it at his will. He was chivalrous and suave. He had a great deal of respect for the institution of marriage insofar as it seldom hampered his pursuit of a woman. He hadn't been allowed the privilege of marrying for love; he had had to marry for an entire empire. It would have pleased him to have found a sensual woman for a wife, one who bore him children and met his sexual and emotional needs, but he was not so fortunate as that.

The princess he made his queen was prudish and barren. He never blamed Catherine, for she had endured years of religious lies that had molded her into the modest and subdued woman she was. That she was barren was another misfortune that plagued her painfully and was not her fault. He could have been relieved of this albatross of a queen and many encouraged him to be so, but he was not so heartless as that. He decided to live with this unhappy circumstance as best he could, as he lived with other things he did not like. But he sought pleasures elsewhere.

There came a bonus in living in such a manner that Charles did not cherish. His mode set the standard for the court and he had no wish to either change his habits or be a moral exemplar for others. He had learned the pleasure of loving at an early age and could never think of a very good reason for giving it up. He watched as the years rolled by, his court becoming more degenerate and perverse while it pursued the pleasures of the flesh to an insulting degree. He was totally aware of it and opted to go on, living in the manner that suited him best and letting other fools kill themselves trying to keep up with him. He would not blame himself. He never forced a noble into bed with a whore and never conspired in a plot from under the skirts of a grande dame. Whether he had been born to a crown or a piece of land to till, he would have had a drive within him that could not be ignored. He would always fill his leisure hours in the arms of a loving woman. If the punishment for fornicating had been death, he would likely have met his death before he started to shave his face.

Whitehall was a den of iniquity. There were a lot of bored people in the cold of winter, with little diversion outside their walls and every conceivable type of indoor entertainment already tried. The faces had started to blend together and looked remarkably the same. When the earl of Bryant brought his lovely young wife to court everyone noticed, especially the men. Charles Stuart was no less a man in this respect than any other.

King Charles immediately counted her among the most beautiful women he had ever seen. There were a great many in that number, but that did not lessen her desirability one bit. Her petite beauty and large, soft brown eyes held a sensual quality that radiated from her. On her third visit to Whitehall Charles defied custom and asked her to dance. The sharp piercing stares from the women and the concealed chuckles from the men, coupled with the lack of concern from the earl of Bryant, indicated that everyone present thought he had chosen yet another mistress. They troubled themselves silly again as the king practically ignored her presence on her next half-dozen appearances at court. The truth was that when Charles danced with the little countess she had trembled and stammered so, he decided to give her some time to acclimate herself to the court before forcing his presence again. She was immature and a little shy. There was not a more patient man on earth than Charles Stuart — nor a more selfish.

Tonight, in the queen's drawing rooms, he watched her again, and again from a safe distance. She was greeted now with more familiarity, the men beating their way to her with great expectations and the women retreating. The earl did not hover over his young wife, but the anxious glances he threw in her direction were not lost on Charles. That was another reason for his distance. The fact that he liked Hawthorne was not so important as the fact that he detested a fuss, especially over a woman. If Bryant had a possessive nature where his wife was concerned, Charles would retreat.

He made his way to Bryant and struck up idle conversation.

"It seems the lady is much in demand here," Charles said, gesturing toward Chelynne.

"It seems, sire."

"She's lovely, Bryant. Your good fortune with women never ceases to amaze me."

Chad eyed his king suspiciously. The mischief in Charles's eyes told of the train of thought. Charles would consider Chad a lucky man, loving romance as he did. Chad had successfully eluded attachments for many years and his accumulating wealth and prospective inheritance had made him a much sought after catch. Now, though no longer in good prospect for matrimony, he had one of the most beautiful women in England for his bride.

"The countess seems well acquainted with the baroness," Charles observed.

Chad looked to where Chelynne stood chatting with Lady Stelanthope. "It seems my wife spent many years abroad and in the homes of Lord Mondeloy's acquaintances for her education. Lord Stelanthope and the baroness are old friends she visited several times. The countess was orphaned at a very early age."

"Then they would seem like family to her. She has precious little of that, I imagine. Have you introduced her to your other friends?"

"I hadn't found the need, sire."

"Bringing her in here like this, my lord, is much like cornering a fox in the hunt, wouldn't you say?"

Chad raised his brows suddenly. "There seems to be plenty of space, should the fox decide to run."

"And if she doesn't run?" Charles asked, looking all the while at Chelynne and not Chad.

"Then as in the hunt, sire. Not much pleasure comes from trapping lame prey. Would you have me lock her up?"

"Ods fish, and deprive us all?" he laughed. "You're not so heartless as that, are you, my lord?"

Chad bowed. "Indeed no, Your Majesty."

"But neither are you foolish, Bryant. If she is anything to you, you don't show it."

"I have never been much for show, sire. Not even in that," he returned, indicating the little countess with his eyes.

The conversation could have gone on and on, each trying to guess the other's thoughts, but Charles was beckoned by some gentlemen. Chad took the subtle hint and sought out his wife, still talking to Lady Stelanthope.

"I'm glad you've come about, my lord," Chelynne greeted him

brightly. "Have you made the acquaintance of my lady Stelanthope?"

"I've had that pleasure," Chad returned suavely, bowing over the woman's hand. Lady Stelanthope curtsied and her eyes warmed with admiration.

"Chelynne has been special to me for a long time, my lord," the good lady said softly. "It pleases me greatly to see her married so well and to a man I've personally admired."

"You're too kind, madam."

"I had no idea," Chelynne said with delight. "How long have you known each other?" she asked Chad.

"Longer than either of us cares to admit," he said lightly.

"Then our paths might have crossed even before . . . ?" She stopped herself and tried to wiggle out of that slip. "I did spend a good many summers with Lady Stelanthope. I fear I was much her cross to bear. My uncle thought to have me schooled in the graces, but . . ." Her eyes grew warm with fondness. "I fear my lady Stelanthope was schooled in tolerance. Those days must have been a trial to you."

Chad's expression was passive. Chelynne apparently did not know about the real Lady Stelanthope. She was not so kind and virtuous as Chelynne thought. Had their paths crossed before the carefully arranged marriage it could have been rather embarrassing for all of them.

"You've made me a proud teacher on this occasion," the good lady returned, acting out her part beautifully. "I've brought someone with me this trip, my dear. I heard him singing in his leisure time and have had him entertaining for me this past year."

"Who?" Chelynne asked quizzically.

"Reuben. The gardener," she said, one brow raised. "Do you perhaps remember him?"

Chelynne blanched, and fought to recover herself. "Of course I remember him," she said softly.

"Why," the baroness said as if suddenly remembering. "He was a playmate of yours, wasn't he?"

Nothing quite so innocent as that, Chelynne thought. "Yes," she fairly whispered. She had been young then but not all her ways were childlike. It was Reuben, dear Reuben, who was the first to ever desire her, pursue her. He loved her in a desperate, hungry way. It was after one of their secret encounters was found out that Chelynne was sent from Lord Stelanthope's home. Chelynne silently prayed that Lady Stelanthope didn't remember and that if she did, she wouldn't speak of it.

"Ah, I think they're ready to hear him now. Won't you join us, my lord?"

"With pleasure," Chad returned, offering Chelynne his arm.

Chelynne was seated in a chair very near the entertainer and Chad stood behind her. Reuben sat on the floor, not taking notice of her then. He was dressed as a jester, with multicolored chausses and a silk jerkin covering his broad chest. He looked so strange in this garb, so out of place. He was a laborer, filling the days since early in his youth with much hard physical work. To be placed in a manor house instead of the fields was quite a lift in his status, but still he was common. His large muscular frame in this entertainer's costume belied his position as minstrel. But he was handsome. More handsome than ever. He would be now twenty-one years and there was not a youthful or boyish affectation to his appearance. He was every inch a man.

Chelynne hadn't imagined his voice for he never sang to her, but it was glorious. The rich tones floated through the drawing room and those present praised his efforts loudly. Reuben, possessing now the enthusiasm of an entertainer, played another song and his rich baritone enthralled them all.

After the third song a stool was brought for him, and more people gathered in the small audience. He was prepared to begin when his eyes caught sight of Chelynne. To her complete dismay he looked pointedly at her, his eyes glowing with emotion. He looked nowhere else as his fingers sensed the strings and a lilting melody floated through the air.

A summer's day a-passing,
I blew away the clouds.
On cupid's back she came a-riding, a-riding,
To steal my youth away, away,
To seal a man to stay.

I knew no kindled fire,
Till she brought me to a touch,
And she lingered for a moment, a moment,
To creep into my heart, my heart,
To creep into my heart.

I longed to hold her to me,
To love her all I would,
To fill her with a promise, a promise,
To claim her for all time, all time,
To make her truly mine.

I took her to the mountain,
I took her to the sea,
I took her to the heavens, the heavens,
And she flew away from me, from me,
She flew away from me.

The applause was subdued and the room fairly quiet. It was the lonely tale of a man who had loved and lost . . . and seemed to be meant for the countess of Bryant. Their eyes were betrayingly glued together.

From where he sat Reuben slowly raised his gaze from Chelynne to one directly above her, the hard steely flint of the earl of Bryant. Immediately Reuben shifted his eyes to Louise and sought to woo the king's mistress with an equally beautiful song about a sailor and a mermaid and their tireless romance.

Chelynne never suspected or worried that Chad had a jealous twinge, or even cared that she had been moved by the romantic lilting of Reuben's voice. She was lost in thought, all of which was of Reuben and his powerful effect on her.

She wished now that she had yielded to him on that grassy bed of nature's own home. She longed for the chance to caress that muscled back and feel his hands on her again. She grieved that she was bound to jewels and dinners at Whitehall, thinking only of the bliss of being a simple lass and wed to a yeoman. It would seem gay to know no burden above the mashing out of the next meal and the swelling of a child within her.

Her eyes closed as she imagined it. Never did a simple man's wife wonder where her husband took the night, never did he have to guess whose child she carried. Their virtues were their strength and their wealth came from their labors. Reuben's voice played the background for her daydreams as she imagined him holding her naked against the fresh, sweet-smelling grass, touching and caressing. She might as well have been alone in her fantasy for the reality of it. He rose over her and she gently smoothed his cheek . . . but the face did not belong to Reuben. It was Chad.

Her eyes popped open in surprise and she quickly discounted the entire experience, flushing it from her mind.

Reuben pleased his audience well, which was all he wanted to do, but after another song he was dismissed. They were bored with the beauty of his talent. It was so typical of this group; always bored, always seeking new diversion, never satisfied.

Chelynne knew better than to approach Reuben, for his safety as well as her own. She waited for a long time before making her way to Lady Stelanthope. Chad was busy at the gaming tables.

"Madam," she beckoned softly. "Does Reuben stay in London with you?"

"Ah, so it was for you . . . the song. Shhhh. Say no more and let me warn you once. The past is over and you must not speak of Reuben or to him. You would be branded forever for trifling with a gardener."

Chelynne lowered her eyes in embarrassment she would have much preferred to be private. "I don't wish to see him," she murmured. "But it would please me if you could tell him . . . tell him that I enjoyed his songs."

"If you wish it, darling," she sighed, brushing a sympathetic hand along Chelynne's arm.

" 'Tis a pity," Chelynne started. She stopped her words. There was nothing she could say. She missed the narrowing of Lady Stelanthope's eyes. Chelynne had no idea that Lady Stelanthope was not so moved by Reuben's voice as by other things.

"A sad state of affairs, this," came a voice from behind. Chelynne turned to find herself looking into the laughing eyes of the king. "Is there nothing here to amuse you, my lady?"

"Of course, Your Majesty," she said quickly. "I . . . I'm having a wonderful time."

He shook his head skeptically. "It doesn't seem so. What would please you? I'll see it's provided."

"Why . . . nothing more, I assure you."

"You liked the minstrel?"

"Of course," she said softly.

"I thought you did. I believe he had a song meant for you."

She worried over her reply. Lady Stelanthope had retreated and she saw no sign of any acquaintance. She was alone with him, what she had longed for and feared. "It would seem so, sire."

"Are you still so uncomfortable with me, my dear?" he asked softly.

"No, sire," she replied, though she could not look at him.

"I think you are, though I wish you wouldn't be. I should like us to be friends."

She looked at him then with open adoration. How kind he was. How thoughtful, gentle. "There is nothing I should like more, sire," she sighed, completely lost in his dark features. There was nothing about him to fear, from what she knew of him. But she had this awe because of his status; he was so powerful and unattainable. Now, so close to him, she wished for nothing so much in her life as to get to know him . . . be his friend. She had a sudden vision of him without his periwig, completely bald. A giggle came to her lips and he raised an eyebrow in question.

"There is something amusing, madam?"

"No, sire," she murmured, embarrassed.

"Of course there is. Won't you share it with me?"

"I'm sorry, Your Majesty. Please forgive me."

"I'll not forgive you until you tell me what set you to laughing. Ods fish, I could use a decent joke!"

There was a merry twinkle in his eye and a smile on his lips. The picture of him with sinister brows and shining pate came again to her mind and the giggles took over. "Oh, forgive me," she apologized, wondering what madness had seized her. She knew no recourse but to tell her thoughts and hope she hadn't angered him too severely. "As I looked at you then, I thought that perhaps . . . well, when the periwig is not in place. . . . Oh, sire, I only wondered what your hair is really like. I'm sorry." But still she giggled.

"What do you imagine it is like," he asked good-naturedly.

More giggles. "I . . . I couldn't say. Perhaps just as now."

"That wouldn't be amusing. You thought it light, perhaps? Like York's?"

"Yes," she laughed. "Yes, that's it."

"No, I think not." His finger touched his lips in thought. "Badly grayed and thin?"

"Oh, no, sire," she said strongly, for she wouldn't have him insulted for the world. But once again she laughed, trying desperately to stop. She wanted to kill herself for this wicked affliction.

Suddenly both his brows arched as the thought came to him. "You thought there was none!"

She gasped and covered her mouth with her hand, her eyes large and round. She had never seen him angry, but she greatly feared being the one who would anger the king and therefore sent to the Tower for insolence. But he laughed uproariously and drew all eyes to them. "Then you shall have a look," he said, snatching the wig off his head and bowing low so she could have a good look at the thick black locks he could still call his own. When he straightened he was laughing still, but more from the shock on her face than from his own mischief.

Soon the people in the room were all laughing and before she could fully comprehend the situation periwigs were coming off all around them, young men ruffling their own true locks and older men refusing to part with their hair.

Chelynne melted into uncontrollable laughter. Forgetting herself and her station she dropped to a stool to hold her sides, painful now from hearty laughter. How ridiculous the whole thing had become, how silly. She never expected the king and all his courtiers to behave like such comedians.

A still chuckling sovereign settled beside her, a periwig still slightly askew crowning his head. "Now you shouldn't wonder at it any longer, madam. Is there anything else you wish to know about me?"

"I think not, sire," she said with good humor. "Lest I should ask and you take off your —" She stopped abruptly and eyed him carefully. What might she have said? She realized with horror that to have finished her statement in some way, any way, would have been better than to leave it as she had.

The king touched her hand briefly and muttered, "That, madam, is the talk of the town."

ELEVEN

TO HAVE JOHN BOLLERING out of London left the earl of Bryant with a great many matters to pursue. He had had no word from Bratonshire and the plan was still delicate enough that there was no one but John to see word delivered. No other confidants knew of Chad's interest and involvement thus far.

In the matter of Harry Mondeloy, Chad moved slowly and carefully, confiding his interest to no one. He found that Harry was indeed in the city, having located his lodgings and caught sight of him a couple of times. Harry spent his time with a group of young fops, drinking, gambling and wenching. There would be, no doubt, a huge debt for Lord Mondeloy to make good. Chad laid the groundwork for obtaining more information and would wait for the proper time to face the young sot, preferring to have the advantage before entering any confrontation.

Chad visited his son almost daily, personally keeping tabs on Kevin and his welfare. There was little time for childish things, the boy already reading, scratching out crude little letters on a slate, and sitting astride a horse. But the moments that Chad spent with his son were the only ones in which the earl let his guard down completely, forgetting his preoccupation with business and duty and enjoying totally the precious time they had together.

The lad had the heavy dark brows of his sire, the brooding in his silver eyes that was Chad's, and his hair was fast becoming that same raven black in color. But his smile, the bright and wild smile, was completely Anne's. It was a rare and odd combination, almost unearthly at times. To Chad it was a wondrous miracle. Kevin was the core of his existence.

Winter was coming down upon England now and soon travel between the country and city would be difficult. Chad looked to the sky often in hopes of snow, but thus far there was only rain.

Some special correspondence the earl had sent off had finally been answered. It pertained to his father's manservant. Strangely, he had word sent to Sebastian at his own home via messenger and asked the old man to travel to an inn to meet him. The ordinary was out of the city and Chad sought out a dim corner to await Sebastian. When the man entered the dark room he doffed his hat, took a seat opposite the earl, and waited. There was no word of welcome, acknowledgment of title or position. Chad smiled. It was as if Sebastian read his mind.

After a tankard of ale had been delivered to the newly arrived patron, Sebastian spoke. "I'm thinkin' there's reason, lad, but I canna say why ye'd be callin' me here."

"There is, Sebastian. First, I've purposely neglected thanking you for tending John. His friendship is valued and therefore his life is more than a little important to me."

"The lad's a mite important to meself, sir. I'd have taken the time without yer approval."

"Aye, I believe you would have. You remember him well, I think. And if I don't miss my guess, you'd remember his father."

"I do."

"You've not had much to occupy yourself since my father's death, have you, Sebastian?"

"I wouldna complain of idleness, sir. I'd sooner have labors to hold off the time, to be tellin' ye true. If there's some chore —"

"There is, Sebastian. An unpleasant one. I can count on one hand the number of people I would trust to do my bidding and you are here," he said, raising up his index finger. "Do you remember when Bollering lost his estate to Shayburn?"

"Aye. It could've been yesterday."

"The family is taken care of now. Difficult as it was, the men are content and have made their way and the girls are married and married well. There's a single one in that family who is not satisfied with the present state of affairs. Do you follow me?"

"Aye, sir. Young John would not take the leavin's of that snake."

"John's been busy these past years, earning his coin. He doesn't have to come back to England now. Lord knows there's better for him in other lands . . . but, as you've witnessed, he's back."

"Aye, sir. He's pirated his way back, as it's told. Thief, pirate . . . ah, the land's not had a lot of pretty tales about him."

Chad laughed. "Intentional fabrications, Sebastian. He had His Majesty's leave for privateering and has not stolen a cent that I'm aware of. Just the same he has managed to accumulate a fair amount of money. Would it surprise you to know John has been most often with me?"

"Not now, sir. But the story had it ye'd fallen out with yer friend and parted ways."

Chad nodded; it was another intended tale. "It seems there's a matter in England plaguing his heart. He's thought to be out of the country, pursuing other interests. Have you mentioned seeing him to anyone?"

"I'd 'ave burned first. I know what the lad's about."

"You do?"

"I do, and I wouldna be sayin' so to yerself but that I think ye're bent on one purpose here. Have ye taken the part of the lad's plight?"

"What do you mean, Sebastian?" he asked, but he thought he knew well enough.

"I came not alone to His Lordship, sir. I brought to England brothers and one sister. We were farmers all and when His Lordship caught wind of the care I gave a sick farmer he brought me to the manor. The others settled and worked Bollering lands. I've lost some to the scoundrel that run him out."

"You never made mention of family, Sebastian."

"I didn't think it wise to be doin' so. To be tellin' ye true, I changed the name and was careful no one knew of the kinship. It's better in seein' to 'em. They serve Shayburn now."

"So . . . that is your interest."

"I've taken care not to be noticed about that shire, lad. But I've heard of a man comes to them in the darkest part of night, carrying no name. He promises a time they'll not answer to the baron, but to a new, fair lord. But there's a price."

"Price?"

"Aye, the fair amount of sufferin' to the end he's bound. I've a notion who the lad would be, but I've not made mention. Could be one and the same I took with me and my own charge to huntin' and gamin'."

"You are hot to it all, aren't you?"

"When I saw the lad's face, sir." Sebastian smiled, his ruddy face lighting up. "Ye couldna be keepin' secrets from the same one who rubbed goose grease on yer skinned-up knees."

"I think it's time you found employment elsewhere, Sebastian. Everyone knows of your loyalty to my father and my ill will toward him. As it happens I've received an answer to an inquiry on your behalf and the news is good. My lord Shayburn is in dire need of a good medic."

"Aaiii, to be tendin' His Lordship's hurts will smart," he groaned.

"I will not insist, Sebastian. It's most likely he'll test your loyalty harshly and it could be dangerous. Should you make any mistakes it could even be fatal. What say you?"

"I couldna be havin' more friends on earth than I have in heaven now, lad. I'll do it."

"It seems his rote to have servants deliver punishments in his stead. You could be put to the task of hurting your own family. If it comes to the point you cannot carry it off, head out. He would, and has, killed without hesitation. If he should trace you to me and me to John, it's over for us."

"My family has had their share o' trouble, lad. It does naught but make a man stronger in his purpose."

"Fine. Now, do nothing but keep your eyes and ears open. There is a laundress in Bratonshire who comes often to the manor.

She will find you when the time is right and tell you whatever John wishes you to know. Should you have something, she will be your only avenue. Trust no one else. And for God's sake, take care. Don't let them find you out."

Sebastian nodded and took a heavy draught from his mug. "When 'tis done, will I be comin' to the Hawthornes again?"

"If that would please you, Sebastian."

Sebastian had his huge fist wrapped around the heavy tankard and lifted in salute. Chad gave a nod and watched as the old man drained the mug. Without further discussion Sebastian was on his feet. There were no farewells. Chad watched him leave.

Chad couldn't guess the manservant's age, but neither could he remember when Sebastian hadn't been around. He was never young. But he was fit and strong and grotesquely large. His hands alone could wrap around a melon and crush it, but when tending some injury his touch was gentle and soothing. It made him a much sought after servant, his skill and experience well known in the country.

When Chad returned home he went directly to his study, which was his habit. He shuffled through some papers and grew restless. His impatience was from lack of information, from being left in the dark and having business unfinished. He began to roam around the house, which was not his habit. It was quiet, cold and unhappy. Everything was polished and shined, with not so much as a speck of dust on the floors and furnishings.

He climbed the stairs and passed his wife's rooms and found it was quiet there as well, no voices, no sign that there was any life in the house. From a window on the second floor he could see the courtyard. It would be flush with flowers in the spring, but now it was brown and dreary. Chelynne sat there on a bench, her cloak pulled tightly around her and her hood covering her hair. She stared at nothing in particular, shivering now and then with the cold.

He stood and watched her for a long time as if witnessing her loneliness personally. Finally she rose and started toward the house, looking up for an instant to spy him there, observing her. A small hand sought its way out from under her cloak and half rose, as if in greeting. His did the same, unconsciously. They looked at each other for a moment, each painfully aware of the great distance between them, and then she lowered her eyes and walked into the house.

Chad went to his room, closing the door behind him and leaning against it. He heard the soft clicking of Chelynne's feet against the stone floors as she passed, paused uncertainly, and went on to her own room. A heaviness threatened to lie on his heart. Guilt and remorse spoke to him in his conscience, but he would not hear it. Unable to bear the weight of the quiet house and the desolate look on his wife's face, he found his coat and left again.

Another fortnight passed with no word from Bratonshire and Christmas drew near, but the earl hardly noticed. He attended the social affairs with his wife but did not celebrate with the same vigor as the rest of London. His mind was on other things.

The ground was hard and the fog thick and pungent in the city. Daily the weather worsened. Chad sought out a dingy tavern that spilled noise from its stone walls in that afternoon. He spoke quietly to a serving maid in the hall and she nodded once toward the stairs. He put the steps behind him quickly and gave a light, anxious tap on the door.

"What's it now?" came the shrill, sassy reply.

The little witch, he thought angrily. She knew he would be coming now; would she have him shout his presence to the world? He opened the door to the drab little room and strode in, finding the woman who had answered his knock lying on the bed and eating an orange. Her hair was tangled, and clothing was strewn about the bed and floor. There was no resemblance to order in her or in her habitat. A thin dressing gown was all that covered her body, though the room was far too cold for one to be so meagerly garbed. He snorted distastefully at the filth that surrounded the wench.

"Ah, it's you, milord," she giggled.

"Have you had the opportunity —"

"Aye, 'e just left, milord. A bit sooner and you'd 'ave passed 'im on the stair. I'll 'ave me money first, milord."

"Then you have something to tell me?"

"I do, but I'm not 'bout t'be spillin' me guts without me coin. An' I'll not be takin' that stinkin' swine to me bed again. 'E ain't no gentleman. 'E's right mean, 'e is."

"Did he hurt you?"

"Aye, 'e did! I'd 'ave turned the beastie out but fer the twenty pound ye said was mine if 'e talked. Squeaked like a parrot." She beamed.

Chad pulled a few coins from his purse and threw them to her. He was hard pressed to bear the stench in the room and wasn't about to move any closer to the wench. He wished sincerely that Mondeloy had either more money for his wenching or better taste, for he hated doing this kind of business.

"Well?"

"Spillin' your name like a drunken fool. Says 'e 'as somethin' the earl'd crawl on 'is belly for . . . says 'e'll be rich enough when 'e's 'ad his fun. Never did say what it was. What's 'e got, milord?"

"Never you mind. Is that all?"

"Says you love what 'e's got better than the countess's privy arse, an' would pay a better sum, too."

So, Chad thought, he did keep the record. It made a lot more sense than anything else he'd done. "Did he mention the countess any other time?"

"Aye, called her a bitch, an' other things. Says 'e's bound to put 'er in 'er place along with yourself, milord. Beggin' yer pardon, but that's what 'e said."

"Is that all?"

"Aye, that's all, milord."

"That's fine. Now say nothing of our business."

"I won't be sayin' nothin', milord," she said with a giggle and a mischievous gleam in her eye. Chad walked a little nearer and reached out a hand to touch her filthy hair. She squirmed a bit closer, always the eager business woman. He grabbed her sharply by the hair and brought her to her knees. He almost shuddered at the foul smell of her unwashed body, but brought her face dangerously close to his.

"Ayeee! Leave off, ye bloody well rat! Yer 'urtin me!"

"Quiet! Listen to me, because I'll say this only once. If I ever hear that word of this has passed your lips, you can be assured I'll be back to fix up that pretty face of yours so that no one would pay for a toss with you. Do you understand?"

She nodded quickly and he released her, letting her fall back into the bed. He took one last look about the crowded little room and left, slamming the door as he went.

Necessity demanded some foul dealings from time to time, but the earl decided it was worth the twenty pounds and aesthetic insult to learn that his marriage record was intact. Bribing a whore was still the fastest way to do business. Why hadn't men learned, after all this time, not to let a woman goad them into spilling out their most carefully kept secrets?

Now it was so easy, knowing Mondeloy intended to put a price on his possession. How the man would chafe to know what he was to the earl of Bryant: not even a danger, simply an inconvenience. And it didn't cause Chad any pain to know that Harry sought to hurt Chelynne. It actually made him feel good. Chelynne's points were quickly stacking up in Chad's mind.

When he returned home that day he went directly to his wife's rooms and opened the door a small crack. He placed a small furry creature on the floor and waited there while the pup scampered around the room. He heard his wife gasp in surprise and listened while she chased the little spaniel, fussing and wooing it into her arms. Finally she came and opened her door completely, a bright smile on her face and a golden puppy in her arms.

"Did you bring it?" she asked, smiling.

"I thought you might like a pet." He shrugged.

"He's beautiful. Where did you find him?"

"His Majesty's litter. Do you like him?"

She nodded and went back into the room, leaving the door ajar so that he could follow her in if he chose. She went to the window seat, sat there, and fondled the puppy playfully, more than pleased with the gift and the giver. She looked to where her husband stood in the doorway, her bright little face melting the ice that covered his heart. He sighed from somewhere deep inside and, defeated, threw his hat into a chair and went to sit near her.

"Does he have a name?" she asked.

"I thought I would leave that to you."

"It has to be something special, something with meaning. He's golden like Summer. And so sweet. As sweet as honey," she chattered. "Honey, that would be a thought . . ." Chad chuckled softly at her pleasure and rose to pour himself a drink. The small supply of wines and liquors were for his consumption but he rarely partook since he routinely avoided this room. He poured a small draught in a glass and went back to her.

"Brandy!" she cried happily. "Yes, that's what he's like; Brandy!" She turned her sparkling eyes on him and whispered softly, "Oh, thank you, my lord. I'll treasure him always."

He was caught there, feeling her spell twine around him like ivy. He longed to crush her to him, taste that delicious mouth again, and woo her gently for the maiden she was. He felt giddy as a virgin lad this near to her, awkward as a newborn colt. How the tables had turned. She was cool and at ease and he felt his heart thumping and his hands trembling.

"He's a puppy, Chelynne. Not a treasure of great value."

"Treasures are different things to different people, my lord." She shrugged. "Stay and sup, Chad."

"I shouldn't," he began. "I have some business . . ." The instant disappointment registered on her face, her eyes brooding now and no longer carefree. He felt like an ogre for crushing her brief delight. "To hell with business. I'll stay."

She brightened immediately. Her play with the pup resumed and Chad leaned back in his chair to let the scene relax him and remove the distaste from his afternoon business. She giggled as Brandy playfully nipped at her and mocked discipline in a little swat. Suddenly she shrieked and held the puppy away from her, the little creature seeming to have sprung a leak. Chad roared with laughter and soon Chelynne could do naught but join him. An almost silent young maid stooped to mop up the floor and Chelynne assessed the damage to her gown.

"Oh, see," she sighed, looking down at the length of her. "Will you unfasten me, please?" She turned her back to him without waiting for a reply. His fingers undid the small fastenings as quickly as he could manage. A man's hands were not made for this chore, he decided, or he was painfully out of practice. But soon she was able to step behind her screen and emerge moments later in a lovely dressing gown.

Chelynne took her place again on the window seat, but this time a towel was brought to cover her lap so she could play with her puppy. When Chad leaned close to tickle Brandy's ear, Chelynne turned her face to come close to his. He trembled slightly with her nearness, letting his lips brush against her cheek to test the smooth sweetness of her skin.

"It will be nice with the fire tonight," she murmured. "See, it's begun to snow."

He looked past her out the window and saw the heavy flakes. The first snow, a sight he had been waiting for. "I hope it's snowing in the country," he thought aloud.

"I miss the country, Chad," she whispered. "It's just not the same here."

"I know," he said, taking her hand in both of his. "It's not the same for me either, Chelynne. But it's necessary. The country will always be there, love. We'll get back to it."

In the small burgh of Bratonshire a young maiden ran through the snow with her cloak pulled tightly around her. She looked over her shoulder a number of times to be sure that no one followed her and then crept into a barn that was near the outskirts of the town. She nestled into a small mound of hay to keep warm while she waited.

Little sounds in the night alerted her to false dangers again and again. She was on edge and nervous, yet steadfast in her decision to go through with this plan. At long last the door to the barn creaked open and she caught her breath in anticipation.

"A fine summer's night," came the voice in the darkness.

She let out her breath in audible relief. "And hear the night-bird's song," she whispered back.

"Ah, sweetheart," John Bollering breathed, coming forward. He deeply regretted the dimness in the barn and the necessity to have no light. He would have dearly liked to look on the lovely face of the young woman who waited for him. "You did come. And early."

"And you."

"Are you cold?"

"No more, John. There's time . . ." She gulped, steadied her voice. "All is ready."

"You shouldn't have come, Tess. It will hurt me to hurt you."

"I know what must be, John. It happened in truth to many here when Shayburn took this shire. Our play will come to good ends."

"Has your father agreed to this? He knows you're here?"

"Aye," she lied. She had been forbidden this, but managed as she knew she must. The woman who had agreed to be the victim of this attack was a little frightened and easy to persuade. Tess was supposed to be at the home of a neighbor, and in the confusion of getting ready for this event her father had neither the time nor the inclination to be sure of her whereabouts. "I would ask one thing of you, if it can be."

"What then?"

"For just a little while . . . before you hurt me . . . hold me? Please?"

"Sweet child, I know the limit to my courage when I think of smiting your lovely face."

"Take me gently, John . . ."

"Tess, it need not be. A bruise here, a tear or two . . . tell them what you will."

"Nay, it cannot be. It must be done."

"Tess," he groaned suspiciously. "What are you telling me?"

"There is no gallant way to rape and beat a maiden," she said softly.

"What've you done!" he cried angrily. "You may have ruined it all! We planned it carefully. There was to be a woman well advised, married if possible, waiting here for me! Now what've you done?"

"John Bollering," she sighed. "Must I seduce you as well?"

"Damn you! I won't do it! You'll go to your betrothed for your evidence!"

"That is not the answer, John."

"You're promised to another!"

"There are not many to be trusted here. Not because they are loyal to Shayburn but because of their fear. My father would accept no one but his own kin. My betrothed will take me as I come to him."

"Nay! Go back home. Tell Rath again in a fortnight. I will not have you on my conscience!"

"Sir! My mother has smuggled small pieces of clothing in bread baskets to her sister as she would dare, hoping to save some goods for our family after our home is plundered. She has buried her possessions in the earth believing she will dig them up in the spring. Our neighbors will touch the torch to their homes at the sound of my screams. Do they do all this so you can tell them to wait? Have they not waited long enough?"

"Tess, dear Tess, you're a dream-struck lass. You've come with thoughts of love and tenderness that are not for me to have. The young heart oft cries out for what it is denied. No, darling, I will not ruin a maiden."

"And so you do not," she breathed.

"You're an innocent child —"

"Child who called after you night upon night? Dream-struck lass who chilled your ale and loved you from afar for months? Foolish heart who chased you down in the dark of night for one small chance to feel your touch? No, you do not believe that John, because it is not so."

"Tess," he said huskily. "A woman barely blooming, but that doesn't make it right to —"

She drew his hand to her breast. "Will you deny that you know of my love for you? I have loved you always. As I was a child awaiting your return . . . I loved you."

"And what of your betrothed?"

"He is a good man but I do not love him. Have no fear, John, I will be a good wife to him and I will not betray you. I will spill you no bastard, for the wedding will be set after this — my father will see it done. If I am lucky even I will never know. . . . But John, however I love you it can never be. But I can know the truth to what I feel this once, and I will never regret it."

"A pretty romance," he said bitterly. "A lovely fornication, truly. God, how low can you bring a man?"

"To touch me is so low?"

"Oh, Tess," he groaned.

"Why do I want you still? You are not so gallant! Pirate, thief, rapist, murderer . . . there is nothing about you to love! You ride to us in the dark of night as some mongrel knight, sneaking about with no thoughts of goodness but a vengeance burning in your blood and a lust for your due! You have no silk or wig like yon baron. No lace falls under your chin or over your wrists. Sir John, knight without a lady, knight without lands! You are not so grand! Can I have nothing of you but pity?"

He came down on her mouth, bruising and crushing her lips angrily. He groaned deep inside his throat at the robust pleasure the taste of her mouth brought. In the cold night, in the dark of the barn with no bed but that of hay, the gentle maiden yielded to his cruelty with softness. Repulsed by duty he tore the bodice of her simple dress and bit at her breast. He growled in strange madness as his desire grew even as he hated himself for wanting her.

"Dear John," she whispered. "Do you hate me so? If there is any tenderness in your heart for me . . . do not hurt me until you must."

His wall crumbled and a choked sob escaped him as he found her mouth again, softer this time, tenderly, gently lowering himself against her and holding her carefully. Her small hands, roughened from her toils, were gentle on his back. Her skin was soft where it had not been exposed to the elements and burdensome toils. Her breasts were full and round, her hips the perfect size for a man's hands.

He found her as he knew he must and accomplished the thing hard and fast, feeling the resistance give way. She made no cry, there was no tenseness in her small form. "There had to be pain," he muttered thickly.

"There was no pain," she breathed. "Fear is pain. I was not afraid. I have never been afraid of you, my darling."

"Tess, don't. You'll make it worse."

"Please," she murmured piteously. "If it can never be so in truth, let me pretend you love me tonight . . ."

"Then pretend," he relented. "I'll help you pretend. I love you, Tess. I want you, darling."

With a sob she clung to him, straining against him and moving with him. His large practiced hands brought every touch to thrilling heights, fulfilled every expectation. He didn't have to really love her; he did truly want her. He didn't have to pretend this, the exhausting labor he worked on her. She climbed to the fevered pitch she knew he held effortlessly.

For long moments they lay entwined and touched each other with curious fingers. Loving strokes as the embers cooled, the blaze dead while the warmth lingered. His lips touched her throat and ear and he tasted the salt of tears.

"Why do you weep?"

"At dawn's first light Shayburn's men will come into the town to take rent and goods from the people. Little good would come of letting them find a lovers' tryst. They must find ashes and blood. You know it must be, John."

"Who is your betrothed?"

"Stephen Kilmore, farmer."

"A decent man," he admitted. He kissed her again.

"Tarry no longer. The truth is hard enough without delaying it."

He paid her no heed. He touched her again with passionate intent. Again she submitted unselfishly. She closed her mind to what would come in the morning, her whole life's dream bent on now, tonight, this forbidden lover who was hers for a brief space of time. This she might never have known had it not been for Shayburn's merciless attack on Lord Bollering years ago.

And when this man who so tenderly loved her was seated again in the Bollering manor she would know him only as master, ruler, lawmaker of his land. Her husband would bend to his demands and yield his coin for rent, tax and tithe. But John would be a fair and just lord and would protect their shire from villains. They could live in peace instead of pain. There would be contentment to replace their fear. And her contribution to this effort was that she should have this gift of love.

When he stood to pull on his cloak she shivered with the cold. He was again as she had seen him most often, self-confident and strong, his features hard and sure. Tenderness was his concession to her on this night, but in truth he was not a gentle man. He was a warrior.

He reached down and grabbed the cloth of her skirt sharply. When he made love to her he had gently lifted the hem, but now he gave it an angry jerk, leaving her exposed. She saw the white of his teeth in the darkness as he smiled.

"You've submitted bravely, lass," he murmured, his voice deep and gruff. "There is more of a sacrifice you must make to this cause."

"If it be in my power, Sir John . . ."

"Do not give yourself in marriage to this Kilmore boy."

"It is done. Our fathers have pledged it."

His hand came out hard against her face and she yelped in surprise and pain. Half her face was frozen from the blow and her nose and lip bloodied. Her eyes clenched, she did not see him wince as he struck her. When she opened her eyes to look at him again she saw that same sure face, hard and impassive.

"I am the law of this land, wench," he said harshly. He bent to one knee and touched the cheek he had just bruised and his voice was strangely subdued and low. "And no one shall have you but me."

He rose after placing a swift kiss on her cheek. He towered above her, his hands on his hips and his feet braced apart. His laughter rang out in the small stable, vicious, frightening laughter. He appeared to her as some majestic and horrible beast, godlike in his immensity from where she lay on her bed of hay.

"Never question my ways, wench, but heed them true. For every time you let another man fondle you the lash will fall once upon your back!"

Her mouth stood gaping as her wide eyes questioned his sanity. He laughed again, that same laugh that reminded her of an animal cornering his prey.

"Was your fantasy worth your pretense, maiden?"

"Yea," she said bravely, though she was frightened of him now.

He bent from the waist, bringing his face down close to hers. With a strained whisper he said, "I was not pretending."

He straightened abruptly, strode the distance to the door, and whirled around to face her one last time. "Mark my words, Tess. Never betray me to another." He laughed again and was gone, leaving only the sound of his rapidly departing footfalls ringing in her ears.

Tess lay there stunned, making no sense of him at all. Would he give her these parting threats to ease her disappointment? To lessen the burden of her guilt and give her false hope? Would he have her wait in truth and take her as his acknowledged mistress?

Silence. She sat up and listened. The dark night was frighteningly silent. There was no sound of horses' hooves; no one stirred. She screamed, a practice scream, and the sound of her own voice chilled the night and she was suddenly half out of her mind with fear. The warmth from her brief touch with love was gone and she screamed again, and again, and again, blood-chilling screams that could frighten the stars out of the sky.

Voices insulted the night. Running and hammering and more screams split through the little village as if armies battered them. Horses were loosed and ran wildly away. Tess moved hesitantly near to the barn door and peeked out to see the street alive with light and smoke. Women rushed madly about, tearing their hair and weeping in fright.

Hysteria gripped her from the reality of the play. The baron would be convinced, for it was enough to convince her. John had seen Joanna Todd and her two small children safely delivered to London and housed there while the bodies of three not long dead were placed in the house that Gaston Todd set fire to himself. One rape, three murders, many precious things stolen and several houses burned. There were several hundred residents in this little burgh and only a few dozen knew of this plan.

Neighbors, ignorant of the circumstance, comforted Todd as he sank to his knees and wept real tears over his loss while his family lived in the finest house they would know in a lifetime.

Talbot Rath rushed to where she stood and stared down at her with disbelief in his eyes. He held a torch in one hand and studied her closely. The voices of the people seemed distant to them both now. Tess could read her father's mind. She had defied him. Betrayal. Talbot threw the torch into the barn and lashed out at Tess, striking her hard and knocking her down. He had never in his life hit her before now.

The barn took light quickly and he bent to gather her up in his arms, holding her close against his chest as she sobbed from the agony of his blow.

"There, lass, 'twas not in anger. Good John could not hurt you enough to convince the baron. And I cannot strike my own dear again."

He carried her toward the village, where there was a mad scurrying to put out the fire, those holding the buckets taking care not to extinguish it too quickly. The pounding of horses' hooves increased the action of the townspeople and the effort looked real, for it was safe now. There was little left to save.

Tess looked up into her father's face and saw in the darkness a slow smile grow as he looked on the holocaust all around him. Success.

TWELVE

AIN WAS A DAILY AFFAIR as winter threatened to leave England early. A heavy cover of drab clouds and constant drizzle caused the thick smoke from the cooking fires to hover over the city and mingle with the gutter waste to offend the senses. Coaches moved at a faster pace and people darted about the streets swiftly to keep dry. Every cloth felt damp and mold grew thick on the stone walls until it had to be chiseled away.

If the sun shone through for a brief time great throngs of people filled the London streets to shop and barter and gossip. Popular lampoons were passed around and crowds gathered to enjoy the latest slander. Rumors and character assassinations were ever the popular sport. Only last spring the king's sister had visited and when she returned to France she found her death. Minette was the only woman on earth Charles had truly loved, and her death brought him much misery. It was said that her husband's homosexual lover poisoned her in a jealous rage. Charles was inclined to believe it, though it was not proven. His remorse was matched only by his anger. In an effort to placate the sovereign, Louise de Keroualle had been sent to the English court from France.

Charles seemed not too displeased with his gift. He had admired Louise during Minette's visit. And Louise, who had been raised among nobility, slid into her position as the favored mistress to the king without trouble. It seemed to matter little to her that the people of England disliked her for being French, Catholic and regal. What did matter was that the king's other mistress, Nell Gwyn, the opposite of Louise in every way, often harassed her regal counterpart.

Rumors of divorce were as popular as ever, many wishing the king would be done with his barren queen and remarry, getting at least one legitimate heir for England. But, as in the past, nothing materialized, for Charles was not a man to treat a lady unkindly.

This hysteria was typical of London, of the court and its people. The earl of Bryant watched his wife receive her very liberal education. He had no idea what she was making of it. It seemed she closed her eyes to it, pretending everything was on the square when truthfully nothing was fair or decent or honorable. He pondered as he rode toward his home in the city that he had helped her in a way. He had set her aside, publicly as well as privately, and so many assumed her to be unimportant and harmless. She was left alone then. She was not drawn into their way of life or their perversions.

A matter that troubled him in no small way was his king. Charles paid Chelynne much courteous attention. The countess seemed flattered to be even noticed, as if completely unaware of her rare beauty. Charles, true to his reputation, was gallant and chivalrous, but he looked at the young countess with something other than platonic intent. He was not a man to be troubled with a rule, a husband or other such trivialities. He was moving cautiously and Chad was keen to the fact that it had nothing to do with him. It might be because Chelynne was somewhat retired, because Mistress Gwyn and Louise kept His Majesty occupied, or because Charles liked the chase as much as the conquest.

When Chad arrived home he went directly to his study, threw off his coat and wig, and went after the task of clearing off a large accumulation of papers on his desk. There was a letter to his overseer to be answered, letters to merchants, friends in America, a message sent to Bess, who would see it got to John; a thousand things burned in his mind. He couldn't seem to juggle his thoughts and arrange them in a more suitable order.

He had not accomplished much when he answered a light tapping at his study door with a curt and exasperated consent to enter. Chelynne stood timidly in the frame of the door, twisting her hands nervously as she judged the scowl on his face.

"If this is a bad time . . ." she started.

"Never mind. What is it?"

"Well, there have been some invitations I would like to speak with you about."

"Yes, yes."

She pointed to his desk and said softly, "They're all there. I don't know which you'll want to attend."

He gave an exasperated grunt and fished beneath his pile of papers in search of the invitations she spoke of, annoyed with this trivial nonsense. She sensed his agitation and moved to the desk to find them and put them before him. In doing this she bent over him, brushing his shoulder with one full, round breast and leaving that bounty clear to his chance gaze. She straightened after accomplishing this and found she was slightly dizzy from the brief contact. His eyes were glued to her bosom, his hand straining to rise against his will and fondle one of those delicious breasts.

Reluctantly he looked over the invitations, idly leafing through them and throwing them back down. "Is there something here you cannot live without attending?" he asked with impatience.

"N-no, sir," she stammered. She took a breath and attempted to enlighten him. "There's a dinner at Whitehall. The king will be there and he remarked the week past that he sees little of you . . ." She was leaning over him again, fishing for that invitation, her perfume encircling him and her lovely body altogether too near. Finally she found the piece she was after and placed it on top of the pile,. straightening again. Chad found more with each passing day that he could not be in the same room with her without misery. She was so ripe for the picking, so damnably desirable. He needed to have her out of his study, out of these cramped quarters, before he lost control. "I don't know if I shall be able to attend or not," he said brusquely.

"Should you like me to go even if you're not able?"

"I don't care."

"Shall I make arrangements for an escort? I could perhaps ask you again tomorrow and see if there is a change in your plans." She took a seat, perched on the edge of the chair directly opposite his desk, staring at him with that sweet, innocent face of a child, those heavy breasts threatening to spill out of her dress. The door was closed, there were no servants around, and she seemed to have no intention of leaving.

"Yes, ask me tomorrow," he said, turning back to his work and brushing the invitations off to one side. Her presence seemed to surround him.

"There's an invitation to go with the king's party to the theater. I put it on your desk several days ago."

"I haven't been here," he said almost angrily. "I've had too much to do at the wharves to even come home. Didn't I tell you there were ships coming in?"

He had mentioned it in passing. "Yes, but it's just that the invitation is for today and I didn't know —"

"Well, madam, I can hardly give it my attention when I'm not here, now can I?"

"No, but —"

"And if it's for today I cannot go! I have work to do . . . or did you perhaps think I was writing lampoons?"

"No, sir," she said softly. She rose to leave and he gave an audible sigh of relief. "Should you like me to go in your stead?" she asked from the door.

"Madam," he snarled, tossing the quill into the well and stabbing her with the sharp gleam of his eyes. "I don't care."

"If you would not be pleased to have me abroad without —"

"Chelynne! For the love of God, do what pleases you. You're not a child to need me as a constant chaperone. Now if I didn't have work to do I would be pleased to escort you, but as you see, I cannot. If you wish to go, then go. If you wish to stay home, then do that!"

He turned to his work again, but sensing that she had not left even now, he looked up to where she stood by the door. "It's only that I enjoy your escort on occasion," she said softly.

"Then you should have married someone who has nothing to do but attend parties. My life's breath does not rest on seeing a play!"

The door closed behind her quickly with that, and Chad turned again to his letter. He started anew several times, making a foolish error or wording it wrong repeatedly. Finally he threw down his quill in exasperation and rummaged through his desk for some tobacco. Smoking was not a particular pleasure of his, but he filled the study with the rich and heavy odor just the same. Then he took up the quill again, but the sweet, enthralling scent of roses lingered.

He turned his thoughts to ships and cargoes, putting aside his letter for a time. He thought of the merchandise coming into port from Virginia and scribbled a few figures, but his imagination turned to sultry brown eyes, moist with emotion. He looked to the chair where she had sat and then to the door, as if replaying the scene in his mind. No, he had no time to be bound to petticoats, to be led around by the nose by a female. Why were there no windows in this room? With a growl he was on his feet and pacing about the confining space.

It hadn't been like this in years. He couldn't seem to get her out of his mind. She was always posturing before him, the patient princess, the goddess of purity. He simply didn't have time to toy with her now, courting her and leading her to parties and plays. He didn't need a woman in his life, he never had. Even when he had Anne he was too busy worrying about supporting her to enjoy the pure pleasure of loving her. Chelynne would just have to wait.

But she wasn't waiting, even if that was what he intended her to do. She was here, at his command, ever under his nose and around his house. He heard her rise in the mornings and go to bed at night. She sought out his approval on every matter and struggled not to bring a slight to his name through her innocence and lack of worldly knowledge. It was difficult to ignore someone who wanted to please so desperately.

Chad turned his thoughts to his son, to his dead wife, to any escape from the emotion that was building up in him. There was no respite for him there any longer. He would never stop loving Anne, but she had been gone for a long time and he had begun to see he could never have her back. And instead of seeing a poor, slighted son, he had a vision of a boy without a mother finally acquiring one. He saw Chelynne sitting on the grass, looking more natural in simple garb than in her burdensome gowns and bone stays. She was laughing with a small boy, letting the sweet simplicity of her love lead him as perfectly as a natural mother's love would.

The boy in the vision vanished from his mind and he was faced again with the seductive beauty of his wife in another setting. He saw her rising from her bath, waking from her sleep, playing with her puppy.

"Hell," he thought. "If it's come to that, so that I cannot even put my mind to business, it's better if I take her and have my fill. Then perhaps I can think."

But he stopped short with a startling conclusion. He had put her aside for so long, declared his indifference for so many months that he didn't even know how to approach her. Go to her like a dumbstruck lad and tell her he couldn't wait any longer? Frighten her and take her quickly, having her despise the thing and him? In avoiding her his actions had been harsh and almost cruel. How to undo that now?

He sat and thought heavily. He tried to figure in his mind when he could take her out of the city. He and John had hoped the spring would resolve the matter of Bratonshire, but it could be years actually, depending on how clever Shayburn was. If he could take Chelynne home to Hawthorne House and bring his son, he could explain what business and problems had beset him. In the quiet of the country he could seduce her and lead her gently where he meant to have her. It was not a matter of trusting her; giving her information now might in fact injure her. She could not inadvertently tell what she didn't know.

He set his mind. It seemed to be in his best interest to begin smoothing over his harshness and bringing her closer to him now. He had burned some very important bridges and must begin busily rebuilding. He was a very practical man. He didn't have to love her. She was comely and gentle, almost exactly what he would have chosen himself for a bride. Whoring had never quite helped him and he had long ago realized that a lasting relationship was better for his needs. He could claim this one and be content. It would make for a comfortable situation.

He never considered that he needed the ease she could bring to set aright something within him that had been troubled for too many years. He never considered love.

He plopped his wig on his head and took up his coat. He would delay no longer. Even in this, in seeking out his young bride to begin something between them, he acted the part of a determined businessman.

Stella confirmed that Chelynne had gone to the theater and he would find her there. Just as he was leaving his house a young boy approached him. There was a message for him from Bess. He dropped a few pence in the lad's hand and read the thing. It was the name of a tavern and a time. John. But he still had time to deal with Chelynne, and went quickly.

It was as if fate itself would play against him when he set out. Going into the theater he met Gwen. She was on the arm of a young gallant whom she abandoned at once in spying Chad.

"How grand to see you, my lord. I swear your company has been sorely missed of late. I was about to send word to you. Pray sit with me and let us have a chat."

"I believe the countess is expecting me, Gwen. Another time, perhaps."

"I've a matter that should interest you," she wheedled.

"I can't imagine what that would be," he returned flatly.

Gwen sensed her advantage slipping and flaunted her knowledge straightaway. "I've made a good friend of your wife's cousin. It seems he has something of yours."

Chad's brows arched in surprise that was wholly genuine. Gwen was a beguiling little sorceress. He had been watching her sashay her charms between dukes and earls for years; it shouldn't have surprised him to learn that she could condescend to the likes of Mondeloy for something she wanted. In truth, she spread herself so thin over plots and affairs he couldn't imagine how she kept them all straight.

It was a time when he didn't want to be seen in her company, didn't want to be bothered with playing her games, but he was trapped. If he didn't find out what she knew now he might have missed his only opportunity. Gwen was coy. He gestured with his eyes toward his coach and she shook her head negatively. He offered his arm as an alternative and she walked with him into the theater.

From where they sat Chad could see his wife. She was in very impressive company and he hoped to get out of the theater before Chelynne saw him with Gwen.

"What is it you wish to tell me?"

"The matter *does* disturb you," she said with a smile. "I was so disappointed, darling, that you never confided in me."

"We were never so close as you would have the world believe, Gwen. There is nothing I wished to tell you that I did not."

"You have dealt with me quite cruelly, my lord," she said with a strained whisper, her eyes gleaming angrily. "At every turn of the hand you have thrown out your insults in the presence of family and friends. There was a time when I thought you cared for me! If you can think of a time when I have done you some injury, I pray you tell me now so I may make amends. I cannot tolerate your hostility any longer."

"At present a very important matter comes to mind. You have knowledge to share and yet you toy with me."

"I thought to help you come by that paper you desire! You would cheapen my meagerest attempt at reconciliation."

"How can you help me?"

"You know that I can," she said, turning her eyes away from him.

He conceded. She could wheedle information out of anyone with her charm and quick thinking. He had no admiration for her morals or methods but he gave her credit where it was due for getting what she wanted. Especially from a man.

"And what do you want in return?"

She stiffened. There was visible hurt in her eyes. "There is nothing more to consider, my lord. I'm quite unwilling to share my confidences with you. Go, seek out another gutter trollop to do your bidding. I'll have no more of you."

"Gwen," he said softly. "Admit to me at least that I have some small reason to doubt your earnest. You've not played the coyest of maids nor have you treated my wife and marriage with much respect. Now you would have me believe you simply wish to help me?"

"I loved you!" she bit out, tears showing in her eyes. "Can you blame me for seeking to share something of your life even though you sought out another name, no greater than my own, to take the position of your wife? Was it so kind that you sampled my affections at will, swearing you could not marry, only to seek out Miss Hoity-Toity to wed? A wench you didn't even know." She laughed bitterly. "From anyone else it would much befit the standard, but you —" She shook her head dismally. "I thought you were different."

How convincingly brokenhearted she was, Chad thought appreciatively. Had he not been desperate to know what information she held he would have risen and applauded. Or at least reminded her of the great number who had occupied his position in her life and asked how he should know he was special to her. She was a superb actress. Another man might be on his knees begging for forgiveness for so brutally abusing her honor. But Chad had known Gwen for a long time. He had even witnessed a similar play for her husband when she sought to placate him. If there was enough sensitivity beneath her cover to really feel that kind of hurt, he would be truly amazed. He could almost believe that she at least thought herself to be in love with him; she responded to him totally. It was more likely bitterness at having not achieved something she thought due her for her sacrifices. Yes, she could help him, her acting ability being above that of the whole company who at this moment entertained the king. He would play this game to whatever end.

"Gwen, I'm sorry that you've been hurt. You should have taken me at my word when I said we would never marry. I am married now at my father's insistence and it cannot be changed."

"Had there been time to think the matter through I would have used better taste. But your animosity, your cruelty! How could I understand? How could I ease the hurt when you never turned a nice word to me?"

"Then I'll take blame where it's due. I should have come to you and explained the circumstances, but I considered Lord Graystone. Let us leave it alone. Henceforth you must not seek to injure the countess as you have. She is inexperienced here. She considers marriage a sacred institution."

"And you?"

"I?" He smiled and ran his eyes over her slowly, noting as he did so that she relished the close scrutiny. She was so unbelievably brazen that he almost lost sight of his goal and laughed out loud. There was a spark deep within him urging him to curb his instincts briefly and enjoy her for exactly what she was. She would yield to him instantly.

But disgust filled him at the thought. It had long been his curse that he could not separate the personality from the body. He couldn't gain enough satisfaction from her sensuality without some appreciation for her character. Thus, Anne, and now, he thought with some surprise, Chelynne. But hiding his true feelings, he faced her and met her eyes. "I have always done what suits me, Gwen. I thought you understood that."

"I had begun to wonder. You play the gallant husband so well."

His wife would beg to differ, he thought. But there was truth enough to that. Not many thought his blasé treatment of his wife out of place. It was the way here. "Do you honestly think I take any obligation lightly?" he asked her. "I play the husband when it suits me, as it suits me. Now, that paper. Will Mondeloy turn it over to me?"

"He plays with the thought. He seeks compensation, but I've not been able to learn his plan."

"The very fact that he has it proves he's had a hand in murder. Does he have no fear of the penalty?"

"None. He has covered his tracks well. He claims to have purchased his parcel from a highwayman and his friends will swear they rode with him. But no one has seen the thing. It is hidden and I have no idea where. Did you know, my lord, that he was playing the innocent guest in your own home when he rode out one day and came back the next with the paper on his person? For a long while he housed it with you."

"I was able to deduce that much, from the date of the priest's slaying." And he had been able to deduce something more. The knowledge of his marriage, of the missing record, was not widespread. Gwen couldn't have stumbled across the information, he cautioned himself. She had sought out Mondeloy, likely hoping to find something to deal with, something she could use to hurt Chelynne or himself.

"He has planned carefully," she commented. "But he has confided in me and it will not be long before I see the thing. Mondeloy will not be injured if I'm able to carry out my plan . . . but then neither will you."

"I would hear of this plan," he said.

"Not here. Not now. I have been foolish to say so much surrounded by ears that are not deaf. Come, take me home and I will speak to you there."

"Gwen," he groaned. "Let me come later. My wife is expecting my company."

"No, she isn't. That group," she said pointing to the king's party, "plans a visit to the Fox and Hounds to sup."

Momentary shock revealed itself in Chad's expression. He was to meet John a short distance from there and it was not a safe part of town. He was painfully aware that nobles often frequented inns and taverns of poor quality for sport, but he didn't like the idea of Chelynne going there.

"I think I shall have the countess delivered home before that party begins."

"I swear she couldn't be in safer company," Gwen argued. "Who would accost the king? There are escorts aplenty."

"Not always," Chad muttered. He knew of more than one occasion when Charles had gone into the city without the star and garter, without royal robes and guards, supping and drinking with the common folk and never being recognized until the adventure was at an end. It was usually the day after when the rumors went wild and Charles confessed.

"Are you not included in that adventure?"

"I would not be missed," she replied. That admission was humbling to Gwen. She would greatly love to have arrived at a position where her presence would be depended on if not commanded. But that did not interest her now. She had come to learn that one duke's night of love and many promises meant little at morning's light. She was growing old. She had tired of the court life, finding it constantly ambiguous and undependable. She set her sights on a more permanent arrangement. Any way she could connive it would suit her fine.

Chad nodded his head in assent and they left quickly. He wanted this business done with haste.

People wandered in and out of the theater. Being seen and seeing was the great fascination; the play was a secondary consideration. He was just handing Gwen into the coach when his arm was brushed by someone passing. He turned to find himself eye to eye with the earl of Rochester and there, on his arm, was Chelynne. He looked around. There was the entire party: Charles and Louise, Chelynne, Rochester and others. He was trapped.

He first bowed to his sovereign and rose to see the king's lazy eyes drifting past him and into the coach where Gwen sat. Chelynne's wide eyes confirmed that she, too, made that observation. His circumstance could not have been more embarrassing had he been naked.

Left without recourse, he bowed over Chelynne's hand and brushed his lips there with a great show of courtesy. "Did you enjoy the play, madam?"

She forced a smile for the many onlookers and held her little chin in the air. "I did, sir. And you?"

"Most certainly," he answered, though he hadn't seen a thing on the stage. "I've chanced to meet my lady Graystone and there is a matter of some business I must speak to her about." His complexion darkened somewhat as a hum went through the crowd. He would have preferred standing there in the buff to putting Chelynne through this sham. But his eyes glowed proudly as he observed his wife's sweet smile and gracious manner. She laid a possessive hand on his arm and her words seemed almost sincere.

"Of course, my lord. Perhaps you'll be free later."

He was amazed by her poise and dignity. His eyes warmed. "I assure you, it is a matter of business I will conclude as quickly as possible."

There was a grunt and then a coughing from the king, the man who invented this inane game. Chad turned to see the twinkle in the man's eyes, but Chelynne gave it no regard. "I await your pleasure, my lord."

She curtsied, flashed him a soft, sweet smile that caught at his heart and tore at it a little, melting every sliver of ice that had shrouded him for years. He watched her walk away on the arm of Rochester, her chin high as she nodded and smiled to their audience. Snickers ran through the crowd as if they had all just witnessed an adultery. Charles threw one last look over his shoulder at the earl of Bryant. Chad could read the expression as if it had been written in script for him to study. The king thought him a complete fool. The king was absolutely right.

Through some manipulating that was not very difficult, Rochester managed to get himself quite alone with the countess of Bryant in his coach. The moment the horses started he turned to her. "God's bones, darling, but you've a lovely handle on things. Is it possible you and the earl have an understanding in your marriage?"

She smiled, though tears stung her eyes, and replied softly. "Did you suspect otherwise, my lord? I would say it's obvious to the world now."

"It seems so. Lord, sweetheart, it's not a common thing, that's all."

"Why, there's little reason to go about sneaking and spying when two people are of like mind, don't you agree?"

"Of course I do, but there's still a great deal of fuss over the smallest fornications, darling."

She refused to show her pain. "Of course we could battle over such things and be miserable. Would that be better?"

Rochester chuckled. "So, he does not fight over your honor?"

"My lord, he does care for my welfare! I didn't say there were ill feelings between us! Should I inform him of some abuse he would do whate'er he must. What I do of my own is unchallenged."

"So very simple," Rochester murmured, a new warmth to his usually light and humorous voice.

"Did you witness any hostility between His Lordship and me?"

"Indeed no."

"Then you may take me at my word. That is our way." She turned from him to look out the window, a pain gnawing at her stomach and her throat feeling parched from strangling the cry that would fight its way out. A pretty set of lies, she thought bitterly. What choice was left her? To blanch and faint from the display she witnessed? To shriek in rage and tear the whore's hair out by the roots? Nothing but mock dignity could save her; and in saving herself she freed her husband to his mistress.

There was a hand on her shoulder turning her back to the earl. This usually smiling man was not smiling now. He pulled her slowly into his embrace. This was another benefit of the little scene. She would be considered fair game from now. He covered her lips and she allowed him. This brief romantic yielding held much reason. She needed comfort, confidence, and something else she couldn't identify. Something began to stir in her. Rochester was handsome and witty and good company. She liked him a great deal. He would not have to be persuaded; she could learn now about the special thing that could free her, that had eluded and mystified her for so many months.

But there would be nothing to hold. There were too many things she had to forget first before she could give herself. When the time did come, it would not be for another of the court's amusing adulteries, it would be for something more meaningful and permanent. Not yet.

She pushed him away but he was reluctant to free her. "Please," she said more sternly. "My lord!" she cried as a hand crept under her cloak to inspect more closely a prize.

Rochester settled back, bemused by her reaction. "You take too much for granted, my lord," she said quietly. "To have an understanding is one matter. To have no discretion whatever is another."

"You have no fondness for me, then?"

"Of course I do," she argued. "But would you even want a woman who would yield so freely? Nay, there is time enough, I think."

"I see," he said, a trifle piqued by her hesitation.

"I don't think you do, kind sir. I delay your affections, true, but not for lack of fondness. I am not a whore."

He chuckled, cocked his brow, and spoke the naked truth. "It makes no difference to me, my lady. Whether you are whore or vestal virgin, I await your pleasure."

Chelynne's insides were caught in a knot. She twisted and turned until she thought she would be sick. How did the queen do it? How did she sit so patiently beside her husband, watch him go off with his mistresses, and play the part of purity, submission and blind tolerance?

And Chad moved through the scene so easily, so sure of himself and her. He thought to find no anger from her. She had no right to be angry. He had never lied to her about his intention. He did not wish to be saddled with a youthful bride and would not cater to her. She would have to manage as she could without husbandly support. They did indeed have an understanding, only she had just begun to understand it.

Night fell over London. John Bollering lingered in the tavern long past the hour Chad was to have met him. When Chad had delivered a message for John through Bess he no doubt expected it to be sent to the country by courier. But John was safer here, in this crowded city.

Chad's message had informed him that Shayburn had requested aid from Bryant. John knew what Chad would have done. He would have informed the baron that gold and supplies would be sent to Bratonshire. The gold would be stolen en route, thieves and highwaymen were so prevalent. Times were hard all around. The supplies sent to replenish the badly damaged village would make the trip safely, however. And as for force of arms, the earl would send his own men to ensure the safety of that village. And with them would go explicit instructions as to their duties. John would have foreknowledge of their positions so as to get quietly around them. All was going as planned. Shayburn was falling into the trap perfectly.

John was not a man to rejoice prematurely. The fact that this retaliation was as fair as what had happened to his father did not make it legal. Should John be caught in the act of terrorizing that town he could be brought to trial himself. That was the very reason he was in London now, anxious to talk with Chad. The word was about Bratonshire that Shayburn thought this attack could be suspiciously linked to John. He was openly inquiring as to John's exact whereabouts, looking for some connection. He had even hesitated to ask Bryant for support. What would his reaction be to find Chad so eager to lend aid? Would he believe that Chad was no longer interested in the old Bollering estate?

There were many sailors about, gambling, drinking, and tussling with women. John had chosen sailor's garb for himself and was unnoticed here. He finished his ale and headed out into the night.

It was in his mind to seek out Bess and leave another message for another time. He could afford to spend a few days in London now and it was imperative that he meet with Chad.

He would walk the distance to Bess. A sailor could ill afford a hell cart and he was not inclined to lead anyone to suspect his circumstance. 'Pressment gangs would not trouble a man in sailor's dress but thieves would not be hindered. His eyes burned on all sides of him, aware of eyes where he could not see faces. So many years had molded his warrior's instinct for the enemy that John could be roused from a sound sleep by a falling leaf or breaking twig.

A squeal split the night, and he saw a young woman engaged in a tussle with a mangy character. He wouldn't interfere. There were two companions to this aggressor that wouldn't take kindly to any gallant gesture from him. She kicked at her assailant and her cloak was flung wide to expose a gown of some expense. His curiosity stirred as he thought of a woman of quality in this part of town. He couldn't help remembering the night he found Chelynne in similar straits. Her vizard was ripped off. He was regretting more with every step that he must pass this riotous scene to get to Bess. He hoped he wouldn't be pulled into the fray just for his chance presence.

He fought reality against the stirring memory and then with a start he realized his mind wasn't playing tricks. It was the countess, again, grappled in the hands of thieves. A quick survey told him there was no coach, no escorts.

John found his knife and with a cry that sounded like a wounded beast's, he flung himself on her assailant and felt immediate penetration. Chelynne fell to the ground and landed with a thud. John stood ready, knees bent and arms wide, anxious for the challengers. The look of pure rage in his eyes and the scowl on his lips sent the thieves fleeing in one direction and the countess off in the other. Everyone but John was running.

Chelynne was dodging down the street frantically and with great speed, leaving John no choice but to follow. He called her name but she did not slow her pace. The jagged street caught at her shoes and she stumbled but kept up the flight. Hysteria gripped her and she was running madly, no light to guide her but what little bit showed through covered windows and doors bolted early against the dangers in this city after dark. Her screams could be heard as she flew down the street but not one door opened to give aid.

The footfalls were close behind her as she passed a last dwelling and the road became a dirt path to the river. That was where she fell, defeated, with an aggressor close behind. She gave up, totally beyond caring what happened to her now, and sobbed into the dirt beneath her.

John looked down at her, watching the little body racked with frightened sobs and, with a sigh, dropped down beside her. He wiped the blood off his dagger and replaced it in his boot. Feeling helpless when faced with a woman's tears, he touched her back as if to comfort her.

Chelynne rolled over and looked at him. "You," she breathed.

"Come on, sweetheart. Tell your gallant knight what's caught you this time."

She sat up and wiped her tears away, looking at him in wonder. "I had no idea it was you," she said, still stunned. She shook her head. What strange plan put her in dire straits twice, and both times this simple man was the one to risk his own life to save her?

He stood and drew her to her feet.

"Looking for your earl again?"

Her chin trembled like a frightened little girl's and large tears fell from her eyes. She could manage only to shake her head while twisting her hands. John opened his arms to her and she fell to him gratefully, sobs shaking her. He gently stroked her hair, giving comfort and time and companionship, filling three of her greatest needs. When she quieted again he held her away from him and looked into her eyes.

"All I've ever asked for my services is your explanation. Tell me what happened."

"It was a foolish thing," she replied with a sniff. "I was with a party of courtiers to the Fox and Hounds. We'd been at the theater and his lordship . . . my husband, was there with his mistress." She shrugged and said simply, "There was no choice for me. There were so many witnesses to my husband's indiscretion that to save my own pride I explained ours as a marriage of convenience. While he assured me it was only business, he felt free to leave me there, taking away his friend, one of London's most well-known whores."

"And that brought you here?"

"Oh no," she assured him. "We supped not far from here and at the tavern Rochester made quite a play of our marriage. They were cruel, making Chad . . . His Lordship the world's greatest lover and me . . . I dare not say what they made of me! I had to be away from there. I took the first offered escort home."

"I think I can see now. You were put upon at once?"

She sighed and lowered her eyes. "Before the door was closed to the coach. What was I to do? I made such a struggle that he couldn't be bothered and let me out. I thought to find a hackney and — and — well, you saw the rest."

"Wouldn't it have been better to have gone back into the tavern? You could have awaited another escort home."

She shook her head dismally. "I think not," she murmured. She was quiet, not daring even to look up, and then her voice began slowly, the pace of her words building with anger as she spoke. "He's brought me to this and how I hate it! See your simple garb. Do you think yourself unfortunate? Look at my rich clothes, my fine fur. Oh, God, how I hate this game we play."

"Who, darling? Who?"

"He has never loved me, never wanted me! He is not even embarrassed to flaunt his mistress before the world! That is the way here, every man takes a whore, a mistress and another man's wife!"

John laughed, softly so as not to hurt her. She had a very accurate perception of the court. "I'm your friend, sweetheart. Talk to me."

"If you are truly my friend, take me away. It's killing me. Oh, John, it's like living without food. Truly, the pain of his indifference is worse than a thousand beatings."

"I'm not that kind of friend. Not the kind of friend who takes a woman from her husband."

"He would sooner be rid of me."

"If that were so, he would be, don't you think?"

She looked at him with such a sad face, her eyes red and swollen and liquid with unhappiness. "Why, then? Why does he even bother with me?"

"Darling, would I know his mind? When a man does not care for his wife he sends her where she would be no trouble."

"John, did you meet the earl?"

"I did." He nodded.

"What did you judge his character to be?"

"Kind and fair, so I thought."

"Does a kind and fair man use his wife as he uses me?"

John chuckled and touched her face. "How does he use you, darling? Does he clothe you in rags? Are there bruises on your body?"

"I am a virgin," she said softly, lowering her eyes.

"Christ," he breathed, understanding Chad better now than he had in years. "A virgin bride." He raised her chin with a finger and looked into her eyes. "And you love him?"

"I don't think I can any longer, John." She shook her head. "No, I loved him once. I wanted him, wanted to bring him happiness, give him a child." She touched his arm and the question in her eyes overwhelmed him for a moment. "I spoke of a child once, a son, and he was so angry it frightened me. I didn't bring it up at all," she said in confusion. " 'Twas him mentioning a son and I . . ." Her words trailed away. "But the marriage was forced and he does not desire it. In time he will send me away and it will be over."

"I think if he was of a mind to send you away, he would have done so."

"Then why would he keep me here and hold himself from me so purposefully? How long am I to endure this?"

John shrugged. "Is it possible that time will see his manner change?"

She laughed a little bitterly. For someone who knew nothing of her husband he certainly sounded like him. "A warrior goes into battle again and again, suffering his wounds and healing and doing battle again. Is it for the end glory, the final victory that he fights, or is it for the love of war? Truly, which?"

"I think for both," he said truthfully. "A man who does not cherish fighting cannot do so and stay alive."

She gently touched his hand. "John, a woman's purpose is not to war, not to exist among hostile creatures. My purpose on this earth is another entirely. 'Tis love and warmth that would see me flourish. If a warrior is maimed and can battle no more, his purpose is done. What of a woman then, whose love is bent and torn? Sullied and decried? Now my husband's standards have been witnessed by so many that they all assume I am likewise engaged. My own doing, for I stood quietly and watched him take his pleasures as he would. But I cannot stay them as Chad stays me. Tonight proves that. What am I to do now?"

"Then you are certain he has a mistress?"

"Oh, many, I am sure."

"He is a condemned man," John sighed.

"What do you mean?"

"You have no proof and his very word denies it, yet you have condemned him. Is that how you play the understanding wife?"

"Oh, trust you see my plight clearly!" she cried. "The man has not shared my bed, fool! What more proof is needed?" With a choked sob she pressed the back of her hand to her mouth and again the tears crept out from pinched lids, trailing in painful streams down her cheeks. He drew her to him and held her, letting the pent-up emotion spend itself.

"As I hold you so near I wonder if there is some name I might put to you, other than this title you wear?"

She looked up at him. "Aye. Chelynne," she whispered.

John tilted her tear-streaked face up to his and planted gentle kisses on it. She was soft and lovely and hurt, so vulnerable. They were secluded and she was needing love too desperately. She responded to him and encircled his neck with her arms. So hurt. So beautiful. His best friend's wife.

"You want me to make love to you, don't you, Chelynne?"

Her eyes dropped and her arms slipped slowly down to her sides. She couldn't look at him. "Forgive me," she mumbled despondently.

"You needn't be ashamed, darling. Wanting, needing, it's very natural and would not be thus if you were tended by the man you love."

"But I am ashamed! I have toyed with the feelings! He touches me, leads me, and halts himself! If he had a favored lackey I wouldn't think him even a man, but I feel his desire and I've wanted him, too!" She was crying again, those same jagged sobs that seemed never to be done. "That's all I am left with, John. That shameless wanting . . . and I'm not at all sure for what. I . . . oh, I don't even know what to do!"

Had there been light enough he would have seen the dark flush creep over her face as she choked out her words. She burned with it. She was ashamed first, then sorry for having divulged so much personal information, and now humiliated beyond anything she had ever known for the whole of it.

"It's going to be all right, Chelynne."

She hugged her arms about herself and mumbled something unintelligible.

"You're shivering," he observed. She could not look at him or answer. "Come, we've got to get you warmed, you'll catch your death."

"I can't go back."

"I'm not taking you back."

"Then where?"

"I'll take you home with me. We'll find a hell cart. It's not far."

"I can't, John," she said, pulling back a little. "Stella would be frantic."

He pulled her to him and stood there, very close to her with one arm around her waist. "You're coming with me, you know that, don't you?" She nodded. There was nothing else to be done. "And you're going to be mighty displeased with me later. There's quite a lot I have to tell you and you're not going to like my deceptions."

"We hardly know each other. How can you deceive a stranger?"

"When you're warm and dry I'll tell you a story. Until then let's make walking our task."

John's arm gave aid. Her slippered feet throbbed from the stones beneath. They passed several surly characters and John's tense body close to hers gave her comfort because she knew he was constantly ready, alert for any danger. It had been a very long time since she had been purposefully protected, a long time since she had felt there was nothing to fear.

It seemed they went a great distance before they came upon a coach for hire. John gave instructions to the driver and there was one stop. He left her in the coach and went to the door of some private residence. It did not occur to her to question this, but she was very conscious of the fact that he did not enter or take his eyes off the coach where she waited. It brought a flood of reassurance that she had not felt since she was bounced on her uncle's knee.

"Now we'll go. Don't expect much. It's fairly humble."

"I must be mad to go with you," she mumbled.

"Or just very confused."

"You could be quite dangerous," she thought aloud.

"You don't think that. Indeed, you've little reason to fear me, but perhaps you should."

"Should I, John?"

He leaned the short distance across and looked at her, gravely serious. "I know that even if I give you my promise that you'll be hurt, you will still come with me, won't you, Chelynne?"

She gave a weak affirmative nod, not even knowing herself why she was doing this.

"I'm counting on you, Chelynne. I'm hoping there's more sense in that head of yours than you've shown by wandering the streets and dark alleys late at night. Anyway, it's too late now."

"It was the circumstance —"

"No, it wasn't," he said sharply. "Had you taken a moment to think you could have prevented all that's happened to you. You could have sent word to someone from the earl's household to fetch you, if not himself. There were a dozen ways you could have spared yourself. Foolish impulse is what got you here, and the only thing that will get you out now is some clear thinking."

"It wasn't simply impulse," she argued.

"Wasn't it?"

She thought for a moment. She started another quick denial and then remembered some other things. There was servant's garb to conceal her identity from her own bridegroom, wild rides to free herself of pent-up tension, following Chad into the night to catch a glimpse of his mistress. Most of what she had done had been impulsive.

"I suppose," she sighed.

"And that's a thing you're going to have to give up. You have a brain; use it. You can find a good sense of reason in that mind of yours if you try. Rash impulses such as this will never help you to find happiness here."

"And going with you now . . . is a rash impulse."

"Perhaps, but it's too late now. The choice is no longer yours."

The coach halted and John led her up a dark stairway to a second-floor room. "Humble" was a kind word for his dwelling. The room was bare but for a small table, chair and bed. A few of his belongings were stacked against the wall and the tabletop was cluttered with papers that he quickly rolled up and put from her sight. Though bare, it was scrubbed clean and had an odor much like what she remembered from when the cook house was cleaned at Welby Manor. She shivered again and John was quick to start a fire in a small and inadequate stove. He left her for a short time and she huddled near that strange creature to absorb any heat she might, wondering all the while what insane notion had led her here. There was only the single resting place and they could not share it without a great deal of physical contact.

But then that was what she expected, she thought dryly. She could try to tell herself she didn't want anything to happen, but it would be a lie. She had wanted something like that to happen for a very long time.

He brought her a hot drink from somewhere below, a milky concoction with a strong odor and a pleasant taste. She wrapped her hands around the mug and sipped, watching him move around the room, removing his cloak and putting things away. She wondered again why she was comfortable in this man's presence.

"Are you warmer now?" he asked.

"Yes," she murmured, taking another sip of her drink. "Did I remember to thank you?"

"But I must thank you, my lady. You see, it was coincidence that I saw your trouble, but it was not coincidence that I helped. Even in your first plight a few months ago I lent aid only because I knew who you were. It was the same tonight. There are no gallant strangers in this city looking for three-to-one fights to save a beautiful maiden. And my purpose is purely selfish. In helping you, getting you here, I find a means to solve some of my own problems. I confess I've known your husband for many years. You are not a stranger to me at all."

"You know Chad?"

"Aye, very well."

"And you were silent! Why have you led me so?"

He shrugged. "It's a friendship neither of us cares to acknowledge."

"Then you *are* his friend?"

"We were. Before tonight."

"What has happened?"

"I have his wife in my room. For all he knows, in my bed."

"Do you think he would care?" she laughed. "He won't even have to know. There will be no suit against you, my friend, for you have shown me only kindness. There is no need to tell him where I had the night. I'll take a coach in the morning and never confess the truth."

"Oh?" He grinned mischievously.

She gulped. "That is . . . if there is . . . oh, please! I think you're trying to frighten me!"

"Perhaps I am. You're a foolish little minx, you know. Had I not seen you, you would likely be floating in the Thames right now."

"I've already heard your lectures and I cede your victory," she said with a pout.

"I'll make you a gift, my lady," he said, reaching down into his boot. He pulled out the pearl-handled knife and held it toward her. She couldn't help remembering that little weapon. "I trust you can carry this somewhere and if need be, use it."

She looked away from it, mumbling, "I don't expect myself in that position again."

"Just in that event," he advised. "I want you to have it. I'll collect it back from you someday . . . when you've put your affairs in order."

"I doubt that day shall ever come," she sighed wearily. There was a moment of silence and the flicker of a memory across her eyes. "Do you know, there was a time when he was kind to me. When first we met he thought me to be one of my own servants. He pursued me. Seduced me. He tried to make love to me on a grassy knoll away from all eyes. Had I not known who he was I would have clawed him, but I loved him instantly."

"Now that sounds more like the Chad I know," John laughed.

"But now I only play hostess for him, seeing to his needs, managing his home and watching him play with another."

"You're so young," John sighed. "Chelynne, has it never occurred to you that he has a very good reason for his behavior?"

"I can think of none. I would gladly share his burdens."

"And if that is not what he wants? Maybe it is in your best interests and his to keep you a great distance from those burdens. He is not a common farmer, darling. He is an earl. He does not play at planting and harvest, letting his lord make his decisions. He plays at political games in which death is not an uncommon reward. Didn't he ever tell you that he has important business?"

"Aye, he did. Is he in danger?"

John laughed. He folded his arms across his chest and leaned against the small table. "Just a while ago you claimed to love him no longer. Why do you fear for him?"

"John, don't play games with me! Is he in danger?"

"That, sweetheart, is a constant possibility when a man is not careful. The business at hand is indeed dangerous. I think the wisest thing he's done in his life is to keep you far from it. And you don't even realize that you're lucky."

"But I've an interest in his business. It could at least help me to understand. But that is not so important; it is his attention I would have." Then more softly, "Some small bit of it."

"Yes, well, I have a great deal of respect for the man, but sometimes he is not the wisest I know. But I will tell you something and trust you to think on it carefully. He is a good man, kind and fair, but I do not know of one more dangerous in battle. He is strong and brilliant, though a little shortsighted in affairs of the heart. But then, there is good reason for that as well."

"You make him sound quite unlike the forgetful and indifferent man I live with," she sighed.

"I believe his indifference to be a conscious thing. It must be because of his strength of will. If he desired you gone, you would be. That he keeps you here is evidence enough that he wants you near."

"For what purpose?"

"Chelynne, I don't know the man's very mind. I suggest you calm your suspicions and fears and let him settle his affairs. I think in all good time you will be glad that you did. And for God's sake, stop jumping to so many conclusions! I know you're young and it's frightening to think of a lifetime of such discomfort . . . but I strongly doubt that it's forever. Give the man some support. Put your loyalty in your husband, if not for love, for duty."

"I'd have more future in loving a mule," she murmured dispassionately.

"Chelynne, whatever happens, put your faith in Chad. Remember that I told you that. And no matter what, I promise that one day I will come to you and beg your forgiveness for whatever pains you've endured because of me. Please," he said, tapping her lightly on her head. "Whatever foolishness goes through there, remember that I promised, no matter what."

She nodded, though she was bitterly confused. He threw an arm wide, indicating the bed. "There's only itself there," he said with a smile. She blanched, not quite ready for all that was happening.

"Come now, I'm not going to hurt you, we'll simply rest. But I'm afraid you'll have to disarm yourself a bit."

She cocked her head, wondering what he meant, and then with a small laugh she realized. There were heavy pins in her hair, great layers of her gown, the bone busk and other unnecessary raiment. The procedure of freeing herself took nearly as long as the coach ride had. John couldn't help chuckling at the many unnecessary stays, ties and hooks. He found he had to help her with many of the fastenings and there was no way for her to lift the heavy gown over her head without the strength of his arms. When at long last she was down to the simple chemise, bereft of starched petticoats and busk, his eyes warmed at the sheer petite beauty of her.

While she sat on the edge of the bed he pulled off the dirty slippers that told of a flight down a dark, muddy street. She put her fingers to the task of untying the garters that held up her stockings and his eyes were glued to that sight. When he looked up into her face she smiled.

"Do you seduce me, John?"

He sighed, then took a seat beside her on the bed and pulled off his boots. "It is as much the other way around," he muttered. He pulled off the leather jerkin next and his linen shirt followed it to the pile on the floor. He looked at her and shrugged. "You'll never believe me if I tell you —" He stopped, looked her over again, and let out a deep sigh. "Come, love, there's no help for it."

She was pulled down beside him on the bed and neither of them stirred. She did not think her simple shift and his breeches protection but neither did she feel threatened. When he finally pulled her into his embrace it was carefully, gently, and she snuggled against him in comfort.

She shuddered slightly as his hands began to touch and caress, but he calmed her with soft words. "I'll not hurt you, darling." His hands moved over her with more serious intent, and she was sure beyond a doubt that her maidenhood would end here. She was pleased with the sensations he evoked in her and she reached out to touch him, to reciprocate, but he stopped her abruptly and bade her not touch him again. A groan came from somewhere deep within him as he continued to bathe her in delicious ministrations. By the light of a single candle she could see his features hard, his jaw tight and eyes clamped shut.

Worry tensed her, for though the decision had been made in her own mind to explore this desire she had so frequently felt, she had no idea what she should be doing. She moaned in her own confusion and he silenced her with his mouth. His touches sparked excitement in her she had never before known and all reason was lost. It was that same wave of desire that plagued her dreams, the same quickness that crept over her when Chad was too near. And now with the contact, it was out of control. Every place his fingertips tested tingled and then burned. She was writhing and turning in his embrace and he became rougher, more determined. She could not fathom where he was leading her but earnestly hoped they would soon arrive.

Her ignorance played against her. He had not disrobed; his weight didn't press her down or hold her. She cried out in exquisite agony as all at once something exploded inside of her, her world going instantly black and dragging her under a heavy curtain of blinding pleasure.

She drifted back slowly, her confusion dulled only by the magnificence of the moment. She turned to look at him. His expression was serious and calm, and he gently kissed her lips. Her mouth formed a silent question.

"Shhh," he whispered. "Don't think about it now."

"But why?"

He shrugged and pulled her closer to him. "That was the thing you've wondered about, darling. That was the most immediate problem."

"But there's more . . . I know there's more . . ."

John groaned. "Aye, a great deal more, but not for me. You are not mine."

"I am more yours than anyone else's," she murmured.

He gave a short, unpleasant laugh. "That will be remedied."

"Does this mean you love me?" she asked timidly.

"No, darling. I don't love you. And neither do you love me. This has nothing to do with love. This is nature, that's all. Love is separate. The true joy is when the two can come together."

"Only a common whore would —"

"Neither that, Chelynne. I wanted to pleasure you."

"And you?"

"A kind of misery I could never expect you to understand." He laughed ruefully. "Such an unselfish bastard am I."

"What am I to do now?" she asked with a sob in her voice.

"Nothing."

"We just go our separate ways? As if nothing —"

His face was above hers, his features sharp and strained, his voice gruff though he spoke in a whisper. "There is nothing binding in this. Bonds come from the heart, Chelynne, not from a simple touch. Let this teach you. The easing of that need is a simple thing. Love is a great deal more complicated."

Every inch of her being was undone. To be so careless, so casual with this emotion that seemed almost sacred; it was beyond her comprehension. How removed he was, how uninvolved. "Better I should not have known," she murmured.

"Don't worry with it, love. It's not going to happen again. From now Chad would not allow us in the same room together and it is certain he will be keeping a closer eye to you."

"He won't even know," she huffed, turning away from him.

"He will know," John returned, gently touching her hair.

"He wouldn't care if he did," she said dejectedly.

"You're wrong, darling. For this he will kill me."

THIRTEEN

A BRIGHT MORNING SUN brought Chelynne out of her sleep. The sight of the little room and the memory of what had taken place there made her shudder. There was such a look of poverty about it that she winced at the thought of herself in this atmosphere, in this bed. John was just a few paces away, scraping off his whiskers in front of an old, cracked mirror.

Her entire body burned with fear and shame. How could she placate Stella? And if he should ask, what would she tell Chadwick? What had she been thinking of? She was totally humiliated and then she thought of John's confession, his friendship with her husband. She sat up with a gasp.

"Good morning," he said brightly as he turned toward her.

"I've got to be out of here," she declared, bounding out of the bed.

"Get dressed, then, and I'll see you home."

"Are you mad? I'll see myself home and I don't wish to see you again. Stay clear of me, d'ye hear? I don't care what trouble I'm in, don't come near me . . . not to save me, not for anything . . ." As she ranted she was frantically collecting her garments, every burdensome layer and every starched piece. Her hands shook as she sought to fasten the many little ties and hooks and bows. She finally achieved some measure of her dressing and had come to the gown, the heavy velvet burdened with far too many fastenings.

John noticed her trouble in catching every one and brushed her hands aside to give assist. "I won't be seeing you after today, countess. Later, someday when all is well with you and you're bearing your first little lord, mayhaps then I shall pay a visit."

"You're insane," she murmured. She shook her head and grabbed for her cloak, which hung on a peg near the door. "I can't make any sense of you at all, talking in your riddles. I can't imagine why I've —"

"It won't make any difference now," he laughed. "It's done and I'm taking you home. I think perhaps the earl will keep a closer eye on you from now."

"He'll have to have mighty good eyes," she huffed. "This entire city is in a state of lunacy and before I have any more reason to wish myself dead I'm going to the country, whether or not His Lordship approves." She had succeeded in fastening her cloak and pulled on her gloves. With a shudder she thought aloud, "Damn, I've no vizard."

"No matter, countess. No one will recognize you on this side of town. Let's go."

"You are mad!"

"Let's go. I'm taking you home."

"I'll take myself home! You can't possibly be foolish enough to let yourself be seen with me! Now?"

"I'm going with you," he said slowly. There was a hardness to his blue eyes that froze her for a moment. His usually grinning face was taut and determined. She watched dumbly as he pulled on his coat and took her arm to lead her out.

On the street she saw a coach waiting, evidence that he had been most deliberate in his plan. He must have left her when she was still asleep and either sent someone off to fetch it or gone for it himself. The entire journey was one long argument in which she pleaded with him to stop and get out, leaving her alone to explain her absence as she would.

"If not for yourself, then for me, do not face my husband. I couldn't bear the humiliation of being delivered home like a naughty child."

"But that's exactly what you are."

"How dare you!"

"How dare I? My sensuous little kitten, ready and willing to place yourself trustingly in any hands that can deliver you pleasure. You've played the game with the gallants and complain of your husband's lack of interest. His husbandly virtues are condemned and I have yet to see wifely talents from you."

"How cruel," she gasped, looking into the fire of his hard blue eyes in wonder.

"Not so cruel. Honest. Go home now and act better the wife. You put your trust and confidence in a total stranger and ridicule that man who supports and cares for you."

"You don't understand," she cried with unrestrained fury.

"I understand better than you think. I understand that you are a spoiled and ungrateful child, pouting and fussing whenever the situation does not please you. Do you think you're the only grande dame who puts up with a less than perfect husband? Do you think that in marriages that are arranged there is instantaneous love and devotion? Why don't you try accepting your circumstances, and instead of criticizing his every move, give your husband some wifely support?"

Her eyes were wide and surprised with the insensitivity of his words. Tears welled up in her eyes and traced slow paths down her cheeks. "Strangely different course you take with me now, sir," she murmured, the hurt apparent in her words.

His grin mocked her. "It's a different thing I need now. My words fit the occasion, that is all."

"I . . . I thought you cared . . . some small bit . . ."

His laugh was loud and cruel. "And you will think the next sweet-tongued lad loves you too, I suppose. Take care, my lady. There is only one man who gains nothing by using you and that is your husband."

She sniffed piteously, wondering how her heart could have been so wrong, how she could have misjudged his character so completely. His touch was now a sinful and vile thing in her mind. How could he use her so cruelly, humiliate her so totally without remorse? What did he hope to gain?

"Would you stop that insufferable weeping and calm yourself? We've arrived. At least try to give off some resemblance to a woman instead of a babe in arms!" He looked away from her briefly and then with a sharper edge to his voice, sounding as though he was disgusted with the very sight of her, he added, "God, but there's nothing grates on a man like that constant sniveling."

She gave a loud silencing sniff and lifted her chin, more angry now than hurt. He jumped down from the coach and then helped her out. Swiftly he walked to the door and three loud and impatient raps opened that portal. Bestel stood there instead of the steward. Instant relief showed on the manservant's face.

"We've been a mite worried after ye, mum," he said, a light admonishing tone to his voice. " 'Is Lordship's been up the night steamin'."

"Oh, my child. My baby's safe!" Stella's fretful squeaking went almost completely unnoticed by Chelynne, for close on her heels was Chad, stone faced and anxious. Chelynne wiggled free of Stella's confining embrace to watch as John bowed briefly and faced Chad.

"Once again you have delivered my wife safely home, Sir John," he said in a strained voice. "My thanks."

"It was my pleasure, Your Lordship," John returned with an insolent grin.

"When did you come across her?"

"Why, last night, as a matter of fact. It was quite late."

Chad's cheek twitched nervously. He eyed the man up and down and his anger was mounting. He turned to Stella, hardly regarding Chelynne at all. "Take Her Ladyship to her rooms and see to her. I will see Sir John in my study."

Chad did not wait for any response. He turned on his heel and made long strides to that appointed place, John falling in behind. Chelynne gave a gasp and wiggled away from Stella again, running after the men. She didn't catch up until Chad had entered the study and was just about to close the door after John. "Chad, listen to me. There's nothing amiss here, I swear it. It was too late to find a coach and Sir John found me a room in an inn."

Chad looked between John and his wife and then slowly closed them into the room. "Do you insist on staying through this discussion, madam?"

"There's no need for discussion, as I've tried to —"

"Be silent or leave," he snapped. Her mouth went instantly shut. There was a sternness to Chad's expression now that frightened her more than anything he had done in the past.

"Where did my wife stay the night?" he asked John impatiently.

"As she said, Your Lordship. In an inn."

"There would have been servants to be found there. Someone could have found a coach or delivered a message to me. Why was this not done?"

"The hour was late. She confided you would not wonder at her absence."

"There was no inn," he accused.

"I confess, there was none," John relented with a mocking grin.

"Where did you keep her the night?"

"My own room."

"And did you take advantage of her circumstance?"

"I did not!" John shouted boldly.

"Chad," Chelynne broke in fearfully. "Stop this madness. He rescued me from a dangerous situation. He did not abuse me in any way."

"One situation in need of rescue is believable," Chad said slowly. "Two coincidences such as this is quite another story. Now be quiet or leave."

He turned again to John and spoke in low, menacing tones. "I am forced to believe that you have desired my wife since first meeting her, Sir John."

"Never mind the formality, Chad. I've told her we are old friends. I apologize for this embarrassment and will leave you to your wife."

"Just a minute." Sitting down, looking perturbed with the inconvenience, John waited for Chad to speak. "I have known you for a long time, friend. I daresay there has been a time or two we've courted the same lady. Am I wrong?"

"Just what are you getting at?"

"You stayed the night alone in the same room with my wife. Did you touch her?"

John smiled, a lazy and wicked smile. Chelynne blanched. What was he doing? A quick denial sprang to her lips but Chad cast her a quick damning glare to cut her off.

"Well?"

"I did not press the countess into any submission," he said easily.

"Then you did —"

"God's bones, Chad! Anything the lady and I shared will not be made public and is better forgotten. I'll not darken your door again. End this!"

"I must demand satisfaction."

"No!" Chelynne cried. "Why? Why would you even care? Leave it, I beg of you, Chad. Just let him go."

"Go to your rooms. Now!"

"No! You can't force me away like that. He didn't touch me, and you know I couldn't say that if I couldn't prove it. You know!"

"My wife pleads with me, John. Why?"

"Perhaps she has a gentle nature and does not like bloodshed. Especially blood spilled foolishly."

"Ahhh," he breathed thoughtfully, as if weighing the argument in his mind. "Then I offer you this compensation. Two years' work on my plantation in Jamaica, well out of the country, and I will pay you fairly."

"Are you so afraid I'll accost your wife, pursue her again? Really, Chadwick, there's no need to treat the matter with such importance."

Chad's jaw tightened. "Do you refuse this offer?"

"Refuse indeed!" John laughed heartily. "I found the little vixen on the street! I apologize for the inconvenience and that is all!"

"You have learned little about respect for another man's property."

"If she is yours and you treasure her, why does she run about the streets of London in the dark of night with no protector? You have learned little about the care a man should give his property! One man cannot abuse another's holdings unless the first allows it!"

"John, you push me too far! By God, you'll pay for this affront!"

"Pay? Will you swing your mighty sword or crush me with your earldom? I've had a bellyful of your blasted nobility! We were good enough friends before your father died and left you so mighty! Now you are above me and I've choices of punishments for saving your wife's precious little backside. Is it truly her honor you defend or the embarrassment to your name?"

Chad leaned across his desk and stared coldly into John's eyes. "Curse you, you bloody pirate! You're never satisfied until you've goaded a man into trimming your ears! I'm sorry now that I passed up my last chance."

"You pulled rank on me there, too, as I recall. You spared me because of my unfortunate lack of coin and arms. What excuse will you give for sneaking out of a fight this time?"

"What is this?" came a shrill and demanding voice. "What the devil are you two bantering about? I am the lady in question and I am neither dishonored nor abused. Chad, cease this madness, I beg of you!"

"This is no longer your fight, sweetheart," John said.

"Sir, how do you address my wife?"

"A pet name for her I've come to adore." He shrugged insolently. Chad's fist hit the top of the desk with a loud bang. "The challenge is issued. Your choice of weapons —"

"No," Chelynne shrieked.

"This is no time for your hysterics, madam. Go to your rooms now or I shall have you carried there!"

Chelynne stared at one and then the other in disbelief. With a horrified gasp she ran out of the study and made for the stairs. Chad came around the desk with amazing calm and watched her flight, noticing that more than one servant skittered away from the study door. He closed the door quietly.

"Should that suffice?" he asked John.

"Were we overheard?"

"Well and good," was the reply.

"Comfort her if you can, Chad. It's a dirty trick. I had not intended to hurt her, but perhaps she'll take more care from now on. It was truthfully another narrow escape. When did the message come?"

"Not until this morning. Lovely little code you used. I wasn't sure what you were after until you started chiseling away at my wife's morals."

"You weren't worried about her last night?"

"Christ," he muttered. "I spent more than eight hours walking London streets last night. I toured more dingy ordinaries than is to my liking, not to mention searching the riverbank a few times. I didn't know you were in the city until yesterday and visited your sister late last night to see if she knew where you kept lodgings. I had every intention of getting your help in finding her. What is your problem? Exactly."

"I've been recognized by one of Shayburn's men. There are bills posted and I'm as good as caught. We can't be seen together on friendly terms. I was at a loss as to what could be done to turn it around, until I came across Chelynne. Truthfully, I'm better off dead."

"Then I shall oblige you, my friend. This afternoon?"

"Good enough." They shook hands. John was about to leave and then stopped, turned, and smiled a little sheepishly at Chad.

"John, did you touch her?"

"I certainly did."

Chad stiffened. "Then you never shall again. I mean that, most sincerely."

"Then keep her better, my lord."

"You've never lied to me, John. Did you take her?"

"No."

"But you toyed with her?"

He nodded. "Expertly," he added.

"Why?" The question was not asked angrily, nor placidly. John eyed Chad carefully and saw that he was feeling something, feeling it deeply. It was beginning to show on his face in spite of his efforts to conceal it. John felt sympathy for his friend, but sympathy would not help Chad . . . or Chelynne.

"Because she needed it. And because you've been a hellish husband."

"You're not very flattering."

"And you're not very smart . . . at least where women are concerned. Christ, Chad, she needs tending, and badly!"

"You're an expert on that, I suppose."

"Not at all, Chadwick." John laughed a little indulgently. "But I have no blinders on my eyes. I can at least see."

"And I cannot see? I have blinders?"

"Aye, the worse kind. Memories like thorns. Suspicions like barbs."

"I think I can manage without your wealth of wisdom on the matter."

"I hope so." A memory came to him of the innocent and fiery sensuality of this maiden untouched who responded so totally. "You lucky fool," John remarked, slapping a hand on his friend's shoulder.

"Watch the blade of my sword, John," Chad warned.

"Strike here," John said, pounding a fist to his heart. "End Bollering and all his troubles. The earth thaws and I'm anxious to be planting."

"You'll regret this, Bollering," Chad shouted as he opened the door. "I'll run you through."

John laughed loudly. "If I feel generous enough to give you a gift, my noble fool, I shall let you draw one drop of my blood before you die! Good day!"

Bestel stood inside the doorway in some confusion, hearing the harsh exchange between these two lifelong friends. He looked at John as he walked out of the house, but John totally ignored his presence. He looked now to his master for some reasonable explanation, but Chad was not so kind.

"Take dueling swords to the Bayberry copse at the edge of London and see if you can find me a good second. It's to be out today."

Bestel shook his head in sheer upset. He had been with Chad for a long time and was aghast at what hardship might befall this old and valued friendship. But Chad walked away without further words and he was left with no choice but to do his master's bidding.

Chelynne paced nervously about her room, the area seeming small and cramped to her now. Stella babbled, questioned and prodded, but Chelynne could not speak. She simply mumbled and fretted, twisting her hands, and wiping her brow with a lace handkerchief.

A light tapping came and Stella admitted the earl, Chelynne running her eyes over him with obvious contempt.

"Leave us, Stella," Chad said calmly, looking only at Chelynne. The old woman obeyed quickly, leaving the two alone to stare at each other.

Chelynne spoke first, taking the first verbal swing. "Will you tell me what in God's name you were doing?"

"You were there, madam. He wanted to fight."

"What difference does that make? Blessed Christ, Chadwick, you've no cause to fight over me. You'd be doing it for nothing!"

"You are my wife, madam. If you are insulted, I am likewise."

"I was insulted with that trollop you brought to the theater, which is the reason all this is happening."

"What does that have to do with this?"

"You put me in a most embarrassing position, my lord. I could only explain away your display by acting a certain part and now all the court thinks I share my lady Graystone's morals. 'Twas Lord Courtney who truly accosted me and sent me running to save my worthless maidenhood! John only came to my aid!"

"Chelynne, stop this damning of me! You were there; he goaded me into a challenge. He hinted that you were intimate with him, and even if you weren't I can't stop the gossip now."

"But you can stop a duel! Don't do it, I beg of you! Don't fight him!"

"Are you so afraid?"

"Yea! I have never known such a bitter fear! Whichever of you is wounded, the blood is on my hands! If you have no mercy for him, then for me, Chad, please —"

"The terms have been established, madam. We duel to the death."

"You're mad," she gasped. "You're both mad! Oh, my God," she choked, tears spilling over. "I listened to him speak of you so admiringly. What insanity makes a man boast of fond friendship and then invite such hostility? Chad, there is no reason for this, no reason at all! You do not love me so heartily. You have never spoken of love at all! I beg of you, my lord, do not kill a man because of your wounded pride!"

He watched her in numb wonder as she ranted, and when her tirade was exhausted he moved closer to her and touched her cheek tenderly.

"Were his kisses so sweet, cherie? Was his touch that delightful?"

She took his hand in both of hers and looked beseechingly into his eyes. "You've done naught but push me aside, Chad. Pray do not condemn another for showing me kindness."

"Was it kindness . . . or passion?"

"Kindness!" she insisted. "Anything . . . I'll do anything to prevent this!"

Chad laughed bitterly. "What will you do, love? Will you stand in his stead? Will you take my sword?"

"Do not mock me!" she screamed. "I've been crawling to you; have pity at least! Forget this and I'll never leave my rooms again! I'll stay right here until I die. . . . Oh, please . . ."

"He must have indeed shown you passion," he muttered hoarsely.

"What makes you so damn certain he made love to me?" she cried furiously.

"Just a guess." He shrugged, a hurt smile on his lips. "You never considered that I might be killed."

"Oh, Chad —"

"Never mind, it's too late now. There is nothing that can be done to change his mind and Bestel has gone ahead to stand ready. I have business, and I do mean business, before I meet him. He wouldn't even consider waiting until tomorrow, so it's to be out today."

He started toward the door to leave, then turned to face her one last time before departing. "You're not to leave the house. If I'm fortunate today I will be able to tell you of the outcome later."

"Chad!"

He did not turn back to her. With horror she realized what she must have sounded like to him, pleading for another man's life when her own husband was in danger. She could do nothing, and the tension threw her into hysterical sobbing.

Chad heard the broken sobs from just outside her door. He hated what he had to do to her, but he was not entirely selfless. He hated her a little for what she had done to him, too. He wouldn't have minded too much if she had flung herself on him and begged him to forfeit for his own safety. She worried for John, and that stung him deeply.

Chad envied John. John was poorer, had a great many more troubles, and yet was always more sure of himself. He was sure enough of himself that he didn't bother with that cold and suspicious part, like what Chad played for Chelynne. John knew how he felt, always. Chad didn't always know if he was capable of feeling anymore.

He left the house and went to the home of a good friend, a surgeon.

When the sun was low in the sky and the mist had settled into the shallow valley braced by rolling hills in the English countryside, John Bollering listened to the swish of his sword as he was set in mock battle. He practiced before his opponent arrived.

Six men stood about in wait for the earl of Bryant. The surgeon, to examine and hopefully mend the loser, or, if the battle was bloodier, mend two men or pronounce one dead.

Colonel Debonet, officiating the match, wiped the sweat from his brow for the tenth time. Lord Mayer, witness, chatted with Sir Thomas Michaels, Chad's second. Bestel was ready with the swords to be used in the duel, his face red and troubled. He couldn't even bring himself to look in John's direction.

John smiled at the manservant's dread, for if in truth they were to duel, even John wouldn't dare to bet on the outcome of this meeting. He and Chad were equally expert with the swords, both more than a little practiced. He was grateful for the dullness of light and evidence of fog.

Pounding hooves alerted them that the challenger had arrived. Chad jumped from his horse impatiently, seemingly eager to have the contest over. He accepted a small draught from Bestel to calm his nerves and warm his blood. John declined the offered drink since the cup had been used by Chad. Bestel bristled uncertainly at the insult.

The colonel quickly positioned the men and at the drop of a silk kerchief they met. Swords clashed and locked, clashed and locked. Chad's guard was down more than once and he seemed not to be serious about the fight. John had to lunge aside and purposely miss more than once.

Chad came upon him hard, his sword flashing past John with a whir between his arm and waist. A slow smile spread across John's face as he assumed Chad was ready, but again at his advantage, Chad was dangerously in the way of John's sword. They met and locked and John's face was close to Chad's. "Watch yourself, you fool," he bit out through clenched teeth.

Chad laughed low and menacingly. John lunged again, and again the miss was too close for comfort. They met and locked. "Damn you," John muttered. "Have done with this play!"

With an artful sway Chad's sword found its way around John's and with a noble bit of footwork he took off a button from his breeches. A scowl broke over John's face. This game could best be preserved for the days they were sorely bored with their toils and had little to do but jest. With like finesse, John returned the favor. He sliced Chad's linen shirt free of his chest without so much as a scratch applied to his flesh. This time when they locked swords, it was Chad who whispered: "One mark, for my lady."

Both men were now in a sweat, each battling to keep up the play without damaging the very important oil-skin bag that was tied under John's armpit. Should the bag break without the sword seeming to go straight through him, chicken's blood would explode all over John. The match would have to be called a hoax.

Impatient to have the thing done, John made a quick stab and managed to take Chad in the upper left arm. Chad's sword went down and John hesitated. The crimson flood that was running down Chad's arm onto his hand showed that the injury was worse than either expected. They met again, and putting on a frown that bespoke fury, Chad ground out, "A *mark*, I said!"

John's vicious laughter rang out in the dreary field. It looked to all as though Chadwick would lose the contest. With a quick and merciless sweep, Chad's sword hit the bag and dug through. Sensing the culmination, John went stiff, his weapon falling from his hand, and Chad slowly drew out his blade. Bright red evidence spurted out over John's shirt and he fell to the ground, face down and limp.

The surgeon rushed to the side of the motionless man and rolled him over. He looked to the witnesses and shook his head. Chad dropped his sword near the body of his friend and walked away from the scene, a look of utter contempt on his face.

The earl shook a few hands and accepted congratulations with his right arm while Bestel worked with urgency on his left. The manservant mumbled as he worked, horrified with the scene, and stammering about His Lordship's injury, which was a damn sight more painful than Chad had intended it to be. When John's body was taken away, hidden under a sheet on a cart, Bestel and Chad were left alone in the wake of the duel.

"Tether yer horse, milord, and ride with me. You've lost a bit o'blood and I wouldn't think ridin' a healin' potion."

"I'm fine," Chad muttered, watching the cart disappear down the road.

"A fine thing me old eyes are seein'. I would've put me trust in the little mum ye took fer yer own, and now it's come to this, it 'as. Aye, I never thought I'd see the dame what could set ye again' yer own good friend."

Chad looked around suspiciously. "Bestel," he said softly. "Do you think I'd kill John?"

" 'Opin' I were blind I seen ye do the thing. Milord, is the mum worth it?"

"Indeed," he said with a raised eyebrow. "She's worth a life or two, and don't you be forgetting that, you hear, you old mule?"

"Aye, I 'ear ye and I'll tend ye till I die, but I'll not believe there's a sweet dame alive worth Master John."

"There is, Bestel. But John did not pay. Not this time."

"What're ye sayin', lad? The boy's cold as fish."

"No. He's fine. It was a play . . . for Shayburn."

"Saints be praised," Bestel breathed; he understood at once. "Milord, ye 'ad me in a fit."

"I should have given him a reminder that I'm not so doltish with my talent. He took a healthy piece of my arm."

"That 'e did," Bestel laughed, his eyes crinkling at the corners from happiness once again. It was a long day on that tired heart, seeing these two go after each other so fiercely. "Aye, that 'e did."

Chad arrived home well ahead of Bestel. The wound was tightly bound and no sign of the injury showed through his coat, but the loss of blood along with the tensions of the day had left him weak and tired. He bumped the sore arm on the doorframe as he entered the house and a muffled oath left him. "Curse that bloody pirate!"

The stairs to the second floor were longer than they ever had been and he took them slowly and wearily. From his room he could hear a great deal of commotion in his wife's bedchamber and surmised with a bitter feeling that Her Ladyship was making ready for bed. He obtained for himself a badly needed drink and had just tossed it off when there came a light tapping at his door.

"Come in."

The door opened and Chelynne stood there for a moment without speaking, a stern and serious expression on her little face. "I'm glad you're safe," she said quietly.

He disregarded her and went for another drink, the arm paining him worse with every passing second, and his nerves totally unraveled. He downed it quickly and waited with teeth clenched and eyes closed for some anesthetic effect.

"Please," she beckoned softly. "Tell me."

Chad looked at her with the cold hard eyes of the victor.

"No," she whispered.

"Yes. I killed him."

"Oh, why," she sighed pleadingly.

"Because he would not yield the fight until one of us was dead!" he shouted. "I'm sorry for you that it couldn't have been me!"

"Chad, I didn't want that."

"No? You've a mighty poor way of showing it!"

"My concern was for John because he told me himself that you were the most talented with a sword he knew. Knowing you had the advantage, it was like murder to —"

"Madam! What he told you was a modest lie! I've fought beside the man on several occasions. There could not have been a more equal match! He could well have been the victor, but he was not! It is done!"

She was silent for a moment, eyes cast downward. When she looked up he was draining his glass of another hefty portion of liquor. "I'm leaving, Chad. I'll be gone in the morning."

"Leaving," he repeated, her image starting to blur.

"Leaving. I cannot stay here another day. It's more than I can accustom myself to. Everywhere I look there is corruption, even in my own home. Duels for no just cause, attackers whenever I step out onto the street without protection. I'm not strong enough for this."

"And where do you think you're bound?"

She stared at him for a moment, knowing there was no way to reason with him in his angry state. She turned and walked out of the room.

Chad poured another drink and followed her, wavering slightly. Within her room there was a mad scurrying. Many trunks sat open while Tanya and Stella carefully folded things away. Valises stood packed and her dressing table was naked of adornments. He leaned against the doorframe, fighting the dizziness that was fast overtaking him. Sick and tired, he cleared his throat and all eyes turned to him. "You will leave me alone with my wife," he commanded.

Chelynne stared at him coldly while her women left her. At this moment she felt outrage and hatred for the man.

"Where do you think you're going?"

"To Hawthorne House."

"The answer is no. You'll stay here."

"No, my lord. I shall go."

"Chelynne, you may not go and the reason is this: Shayburn's lands have been overrun by bandits. He is being burned out and the country is in a turmoil. Your coach would be halted and even if you did manage to arrive safely, you could be rousted from your own bed. You will have to stay here."

"I would be safe once there. There are servants and —"

"There are not! The house has been closed up and most of my men sent to Bratonshire to provide protection for the baron."

Her eyes widened considerably. "You've sent men to protect that heathen?"

"Madam! It is not the baron I am concerned with. He can go straight to hell for all I care! The people of that shire have suffered enough and it is the people I would see protected. How many times must you be warned not to make hasty judgments on matters you know nothing about?"

She swallowed hard. It was twice now that she had totally misjudged him and consequently hurt him. Twice in the same day she had lashed out at him cruelly, as if he were a fool, and both times he had been acting either in his own defense or in the defense of innocents.

"I'm sorry," she murmured, knowing it was inadequate. She turned back to the gowns that were spread across the bed. "Then I shall go to Welby Manor."

Chad stared at her back for a moment and then asked softly, "You are so anxious to leave?"

She turned to face him. "Yes, I am," she said slowly.

"Well, I forbid it. You will stay here."

"I beseech your kindness, Chadwick," she said with quavering voice. "Let me go home." She fought the urge to cry. Her head held high, she was determined never to shed another tear over this man. She hated him more fiercely than she had ever hated in her life. "I've had the limit I can endure of this, Chadwick. Let me go to the country . . . please . . ."

"I cannot. It is for your own good."

"Bah! If you knew the number of times that has been dealt me!" she spat, losing control at last. "What is supposed to be my own good as far as others are concerned brings me naught but misery. I've watched the husband I love take up with any trollop of the eve, holding myself with the hope that one day he would heed his vows and turn to me, take me in truth as his wife! This life is a sham! Had I the option I would travel in a wagon and reap my rewards in dry bread for the love of one simple man slumbering at my side!"

"One simple man?" he sneered. "In the form of John Bollering, perhaps?"

"I have been true, though that would not win me much admiration from your stately friends! Indeed, they think me quite the noble dame now that they believe we have an open marriage." She strode closer to him and placed one hand on her hip and smiled devilishly. "I have not been unfaithful and you could determine the truth for yourself. Are you even curious?"

"It doesn't matter to me who you've had," he snorted, turning away from her and walking back to his bedroom. She followed him and stood in his open doorway, watching as he tossed off another drink.

"Decide with me," she said evenly.

"Decide? What is to decide? We have been thrust together and have dealt with it admirably, I would say."

"Perhaps you have. I have not. I am sinking, and this play we engage in every time we meet is destroying me. If you care for me and the vows we said, then take me to wife and play the lover. If you cannot, then tell me your intention and be rid of me. Put me out of my misery as you would a wounded mare and at least let my soul seek peace. If you have no respect for my life, I do!"

Chad's head pounded and his vision blurred. He heard her words but they did not register very plainly on his brain. "Put it from your mind."

"I demand you deal with me now!"

"Chelynne," he groaned. "Have done with this outburst. We'll talk tomorrow."

She strode into the room until she stood directly before him. The vision of her swam before his eyes. He needed to be rid of her so he could fall into bed. Had he not been holding onto the table he might have crumpled to the floor.

"This is not a fit of temper. Chadwick. You are not such a great prize to forfeit."

Her bosom heaved with anger and her brown eyes flashed a warning. This was no show for his benefit, no tantrum. She meant every word. Her cheeks were flushed with color and she stood her ground impatiently awaiting some response from him.

Chad's head pounded painfully, and reality merged with fantasy. He was slipping into a fog of confusion, wondering where he was and with whom. Suddenly he slipped an arm about her waist and crushed his mouth down on hers, savoring the wine-sweet flavor, loving the feel of her against him. What promise was this? What madness? During that brief kiss he alternately believed he would die and felt the strength to carry her to the bed and force her with his manhood.

Chelynne weakened under his flaming lips. Every bone turned to fluid, every nerve came alive. Just when she thought that last part of him dead in her he would bring it to life, as he did now. And then he would begin to destroy it, hurting her again. He released her and her fears came true. There was no softness in him, no tenderness. His eyes were again that hard gray flint.

"You would play the virgin lass until the end of time, my love. You have yet to tell me what your story will be when I test the parcel and find the game a fraud."

"Try me," she blurted with bravado.

His laughter rang through the room. "Is there some magic spell inside your thighs to bind a man? I doubt it! If you have not yet tasted the nectar then pray do not wait upon me. Test your talents! You have but to choose!"

"You cast me aside and mock my virtue cruelly, my lord," she said softly. "I will not stay and watch you laugh as my years waste me away under the fine comforts of your holdings. Never did I ask for this. Only for the goodness of your love did I speak my vows."

Chad snorted, the pain growing almost unbearable. " 'Twas the size of my purse that brought you and the size of my purse will hold you."

"Nay," she cried, insulted now to the depth of her endurance. "Whatever painful memory pricks your mind so that you cannot find any peace within yourself is beyond me. But hear this, my lord fool: I will not withstand one more test for your satisfaction. I repeat, what you have to offer is no great prize to forfeit!"

She turned on her heel and stamped out of the room. She heard the smashing of glass and stopped in her tracks, a slow smile spreading over her face at the thought that she had touched him at last. Her smile faded as she heard a low moan come from his room.

Turning slowly she went back to the open door to peek into his room. Chad was slumped and holding the wall for support. She eyed him quizzically, wondering at his strange behavior, and then he fell to his knees. "Chad?"

He turned glassy eyes in her direction and held his upper arm with his hand. Then he pulled his hand away from his injury and viewed with some distraction the bright red that stained his palm.

"You're hurt," she breathed, rushing to him. "Oh, Chad, why didn't you tell me?"

He sat back on his heels and allowed her to help him out of his coat. The wound had begun to bleed profusely, and the bandage and white linen shirt were red with his blood. "Come, you've got to help me," she urged, pulling him to his feet. With a great deal of effort she managed to get him onto the bed, muttering distractedly the entire time. "Oh, why has Sebastian left us? Perhaps Stella could . . . no, she is weakened by the prick of a pin. Bestel is not here. Darling, you've got to help me a little . . ."

Chad couldn't focus on her features but did as he was directed. The touch of her soft, warm hands stripping away the makeshift bandage was comforting. Feeling the softness of his bed beneath him and hearing the lulling voice of his wife, he let his eyes close and allowed his body to untense.

Chad could feel the bed rise and fall as she flitted away and returned. There were more people in the room now. Water and fresh bandages were brought for Chelynne. He felt the edge of a glass being pressed to his lips and obediently he drank the brew for a greater numbing effect. The wound was cleansed and oddly he felt no pain, just a hazy brushing against that tender place, the tiny pricks of mending as she tended him.

Much pleasure was coming from this injury, he thought in hazy delirium. Her voice had become a lilting melody for a troubled man. Her presence and the fact that she was so intent on helping him brought bliss. He was still and quiet and let her work her will.

The room had been quiet for some time and he had not felt her presence. He dared to open one eye slightly and saw that she had pulled a chair to the edge of the bed to keep a vigil at his side. Her velvet gown had been replaced by a light and lacy dressing gown as she hovered there, carefully guarding him. The image was clouded by his lashes but he could see the soft, light-brown hair tumbling to her shoulders and disappearing down her back. And there was a sweet frown of concern troubling her brow.

"Can you open your eyes and at least show me you're all right?"

Chad lay quiet and unresponsive. She touched his hand and it was warm and still. He couldn't spoil this moment. He refused to open his eyes or his mouth and ruin what was for once a lovely relationship between them.

"You've been a fool," she muttered to his sleeping face. "To let him hurt you when you could have prevented it." Still there was no sound or movement. She gave a deep sigh. The injury, the many heavy drinks — it was no wonder he slept so soundly.

"Do you know what life with you has become, Chadwick?" She looked at his peaceful face and sighed heavily. "Life with you is one long series of contradictions. You warn me for my safety and then tell me you don't care what I do. You promise never to duel over me, and then kill a man for even intimating desire for me. You tell me the day will come when business is done and you will tie yourself to a marriage, yet you make no effort to secure that day."

The deep, even breathing from her husband was his only response. Chad had physical reason to be this exhausted, but Chelynne's tired body cried out for rest only from the emotional tensions of the day. She had seen a little too much now to go back to that quiet and naive young virgin who had offered herself so trustingly into this marriage. A great many things had passed between Chelynne and her husband and precious few of them had been pleasant.

"I once longed for love," she said to her sleeping husband, her voice soft as a whisper. "But I only fear it now." There was a long pause and then she went on decidedly, though quietly, to explain to this man some things that she would lack the courage to say if he were in an alert state. "We have reached a barrier, I think, that will either be impossible to pass . . . or will be the starting point for a new relationship between us.

"It has been a most painful thing, loving you. I can't count the number of pleasurable moments, there haven't been enough of them to recall. And hating you, it's so senseless, so futile."

Bestel had been sent on some errands following the duel and was only now returning to see to Chad. The door to the bedchamber was ajar and he heard the soft voice from within. Assuming Chad was in a conversation with his young wife, he paused before entering.

"You have so much and yet seem to be such an unhappy man. Is it a painful past that plagues you? Conflict with your father that was never resolved? I can understand some of that now, truly. You see, I waited for love, the idea of how it would feel firm in my mind. Now I have learned the truth to it. It is a fantasy for young hearts; there is truly no such emotion. My uncle does not love my aunt, the king does not love the queen, there is none of that for anyone. Desire that was once an honest and beautiful thing is now disgusting in my eyes. Now that even that has been destroyed . . . even that . . . what more is there?"

Bestel made a move to knock or creep away, but the voice came again from inside that room and he was frozen. He could do nothing but listen. "There is no choice, Chad. I have no place to go. I would not shame Sheldon and flee to him. From now I suppose it will be as you wished it, we simply exist, feeling nothing, showing nothing, sharing nothing. I will wonder as I rise in the mornings if this is the day you hold me, or lash out at me in anger. I never know if we will dance in harmony or duel with hostile words. I will wonder, husband mine, as in the past, but no more will I pursue you. No more will I cry."

Bestel knocked quickly, unable to bear much more of this eavesdropping himself.

"Yes," came her quick response.

"My lady? Might I see to 'Is Lordship now?"

"Of course. Were you aware that he was injured? Were you the one who tended him?"

"Aye, mum." He nodded.

"Well, it's worsened and I mended it as I could." She gave a soft, embarrassed laugh. "I'm not accustomed to that fabric type but it will do."

"You've sewn it?" Bestel asked, shocked.

There was a quick but slight movement from the bed and Bestel warily stole a glance in that direction. He had been with Chad through the worst of times, through wars, crises on his plantation, disasters on shipboard. He had been shot through the stomach, stabbed more often, fallen from horses — yet he had never lost his consciousness completely. Chelynne did not notice the movement. She simply shrugged. " 'Twas a necessity."

"Aye, mum."

"I'll look in on him in the morning, then, if you'll stay with him now. I'm so tired I could sleep in the chair, but would prefer a bed."

"Aye, mum. Don't worry fer 'im, mum. I'll see to 'im now."

She nodded, placed a light kiss on her husband's brow, and left the room. Bestel stood and looked down at His Lordship's sleeping face and saw a slow, almost imperceptible smile grow there.

"Aye, the little mum was dishonored, right enough, but not by Master John." A faint frown replaced the smile, as though the man were troubled in his sleep by a fleeting thought. He made no other movement.

Chelynne went to her room, blowing out the candles on her way, and she found her own private resting place had been cleared by her servants so she could sleep.

She was so tired that her resolution to spend the rest of her life void of feeling seemed an easy endeavor. She even found some comfort in it.

She slipped out of the dressing gown and into bed, sleep greeting her immediately as she closed her eyes. In her dreams, gentle hands soothingly crept over her body as fiery lips teased her. Pleasure tingled within her again and when she looked into the face of this delightful lover . . . it was Chad.

FOURTEEN

CHELYNNE HAD HOPED the morning would come and give her strength in her new resolve. She was wrong. The same worry and fretfulness encompassed her, the same feeling of depression was there. She bravely disregarded it and found comfort in her routine. She bathed, dressed, and breakfasted. Then she took herself to her husband's room to see to his well-being.

She saw what she had expected to see in his bedchamber. He was up and dressed, drinking his coffee. The only sign of his injury was the linen sling that supported his injured arm. There were no lines of tension on his face, no shadows of fatigue. He was refreshed and once again in control of his situation and his surroundings. It was the image of him she had had since their first encounter. He was a warring machine, never troubled or confused, never flustered or pained. An injury that had brought him to his knees the night before had been tended, and with the aid of a brandy and a few hours' rest he was completely mended and revitalized. He could be weakened temporarily, but he could not be disadvantaged for long. He was like a jungle beast, a man whose challenges and beatings only made him stronger and more determined. So how could a mere girl, a woman child, expect to affect him very much? How could she have thought to tempt him, gain his affection, be of any real importance to him? Is that not what a woman really wants when she seeks love? To dominate a man's heart, if not his mind and soul? So she had thought, unconsciously, to do. To dominate at least a part of him, of his life. But no more. He could not feel. She would have more promise of success in trying to collect a wild boar from the forest and keep him as a pet in her house.

"You're looking fit, my lord," she said.

"I'm feeling well enough. I commend you for your fine stitchery. It does not pain me much."

"Good, then. Might I ask you something of . . . of a delicate nature?"

"Of course." He nodded, businesslike.

"Will you be attending the burial of Sir John?"

His brow creased into a frown and he muttered under his breath. "I think not."

"Shall you be offended if I do?"

"I think the gossip should be sufficiently horrible without adding that to the tale. I would much prefer you pass that affair by." He looked away from her for a moment and she remained silent. Looking back at her, he added, "I'm certain his body will be taken out of the city. His people were from the country."

"Very well, I thought only to have your opinion on the matter."

"Regardless of what you might think, my dear, I do not take the incident lightly. Killing has no appeal for me, even with just cause. And especially one such as Sir John, who was a friend of mine. I would have much preferred another course."

"I know that he insisted," she murmured. "I cannot fathom the reason."

"It is of a bitterness you couldn't understand. He's had much misfortune in his time and has come to resent anyone of the noble class. I knew him at a time when he did not do such dramatic things, when he had a good head for sense."

"Sound reason," she mumbled as the memory stirred.

"My dear?"

"Nothing, my lord. What more might come of this, Chadwick? Shall you suffer ill from the duel? Will there be a harsh penalty?"

"Nothing of that sort, I assure you. But you'll favor a new treatment from your courtly friends. I should think they will leave off forcing their affections."

"I hadn't thought to pay such a price," she murmured.

"I'm afraid you'll have to accept something here and now, Chelynne, for your own peace of mind. John Bollering used you as his excuse for a fight he'd been wanting. As you might have guessed, it was not the first time we've had differences. In all actuality it had nothing to do with his or my affection for you. I can bear the insult of another man touching what is mine, without killing him. I met him because he insisted; that is the only reason."

"Then you would not have met him for my honor?"

"I'm afraid not."

"That is the answer I expected," she said softly.

"You are a very guilty woman, madam. You are guilty of judging harshly and without much cause. I would protect you in any circumstances. I would kill any man to prevent him from abusing you, from using you against your will. But I am not a fool. I would not seek to rid you of the lover of your choice by the sword. I know better than to think that would gain me favor with you. Do you understand?"

"He was no lover of mine."

"And he was not killed because I thought he was. He was killed because in his foolishness he sought death, or victory, for —" Chad's voice had a harsh tone that had become louder and louder as he explained. He checked himself, then calmed his tone and went on in a more dignified manner. "For old causes that were not worth the price."

"What causes? By my word, Chadwick, I understand nothing of this!"

"That is all I am prepared to say, Chelynne. Understand this: he was not killed for the reasons you think. Whether or not you had gone with him to his lodgings, he would have found a way to battle this out. He was determined."

She opened her mouth as if to speak but a knock at her husband's door held her silent. Chad called out his consent to enter, and Bestel came hesitantly into the room. He noticed Chelynne and addressed her reluctantly.

"There is a caller, madam. For you."

"Who calls at such an hour?" she asked quizzically.

"Manservant to your uncle, my lady."

"Then they've arrived at last," she cried, not concerning herself with Bestel's formal announcement. To her this was like a lifeboat in a storm, at precisely the time she needed something like this, something like her uncle's dauntless love to give her ease and confidence again. "Excuse me, Chad. I'll see him at once." She whirled and was gone, excitement in her quick step and happiness lighting the features that a moment ago were confused, sad.

Bestel looked at his lord, a cloud of doubt crossing his eyes. "He brings the mum bad news," he said simply. Chad rose and followed. At the bottom of the stairs Chelynne had only just faced Gordon.

"Has Lord Mondeloy just arrived?"

Gordon was uneasy. He looked between the earl and the young lass he had watched grow up. "Last night, my lady, but—"

"How grand! Where are they? When may I call?"

"My lady, Lord Mondeloy shouldn't have made the trip. He was ill and . . . and we had to stop several times. He insisted on pressing his health, determined about some business here . . . and would not return to Welbering as he should have."

"Is Uncle Sheldon ill? May I go to him now?" Gordon looked helplessly at Chad, his face twisting with pain. "What is it?" she demanded.

"In the night, madam, when we'd only just arrived. . . . He's dead, my lady."

Chelynne swayed slightly, taking a step back, and Chad instinctively moved up behind her to give aid if necessary. Her hand began a journey to her mouth to stifle her cry of grief, but there came no sound. Instead, both hands returned to her sides and her fists clenched. There was a movement from her, but so slight it was almost unnoticeable. Her eyelids were pinched closed. She was reaching deeply within herself for strength. For Chad this stirred a memory. It had been a day of battle when he was suddenly aware of all the cruelty that existed on earth. He remembered thinking that he hoped the men he slew had believed in God; how frightening to think he would send a man to Hell. He could not remember the exact moment or the particular crisis, but there had been a time when he had decided that he must endure and accept this agony of living or simply lie down and die.

Now, watching his young wife, he knew that she had come to that same position, though the circumstances were very different. This must be the very grimmest moment of her life. She would have to be strong, endure and accept this or give up.

"Do you know the cause?" she asked.

"Nay. It was not swift. He had been ill."

"Are arrangements being made?"

"Aye, Lady Mondeloy and Ha— Lord Mondeloy will have everything done. Service for His Lordship in the city and then to Welbering to the family cemetery."

She nodded and looked to her husband. There was sympathy in his eyes but she was not looking for that. She could not think beyond control now. There was absolutely nothing anyone could give her. "I will go to Lady Eleanor now, my lord, with your permission."

"Of course."

"Will you wait for me, Gordon?"

"I'll take you there, madam," he returned with a slight bow.

Chad gave her a moment alone in her room before going in. She had little to do to make ready. He entered then, this time knocking first.

"Should you like me to accompany you?"

"It's kind of you to offer," she said somewhat blankly. "But this time I would like to go alone. My family may have need of me."

"I would not consider it an imposition, Chelynne. I would be happy to lend my support."

She did not respond to that statement. "I shall go to Welbering."

"Then I will make ready."

"No, Chadwick. This, too, I do alone."

"The roads are not safe. I shouldn't let you go without —"

"Hire horsemen, then, if you wish. My purpose is not to aid my aunt or cousin. Indeed, they will not likely be pleased with my presence. I was not well loved by any but Sheldon. I would like to go through the house to see if there is anything left of my parents before Harry or Eleanor destroys anything I have right to out of cruelty."

"You think them capable of something that low?" he asked incredulously.

With amazing calm she faced him. "I have no delusion about their affection for me. Yes, Harry has done that very thing in the past with no other motive save causing me grief. Lady Eleanor is much like her son in her lack of compassion."

"I could go and lend my support there as well."

"There are times," she said with an air of melancholy, distant and somewhat detached, as if she were speaking for someone else, as if she had no feeling. Her voice drifted away for a moment and then drifted back in the lifeless tone. "There are some times, some things that one must do without aid or counsel. I pray you try to understand my circumstance. He . . . he was my only living kin, and is now gone. There is a task at hand and grief. Both of those I consider private now." Her eyes went up to his and she spoke quickly. "I will take great care and return to you swiftly."

There was a kind of command in her words, but that was not what persuaded Chad to give his consent. It was a decision on her part that was important to her maturing, and one that brought back memories of the time when he took the matter of his own life into his own hands and denied interference. It was important and necessary to her. Having been there himself, he couldn't deny another the time of seeking and finding — not even one who was sworn to dependence on him by law.

He put his hands on her shoulders and stared into her eyes. "Times have not been the best between us, Chelynne. I am a hard man, and I know that about myself. From now, if you need me, come to me. I am at your call."

He wished she could see this as a great sacrifice, the beginning of something. But she only mumbled, "You're very kind, my lord."

It had been Gordon's intention to drive Her Ladyship to the

Mondeloy residence, but Chelynne coaxed him into her own coach, leaving his behind, so they could talk during the ride. She faced Gordon with a commanding air and spoke quickly and in hushed tones. The discussion was brief and the servant only nodded. He neither questioned nor argued.

The body of the baron did lie in state and there was a service in London. Finally the priest said his words over that sad corpse and blessed the passing. Chelynne sat with her husband or stood at his side during the tiresome affair of death and mourning. Many nobles attended, the funeral being as much a social affair as a ball — to be seen, if the queen was; to be present, if others of importance were. Sheldon was not well known or greatly missed, but it was like other things at court, very much a matter of appearances. And it was typical of Eleanor, pompous and extravagant. In their black with heavy veils the women were not known but by escort, and their grief was announced by the color and sternness of their garb.

Chelynne was not moved by any of this display. She had come to loathe the pomp and ceremony with which the slightest daily habit was treated. The black couldn't show her grief as acutely as she felt it. She couldn't rend her clothes or tear her hair to mourn her uncle properly. The ache in her heart was the only true grief, and it was a thing she could neither share nor display.

The family separated as they made ready to depart for Welbering. Chad insisted on sending his own men, more than a score, to ride with the Mondeloy party. They had gone ahead to prepare to ride escort once Chelynne's coach joined Eleanor's. The Hawthorne coach was readied and parcels were loaded. Summer was tethered to the rear.

Stella, Tanya and Chelynne stood ready to board when Chad lifted his wife's veil to place a farewell kiss on her brow. Chelynne didn't notice the worry that was as plain as the nose on his face.

"You're sure you don't want me to attend you?"

"I'm sure. We'll take care."

"Chelynne," he began, uncertain. "Chelynne, if you're sure Harry wishes you ill, keep an eye turned to him. Don't let him —"

She placed a hand on his arm and smiled. "Harry is troublesome, to be sure, but he is not smart. I will keep careful watch."

"The men I've sent are ordered to do your bidding. If you need their aid, even to protect you from your own kin, they will do as you command them."

Chelynne smiled, and had turned to enter the coach when Chad stopped her by pulling at her arm. "You will not stay long?"

"I should like to ride about Sheldon's lands and for that I take Summer. I've come to cherish her. I will visit some of the people there I have known since childhood, but I will not overstay."

"Chelynne . . . take special care. And hurry home."

"Soon," she said simply, ready to leave.

Chad held onto the door of the coach, reluctant to have her go. He had an ill feeling about this trip she was so set on. "Chelynne . . . if you need me . . ."

Again, she failed to see this as offer of a commitment, a reconciliation. "Thank you, my lord."

The coach pulled away from the earl of Bryant. The shades were pulled tight, allowing no interference to enter from without, no secrets to leave from within. They were to join the retinue traveling to Welbering and make their long, tiresome journey to see Lord Mondeloy laid to rest on his own property.

But they had barely started moving when Chelynne threw up her veil and moved to the edge of the seat so that Stella could unfasten her. "Hurry, Tanya," she urged.

The servant girl eased out of her own dress with haste and in just moments the two had exchanged clothing. "Lady Mondeloy will be much upset when she arrives home," Chelynne mumbled without much concern.

A black garter could be seen on Chelynne's thigh as she quickly disrobed. A few quick stitches the night before had made it a handy place to carry a pearl-handled knife. "Guard yourself, sweetheart," Stella murmured. The coach stopped and Chelynne turned her back to her woman so she could fasten the last remaining hooks.

"Tanya, don't lift your veil, not even when you stop to eat. Stella will carry food in the coach and you can have your meals in private at the inns. Don't let them suspect it is not me. Take care."

She placed a quick kiss on Stella's cheek and patted Tanya's hand.

When she climbed out of the coach, Gordon was standing beside the two mounts that had been hurriedly saddled. Without a word she was given a lift up and they started on their way, two riders alone, a mature man in simple garb and a young woman in a heavy, functional dress — average English personages traveling, nothing more.

The first stop was some six hours down the road. Here a groom had been paid no small amount to secure their horses for the return trip and provide them with fresh mounts. Chelynne was intent on speed for this excursion. So much so, that she could hardly be persuaded to sit and sup. Her young body was taut with nervous energy, strong in her purpose. She thought constantly of the possibility that Harry or Eleanor would discover her deception and hasten their own journey to prevent her from combing the house.

And that was perhaps the strangest thing of all. She had no idea for what she was looking or why she was driven so. She had nothing but suspicion where her family was concerned, and she couldn't ignore it. Sheldon had lied about what of her parents remained, though she understood that he meant only to protect her. But there had been the letter . . . and perhaps there was something more.

The servants were her friends. In Welby Manor all the loyalty was for the baron, Harry and Eleanor earning nothing from the staff but their contempt. Chelynne was certain she would be aided there and that those who aided her would remain silent for as long as that was possible.

Though impatient to be going and far from hungry, Chelynne took note of Gordon. He was no longer an agile youth and the ride was showing on him. He was moving slowly as if his muscles were stiff and sore and there was a tiredness about his soft eyes that caused her to yield and allow a short repast at the nearby inn.

When the sun was low in the sky they stopped again, in the next village en route. They would be allowed no more safe travel time that night. All airs were cast aside. They shared a room, the only one available. The meal was taken quickly and Chelynne occupied the bed at Gordon's insistence while he took a makeshift pallet on the floor. No clothes were removed and carefully placed away, no toilette done by doting servants for Her Ladyship. There was little conversation, just each inquiring of the fitness of the other.

At dawn's first light Chelynne was up and calling for breakfast. She splashed some water on her face and tucked her hair under a hat, with no fuss and no bother. Gordon rose a bit more slowly.

"Are you up to the ride, sir?" she inquired.

He nodded simply with his mouth full of meat for his hasty breakfast, but his eyes spoke otherwise.

"I've no wish to press you, Gordon. It's a taxing trip and I'm certain I could hire a trustworthy escort."

The man swallowed and cleared his throat. "I'll not allow you to go without me, madam. I've spent too many years with you and your uncle to take any chances on your safety now."

She smiled her thanks but said, "You'll be little protection for me if you're completely exhausted. Think a little on that, Gordon."

"I'm no longer a lad, madam, but still I can raise a strong arm in your defense, if need be. I'll not stay behind."

"I couldn't have done this without you. I'll find some reward that suits your loyalty. I promise you that."

He laughed low in his throat and looked at her with a gleam in his eyes. "I was hoping you would."

Chelynne started a little, for though she had fully intended a reward, she never expected a request. His loyalty was too strong and his nature too unselfish. "Would you explain what would please you most?"

"Of a certain," he replied with enthusiasm. "I don't think my place is with the new lord of Welbering. I'll be seeking a new position."

Of course. She had been foolish not to assume this. Harry would never make life bearable for Gordon, especially since he had done this kindness for Chelynne. "There will be a position for you in my household for as long as you want it, Gordon. Will that do?"

He nodded, came to his feet, and they were off again. The day was the same as the one before. A few hours passed and they stopped for horses. Little changed, only the scenery and the people they passed. The next day was equal. Then in the afternoon sun they came to a crossroads and Chelynne paused. She knew this part of the country. Welbering was in the direction they traveled but not very far down that other road she would find Hawthorne House. She hadn't given much thought to travel plans. She hadn't anticipated passing this way. And here she was, in her husband's holding, only a short distance from his house. She glanced wistfully in that direction, thought of hopeless expectations and shattered dreams.

They hadn't traveled much farther when they came upon a large group of men blocking the road they journeyed down. Chelynne shivered, only now recalling Chad's stern warning of the thievery in this shire. A few men hailed them to stop, while others lounged under trees as if lazily passing the day there.

"Where're ye bound?" one shouted gruffly.

"Welbering," Gordon answered.

"Welbering," the man mimicked thoughtfully, scratching his chin. "An' that be a long ride . . . down this road, seems. There's another way ye might be bound to take, lies to the east and runs through Bratonshire."

"But that's hours out of our way," Chelynne cried. "We would be foolish to waste so much time."

"Well, if yer mind is set to this road there's a meager toll," he advised her. "Two pound."

"Who enforces this toll?" she asked.

"Now, dear," Gordon admonished her. "I've got the sum and we'll pay the toll." Gordon seemed to be the doting parent in this twosome. He dug into his pouch and offered the coin.

"That's a wise old man," came a lazy voice. A man sauntered toward him, with a patch covering his eye and a scarred face that gave Chelynne an instant chill. He looked over the couple astride, a depraved gleam in his eye and his lips parting to show stained and rotting teeth as he leered at Chelynne in particular. His lust was plain and he was completely unabashed. "Be ye 'is wife or 'is brat?"

She pinched her lips against a hostile reply and said simply, "The toll is paid and we'll be on our way."

"Could be the toll's gone up in price," he commented, scratching his lice and eyeing her coldly. One quick look around told her they were completely at the mercy of this band. There was no chance of escape unless they were willingly released. She found her only hope in swinging out at the man with her husband's earldom, in lieu of the sword she would have preferred.

"I'm interested in this toll. Why is the road taxed?"

"We've 'ad our share o' trouble along our roads," he said briefly, in no mood for trivial conversation. She was certain these were not Chad's men.

"And we're still in Bryant?"

"Aye."

"I was told the roads were guarded but I was unaware of the toll. Whose authority have you?"

He chuckled. "A spy, by God." He reached for her and she quickly pulled back, giving the horse a start and leaving it to dance.

"Let us pass," Gordon demanded.

"Not just yet, old man. Lord Shayburn imposes this toll," he said to Chelynne. "What interest 'ave you in it?"

"It's a large sum for passage." She shrugged, playing coy. "And, I was not aware of it."

"Aye, it's a fair sum and likely to be more."

She stiffened indignantly and lifted her chin. "My husband will be interested in this."

"An' who be that, me grande dame?" he sneered.

"The earl of Bryant," she answered clearly. For a moment she had the pleasure of his surprise, but it changed too quickly to that leering grin.

"A pleasure to make yer acquaintance, m'lady." He smiled. "Fellows," he said, turning to his companions, "the countess of Bryant." He made a sweeping bow. "Take 'er down."

"What do you dare!" she half shouted, half cried. But she was not heard. Gordon, too, was pulled off his horse, and she was held on both sides by some of the men. Their leader, the loud, insolent man with the patch over his eye, bowed before her. "Captain Alex. At your service, madam."

"You're not much at my service," she spat. "Unhand me!"

"Now, countess, surely ye know that m'lord Shayburn wouldn't take kindly to sharing a part o' that toll with His Lordship the earl, eh? We'd be most grateful for your silence on the matter."

"Of course, just let us pass."

His laughter was loud and genuinely amused. "In due time, m'lady, in due time."

Chelynne knew her error. Whatever she might have suffered before the announcement of her title, now she would likely be killed instead. They would kill her and lay blame to the thieves that ravaged this land. As if reading her thoughts, Captain Alex declared, "Another crime for that blackguard who defiles our town."

There were eager nods and exclamations from the men and they seemed to converge on Chelynne and Gordon as one. She screamed and kicked in anticipation but at the very moment she thought herself lost, loud shouts and cries surrounded them from all sides.

"Good Christ," Alex muttered, drawing his sword and waving his arms at his men. Chelynne was dragged aside and held still, and in the confusion she saw that a grand, albeit tattered, company of men who must have been hiding nearby had descended on the small party of toll takers. As she studied them she saw that some had actually dropped from the trees, far enough away to go unnoticed. They raced forward like an army of misfit warriors. Most were masked, all were as meagerly attired as yeomen farmers, and of those unmasked she could not recognize one of Chad's men. These must be that band of thieves, she reasoned, come to upset the road guards and collect their toll. Just as suddenly she realized that the thieves were acting as protectors and the hired protectors had been doing the injustice here.

Still her arms were held, but by one lone man now. She could not see Gordon. They were equal in numbers, these two groups, and she wouldn't dare bet on the winning side. She would feel safe as a hostage for neither.

A masked man came in her direction, forcing her captor to loose her and take up his sword or die where he stood. She had a strange and eerie sensation as he approached, a recognition, but her thoughts were fast flying in this mayhem and she didn't think on it. And it was no boxing match. They were, both sides, intent on finishing lives.

She scrambled away and made for her horse, hoping Gordon would have sense enough to follow her if he could free himself. As she prepared to mount she was pulled from behind by Alex himself and thrown to the ground. He held her with a large hand around her throat and fished for his dagger. He sought to quickly close her mouth for good.

She rolled and struggled, unaware of her actions, for the most part instinctively pursuing survival. Her skirts were drawn up in the tussle and her hand found the pearl handle of her knife. She plunged it into the unsuspecting man's shoulder. It felt like nothing else she had done in her life. For a moment Captain Alex stared down at her in wonder and then he grabbed the dagger with his other hand and rolled over.

Chelynne took advantage of her temporary freedom, knowing that if she stopped him at all it wouldn't be for long. She could sense him behind her as she fled toward the trees. Suddenly she heard a loud thud and a groan just behind her. She turned to see the same man who had rescued her from her first captor pinning Alex to the ground.

Alex squirmed under the man's superior weight, trying in vain to throw him off. Chelynne was mesmerized by the sight. Her dagger lay just inches from Alex's hand. But the masked man did not look at Alex. He looked directly at Chelynne, his eyes the only visible part of his face. He held her with the glittering hardness of his eyes for a moment and then almost casually he reached for the dagger and turned his attention to Alex.

Alex ceased his struggle and stared into his opponent's eyes. His mouth opened as if he would speak but the knife was plunged mercilessly into his chest. Chelynne's hand went to her mouth to stifle her cry as she backed away in horror. The trunk of a tree stopped her and she was frozen there. The masked man stood and began to walk toward her slowly, the anger in his eyes making her certain she would be his next victim.

"My lady," Gordon called from the road. Both Chelynne and the masked man looked in his direction. He was astride with her horse in tow. She looked back at the masked man. His eyes crinkled at the corners as if he were smiling. He folded his arms across his chest and she saw that his own weapon was still sheathed at his belt. Just behind him she could see her dagger protruding from Captain Alex's chest.

Carefully she inched her way toward Gordon and after just a few steps she could see that he didn't mean to stop her. He was letting her go. She lifted her skirts and ran toward her horse.

Mounted, she looked once more at the riotous scene. She could no longer tell which of the men had been the one to save her but she silently prayed he would not be hurt.

Gordon and Chelynne rode at a fearful and frantic pace, looking over their shoulders a number of times for following aggressors. When they came upon a town with an inn they stopped in sheer exhaustion, relieved to be among good people again. That was the first time they talked and all Gordon could say was, "What do you make of that, madam?"

She brushed her skirts, thankful there was no blood on her that could not be easily washed off. "My husband must be told at once. He couldn't be aware of their state or he would have . . . I'm certain he would have done something more. The guards are far worse than the thieves."

"Will you tell him?"

"Somehow . . . I shall." They took a hasty meal, and by the time Chelynne had finished she had thought of the best means. She asked the innkeeper for a pen and ink and sat down to write to Chad. It would take all her remaining coin to have the message sent, but they were close enough to their destination to make do on what little money Gordon carried. This would be easier than telling him in person and answering his questions. She explained briefly: they were set upon by guards exacting a heavy toll by the privy order of Lord Shayburn. She didn't mention they were without escort, that they feared for their lives for a time. She closed with the assurance that they would travel wide of that shire on the return trip, signing only her initials.

Gordon had found a lad to carry the message, and he was given careful instructions and some coin, to be doubled when the earl had the message in hand.

"Put this only in the hand of the earl of Bryant," she warned him sternly. "If you find trouble at his house you may explain that it is from his wife, but no place else should you give that information."

"Your Grace," he gasped, dropping before her.

"Get up," she snapped. "Don't you see? Tell no other that you deliver a message for me or you'll likely find yourself hanging from a tree! There are thieves along that road, dangerous and armed. Go wide, and quickly!"

"Aye, milady."

"Have you a weapon of any sort?"

"Nay, milady."

"Well, I can't give you mine," she mumbled with a shudder, remembering all too clearly where she had last seen it. "You must find something before you leave. And travel carefully."

That was the only incident on the trip, but one likely to be remembered by both Gordon and Chelynne for a long time. When they arrived at Welby Manor she was greeted warmly and not questioned about her early arrival. The house was being readied for the arrival of corpse and mourners. Those servants who had only just been freed from the manor to return to their families while the house was unoccupied were back, working in force again.

There was a comfort in the feeling of coming home, but the sadness in doing so was real, for Chelynne knew she could never come again. Once Sheldon was buried she would never view the insides of these walls again. With his passing went her childhood and her memories of the pleasant love that brought her into womanhood. Now she was alone.

When her breakfast was delivered the next morning she called for the head housekeeper. Mrs. Becker had served the baron for many years. She had been a friend and confidant in many instances. The round, happy woman was a good friend to Stella and was not only willing but eager to help Chelynne in any way. But she knew nothing of Sheldon's memorabilia, nothing of what personal effects should rightfully go to Chelynne now. She knew the house, as only a housekeeper could know it. There were large spaces for storage behind certain walls, private cabinets in his study and in the library, an office in the stables and a desk containing important papers in his bedroom. They promised an arduous search.

Every paper was turned, every picture examined, every drawer sorted. Ledgers were leafed through and correspondence looked over. Most of what Chelynne saw meant nothing to her. There were piles of letters, old and new, some of them written by Sheldon's father. Near the end of the second day, pulling books from the shelves and paging through every one, Chelynne began to fear that Sheldon had been honest; there was nothing. But she spent every waking moment at her task, hoping to find something to tell her of herself, if not of her parents. The key to her past.

In her search she came across a collection of papers that belonged to Eleanor. With a morbid curiosity she leafed through the letters. There were none from Sheldon; most were from members of her family and a few female acquaintances from years back. Chelynne noted that the family Sheldon had married into was a good one and the dowry Eleanor had brought him was great. But Eleanor was too old to have married for only the first time. Marrying a woman in her late twenties was like marrying someone's grandmother. Chelynne knew that the dowry, Sheldon's reason for taking his bride, had all been lost during the wars. There was nothing in letters to indicate that Eleanor had been happy, that she had had the love of her husband and a pleasant life. The worn and aged folder was all she had in the way of keepsakes from her youth and it contained nothing.

And then came a document on which Chelynne recognized Chad's name. It caused her to drop the rest and sink into a nearby chair. She stared at it, dumb with wonder, numb with confusion. It was a torn marriage record bearing her husband's name and a woman's she did not know. It was dated over six years back and was appropriately witnessed and signed.

The questions rose without delay. Why was she never told? Had she been marrying a widower she would have been told. Was the marriage perhaps put asunder by a man of the church, declared void? Was there love, honor or something akin to force in this union? Whose possession was this? Sheldon's? Surely not Eleanor's.

Chelynne did not know the name of the bride and what she

knew best, due to her schooling, was names. Oh, names! So important, almost equal to money. Was the woman now abandoned, lacking in name and money?

Chad had never mentioned anything of a wife, dead or divorced. Chelynne knew nothing of him. Who was the woman? Who would he marry? Who would he love? Was it willingly, or unwillingly, as with her? Was it a marriage past . . . or still practiced?

Her mind rambled on and on. For a long while she was immobilized from shock and confusion. Not many of the thoughts she had now concerned her departed parents. She could search no more, confident there was nothing else to be found yet a little fearful there might be something. Carefully she made an envelope for this aged paper. She could think clearly enough to know it had been hidden, meaning to her that it could be destructive if found. Until she understood it, she had to secure it.

She confided her intentions in no one and sought out one stable hand who she knew could not read and whom she did trust. She had known the man Gorely since early in her youth. He and his family had served Sheldon, and though he was paid fairly he would relish a simple chore that would bring him a few extra shillings.

"This is a paper of some importance that I would have taken to Hawthorne House," she informed him. "I would ask that you place it yourself in my coffer. The caretaker will admit you on my letter and give you a bed for the night. My keys will admit you to my rooms and open the coffer where some jewelry is kept. The problem is not the chore, Mr. Gorely, but the roads. There is a great deal of trouble in that part of the country, the reason the house is closed and the guards posted. Some are not trustworthy and will not let you pass, and I cannot tell you which they are. It must be done carefully and secretly or it could be very dangerous."

He made no response to her, waiting for her to continue. He would do the chore if ordered. But Chelynne would not command him. It had to be a matter of choice, especially when she feared going past that part of the country herself, even heavily guarded.

"There would be a handsome reward upon your return. In the event there is a mishap . . ." She stumbled on her own words, wanting to tell him how great was the risk and not able to do so easily. "I would leave a goodly sum with your wife. That is all I can do."

"When would you have me leave?"

"As soon as you can be ready. Take time to speak to your wife, if you must, but I should like to be unknown in the matter. I would think . . ." Again she stumbled, unsure. She had no idea whom she would be protecting. Herself? Her husband? Someone else? "I should think if there's danger such that the paper could be found on your person, destroy it quickly. Yes, destroy it. In any possible way."

He was a large man but very gentle. He stood and nervously twisted his hat in his hands as she gave the instructions. It pained her to think of committing him to any danger, but it hurt her to think of any living creature being hurt. She did not think herself strong. She had always found her strength through her protectors. Being the protector alarmed her. She was not confident that she could play this role for long.

Chelynne helped to apply the precious paper to Mr. Gorely's chest in a linen cover, keeping the rough edges soft against his skin. He admitted his wife could make do without asking questions of him. He could make the journey in two days' time and Chelynne would expect him back in five. She watched him a short time later from her bedroom window. He left Welby Manor with horse and cart, looking like a common traveler, though speedy.

Chelynne did not go back to her searching after that. She sat quietly in her room until Mrs. Becker came and inquired of her.

"Have you given up the idea, mum?" she asked solicitously.

"I suppose I have."

"You seem to have lost the spirit of it. Myself, I wouldn't know where to look or for what."

"It's all right," Chelynne mumbled. "I was told there was nothing . . . but I had hoped . . . some small thing . . ."

Mrs. Becker touched her hand. "I have something you might hold dear." She reached into the ample pocket of her apron and pulled out a small portrait of Sheldon painted not long after he returned to England. There were a great many paintings about the house of himself, Eleanor and Harry. This small painting was not much to cling to, but Chelynne wasn't sure that Eleanor would be gifting her with anything at all. For that reason she took the little portrait with warm thanks and asked if it would be missed.

"It's one he put away," Mrs. Becker told her. "Laid it away, he did, not liking the style. There's others more valuable. Nothing that I know belonged to your own dear parents but for the miniature of your father in the study. That will be yours, but . . ." She straightened slightly and had a light frown. "I'd take it now, mum, if you mean to have it."

"I never knew either of them," Chelynne said with a small, childlike sob in her voice. "There were so many times I wanted to ask my mother . . ." Her voice trailed off, tears coming to her eyes.

"Aye, it's a blessing you've had Mrs. Stella."

Chelynne gave a small nod without raising her eyes. There was no way to explain that what she needed could not be learned from a helpmate such as Stella. Stella's love was grandmotherly. Chelynne longed for the answers to questions only her mother could give. She needed the wisdom of a woman who had lived and loved. Stella had never married and, as far as Chelynne knew, had never been in love. She needed someone bearing a stronger bond than gender — a blood bond, kinship.

Stella offered comfort and love, but for a child. Chelynne remembered when she would sit upon her woman's knee in the cook houses or kitchens, visiting with other servants. Work stopped for meals or tea and they chattered of matters centered on husbands, childbearing, disorders of the bowel or womb, and the latest gossip about their employers. What the servants knew of court life came from washing nobles' finery and delivering meals.

So Chelynne remained as Mrs. Becker left her, depressed and confused. She felt a great deal of animosity toward all those who had fooled her, Sheldon among them. She knew the bitter taste of betrayal, and she had little determination to carry on with such a farce. And there was no solution. It sapped her of energy and left her listless.

Midday next the Mondeloy party arrived. The heavy footfalls on the stairs brought Stella and Tanya to her rooms. They had traveled for almost a week, drearily and slowly, and Tanya had not once lifted her black veil or uttered the slightest word. One she did for loyalty, the other, through no fault of her own, she could not do.

"So it seems, dear heart, you've come off without a fault," Stella remarked.

Chelynne didn't answer but began pulling off her dress so she could don black again for her uncle. She would take up the role of mourner, putting forth the public facade of grief. Her silence brought Stella to an accurate conclusion. "You've found nothing."

"Nothing," she murmured.

"Well, darling, you've had the chance you wished. There's nothing more to be done."

"They'll find out. The entire household knows I've been here and looking, turning the house upside down. Someone will use that as a means to win Eleanor's favor now that Sheldon is gone."

"We'll be leavin' soon enough. Could they come down hard on ye?"

Chelynne shrugged, noncommittal. She simply didn't care. Let them carry on, ply her with questions. What would it matter? She would give no answers. When Sheldon was buried and Gorely returned, she would leave.

The tombstone was unfinished. It seemed strangely symbolic to her. Had he even completed his life? She had the urge to throw herself on the ground, tearing her hair from her scalp and screaming. She would draw him to life again with the sheer bizarre display, frighten him into life. But instead she was composed. Dignified. It was the only honor she could do him in case she was being watched from some other world.

The next day she rode, planning carefully to find some secluded place to heave herself upon the ground and let her body wrench and flounder from the agony of his leaving. She would scream hatred at her abandonment where no one could hear. She would let the emotion pour out and reserve her dignity for those who would look at her and pass judgment.

But oddly, she felt nothing. She tried tears for Sheldon and there were none. She pounded on the earth with a fist, and, realizing the futility, tried to straighten the bent grasses she had injured in her play at fury. There must be something stronger within her. She thought heavy and hard, but in the end she simply rode, committing the land to memory.

She stopped near the place where Sheldon was laid away, but she didn't enter the iron gate, lay flowers on the tomb, or do anything of significance. She stared at the mound that was her uncle and her heart whispered, "I think you've taken my soul, Sheldon. I cannot feel, I cannot hurt, I cannot grieve."

A few mornings later Chelynne found Mr. Gorley in the stable taking up his chores as if he'd never been gone. It had been wise of him not to report to her. He had had no trouble. The countryside was peaceful where he passed and he hadn't been questioned or bothered at Hawthorne House but taken for a servant en route to His Lordship in London. One thing at least had gone well, and Chelynne amply compensated him. She could now make ready for her departure. But first she sought out her aunt.

Eleanor's chair in her bedroom, her private retreat and sanctuary, was as large and imposing as she was. A blanket covered her from her waist to the floor and she sat staring blankly ahead, never acknowledging Chelynne's presence. They had not spoken since Sheldon's death except for the superficial comments people who care nothing for each other make.

"I shall be leaving in the morning, Aunt," Chelynne said.

Eleanor looked at her. She did indeed have the haggard look of the bereaved. Her husband's passing had etched deep lines on her face and her pallor bespoke ill health. "I rather expected you would."

"Unless you need me here to —"

"I shall be glad to have you gone."

"You grieve deeply," Chelynne said more to herself than to Eleanor, making allowance for the woman's tactless tongue.

"And would that surprise you? I grieve more for the many years I've lived in marriage with a man who never saw fit to treat me in a wifely fashion."

"Sheldon was good to you," Chelynne said, coming to her uncle's defense.

At that Eleanor laughed. "Ah, yes, he was so good to me! The kindest thing he ever did for me was to die!"

"Eleanor, please," Chelynne begged, hoping to stop the woman before she said too many things she could not retract.

"No, hear me. Hear me now while Sheldon is not here to silence me. For all the years I was mistress of this house and lady of these lands I never had his love. Do you think him so noble? So gallant? Then consider this: on the night I labored to give his son birth, he was whispering love words to another woman. All the years I traveled like a gypsy as we fled England he wrote letters to his true love, longed for another, desired . . ." Her voice broke for an instant but returned with clear resentments. "Oh, it was a long time before she was out of his reach, but he did not turn to me then. Then his devotion was for you! His own son could not have the love he gave you! Ah, my regal niece, you've had more of Sheldon than any other. Go! Go to your earl and good riddance!"

The hateful words stung her deeply, but in deference to the uncle she loved, Chelynne turned to Eleanor kindly. "If you should ever have need of me, Aunt, have word sent and I shall come."

"At long last, my dear, I shall have no needs. Now I shall finally gain my due."

"What do you mean?"

"Have you looked upon these lands? Have you not seen where all our holdings lie? Perhaps you thought us wealthy? The Mondeloys have never known wealth! Are our people dressed in rags? Are their houses badly kept? Even the children who will be raised to naught more than simple churls are schooled here. They learn to hold a quill and read in Welbering! They keep a finer share of their crops to barter than their lord ever had. Every man has a horse to ride aside from the beasts to tend the crops. Our peasants are fat and wealthy and the lady of the manor must plead for simple garb from the lord. I've begged shoes for my son while the farmers read in their leisure time!"

Maudlin, dramatic lies, all of it. Eleanor had a shoe for every day of the year and there were only a few in Welbering who knew comforts beyond the norm for a yeoman. Schooling was a thing Sheldon thought of, pursued on a small scale, and had only barely achieved for some of the adult members of his burgh.

"Eleanor," Chelynne hissed in warning. "Sheldon was a fine and fair baron! I'll not let your jealous slander rip him from his grave! He gave naught but kindness and justice here. You've never suffered!" She clamped her mouth shut, though there was a great deal more she wished to say.

"Every spare coin we held was put toward a dowry that would see our regal wench wed to a fine title! We bought your fine marriage with Harry's future, with my mother's jewels! What has Harry now? A piddling acreage and a humble steed! No fine bride with handsome holdings. No lands in new ports! Nothing but a simple farm and an aging mother! It took the smallest and final pittance from my own purse to set him in a house that would not shame our name in London. Do not preach to me of what I have! I know what I have!"

Chelynne shook her head sadly. "He has stolen from you, too? Has Harry cried his woes to take the last of your own gold? I pity your foolishness, Aunt. You should have called him home, gifted him with his simple farm, and challenged him to be half the man his father was."

Eleanor smirked at her niece. "Sheldon paid a fair price for your loyalty, Chelynne. My only reward comes in seeing that at least that was not wasted. How could I expect you to feel shame for what you've taken from us all?"

There was nothing to be said to this resentful shrew. Chelynne grieved all the more that Sheldon had spent so many years living with this. It was clear that had he not seen to her future, Chelynne would have been fortunate to be allowed to empty the slops in this house. She had always known there was dislike for her here, but she had never realized the hatred ran this deep.

"Good-bye, Eleanor. I wish you well."

"Hold fast to your fine title, countess. Take care not to call yourself Mondeloy again. I deny our kinship from now."

Chelynne turned slowly to face her aunt again. "I doubt there ever was any kinship between us, Eleanor. I think you have denied it always in your heart."

"The next time you pillage through my house without permission, I shall have you jailed. Never set foot here again!"

"No matter." Chelynne shrugged. "There is nothing here for me." There were no tears for Eleanor's harsh words, but pity.

Early, as the sun was just rising on the next day, they prepared to leave. There was little to ready, simply servants to inform, horsemen to alert. Chelynne pulled her wrap tightly around her as she watched Tanya leave with the last light parcel. She looked around the room that had been hers when she stayed at Welby Manor. The bed had been made in France, a gift to her on her tenth birthday. The room was done in virginal pink and white, a feminine and pure habitation. She remembered Sheldon's exclamations, for he had had the room decorated to his specifications. "If I surround you with womanly things perhaps you will grow into gowns instead of breeches!"

Sheldon had always said such lovely things about her mother, his hope clearly being that drawing a good picture of Madelynne would help Chelynne to grow into the dignified and graceful woman her mother was. She had at long last given up her boyish antics and impish foolery, but she could never live up to Sheldon's expectations. She could feel gratitude, though, and more profoundly now as she prepared to leave for the last time. She had not known parents but she knew fatherly love. She had never felt protected until the protection was gone and she was awesomely alone.

The only thing she could do for Sheldon now was to take charge of her life and carry on as she had been reared to do. She gave a sigh of resignation and prepared to leave all this behind her.

There was a swift sinking in her heart as she saw Harry in the doorway, lounging lazily against the frame. She would not be allowed to go easily now. He stood and leered at her.

"Will you ride in the coach this time, cousin, or flee on horseback again?"

"I will ride where it pleases me," she sighed wearily.

"Strange, I hadn't thought you so clever, Chelynne. Such a wit. I'm greatly impressed."

"You seem greatly intoxicated, Harry. And so early, too."

"I should like to know if you sought it out, or stumbled upon it?"

"I don't know what you mean, Harry."

"The paper. I would like to have it back."

"What?"

"Perhaps you didn't know it belonged to me, Chelynne. Did you think perhaps it was my father's?"

"I don't know what you babble about, Harry."

"Spare me your innocence," he snapped. "I know you were the one to take it. I want it back."

"I'm sorry, Harry. More of your delusions?"

"The record of your husband's marriage, as well you know."

"You confuse me. You must explain."

His fist hit the door in a sudden rage. "Where have you taken it?"

Chelynne jumped in surprise and turned her palms up in dismay. "I've not left the house since I arrived but for a ride. What is it you're after?"

"I know it's not here, I've had your room thoroughly searched. I mean it, cousin dear, I want the thing!" Her great effort at confusion was not fooling Harry. He was determined and his temper frightened her a little. She was too alone with him. He stared her down and she remained mute, refusing to play this game with him. "Perhaps you thought to make use of it yourself, Chelynne?"

"Make use of what, Harry?" she asked with feigned tolerance.

"Your husband's marriage to Anne Billings. Will you hold it over the earl's head for a price?"

She ruffled somewhat, wondering at his plan. She should have determined this was mischief worthy of Harry, but she had not. She couldn't fathom his purpose now.

"My husband will be angered by your interest in his private affairs."

"I don't doubt it," Harry laughed. "He's taken great enough pains to keep it secret." Chelynne paled and Harry was quick to notice. She was at the disadvantage, knowing nothing of the marriage and little of the man. He saw his chance. If he was correct in guessing, she was ignorant of the whole thing. "It must have come as quite a shock to you, Chelynne. Of course you would be the last to learn of it."

"You're mad," she hissed impatiently.

"I imagine you wish I were. Quite a rake, isn't he? Keeping two wives in the same city and neither of them knowing of the other. You truly never suspected, did you?"

"Harry, I believe the last link has slipped," she sighed, quickly trying to pass him in the doorway. He grabbed her sharply by the arm.

"I pray you remember I have never lied to you, Chelynne. Wasn't it I who taught you of your parentage? Of course I left you the letter in your coffer. I could have held that for a price, but why antagonize the same king I seek favor with? That was better off yours, but this I would have kept."

"For what purpose, Harry?"

"It might serve to see you selling oranges outside the Duke's Theater. Nothing would bring me greater pleasure."

Chelynne was beginning to tremble and prayed she wouldn't faint dead away. To cover her upset she attempted a wicked laugh, but it was little more than a nervous giggle. "Some petty forgery to bring you easy coin, Harry? Do you think the earl that kind of fool? He would never let you embarrass a farthing out of him! Come now, have done with this acting!"

"Bryant is no fool. He sought to have the best of both and before I found the truth to it he was succeeding. Few knew of the lady Anne. There is the woman who gains his love and devotion and here stands the well-bred flower he can take to court. I don't doubt it could have gone on for many years, but now I have an upset at hand."

She blanched, her world beginning to spin around her. It all made sense. He was ever away from the house and she had never shared his bed. Personal problems to set aside? Must he rid himself of the old bride or the new? Whom did he seek to remove? She looked searchingly at her cousin and mumbled, "Why?"

"I wouldn't know his reasons."

Her hand came up to stop him, for he had not answered the right question. With a pleading in her eyes she whispered low, "Why do you go to such lengths to bring me pain?"

The cold gleam in his eyes was so wicked and depraved she was more afraid of his words than she ever had been. He had always been a nuisance and now he seemed a danger. "For the years I've played lackey to a bastard whelp of an exiled king! Ah, the praise and glory bestowed on our sweet Chelynne, with my father's own flesh left to scourge a wasted farmland! I've taken my place behind you long enough, Chelynne. I've lived for the day you'll beg of me a meager rag to clothe yourself, a roof to lie under. I've had a bellyful of your regal airs!" He turned and stamped away but foolishly she called him back.

"And the earl?" she asked softly. "What has he done to warrant your vengeance?"

"He coddles you. And he's an insulting bastard. Reason enough!"

She stood and stared at the now empty portal where her cruel cousin had flung his final blow. Her spirit was so broken now that could she have closed her eyes and sought the peaceful haven of death, she would have done so. It was mad, this. But life did not give one escapes, but challenges. Some were so unbearable that many gave in to the urge and ended the misery of living for themselves. Chelynne considered that alternative.

She made the blind journey to her coach, seeing nothing she passed, not recognizing the servants who turned out to bid her farewell, not glancing back to what she was leaving. The coach waited with her women standing near, pulling their wraps tightly about them, allowing her first entry into her coach. The men were prepared to ride, their horses dancing in anticipation. Gordon sat beside the driver, more than eager to leave Welby Manor. The majority of those attending her journey she didn't know by name, but they served. Regal wench! Countess! Her Ladyship! Her Majesty, the royal bastard whelp of a whore and an exiled king? Her Mightiness, the wife of an earl who already had a wife? Her Grace, an illegitimate peasant who lived not even in sin with a married man she loved? A lie? Everything? All things? What was truth? Her world went black. She hoped death had taken her.

FIFTEEN

ETITIONERS ARE AS COMMON as air at Whitehall. They chase the king down as he walks to chapel, bribe his mistresses for an audience, offer delightful and expensive gifts to his ministers for a kind word on their behalf. And the king is a rare man. He would like to give them all just what would make them most happy.

Those who are close to Charles Stuart know that he is well informed. He knows all the goings-on and is seldom, if ever, surprised. Because he is quiet and solemn where rumors are concerned, those many he has not confided in are never very sure how much he knows and about what. He trusts no one, but plays at trust. He pretends in many instances, or even begins to believe in a lover or comrade, but life has made a realist of him. He knows everyone has a price.

Charles Stuart was urged by one of his friends to grant an audience to an anxious baron. He was not eager to hear what the man needed, but just the same he was curious. There were so many in the palace, in London for that matter, who knew the profit to keeping the king informed that Charles was not in need of information. It was the presentation this man would make that aroused his interest.

The king was in the company of some of his ministers when Lord Shayburn was admitted after a very long wait. The heavy lord found it difficult to bow very low before his sovereign and Charles grimaced as he tried. Charles was in excellent physical condition, athletic and tireless. He found a gluttonous man somewhat repulsive.

"So gracious of Your Majesty to see me," Lord Shayburn began.

Charles did not feel gracious. He felt imposed upon and suspicious. Had he no suspicions he would not have seen the man at all.

"There is something you require, my lord?"

"Ah, sire, yes, there is, though for the good of England, I assure you."

Total tactlessness on the part of the baron, Charles thought. It was usually his first clue that the man had no hope above bettering himself when he opened with such a statement. Everyone wanted the good of England. Few ever did anything that was good for the country.

He nodded and urged the man on. Shayburn was not encouraged by Charles's appearance. The king lounged in his chair, majestically, but lazily. He was already bored, already prepared to doze during this appeal. Charles's position bespoke endurance and tolerance — nothing even near to interest.

"We've had problems in Bratonshire, Your Majesty. Critical problems. You'll remember that our shire is on the main . . . or, um . . . one of the main roads to London from the north. Imperative that it always be a stronghold, er, at least in the position to bear men-at-arms in the event of any pursuit from the north, er . . ." He stopped and coughed, spitting into a lacy handkerchief. He was not doing well. He was not convincing the king that Bratonshire was important — because it was not, to any but himself . . . and some aggressor. He had to make it seem important, worthy of royal support.

"Should there be any attack by aggressors from the north, sire, Bratonshire would be an ideal place to house an army and thwart any such plans. I've had the land in the name of the crown for many years and am in the process of building a castle there. An outpost, if it pleases Your Majesty, in the name of England."

"I'm flattered," Charles drawled.

"Um, yes, sire. But we haven't had the opportunity to make any progress on building since we've had trouble with —"

"When did you start building, my lord?" Charles asked.

"Sire, money has not been . . . that is, we had the plans drawn and that is the extent of it. Building was to start in the spring and it's beginning to look as if that will be impossible."

"There has been trouble," the king acknowledged. "Of what sort?"

"Thieves, Your Majesty."

"Thieves?" Charles raised one eyebrow. Was it customary to trouble a king with a report of thieves in a small, almost nonexistent village of farmers? It seemed, on days like this, that it was customary to trouble a king about which pot was used and when.

"It seems so, sire, but I have my doubts. This is an army of sorts that plagues me now, sire. I've set my own men to guard and patrol and we've had no success in stopping them. They are not only more skilled than ordinary thieves, they seem to be well informed. Knights, perhaps from some foreign aggressor." Both Shayburn and the king knew immediately that this dramatic ploy was a failure. There was no foreign power interested in a tiny, centrally located English shire filled with farmers. There was no industry and not even a fine manor. It was ridiculous to speak of it. Shayburn stumbled for his ground.

"It has been the worst struggle, sire. You may have heard complaints of my management, but the truth to it is that I've paid more privy tax and tithe to the crown than many other barons, and in addition there has been a good deal of prosperity in Bratonshire since Your Majesty's restoration."

"Complaints?" Charles asked.

Shayburn gulped. Charles had heard no complaints? "Perhaps not," Shayburn stammered.

"I should like to know what you suspected I might have heard."

"I've had misdealings with the earl, but then it was a small misunderstanding and well before your return to England. Nothing of any real importance."

"Just the same, what was his complaint?"

"It was insignificant, but if it pleases Your Majesty, he complained that I treated the townspeople unfairly, harshly. Claimed they were overtaxed, but I have accurate ledgers and there was never any . . . that is, there were no further accusations. The misunderstanding was resolved."

"Bratonshire was not your family seat, am I correct?"

Shayburn blanched. He wouldn't have guessed the king would pay much attention to those matters. He thought it well in the past. He had never faced any doubt or question when Charles was restored to the throne, and he hadn't thought to now.

"No, sire."

"It was the Bollering family, is that correct?"

"Lord Bollering was charged with treason, sire." It was overcompensation, he knew it at once. He was defending himself before defense was necessary.

"He fought for the crown. One of his sons fought for me."

"I'm aware of that, Your Majesty. There was nothing I could do to restore his name or clear him short of gifting him with the land I had lawfully acquired."

"And I am aware of that, my lord," Charles replied. "But I am certain that is not why you've come to me. What is it you require?"

"Because we are under siege, sire, I require men-at-arms and gold to back me in defense of my lands. I come to you only after all other means have been exhausted."

"You've gone to others for support?"

"The earl of Bryant and other barons. With little success."

"You're not supported by Bryant?"

"Ah, sire, he has supported me. His support is useless to me. I even suspect —" Shayburn stopped. He reminded himself not to slander Hawthorne to Charles Stuart. The king liked Hawthorne; there might well be coalition there. "He has provided gold and men-at-arms, but I suspect he has little interest in helping me. And neighboring barons are suspiciously unassaulted."

"Suspiciously?"

"It is a personal attack, sire, I'm certain of it. No one else has been bothered. And to hold what is mine I need support. From the crown. Royal support would see an end to this trouble . . . for the good of England."

That always soured the king. He hated the sound of it more every time he heard it. In sincerity it was a noble gesture. It was seldom sincere. What difference to England, after all, did Bratonshire and Shayburn make?

"I appreciate your gallantry, as does England. I shall consider your request and you will hear from me. Good day."

"Thank you, sire. Thank you."

Shayburn waddled out of the room and Charles sat still, watching him. Finally he muttered, "Gold and men-at-arms."

"For thieves!" Buckingham roared with laughter. The consensus in the room was that it would be foolish to aid a baron in holding lands he could not even secure against thieves. But then perhaps it was not holding he sought, but building.

"What do you make of it, George?" Charles asked Buckingham.

"Sounds like a privy squire looking for an empire. Why not grant him a duchy, sire, and see if he can save it from beggars?"

While Buckingham delighted in his own wit, Charles walked to the closet where he played chemist. He gave the matter of Lord Shayburn some consideration while mixing strange concoctions together. Just outside the door Buckingham and York joked over the fat baron's audacity. Charles smiled occasionally at their jesting without comment or even a glance in their direction. It would seem that he didn't even think about the man's request now.

Stuart was not a man to act impulsively where his political affairs were concerned. He was a little curious to see what Hawthorne would do with this mess he had created for himself, but he was not pleased to learn his people had trouble. That was the extent of his consideration. He put the matter out of his mind easily and walked briskly in the direction of a lovely young Frenchwoman's apartments. In politics he didn't react impulsively. In his diversions it was the only way he reacted. He was thoroughly delighted with himself.

The countess of Bryant suffered through a long and monotonous journey home to London. The ride was uneventful and silent. There was a hardness to her eyes that hinted years of trials. More than her uncle's passing was being mourned.

Chelynne couldn't help recalling the other times she had traveled to Chad. The first time there had been a heaviness of heart, but she was prepared to accept her uncle's choice of husband and make the best of a sad situation. And then she had met him and loved him. That was the beginning of her trouble, the beginning of dreams of the day he would love her, too. She thought of the nights she would spend in her lover's arms, of the children she would give him. She imagined the proud set to her husband's jaw as he watched over his sons.

When she had journeyed from the country to London to join Chad there had still been hope. There had been that innocent maid's mind so anxious to win her husband.

The same desire that once filled her with hope had soured. His betrayal was bitterest of all, even though he had never given her reason to expect encouragement from him. Everything she had been through turned on lies and secrets. She had finally learned that. Now she must use the same means, if necessary, to learn the truth.

She made no pause when entering the earl's fine home, but went directly to her rooms. Stella and Tanya were eager to make their mistress feel at home by seeing all her things properly installed. Chelynne was more intent on removing her stays and fillers and being done with the heavy gown. When that was accomplished she wished only to be alone.

More than an hour had passed when Chad came to her. He entered without knocking or announcing himself, standing inside the door to watch her as she sat in quiet repose. Finally he spoke.

"Welcome home."

"My thanks."

"You're tired from your journey?"

"Quite. It was long."

"I received your message. Would you like to tell me about it?"

"There's very little to tell, my lord. We were stopped by a large group of men imposing a toll to pass. They were reluctant to inform me of the man by whose order they did this thing. I fear the mistake that endangered us was telling them I was your wife. It was foolish of me. They didn't fancy having you know of the tax. When I thought my life in danger a band of men, thieves, I suspect, attacked the guard. In truth, I didn't know who to fear more — Shayburn's guard or the thieves."

His expression did not change through her story. He stared at her wordlessly for some time before he broke the silence. "You must have been very frightened."

"I was not at ease."

Again there was silence. Chelynne was uneasy about the strange light in his eyes. He looked to be in a wicked mood. She spoke out of nervousness. "How fare things there now?"

"I've seen to it. There's something that came for you while you were away," he remarked casually. Walking the short distance to her cupboard he drew out a package. Placing it in her hands he bade her open it right then.

"What is it?" she asked.

"It came by messenger. One good thing came of your experience, my dear," he said lightly. "The captain of Shayburn's guard was killed during that conflict. He had a reputation far worse than any thief. His name was Captain Alex."

The words were barely spoken when she lifted the wrapping paper and spied the contents of her parcel. It was the pearl-handled dagger that John Bollering had given her. The sight of it pierced her worse than the point could have. She grasped at composure and covered the thing quickly. "And is that good news, my lord?"

"Indeed. I was fortunate in locating a man who viewed the entire fray. It seems Alex was first injured in a tussle with a simple lass. What was your gift, my dear?"

"Nothing of importance. Is all well there now?"

He sauntered over to her and lifted the paper to expose the dagger. "She stabbed him with a dagger," Chad went on. "Of course the lass did it in defense of her life so it won't sit ill with her. I for one am glad the man is gone. He's caused more grief in Bratonshire than any marauder."

He looked into her eyes and she could read there the completeness of his knowledge, down to the very last detail. She swallowed hard while she waited for his next words.

"She identified herself as the countess of Bryant," he said as he walked away from her. She heard his words dwindling away as he moved across the room, but he was speaking slowly and carefully. "She was not riding in a coach with a goodly number of hired protectors, however." He turned to look at her and she saw rage in his eyes such as she'd never seen before. "But alone, with one simple companion to aid her."

She watched him cautiously but he just stood, looking at her, his anger building. When his mouth opened he shouted with such thunder she jumped in surprise. "What in Satan's Hell were you doing?"

She gulped and stammered and attempted some words in her defense but he was beyond control now, moving toward her quickly. He pulled her sharply to her feet and clutched her to him. She expected him to strike, but he gave her an angry shake and only held her fast again. In his embrace was anger, frustrated anger.

"By my oath, Chelynne, I'll do whatever I must to keep you from your own foolishness!" He held her away from him and looked into her eyes. There was discomfort and confusion in that stormy gray that she had never seen before. "How many times is it now? How many times have you been returned to me on the heels of some threat to your life? Good God, madam! What causes you to be so reckless?"

"But as you can see . . . I've returned safely," she replied shakily. "Surely the story you heard was greatly exaggerated."

"No!" he shouted. "The story was accurate, I would stake my life on it! Will you tell me why in God's name you were traveling thus?"

With a sigh she said simply, "To arrive in Welbering ahead of my aunt and cousin. So I might search the house for something of my parents."

"Why didn't you simply explain that? I could have accompanied you."

"It was my concern," she answered.

"Your life is my concern!" he bellowed. "And since you have such little regard for it, I shall have to make your safety my primary concern! You will not leave this house without permission. Is that understood?"

"I wasn't aware that I was so important to you, my lord."

He looked at her carefully. She struck a dignified pose. Proud. Detached. Unattainable. He bristled slightly at her sarcasm and opened his arms in a bemused fashion.

"So, you've not had much passion in your marriage, but you have little else to complain about. Is it your sensual yearnings that drive you to such carelessness? Can you blame my lack of attention for taking such little heed of danger?"

She simply stared at him coolly, answering his question with her lack of response. A hollow laugh escaped him.

"So I don't keep you well enough, eh, wife? You came to me a child and grew into a witless vixen. It's by the grace of God and some strange miracle that you're alive at all." He shrugged out of his coat, tossing it aside. "I can well understand your lack of concern for my welfare, that much I have earned, but this disregard for your own life . . . by damn! Wandering the streets at night and traveling country roads where thieves and rapists run wild . . ." He was striding toward her again, angry and insulted.

"Nay, Chad! Do not beat me! I will take care!"

He stopped abruptly and stared at her in wonder. "Beat you?" he asked softly, stunned by her fear. He approached her slowly, taking her hand carefully and drawing her closer. "Have I ever given you cause to think I would hurt you? Not beat you, Chelynne. Bind you, once and for all."

She was pulled into his embrace as his lips searched out hers. She could feel the anger drain from him, yielding to another emotion. His lips were warm and light, but she could feel passion growing there, building and spreading from him, through her. Her mind reeled and her knees weakened. The bold hardness of his lean body against hers, the masculine scent of him and the sureness of his muscled arms around her all played against her. A pain grew within her as she realized that in spite of everything that had passed between them, she wanted him desperately.

"How much reason must I give you to take care with your life?" he whispered hoarsely against her ear. "Must I hold you ever at my side? Must you know passion every hour of the day to see my intent?"

Chelynne couldn't silence the screaming in her mind. What game did he play now? Claiming such concern, indeed desire, after these many months? Anger because she might be lost to him? To him; the same one who could not be bothered? She saw a vision of herself falling into bed with him and then watching as he left her to go and seek out another. Someone else who waited patiently for him, always there and devoted.

"No," she murmured, pulling away. Then more desperately she cried, "Nay!" She pushed at him angrily.

He was shocked, cooled by her fierce and sudden denial. She clenched her eyes against her tears, shaking her head furiously. "Never," she ground out.

"What madness seizes you, wench?" he asked angrily.

"Leave me be!"

"You have no right to refuse me —"

"Then you will take me by force! No other way!"

He saw the anger but did not reckon her reasons. He paused, digested her refusal, and then slowly he caressed her cheek. "Do you deny me? Or yourself?"

"How long have you played this waiting game, my lord? How long has my very presence in this house been ignored? Would you have me wait at your call? Am I the whore to be taken on a whim? And what of your problems? Are they finally solved?"

He groaned in some discomfort for he had set his mind to fleshly business now quickly halted. "I must live with mine. What of yours?"

Her mouth took a rigid set. "I must be allowed some time," she said flatly.

The dawning came to him. "So that is how it will be. I've not been an eager groom. You'll turn that back on me now? That is your game?"

"No game," she murmured, shaking her head.

"Come, Chelynne," he said softly. "I regret my reluctance. Let us have done with this hostility."

"Oh, Chad," she sighed bitterly. "Just set aside the months of torment now that you are ready? Perhaps, but not without doubt. And probably regret."

He touched her arm, caressing, sending shivers through her. He was not done seducing her. He was slow, easy and persuasive. "This touch does not burn," he murmured. "It heals. And you've wanted this, I know."

"Will you taunt me now with the months I have wanted you? Perhaps you can laugh at the tears I shed foolishly while I waited so patiently for you to discover me. Or at least gain some mirth from the words your mistress speared me with; they still ring in my ears. I have blood on my hands, Chadwick, for accepting kindness from a man I turned to in desperation. Now that you are ready, am I truly to set it all aside and come to you in passion? My God, you think I am inhuman!"

"I am your husband! You are mine!"

"Not until I yield my heart," she whispered. "Whatever you take by force you can lay claim to, but you'll never truly own any but what I yield of my own free will."

Chad felt aggravation more intense than he had in years. It came to mind to tell her that Bollering lived, to woo her with the truth to his problems, but he checked himself. That was the merest part of the difficulty. He had cultivated this coolness in her over a period of months. It would take time to warm her. He believed himself capable of succeeding. In fact he would succeed if he wooed her now, have her willingly with but a few more gentle touches and tender words. He was sorely pressed not to, his need had grown so intense. Moments, his mind kept urging him, only moments and she would yield. But he knew better of it. She had already decided doubt and regret would be her reward for submission. He could not hold her when it was done and have the moment spoiled by anger and tears.

"So be it," he said in resignation. "Your servant, madam." He bowed. He took up his coat and made to leave, turning back to her when he reached the door. "Tender or cold, you are my wife, Chelynne, and you will do as I command. I will not force you, but neither are you free to run wild. You will stay in this house unless you have my permission to leave or my escort."

"And now I am prisoner?"

He smiled tolerantly and decided to let it go. "I'll leave you now and seek your company when both our moods have settled somewhat." He closed the door behind him and was done with her.

Fists clenched and teeth gnashing, her unwanted tears streamed down her cheeks in spite of her efforts to feel nothing.

The sun had disappeared and Bratonshire was coming to rest. The people were closing shutters against the night and praying for a peaceful rest. Knights in full dress commanded the streets now and took lodgings in stables, spare rooms and in the main hall of the manor house. They bore the crest of the Hawthornes on their shields. The effect was frightening for the simple people, for they could not remember times this harsh since the wars. It was as if an invisible army closed in on their shire. The attackers seemed to sense the short time when the guards would be resting, changing position, or out patrolling the roads.

There were piles of ashes where houses once stood and the graves of those slain were mounting in numbers. It had the look of a ravaged town at the peak of a gruesome war.

In the house of Talbot Rath there was more trouble than just that of thieves. Most thorough in the deception, the earl of Bryant had delivered word through a page, informing Rath that John Bollering was dead. Plans would go on as determined, but another would take that seat in lieu of the avenging knight. Rath had no doubt that there would be careful selection and that the lord would be better than what they had. He trusted Bryant for that. And he was convinced that should the devil himself gain that shire, the people would suffer less than they had with Shayburn. Rath mourned the life of the knight because he had respected him and held his friendship dear.

It was not strange, then, that when there was a knock at the door and Rath opened it to see Bollering in the flesh, his heart nearly stopped. Silently he reached out and pulled the man in, breathing his words in low measured tones. "My God, is it truly yourself?"

John nodded but did not smile. "I should like to have stayed away longer, but I'm here about the trouble in your house. Your family is distressed, I've heard."

Rath looked away in shame and anger. "It's none of your concern."

"Come now, Rath. We both know it is. Why was no word sent to me?"

Rath faced the younger man proudly. "I wouldn't bring that shame on your house and mine. The wench acted out of my authority and refuses her father's commands."

"The truth, Rath. You thought I wouldn't want to know?"

"Aye. That, too."

"And now she thinks me dead?"

"As we all have."

"Did she tell you it was me?"

"She would not say, but I knew the truth. I knew because she's not the whore she seems. She's not been with another man since that night and she went to you then against my orders. She threw herself upon you when there was to be no such plan. She shamed our —"

"Fetch her to me."

"Nay! She took the part of a trollop and I'll not allow her to follow this course! I know what she's done. She lied to you. She misled you to satisfy her own lust. Ah, I could forgive the lass for that, I knew she loved you. But when I sought to ease our shame, she would not take her betrothed!"

"I threatened her. I commanded her to refuse him."

"What're you saying, lad?"

"Fetch her to me. Now."

Rath stared at John in wonder, finally shaking his head wearily and moving across the room to open the door to the only additional room. He beckoned his daughter out.

Tess had heard the voices but no words. There had been months of quiet murmurings in the other room and more often than not she had sought out the bedroom where the other children slept so that she would not be badgered by her angry father.

She appeared at the door and looked across the dimly lit room to see John. She wore a tattered cover held together by a single string over her full breasts, parting to expose her frayed nightdress bulging with the rounding of her belly. She stared at him in wonder. He seemed to fill the room. Tall of stature and broad shouldered, he was a most imposing figure. He was garbed just as she most often pictured him in her mind, breeches of leather fitting him so snugly that his muscled thighs bulged, a white linen shirt hiding the muscled chest and a leather jerkin accentuating his broadness. He might resemble any townsman but for the sword that was strapped to his waist and the dagger in his belt. He was dressed more for war than for tending crops.

Thinking herself in another dream, her hand rose shakily to her mouth to stifle a cry and she shook her head in confusion. Tears wet her cheeks and a faint smile grew on John's lips as he held his arms open to her. No more invitation was needed. She flew to him and he held her clear of the ground while she threatened to choke off his very life's breath in her embrace.

He set her on her feet and let her study him closely with her eyes and fingers, reassuring herself that he was real. Then he kissed her and she melted to him, her tears moistening his face and salting their kiss. He was most reluctant to release her but there was business to be done with this maid's father. He let her go, but held her close at his side. Before turning to Rath he placed a trusting hand on the small obtrusion in her middle and quietly asked why she had not attempted to reach him with the news.

"I did not know what your manner would be," she replied quietly.

"You worry me, Tess. I had thought to keep the number of heirs under a dozen. What shall we do?" She shook her head slightly and love and relief shone in her eyes. "The child is mine, as you suspect, Mr. Rath. I will take Tess with me now and we will be wed."

"She's a good lass and comely, but she is of simple means. I cannot give my consent."

"Do you find it embarrassing to marry into a noble family, Rath?"

"Neither that. The dishonor is in scheming to do so. My neighbors will share that thinking. I am ashamed of my daughter's plot."

An amused expression came over John's face. He turned to Tess. "Shame on you, Tess. You're after my money and pretended it meant nothing."

She smiled warmly. "Does that mean at long last you have some, sir knight?"

"Enough to see you fed. Above that? Not much."

"Sir John, the lass is promised to another. She disgraces us all with this behavior. Your cause will surely be hurt, for you will not be free to seek a maid with a suitable dowry. I refuse permission to you!"

"Would you have me take her as my mistress? Would your wounded pride suffer less then?"

"You conspire with her," he accused. "She is simple bred and can marry none but yeoman!"

"If one nobly born can be reduced to yeoman, then yeoman can in like be elevated."

"Nay. Kilmore will take her as she is!"

"I say you nay!" John shouted, oblivious to any need to be quiet. "What is done is done and the motive matters little to me now! I'll not sit upon the hill and watch my son raised by a farmer when he is within right to stand at my side! And further, it doesn't meet my mood to think of Tess in another man's arms when naught prevents our marriage but a stubborn old man! Bear the snickers of your neighbors as you will. She will come with me and she will be my lady now! It is done!"

"Father," Tess attempted.

"Why do you this, Tess?" Rath asked bitterly. "Why would you give yourself sinfully to a man you have no earthly right to wed?"

She took a steadying breath and looked beseechingly into her father's eyes. "God was most careful to show me my station when he cast me as a daughter to a simple man, but he was not so careful when letting me fall in love. I'm sorry, Papa."

Rath sighed heavily. "Are you bound to have her, lad?"

"I am."

"And how will you take her?"

"By force." He smiled. "But, God willing, you'll be near enough to watch your grandson grow up."

"There's naught I can do to stay you?"

"Nothing."

"It's not right," he groaned, shaking his head in frustration. He looked between Tess and John and muttered, "But it has a better ring to it than bastard."

"Thank you, Papa." Tess smiled. "I never like to battle you as I have."

"You have my deepest sympathy, lad. There's not a more stubborn lass on the face of this earth."

"I know that well enough," John agreed, giving Tess a light squeeze. "Have you something better to clothe yourself with, cherie? I don't want to take you away in your natural state."

"Shall I bundle my things? They are few."

"Nay, a heavy cloak is all. And hurry."

She went through the door to the bedroom swiftly and John turned again to Rath. Now the warrior was at rest and the lad who had done wrong faced an elder. He shrugged innocently. " 'Twas not in my mind to fall in love with her, Rath. It comes to a great deal more than the child. I was bound to have her in any case. And it's not her fault, Rath. You have to believe that."

"I cannot reason this, John. Was it one night bent on love when there were a few simple words between you? You're no stripling lad to know love at passion's touch. There was no courtship, no involvement . . ." Again came the man's confused head-shaking. John stilled him by placing a hand on his shoulder.

"Rath, had I not been cast from my own home as I was I would not have learned what I have of life and this world. Now at three and thirty I know what manner of lass must stand at my side to bring me honor. She must be strong and proud and determined. She must have a good and natural sense of justice and a compassionate nature. What more needs a man then but enough love to keep him warm, and sons? I knew your Tess to be every measure of a man's desire before my lips touched hers." He laughed low and commented, "She only rushed me a bit. My mind was made." He shrugged, his pride showing. "Never fear, Rath. She is stubborn, but I am more so."

Rath nodded and a faint smile found its way to his lips. "Will you tilt a cup with me, friend, and accept my blessing now?"

"With honor."

When Tess came back to the doorway she stood silently, watching John and her father as they toasted, drank deep, and clasped hands in friendship.

The earl of Bryant had been called away on important business. He made his apologies to his wife and departed. It seemed there was a shipping problem that needed his immediate attention and he wasn't sure but that he might have to travel to Portsmouth to see to it. He had not forgotten his decision. Chelynne was confined to the house. His orders were most specific. She was allowed to travel abroad to the New Exchange and the residences of friends during the daylight hours. No evenings out, no theater, no Whitehall dinners or receptions.

In this case, Chelynne sent for Gordon.

"I'm in need of information, Gordon. It must be sought out by a trustworthy person. I deem that person to be you, if you accept."

"If I'm able to help, madam."

"Quite by accident I found at Welby Manor an old document, the record of marriage that my hus— that the earl signed over six years ago."

"The earl had been married?"

"The true possibility is that the earl may be married still. He has never mentioned any of this to me. I'm certain that my uncle did not know or he would have told me for my own protection. I cannot face him with the question in that case, and I must have the answer."

"And how can I?" Gordon asked.

"I have only the name of the bride and the small town in which they were wed. It will take you back to the country, Gordon, and perhaps to an unpleasant sector. There must be family and friends there. You'll have whatever money you need, of course."

"Is there any other clue?"

"None other, to my knowledge. I can give you no advice, no counsel. Will you try?"

Gordon nodded but paused, looking at his young mistress with distressed eyes. "And if the earl's marriage is valid? If he is married still?"

She winced involuntarily at the suggestion and looked away to cover it. "Then that would mean I am not,'"she answered softly.

When Gordon left her she went directly to her husband's study. She placed an invitation on top of his desk. If he returned from his business in time there was a dinner at Whitehall she was determined to attend. Chelynne was done with mysteries. She was bound for answers.

There was little diversion in the large house. She spent the majority of her time in her rooms with nothing to occupy her. The routine tasks being done all around her had gone unnoticed before and now they unnerved her. Tanya's silence grated on her nerves. Chelynne was impatient and harsh, accusing the quiet girl of purposely remaining mute to aggravate her. She was shrewish, and she knew this, but could not even force herself to be polite.

When the earl returned to his home it was late at night. Chelynne heard him moving through the halls, the clicking of his boots making a sound she could never mistake. She pulled on her wrapper and opened the door to her bedroom. She called to him, stopping him before he entered his own rooms.

He paused and turned to see her. He was well worn, obviously tired from a long ride. She was a little surprised to see him in this condition. She had assumed he was in London with some other woman, a mistress or a wife. Perhaps she was wrong on some counts. Perhaps this once he was truly about business.

"What is it?" he asked impatiently.

"There's a special favor I would like to ask of you. A dinner two days hence at Whitehall. By invitation, of course."

"Do you have an escort?"

"I could arrange it," she replied defensively. "But no one has offered and I haven't asked."

"I'll take you . . . if it's so important to you. Where is the invitation?"

"In your study. On your desk."

"I'll find it, then. Is that all?"

She nodded and started to say something of welcome, but he slipped into his room quickly to avoid any further conversation.

Chad leaned against the closed door in complete exhaustion. His arm pained him now, that sore member having been put too soon to the test. He rubbed the wound absently, thinking of the days past.

He had been called to Hawthorne House directly. There he had found John and Tess. While Tess sat alone in a closed-up portion of the great house, John and Chad rode with a few other men to the baron's estates. That house had been closed up as well, but for the part that housed some of Chad's own guard in the main hall.

The reason was obvious. Shayburn was convinced the affront was personal. The elimination of some of his own men, particularly Captain Alex, made it impossible for him to continue to bleed the villagers. He would now assume either that John Bollering lived and continued to ravage his holdings or that Chad had taken up the fight in his friend's stead. They had come to the point they long ago anticipated. Shayburn was not fooled. Their choices were to lie back and let his suspicions cool or move ahead in force. John was too close to lie back. He offered Chad the option of pulling out to avoid possible recriminations.

The earl pulled out his men and sent them home. While Shayburn occupied his safe lodgings in London the manor house was stripped bare. Most of what they removed had been Bollering possessions before the war. They were not taken from the land but placed in an old cook house, hidden within the manor itself, and scattered about the village. They thought the matter quietly done, when the remaining force belonging to Shayburn returned to find them ravaging the manor. They had to defend themselves, and four were killed before Chad and John and their few supporters could escape.

This would subdue Shayburn. He wouldn't be able to function any longer with his depleted manpower, weapons and supplies. He had little land to bargain with and precious few baubles to barter. He was in a state of complete financial ruin. But . . . he knew his enemy.

Chad returned to London with a traveling companion. He settled Tess with Mistress Connolly and his son. John had family in London but the risk was too great. He wouldn't have Tess threatened now.

Chad fell into his bed, sleep overtaking him immediately. He awoke in the same clothes he had worn, ridden and fought in for days. He rose, bathed, and waited. At noon a message he had been expecting came. He gave some instructions to Bestel and went to his study to await his caller.

It was hard to keep from smiling when Lord Shayburn blew into the room. His face was red and twisted with rage.

"Thank you for seeing me, my lord," Shayburn said carefully.

Chad nodded and leaned back in his chair to wait for the flustered man's request. Shayburn was outdone. "Has your lordship been quite busy? I was told you were called to Portsmouth with some shipping business."

"What is your business, my lord?"

"I don't think I have to tell you why I'm here. I think you already know. Do you truly believe you have me fooled? Now?"

"I'm afraid I don't know what you're talking about."

"Why did you pull your guard from my village? From my home?"

"I thought the town quiet enough and I needed them elsewhere."

"You've withdrawn your support entirely."

"That is the fact."

"The house was stripped," he ground out accusingly.

"The family jewels gone," Chad returned with a smile. Shayburn went livid with rage. Nothing that had been taken from his home had belonged to him or to any member of his family. They were Bollering possessions, taken the same way years ago.

"Robbery is no petty offense," Shayburn threatened.

"As I recall . . . sometimes it is completely ignored."

"You have ruined me!"

"You've had quite a time of it, haven't you?" Chad asked with a smile.

"You're quite certain I'll walk out on it all now, aren't you? You think you have me beaten?"

"At your own game, my lord. I am no longer giving you the opportunity. You will make good your debts or turn your land over to the benefactor I arranged for you now. Whatever I recommend will be heavily considered."

"I've been to the king," Shayburn blustered.

Chad smiled tolerantly, but the news greatly upset him. "I hope you haven't made any foolish accusations, ones you cannot back up."

"You bastard —"

"Now see here, my lord. I can't allow you to use such a disrespectful course with me. I am not so coldhearted as to leave you walking naked in the streets, even though I have no doubt you would do that to another. I could easily relieve you of your burden to your satisfaction. You've lost it already, you know."

"Not yet. I still have claim there."

"Where?"

"The land!" he cried.

"Your debts?"

"Time is all I need —"

"I grant no more time. I propose to collect. You're behind in taxes and tithes and have a great many other collectors standing in line. The dynasty has ended, my lord."

"Your proposition?" Shayburn asked reluctantly.

"Virginia."

"Never!"

"You refuse this solution?"

"England or nothing!"

"You are a fool, Shayburn," Chad said easily. "And a coward. But you've sown the seeds to your own fate again. You have fifteen days to meet your debts. And manage this carefully. Thievery and murder to meet your ends will do you no good now. You are being watched. I give you this warning in hopes you make no attempts that will waste lives or property, because quite honestly, my lord, I would relish seeing you hang for what you have already done."

"What are you going to do?" Shayburn asked a bit wearily.

"The people of that shire have suffered enough, my lord. I will make a recommendation to the king but of course the decision is not mine. I deal simply with facts. My advice is that you take up your old profession or accept the offered property in America."

"What do you suppose His Majesty will think of the way I've been burned out? Do you think he will kindly accept the fact that one of his own nobles slit another's throat, ravaged his lands, and murdered his people only to place that acreage in the hands of a well-known pirate and —"

Shayburn stopped as he noticed Chad was smiling, not at all worried about these accusations. Shayburn wheezed and blustered and Chad simply smiled. At last Chad leaned forward in his chair and placed both hands on the desk, looking into Shayburn's eyes.

"In the event that you can prove any of your accusations I must warn you that there are at least twice as many testimonies implicating you in far worse crimes. As to murder, that protest is ineffectual as no murder was done in your shire. Swords were raised only in defense and those portrayed as dead actually live. You have ruined your own cause listening to rumors that Sir John is a pirate when in fact he is a knight of the realm with His Majesty's support and permission in a privateering venture. I suggest you leave quietly, my lord. It is perhaps the only way you will do so alive."

"I demand to know what card you hold!"

"I'm sorry. I've said all I am prepared to say."

"You'll pay for this, Bryant! This is war!"

Chad smiled. "I have paid for this, Shayburn. Many times over. If this is indeed war, it will be the shortest on record."

Shayburn's fury melted into fear. He had so many illegal dealings he didn't know which to fear for most. Financing Dutch troops and vessels? Thievery? Bribing officials? Scanting the tax? The old battle with Bollering?

He slammed his hat on his head and left the earl. Smiling at the quick departure, Chad leaned back in his chair. Slowly the smile faded. He was weary. Tired. He wished only for peace.

SIXTEEN

T WHITEHALL THERE IS CEREMONY and beauty. Artfully garbed gentlemen posture over the hands of exquisitely dressed women. Tables heavily burdened with scrumptious and unusual foods artistically prepared fill the rooms. Large ice sculptures decorate the tables; the orchestra stands ready to play.

But it is an illusion. As one presses one's way into this noble throng the senses immediately reveal the falseness of this beauty. The stench of unwashed bodies is almost overpowering. Courtly manners are contradicted by the sight of a gentleman crossing the room to relieve himself on the wall. Ice sculptures melt to run onto the floor with leftover bits of food and spilled wine. Rodents creep dangerously close to steal a morsel. The people who stand chatting in the corners are usually plotting some way to ruin an associate or seal for themselves a better position at someone else's expense.

Louise de Keroualle was firmly established as the king's favorite mistress. She was surrounded by her own party of well-wishers, her throng of supporters, those who zealously sought her good favors to improve their status. She, however, sat in a pout tonight. The king's other mistress, an actress from the theater, was about her usual mischief, relishing doing things that would embarrass Louise.

Chelynne found her former admirers a little less eager and the ladies a little more responsive. She found a circle of women to sit with and noticed her husband seeking out the king.

Chad stood near Charles, but not too near. Chad didn't like the close contact and hated speaking to anyone who forced his presence closer and closer during the conversation.

"I understand congratulations are in order, my lord," Charles said without looking at him.

"I shouldn't think so, sire," Chad returned somewhat sullenly.

"Nasty business, this," Charles commented with some humor in his voice. "Wears a man out to have a beautiful wife, trying to keep the men out from under her skirts all the time."

Chad grunted his reply, completely unintelligible to Charles. But the king laughed as if he had been let in on some great private joke. Chad looked toward him in confusion and for the first time since their conversation began they met eyes. Amused brown with suspicious brows stared into younger, lighter, gray stones. Chad was seldom at a disadvantage. For his sovereign he was obligated to be disadvantaged. "I prefer my friends handle their problems less dramatically, Bryant. I thought we agreed on that and other things."

"Aye, sire."

"Your battlefield reputation is well known so not many are surprised. But then few have known you as I have. Indeed, you're a mystery to many."

Chad smiled. "And not you, sire?"

"Not I," he returned simply. "But then I have another advantage. I knew Sir John as well as yourself."

"And?"

"And . . . I think it mightily out of character."

"I'd be pleased to make an explanation to Your Majesty —"

"No, I won't hear it. I'm playing at observer, if you will. For now, that is. I'll hear your story when you have a conclusion to it."

"I'm honored, sire."

"Don't be. I am not a generous man, actually. That's a rumor that seems to have gotten out since my habit of gifting women with comforting baubles to ensure their rent. It does not necessarily apply in other places. My reason for leaving you to your business is more practical and selfish. I believe you understand well enough now without need of further compliments to you."

"I will do my best to serve your interests, sire. You can be assured."

"Yes, you will. And I am assured. Do you know why?" Chad did not attempt a reply, for he knew Charles was intent on delivering a little speech without any assistance. "I am assured because if you do not serve my best interests you will be extremely sorry. Thus far we have been compatible because you've managed to better yourself and your king simultaneously. Otherwise . . . will be dealt with otherwise."

"Thank you, sire. I'll heed your words."

"Do you have any idea why I trust you, Bryant?"

"Because I have never betrayed you, sire?"

"That is idle romance. When do you suppose the first betrayal comes, Bryant? The reason is this: already you have more than you want or need. You are an adventurer and warrior first. You're hatefully inept at politics. You see, it's your basic inadequacy that brings my trust." Charles laughed heartily at his own wit. Chad smiled. How could one feel the sting of insult delivered so honestly and appropriately? Charles clamped a hand down on his shoulder and then walked away mumbling something Chad couldn't hear.

Charles failed to mention the other advantages Chad had. He had never been very affluent or influential and therefore never slandered before now. That was one way to measure a person's importance at court. Only the most important were slandered. That Bryant was suddenly taken notice of and an attempt made to ruin his name would only bring skepticism to an already skeptical king. Charles was not a fool.

Chelynne was talking to an older woman whom Chad had never met before. When he approached her she looked up at him and bestowed on him a soft, wifely smile. He fondly touched her shoulder. Then a familiar woman sauntered over to where Chad stood behind his wife's chair and casually looped her arm through his. Chelynne's eyes narrowed and she looked away, disregarding them both and giving her complete attention to the baroness to whom she spoke.

"The countess seems out of sorts this eve, my lord," Gwen remarked.

"She's had her problems," Chad grunted, wishing with all his heart that Gwen would go away. Apparently all of his earlier warnings meant nothing to her, for once again she arranged herself close to him in a most familiar fashion. And again for the benefit of his wife and companions. "Have you anything to tell me?"

"He's not yet returned to London," she stalled. "Black does her coloring ill," she observed of Chelynne.

"She wears it respectfully, my lady," he returned. "And luckily is not bound to it for life." Gwen felt the gibe. It was painfully clear to her that until she could procure for herself another husband she would be bound to her mourning gowns.

"She wears it for her uncle, then," Gwen said saucily. "I thought she mourned another."

Chad's face darkened considerably. "You've a mighty poor way of showing your friendship, Gwen. I thought you wished nothing but goodwill between us."

"Of a certain, my lord. I offer you my sympathy, that is all." She turned her seductive green eyes up to him and said softly, "I know the pain of losing someone you love to another."

"Truly? Then I offer my sympathy to you, madam. I do not."

Gwen stammered as if she would argue the point, accuse Chelynne rather loudly of taking a lover in the form of Chad's own friend. In her confusion she could say nothing. Before she untangled her tongue for a quick response she was aware of a very important presence and held silent.

"You're looking lovely this evening, madam," Charles said, addressing Chelynne with a most personal smile. Chelynne dazzled him with one of her own; warm, sincere and lovely. One that had not been bestowed on Chad for some time. The earl felt a quick twinge of jealousy and as quickly ignored it, telling himself it mattered as little as anything.

"I'm honored that you would even notice me, sire," Chelynne replied.

"Notice you? Would I notice a rose garden in full bloom at Christmastide?" He laughed lightly and took her hand, helping her to rise and stroll with him across the room. All around them heads went together, whispering ensued, judgments were passed. They chatted at a distance from eager ears, he laughing at some comment she made and she smiling at his amusement.

"You're lacking in attention tonight, madam," the king said.

"Think you so? I would say I've the most influential attention in the room."

"You flatter me," he said with a bow.

"You seem to have problems of your own," she commented, indicating the pouting Louise with her eyes. "She appears a trifle sullen."

He raised a brow and smiled. "A common affliction among beautiful women. Sulking. They keep forgetting it gains them nothing."

"She'll adjust, given time."

"Time is about all I have to give," he laughed. It was well known that the king's financial affairs were in a continuously horrid state.

"The pity is the ennui you shall both suffer from her pout," Chelynne dared. "Perhaps you can liven her spirits."

"I leave women to their broken hearts. Most often they are conjured up for the purpose of having their spirits expensively livened." He laughed at himself and she joined him. Then she made her greatest attempt, acting so well that Charles was unaware of her fluttering heart and damp hands.

"So, you've no plans?"

He raised a quizzical brow. "Methinks you lead me on, madam."

"Never that, sire," she said, batting her lashes as coquettishly as she could.

"You've been quite halted in your own diversion, it would seem."

Guessing he spoke of the duel, she looked away for a moment. It still upset her greatly to think of it. But following through as she planned, she smiled into his amused black eyes and replied, "I think not."

"What shall you do?"

"Keep my company to those who would go unchallenged."

"Have you the means?"

"When I set my mind to it."

"Tonight?"

"It would be no problem. Though late, I fear."

"The back stairs. Chiffinch will guide you." He laughed easily, delighted with himself and her. He had long admired her loveliness, desired her. He cast a glance to her husband, still standing with Lady Graystone. He shrugged. "I hadn't thought to put horns on Bryant," he murmured. "But any man with so lovely a wife must better learn to protect his interests."

"My thoughts exactly, sire," she returned, but there was no humor in her voice. She was gravely serious.

There were puppets and acrobats, dancing and gambling. Then came the favorite diversion, when the party began to dissipate and all the elite personages began rushing off to their different assignations. The countess of Bryant had always retired to her home at this time of the evening, but tonight she had an appointment — and her appointment was with the king.

Chelynne went home with her husband. They parted at the top of the stairs and each went off into private quarters. She was feeling shameful about this deception, however sure she was she must go through with it. She let the feeling of guilt swell within her, and then it vanished quickly when she heard his bedroom door close. She opened her door just a crack to see what she expected to see. He was leaving the house.

Her women were dismissed. She did not wish to be aided in disrobing and wished no company in her bedding. She wanted to be alone and not to see a servant's face before dawn. Stella was hurt. It showed in the old eyes and Chelynne touched her arm, halting her departure.

"I'm sorry," she murmured. "I've been a burden to you."

"I worry with your manner," Stella confessed, troubled.

"Stella . . ." she started, unsure. "Stella, you were closer than any to my mother. Did she . . . was she . . . was there ever anyone else for her? Other than my father?"

"My lady Madelynne? Lord, mum, she was the finest, sweetest . . ."

Stella went on but Chelynne did not hear. This was all routine. This praising of Madelynne would never alter or change, not even if Chelynne were desperate. Even if Stella knew more she would not divulge it.

"What is it, sweetheart?" Stella asked with genuine concern.

"It would break your heart," she mumbled.

"What, mum?"

"Oh, it's nothing, dear." Chelynne braved a smile. "But that I'm tired and sore and need my bed. And some time alone. You go on now, and I'll see you in the morning."

So she wasn't allowed to leave the house? There was no command more influential than a few coins. These, placed in the hand of the steward, opened the door quite easily. Gordon, disapprovingly, drove the coach. This time, however, she was well guarded and supposedly secret. She sought out trustworthy footmen who would not speak loosely of her outing and they obliged her to the tune of twenty pounds. She entered Whitehall this night through a door she had never used before. She was greeted almost instantly by Chiffinch. He did not speak to her but simply handed her a candle to light herself up.

What a long way she had come, she thought wearily as she climbed the dark stair. From a careless youth whose greatest problem was what time to ride, to this: conspiring and spying, fighting off bandits with her own force of arms and meeting the king for what he thought would be an entertaining toss with a new mistress. She was at a loss. She wished now that she had paid closer attention to the women who boasted infidelities similar to this.

She found herself in a small anteroom adjacent to the king's apartments. She was alone. There was no sound, no voices coming from any side of her. She tried a door and walked through a gallery to yet another door. She found herself eventually in the king's bedchamber, again alone. She stood in wonder for a moment and then Charles startled her by speaking.

"There you are. I would have come for you."

For lack of an alternative she fell into a deep curtsy and thought at once how foolish she must look. She had come to go to bed with the king and here she was acting as though she were being presented at court. As she raised herself she saw the mirror of her thoughts in his eyes. Gad, how stupid.

"I fear I risk punishment in coming to you in this way, sire," she said softly.

"The earl?" He shrugged. "Perhaps you should have given it more consideration before making your decision."

He did not seem very disturbed and she knew it would be best to state her business quickly. He sat on the edge of the bed and began to peel an orange. He was naked of all adornments and wore only shirt and breeches, no shoes or burdensome robes to hamper a quick undressing.

"The anger may be yours, sire."

"I doubt that, dear. Do you fear displeasing the king?"

She gulped hard. "If you would be so kind, there's a matter on which I seek counsel."

He laughed richly. "You needn't have gone to such lengths, madam. You would certainly have been granted an audience."

Drawing one step closer she tried again. "I thought to see you privately, not in the company of your ministers."

"I seldom have a private moment," he advised her. "And I seldom enjoy a woman freely." Again came the laughter and head-shaking as if in amused exasperation. Then looking at her and raising a quizzical brow he said in a low seductive voice, "Most wait until I'm in a more pliable position, but go ahead."

She flushed scarlet, momentarily unable to speak.

"Well, madam, let's have done with the baiting and get on to more enjoyable matters." He stood and began to undo the buttons on his shirt.

"Might I beg your discretion, sire?"

"You'd have more chance getting that than anything else," he laughed, finding the last button and shedding the shirt.

"It's about my mother, sire," she said quickly. "I had the chance to come upon a letter she had written while she was round with me and near her lying-in. She —" Chelynne stopped and stared as he pulled off one stocking. Her voice went on at an urgent pace. "She indicated strongly that I was not my father's own and that —" Off came the other stocking and he stood. "That the man from whose loins I did come would not be challenged by my legal —" His hands were on the fastenings that held up his breeches, and in equal parts fear and surprise she shouted, "Will you stop that?"

Charles did stop. At once. He stared at her in wonder. That she would scream at him, this mild-mannered flower. "Oh, dear God," she groaned. "Forgive me, Your Majesty. Please . . ."

"A letter, you say?"

"A letter," she murmured. "Sire, it's possible that I am your own."

"Christ," he muttered, sitting hard upon the bed. He grabbed up his shirt, shrugging immediately into it.

"Do you remember, sire?" she asked timidly.

"What would it matter," he said angrily, waving his arm at her. "You've a name right enough. You've a marriage of quality. Can you ever be harmed above a little gossip?"

She hung her head, ashamed now at having thrown this up to him as she had. "I couldn't live with the uncertainty, sire. That is all."

"I'm curious. What is it you want?"

Her head shot up and she smiled at him. She did love him, that had been decided long ago. From the first time she met him she had found him soothing to be near, chivalrous and gentle. She had never been afraid of him; self-conscious and nervous in his presence, but never afraid. "Good Lord, sire! How could I want for anything you could give me? I declare the earl is rich enough. I'll warrant he's richer than —" She stopped and covered her mouth. But Charles laughed.

"I warrant he's got twice my wealth. He's scattered it well enough."

"I've never known my parents, sire. They've been dead a long time."

"I remember them. I seldom forget anything of any importance."

"And you remember her?" she asked, holding her breath in anticipation.

"I do."

"And . . ."

"And . . ." He took a deep breath and looked at her. "I cannot deny the possibility."

She digested that, slowly and with her eyes closed. She had been prepared for that answer and still it struck her hard. Finally she murmured her thanks.

"Things are not often as they seem, madam. There could have been ten others you've never heard of." Her eyes shot up to where he stood and she burned with sudden anger though she dared not show it. "I'm afraid the real truth is buried with your mother. I won't give you airs where there are none. A great many women have passed where your mother did. And I am not the lone rake in all Christendom, my dear. Mistresses of mine have had their own indiscretions, thinking I've never been wiser. The only reason they carry on is certainly because I've never been the knave to chastise them." And then he muttered, "And because I seldom give a blessed damn."

"And would you know of any other possibility?" she asked, her voice barely above a whisper.

He moved nearer and looked into her pretty brown eyes. For a moment he was struck by her beauty and a resemblance. In the eyes, the fine arch of her brow, she resembled a daughter of his by Barbara Palmer. "No, darling, I know of none other. But you must be aware of the possibility. And you must tell me what you hope to gain."

"Nothing but the truth, sire. It would suit me best to have a secret."

"There are no secrets here," he informed her. "What they do not know they will guess. Whatever my intentions were, they have changed because of this development."

"Probability," she corrected him.

"What they do not guess they will invent. All will think we've shared a bed." He fastened the last button on his shirt and grumbled. "Secrets fascinate me . . . because they are so rare."

She shrugged. "It's of no matter to me, whatever is said."

"Women are the greatest lovers of a slander. I hope it does not burn you badly."

"Not I," she said simply.

"As I remember, she was much as you are now. Small and slender, lovely. A quiet woman." He laughed and added, "Now that is rare. She was discreet and modest. I was hardly aware of her, though I was guilty even then of picking out a lovely woman and admiring her openly. I did the same when you first arrived at court." He laughed again, looking her over roguishly. "This is a new twist, however." Chelynne's eyes widened somewhat but he quickly shook his head. "My sins are many but I am not guilty of that horror. Thank God, that won't be among my many counts on the Judgment."

She smiled her relief. "Thank you, sire. You've been most patient."

"Do you know the wrath of a king who's been played for a fool?"

"I've no cause to worry over that, sire."

"And what of Bryant? What will you tell him?"

"I won't tell him. Neither will he ask."

"Oh, I think he will at least ask. I understand him to be a jealous man."

"If that is true, of what I couldn't say. I've —" She stopped, not wishing to divulge too much personal information. Whatever their problem, she didn't want to make things more difficult for either of them than they already were. "He won't be interested, Your Majesty."

"I would have thought he was in love with you."

"I promise you, this once you were wrong."

"That, madam, is not new. This, I think, is best left alone from now. Do you agree?"

She smiled warmly. "My wishes as well."

Charles continued to study her. She had been at Whitehall long enough now to know that he never forgot one of his own. She was fresh and lovely and he felt, strangely, a fatherly pride. But that was perhaps the strangest thing about Charles. He was never too mortified to accept one of his own children, claim them through subtle acknowledgment, shower his attentions on them. He loved children, his own doubly so.

"You're fortunate, I think, that your mother never insisted you were mine. There's nothing pretty about an acknowledged bastard, however I take care of them."

"But they're proud, sire, to be yours."

He smiled at her innocence. He wondered that often. Proud? Hardly proud but certainly excused in lieu of a king's wrath and thought and spoken of with care. A few scattered titles, pensions that could be revoked or ignored with his passing, the arrangement of proper marriages, that was all he could do. He would have much preferred legitimate children, but life was not so kind.

"Am I the bearer of good news?" he asked.

"You've put to rest a grave uncertainty, sire. Good news? I'm not sure. Forgive me, sire, but I'm not —"

He hushed her, waving a hand. He understood that perfectly. However he personally chose the course for his own life, he was a man to greatly respect some moral conviction. "Then we'll live with this gracefully and if possible, quietly."

"There is one thing, sire," she attempted softly.

His brows lifted as he awaited a request, wondering wearily if there was so much difference between women after all.

"We could be friends."

"There are many who would like to befriend me, princess."

"I'm certain of that. More than you prefer, no doubt."

He laughed, his happy and amused laugh. This had been the only way she could determine his mood, the tone and scale of his mirth. So she hadn't greatly angered him. But then she had never known him to be greatly angered.

"Your friendship would be a welcome change, madam. Good night."

The next time she saw Charles he was gracious and attentive. Nearly a week had passed since she made her visit to his bedchamber. She was no longer uncertain and nervous in his presence. She believed they shared a very important bond and it gave her pleasure and confidence. But Charles, true to his manner, never openly admitted what she was to him.

At a crowded affair at the palace Chad blended into the crowd after the entertainment was over. He had moved in the direction of the gambling and Chelynne was left to receive some attention from the duke of Monmouth. He playfully courted her, and having come to know something of his character, she guessed he wouldn't mind a scene with the earl. Indeed, he might welcome it. He was a mischievous man, already accused of multiple crimes, murder among them. But his attentions to her had not been long cast when the king and York sauntered over to them.

"You've a certain determination where this young woman is concerned," Charles told him.

James smiled impishly and returned, "It's most difficult not to, sire."

"Come along, my lord, and allow me some moments of your time," Charles invited.

Chelynne was left in the hands of the king's brother, who tried to strike up idle conversation with her. She couldn't keep her mind on what York was saying because the king had taken his son only a short distance away and stood talking to him. Their talk was brief and in a moment Charles was back and young James had gone away to prey on some other tender heart. And York, discreetly, took his leave and the two stood alone. Charles looked down at the countess of Bryant with a twinkle in his eye.

"You didn't tell him, sire?" she asked nervously.

"No, but what I did do might sit worse with you." He grinned.

"Lord, I don't think I want to know," she said with a gulp. Charles smiled lazily and she felt the crimson flowing to her face, brightening her color and giving her away.

"I didn't say I had. I simply said I had a mind to."

"It shouldn't much matter," she said, suddenly at ease, laughing a little. "It's been decided. Just look around us."

Charles didn't even bother to look around. He knew what he would see if he did. He knew he couldn't carry on the simplest conversation without the rumors deciding his circumstance, the truth to it being the least important thing. "I imagine you'll be counted among that number," he said good-naturedly. The countess laughed a little, accepting her assignment with equal good grace. "I've heard myself to have had women the numbers of which would make me a champion. Do you start to see the disadvantage of being the king's friend?"

Chelynne stood on tiptoe to look all around her. Finally she spotted Chad, a great distance from them, and their eyes met. He was watching her, closely. From what seemed miles across that grand room she could see the hard flint of his eyes. She lowered herself back onto her heels and looked up at the king. She smiled sweetly. "Indeed not, Your Majesty. Thus far there has been nothing but advantage."

SEVENTEEN

OW LONG had the weather been damp and dreary, Chelynne wondered. The beauty of summer, the luscious green was so far behind her she could scarcely remember it now. She smoothed the green velvet of her gown over her lap dreamily. She remembered when this one had been made and she thought it the exact color of the lawns at Welby Manor. Now, with her mood as dull and gray and damp as London, she simply couldn't believe England was that green in summer.

Chelynne confided to Stella that the king had confirmed her suspicions and confessed there was a possibility she was his own offspring. Stella, loyal to the end, swore it was not so. She wept and pleaded with her young ward to disregard this as slander. The outburst went on for a few days with Stella quieting finally but never giving in. She was steadfast. Madelynne was not in love with the king.

"It was never my purpose to decry Mother's virtue," Chelynne told Stella. "I could never lay blame to her for loving one such as he."

"But 'tis not so!" she insisted.

"Nonetheless, he's admitted this. And it's done. And if you did not know it is because my mother was discreet. Let's give her praise for that much and forget the thing."

But the inevitable damage was done. She was marked as being heatedly pursued by the king and probably already a conquest of his. Chelynne didn't care because it was useless to care. And the greatest insult came from the effect it had on her husband. She remembered the first indication he gave that he'd heard the gossip.

Chelynne wasn't sure if he intentionally brought it up or not, for it did seem coincidental to her at the time. They were on their way to a dinner and she was putting forth her greatest effort to be gay.

"You seem to be adjusting to London with more ease, madam. Have you perhaps found something here to bring you pleasure at long last?"

"I confess I find nothing much pleasurable about London, my lord. It might be only that I find no more energy to fight these ways. I'm making the best of it."

"I thought you would, given time."

"Or trouble."

"Or that. But nonetheless it pleases me to see that something makes you happy. Since it couldn't be me."

"Oh, my lord, whyever would you say that?" she returned saucily. "Why, what woman wouldn't be proud to have a husband so handsome and rich? I'm sure I am the envy of all the ladies at court. They would assume I have your affection as well as your name. Wouldn't they laugh to know they have more of you than I?"

"I have been refused, remember that, madam. Now you finally sound like a lady of the court."

He looked away from her and she interpreted this as disgust. She wanted to hurt him as deeply as he hurt her. And she hated herself for feeling hurt, for even being affected by him at this late date.

"And you should be well pleased, my lord. Is this not what you have wanted of me? To be like the rest of them?"

"Regardless of what I wanted of you, my dear, you chose your own fate. You can decide your own destiny. I have nothing to do with that. You cannot blame me for everything and you certainly can't blame me for gossip."

That was when she knew that he had heard the rumors. She jumped at her chance. "Have you been waiting for me to do that, too? Yield to temptation? Take a lover?"

He was not surprised. "Is that what you have done?" he asked with a raised brow and an amused expression.

"And if I have?" she returned, hoping for something akin to emotion on his part. Jealousy and anger would please her. Anything would do, as long as it was not that heartbreaking indifference.

"What could I possibly do about it? Seal you away? You've proven that you know the way to open my doors. The next alternative is to lock you in your rooms and stand guard myself. At least you are no longer so careless with your life."

Unexpectedly she started to laugh. Why in the world was he still concerned about her life? Would it embarrass him to have her killed as a result of her own foolishness? "My willingness to bear your children was long ago rebuked, my lord. What would you have of me now? Ever willing and eager at your call?" He threw her a murderous look that even a few months ago would have frozen her but now only goaded her into more taunting. "Tell me, my lord, would you take the king's bastard under your roof and give it a name?"

Shocked, he leaned forward. "Are you with child, Chelynne?" he asked in a stunned whisper.

Tears stung her eyes. She hadn't counted on her own words hurting her as they did. When she had first determined so long ago that she loved her husband helplessly, the thought of bearing him a child filled her with joy. Now the thought brought sadness, for she believed it impossible. The purpose a woman was specifically designed for was not possible for her.

"No," she replied weakly. "No, I am not so fortunate."

But he was serious. "You want a child so badly?"

"I wanted a child once," she said defensively. "I wanted a marriage and in that, children. I had a great many private ambitions for myself, sir, much as that might surprise you. And none of those dreams of mine concerned the court or lovers or any of your wealth!"

"All lost now, Chelynne? Are there no more dreams?"

"All lost, my lord. I thought I explained that I've reconciled myself to this."

"Chelynne," he said seriously. "Chelynne, listen to me. You must take care. You must not do anything in desperation you may later regret. Many times things seem hopeless, but you're very young and there are years ahead of you. An impulsive action now may result in years of doubt and regret. There are methods, madam, for avoiding more serious complications. You might employ some of them."

Her eyes were wide with disbelief. In duty he could be tender, even compassionate. It was his obligation to care for her if he could, and now it seemed he was advising her to take care in her affairs. He was the most profound mystery in life.

"Are you suggesting, my lord, that I take care not to get us one of the king's bastards to raise?"

"Chelynne," he sighed. "I am trying to understand you. Give me credit for that, at least. I am advising you to carefully think on what you involve yourself in lest it reach a point where I cannot help you out of it even if you want me to. However insurmountable your problems seem now, there may yet be a course to dealing with them."

"You have little reason to worry, my lord. I shan't further complicate your life. I am not sharing a bed with the king, but I do not defend myself to you. Think what you will."

He had no comment on that. He didn't say he believed her and he didn't say he thought she lied. If he was prepared to test her virtue, she was not prepared to yield the opportunity. They did not discuss it again.

Chelynne received a message from Lady Graystone. Gwen wished to visit. Chelynne couldn't imagine why this woman would wish to call on her and she wasn't wily enough to plan out her actions very well. She was prepared for more trouble from Gwen but little else. Chelynne was learning, but she wasn't learned. The ways of scheming and weaving webs of intrigue still mystified her and dealing with scandalous behavior didn't come naturally.

"Lord, my lady, but you're looking fit as ever," the baroness greeted Chelynne when she arrived. "But I must confess I expected to find you in a fit of some kind. You've been about so little."

"I'm more content to stay at home, madam," Chelynne replied.

"And of course I've seen Cha— His Lordship has been about, that is. He promised he would give you my best."

"I thank you for thinking of me."

"Why, madam, you've been much in everyone's thoughts these days. As a matter of fact, you're all the talk. I thought to warn you of rumors lest you're caught unaware —"

"That is no longer possible, madam. I am completely aware."

Gwen chuckled contentedly. "It is not necessary to prepare you, madam; I'm glad of that. Louise is more refined than most, but —"

"You've seen a great many pass through Whitehall, haven't you Gwen?" Chelynne asked in a quiet voice. Truthfully, however she disliked Gwen, she pitied her somewhat. Her lust for power was so obvious and her failure to achieve greatness rather pitiful. She was lovely and accessible. There was no doubt that she would have shared Charles's bed just as many others had, but the lack of a long-lasting position branded her as unsuccessful.

"There have been a few," Gwen answered in an unenthusiastic voice. For a brief instant these two women communicated. Each seemed to know the other's thoughts. But it passed swiftly.

"Well, this will no doubt disappoint you, madam, but if I've caught the king's eye, that is all. I haven't the nerve to make trouble there."

"Trouble," she laughed. "You jest! What trouble could come from being favored by the king?"

"With a husband like mine?" Chelynne countered, knowing how wickedly she lied.

Gwen's eyes were bright with glee. "What harm could he possibly do the king? I know it's thought all the mode to have a man killed over you, but truly, my lady, do you think Chadwick the fool to show his wrath to the king?"

"Certainly not, madam. I believe his wrath would be all for me. I assure you, I value my life more than that."

Gwen gasped. "Do you mean he's threatened you?"

Chelynne sighed. That would be the next thing. Once the all-important position of being worthy of gossip is achieved, every possible slip of the tongue is exaggerated until worn out. "As I told you, madam, he hasn't had the cause. And it is not in Chad's character to threaten. He is a man of action."

Gwen relaxed in disappointment. All the excitement was gone from this conversation. "Well, that isn't the reason I've come. Bear with me, madam, for this is most difficult." Gwen dropped her gaze and took a breath. She looked up to Chelynne again and there was sincerity in her gaze. "I beg your forgiveness for my behavior and would like us to be friends, if it is still possible."

"Whatever do you mean? Have I done something amiss? I hadn't purposely led you to think friendship impossible between us, my lady."

"I believe you've seen through me from the first. I've been quite jealous of you. I honestly don't know what Chad might have told you of me but the truth is, there was a time when we were very close. We've known each other since childhood . . . for a very long time."

Chelynne couldn't believe Gwen would face her this way, this honestly. She couldn't guess the purpose, but it made her very uncomfortable. "Here now, madam," Chelynne said nervously. Gwen actually had tears in her eyes and Chelynne fished for her own handkerchief. "Surely there's no cause to turn to tears. You needn't confess to me. What is done is done."

"I've never been very wise in loving." Gwen sighed dejectedly. "Truly, I thought he had some love for me or I never would have —" her voice broke and she tried to recover herself. "When he told me he could not marry me I thought to hide my shame in marrying Lord Graystone quickly. But it wasn't long before I lost him, too."

"Madam, please, do not weep so. It is best forgotten now; you needn't tell me so much."

Gwen dried her eyes on the lacy piece and behind it she scowled. This little package was certainly not very bright. She went on with her story as convincingly as she could. "When he was leaving me he explained that he couldn't marry me, under any circumstances. Had Lord Graystone not begged for my hand soon after, I don't know what I would have done."

"Oh, dear heaven," Chelynne gasped. "Was there a child?"

"No, there was no child!" Gwen snapped, forgetting herself in mounting impatience. God, but this wench was stupid. If her information was correct Chelynne had the record of Chad's marriage and was totally unsure of his circumstance. "But I suppose that is the reason for my shock and hurt when he took you as his wife without a word of explanation to me. I reacted impulsively and regret it now. I thought he had lied to me and simply couldn't understand. It was most difficult for me. I thought . . . he . . . cared . . . for . . . me." She blew her nose loudly into the rag.

Chelynne sat upright, thinking quite clearly now. "There, madam, dry your eyes. Did he say why he couldn't marry you?"

"Oh, yes, of course." She sniffled back her tears and looked sympathetically at Chelynne. "It was unfair of me to treat you so. I never thought of your misery, I thought only of myself. Please say you'll forgive me."

"Of course, of course. What did he tell you?"

"That he was married. I thought you knew."

"Well," Chelynne said uncertainly, not knowing how to get more information without looking like a complete fool. "He was."

"Oh dear." Gwen straightened as if in shock. "What've I done? Oh, I'm sorry. I meant only to set it aright."

"Madam, what troubles you? What *have* you done?"

"I never intended to make more trouble," she said, rising. "Forgive me. I've said too much. I must be going."

"No, madam, not now. Pray sit and let me determine the trouble."

Gwen sat wearily, a beautifully guilty frown creasing her brow. She had Chelynne's complete interest. "I'm so sorry," she murmured. "I've used poor judgment again. I cannot say more."

"And if you do not explain yourself I shall have to make the problem my concern. That could be a great deal more unpleasant, don't you agree?"

"I cannot forgive myself for this. He'll have my head!"

"Hush," Chelynne commanded sternly. "I won't tell him, I swear. Out with it, madam."

"He said his wife was dead."

"And you know otherwise?"

Gwen gulped, starting to speak and then clamping her mouth shut and turning pleading eyes to Chelynne. "My lady, I've no protector but what servants are still installed. He could have me killed and no one would be the wiser."

"Nonsense. I've given you my word I won't betray you."

"It was just a foolish coincidence, you see, but I happened to lay eyes on his wife. When he wed the girl it was all the talk, his father's anger and Chad's leaving his home. Then the rumor was about that she was dead and he was forgiven by his father and the estate and title would be his. But I've seen her! In London yet! Oh, madam, he'll have me soundly beaten for this!"

"Where?" Chelynne asked impatiently.

"At the 'Change. I wasn't sure, but I followed her. She is quite pregnant. That's my curse, I simply can't leave a thing like that lie without knowing the truth to it. I talked to her. She told me her husband is a merchant who travels often to France."

"And you're sure it is she?"

"Certain. It is Anne. If there was any doubt it was satisfied when I saw the boy. He is the image of Chad."

"His son?"

"Of course you knew about his son," Gwen said innocently. "Why, even I knew of his son. He was being raised in the country since the earl would not acknowledge him."

"Of course," Chelynne lied, as if she were well aware. She had a sick feeling in the pit of her stomach that grew. She didn't see Gwen's superior smile for she couldn't raise her eyes from the lowered gaze she held.

"There is always the possibility that the marriage was annulled, or perhaps there was divorce. There's a great deal of that now . . ."

Chelynne did not reply. With a child so obviously Chad's there would be no annulment and divorce was no simple matter. "Would you be willing to show me where the woman stays?" she asked.

"I couldn't! Oh, madam, it wouldn't do any good to go there! I've caused trouble enough. I couldn't do that, too!"

"Now that you've done this much, my lady, you'll have to see this through."

"Think carefully, madam," Gwen advised. "If he sought to have this secret and you found him out . . . I'm frightened for you, madam. I wouldn't be able to live with myself if you were harmed because of something I —"

Chelynne's eyes narrowed and she rose. "That's very kind of you, my lady. Have you your coach?"

"If you insist," Gwen murmured with an edge of fear in her voice. "But I pray you remember you promised not to betray me to him. Lord, I'm more afraid of that man than —"

"Come along," Chelynne said crisply, already moving toward the door. With an air of command and a great deal of impatience she had someone fetch her wrap and vizard and gloves. Gwen bristled slightly at the haughtiness of this young countess, but her face relaxed into a sly smile as she thought of the eagerness with which Chelynne had lapped up this story.

There was little argument over door opening now, since Chelynne had learned the price and promised the reward. She was freed quite easily and never considered her husband's anger.

Chelynne was quick to notice that the baroness did not travel today with her usual pomp. The coach was not flashy, there were no jeweled horses and it was lacking in familiar markings. Chelynne said nothing and let the driver help her in.

Gwen, afraid of losing Chelynne's credence, wept believably throughout the ride, begging Chelynne to reconsider and not make this further investigation. Finally, having heard enough, Chelynne bit out testily, "Will you please get a hold on yourself! It's not your husband who's married!"

Gwen stiffened behind the now saturated rag, gleaming within in satisfaction. She called to the driver to halt at the appropriate place and pointed the residence out to Chelynne. "It's that house down the street. And I see something far worse."

Nothing more needed to be said. Chelynne had already seen it.

It was an unobtrusive hell cart, waiting. It could be there for any purpose, but it prevented Chelynne from going to the house and inspecting and questioning the occupants.

"Has she servants, madam?" Chelynne asked.

"Few," was the reply.

"If it does not displease you, we will wait," Chelynne said softly.

Nothing could have pleased the baroness more. This was far better than she had hoped for. She had seen Chad enter and leave that house several times, but there was no schedule to his comings and goings. It seemed that he visited whenever time allowed him freedom from his business at the wharves or Whitehall. It was likely he was there now.

"Alms, alms . . ." came a whining voice from without.

"Begone, you impudent scum," Gwen screeched. The poor were completely unabashed at the sight of a coach bearing two fine ladies. They gawked within and bawled and begged. "Whip a few, Ralston," Gwen commanded. "Get them away."

To Chelynne's horror the driver stood and raised a whip. She gasped, appalled at Gwen's instantaneous cruelty. But it went no further, those good peasants never doubting the intent. They moved quickly away. Chelynne grimaced in disgust.

Neither spoke during the lengthy wait. Finally the door opened and Chelynne caught her breath in anticipation. Chad stepped out of the house, hat in hand, and a youngster and a pregnant woman joined him in the street. The boy stood politely beside them as they exchanged a few words. Even at this great distance Chelynne sensed the strong resemblance between father and son. The boy was dark haired and had a large frame. The child looked to be closer to ten years than six.

Chad slipped an arm around the woman's waist. Chelynne's eyes were caught on the rounding belly and the affection in Chad's embrace. She looked so young, so healthy and vibrant. Yet she must be at least in her early twenties to have been married nearly seven years.

Chelynne's throat was constricted; breathing became harder. She ached with fear and rage. The youngster extended his hand to Chad but Chad dropped to one knee and opened his arms to his son, indicating an embrace would be preferred. Chelynne winced at the sight, jealous and forlorn. Then the last hope vanished. Chad held the woman lightly and placed a husbandly kiss on her brow. Then the earl of Bryant, subtly clothed and resembling any London merchant, gave them a brief wave and climbed into his rented coach. It was done. And it was all too real.

Chelynne was frozen. She watched almost blindly as the woman hurried the youngster off the stoop and into the house. Chad's coach disappeared down the street. Still, she could not speak.

Gwen waited. There was no sign from the countess that she was ready to leave. Miffed at this hesitation, she called to her driver and they started away.

"There, madam," Gwen comforted, slipping an arm around her shoulders sympathetically. "Don't be undone, dear. Perhaps there's an explanation. Perhaps —"

"Stop it!" Chelynne snapped, removing the arm roughly. "Stop this play! I'm quite bored with it now. I know it was your intention to have me see what I have, but I don't wish to hear another word! Forgive, indeed!"

"Why, Your Ladyship, whatever —"

"Stop!" she cried. The driver began to slow. "Not you, fool!" The coach picked up speed again. Chelynne looked at Gwen coldly, her eyes near golden with anger. "I've heard as much of this performance as I intend to. You may dispense with all the simpering and whining. It bothers me a great deal more than your treachery!"

Gwen's eyes narrowed visibly. "Now you know what you're facing."

"I know what I saw, or what you intended me to see. I assure you, I will not let that little scene decide every circumstance."

"Now wait just a minute, madam, you promised that you wouldn't —"

"There is no reason I'll have to betray you if you're honest," Chelynne advised her shrewdly. "But if you're lying, you've betrayed yourself." She turned away from Lady Graystone and refused to speak again. When they arrived at the countess's home she made a hasty withdrawal from Gwen's coach. "I'll commend you on an expert piece of spying, madam, and thank you to trouble me no more. Good day."

"Well!" came the insulted voice from the coach.

"Well and good," Chelynne mumbled as she walked quickly to the door. Anger within her was the only thing that kept her on her feet, the only reason she had not fallen to the ground in a fit of weeping. The cad! The monster! That he dared to use her at this rate! To gain reconciliation with his father and obtain his inheritance at her expense! She was gently reared and of some quality. How could the man defile her to this extent? The lies and boldness of his betrayal infuriated her beyond anything she had ever known.

She opened the door herself, meeting the steward, who was guiltily rushing back to his post after sneaking away for a nip.

"Is His Lordship at home?" she asked quickly, removing vizard, wrap and gloves.

"Um, he is, madam, but he asked not to be disturbed."

"Where is he?"

"In his study, madam. With his man."

"Thank you," she replied, going straight to that private hold, intending to disturb him whether he liked it or not. There was a low murmuring from within that wasn't likely to stop her from throwing open the door. The next sound, her husband's angry voice, stopped her at once.

"Christ! What's the bitch been about now?"

More murmurings and then a loud bang that Chelynne imagined was her husband's fist in outraged impact with the top of the desk. "Why the hell would I care who she's sleeping with? That's the least of my worries. It serves to keep her out of my business at least."

The next low tones from Bestel brought even more anger from the earl. "Oh, she has, has she? By God, she's been trouble from the first. I should have been done with her when it first occurred to me. Well, I'll coddle the little whore no more. Thank you, and be assured, I handle this from now."

Chelynne's eyes burned with unshed tears. Be done with her? It was certain he couldn't have been speaking of that sweet young thing he so tenderly kissed good-bye. She turned and walked away, totally dejected now. The anger was gone, replaced by hurt that was not even profound. She felt weak and helpless, more the absence of emotion, passive and immobile.

Within the study Chad turned to Bestel more calmly, trying to subdue his rage. "From now, when Lady Graystone comes to this house, make certain you know what her business is. And I'll see what I can learn of her purpose in coming here today."

Chelynne stayed in her rooms, turning away meals and refusing to see anyone. She had not slept and would not go out. No amount of persuasion from Stella would induce her to confide her hurts. And then Gordon returned.

"It took me not long, madam, to find the family of the girl. She married the earl right enough, and went off with him. Her father was shamed since she got herself with the earl's babe and he was finally forced to leave his holdings from the scorn of the town. Left the earl's lands and moved on."

"We knew they were married," she said somewhat listlessly. "What since?"

"Since then there is nothing. They were said to have come to London, madam. I took it apart, as I could, and couldn't find a trace. There's no record of the birth, no tombstone or remembrance for one departed. I'm sorry, madam. I tried my best."

"You've done fine, Gordon. That was all I expected."

"Is there anything to do now?" he asked solicitously.

"Just be available to me, that's all."

Her voice was so distant and bland that Gordon stayed for a while, waiting for her to think of something for him to do. But Chelynne seemed oblivious to his presence and finally he left. He found as he was leaving that he wasn't alone in his concern for her. Stella stood near the door, shaking her head in a gesture of defeat. Gordon assumed, incorrectly, that Stella was aware of the countess's plight. They exchanged worried glances and the manservant left.

Stella went again to Chelynne to tend her, urge her, but she was waved away for her efforts, excused.

In the days that followed, the earl of Bryant suffered more frustration than he had ever known. Harry Mondeloy had apparently disappeared from sight, for Chad could locate him nowhere. His previous lodgings had been abandoned and he was not seen with his usual group of young gallants.

In pursuing Lady Graystone he met with only confusion. She admitted to having visited his home and taken his wife abroad, but insisted it was all of an innocent nature, the premise social. She gave no impression of either guilt or fear. Chad could not imagine her current plotting, but he knew Gwen. It was bound to be trouble. She held him at bay with the promise that she would contact him if Mondeloy showed himself again.

Bratonshire had turned from an invisible affront to an all-out war between Bollering and Shayburn. It was peaking to a culmination with Shayburn's time drawing to a close. And Chad was being called often to Whitehall for what was either interest or amusement from the king.

He was keeping his composure in the mounting stress, but he scarcely had time to take a meal and change his clothes. He simply needed to be everywhere at once.

Exhausted, Chad went to his study to go over his accounts. Hot black coffee was brought to him. The thought of rest did not give him temporary energy, for he knew it could be weeks, perhaps months before he could relax with his affairs in order. He didn't even know what was happening in his own house. He was at the point where either it would all fail or he would get a grip on his dealings and pull everything off.

There was a knocking at his study door. Interruptions. More little troubles. He ground his teeth in frustration, but bade the intruder enter. Stella stood in the frame of the door, nervously waiting his indication that he could give her some attention. Finally he laid down his quill and looked at the serving woman in some vexation.

"It's Her Ladyship, milord," she said shakily.

Chad sighed and looked back at his work. "What does she need?" He thought of some errand, permission for an outing, a merchant's slip for some article of apparel. He resented women's trifles. He was too harried for nonsense. Thus piqued, he hardly heard Stella's quiet plea.

"She's ill, milord."

He looked up. "Ill?"

"I can't seem to help her, milord. She won't let me near."

"Does she need a physician?" His interest now was drawn from his work and he looked at Stella with concern. She saw the opportunity to speak her mind.

"I don't know what ails her, sir. I've known her since her birth and I've never seen her so. It's worsened since the day her uncle died and now she won't take her meals at all. I know she doesn't sleep. I look in on her through the night, milord, and most oft she's up. She won't let me dress her or brush her hair, nothing . . ."

Chad judged the old woman's haggard face and knew this was no exaggeration. Though on in years, Stella usually had a vibrant, energetic appearance. Now the old face was lined from worry and lack of sleep.

"How long has this been going on?"

"The worst of it came in the last week, milord. It seemed the ague, but the sickness passed and the weakness is worse."

Chad realized he couldn't remember when he had last spoken to his wife. It was at least a week, probably more, since he had actually visited her, and that was briefly. "Fever? Flux?" He almost said green sickness and caught himself.

"Nothing such as that, milord."

"Why was I not informed?"

"She . . . she wouldn't have you troubled, sir. And you weren't about the house often, sir." Her voice broke from worry and from the fact that she lied. The truth was that Chelynne refused to let them bear the news to Chad. She insisted he would not care and threatened them with dire consequences for betrayal. "But we've had to carry her to her bed, milord. Too weak to walk, she was. I fear I've waited too long. She looks the death . . ."

He was up and walking to the study door as Stella finished. He sent Bestel at once for a doctor and then mounted the stairs to look in on Chelynne. It was hard to tell if it was anger or panic that drove him, but he moved with great speed. He cleared the room of servants and went straight to his wife. Those who did not know him well would not interpret that expression sealed in stone as upset. But then he saw her and the hard features melted into something akin to despair.

Blankets were tucked around her but he couldn't believe the face that stared at him. She was thin and pale, her hair matted and dull and her eyes hollowed and tired. The transformation was so complete that she resembled an aging dame more than the bright and lovely young woman he remembered. She seemed to be slipping into unhurried death. He breathed her name.

"Yes, Chad?" she returned softly.

"Is there pain? Tell me where?"

"There is no pain," she answered, shaking her head slightly. "I'm just very tired."

"What is it? What has made you so ill?" He sat now on the edge of her bed and took her small, weak hand into his.

"It's nothing. It will pass." She tried to smile but he could not recognize the effort. She was a different person.

"I've sent for a doctor, Chelynne. You look worse than I expected."

"You've been a long time away, my lord. Is business bad?"

He shook his head dumbly. Where had he been to so badly neglect his own household? Nothing else seemed important any longer. He could not see beyond those glassy brown eyes.

"Don't worry with business, love. Tell me what I can do to make you more comfortable."

There was a shallow sound from her that was almost a laugh. "But I've always wondered about your business. It was only that you wouldn't share it with me. You've shared very little with me . . ."

"Chelynne, rest now. Don't talk."

"I fear I may never get the chance to talk to you again. Talk to me now, won't you?"

He stared at her with disbelieving eyes. He couldn't be sure whether she was serious or delirious from her illness.

"What would you like to know?"

"What you do at the wharves. All those ships . . . would you love to be riding them again, rather than this? Would you?"

Chad didn't really want to answer her. It seemed so ridiculous to be making idle conversation when she was this ill. But those glassy eyes were turned on him, begging for attention, and he was without choice. He sighed.

"I confess, I love sailing, but it was done out of necessity and mine is much the merchant's job now. I first took that profession when I was in dire need of money. I intended never to live in England again, but that was not left to me, either. There is scarcely a place on this earth where I would not be responsible to the crown and it might as well be home. I am neither a traitor nor a coward."

"And fighting?"

"For lack of a choice. For money and influence, that is all. I love it little."

"For loyalty, I thought."

"Yes, for that. But I was not allowed to choose my loyalties. I was born to them."

Her eyes were surprised, but not very much emotion showed. She was too tired and sick for much emotion. "I thought you loved England first. Your king, your title, your lands."

"No, Chelynne. No. But there are things in England I love, that I cannot turn away from. I am bound to it, therefore I find things in it to love and fight for."

"Have you ever been in love, Chad?"

"Yes," he said simply. Why did she ask this now?

"Did it feel wonderful?"

He looked at her pityingly, reaching out to touch her face. She was one of the most beautiful women he had ever known, and sweet to be near. Had she really never tasted love, never flown after it, held it in her heart and felt the intensity of it? He had failed at that, too? In bringing it to her? And she clung to him for support and care. He was totally ashamed.

"No, Chelynne, it was most painful. I loved helplessly and didn't know the way to deal with it. I was too young. I am not young now."

"They say love is for the young."

"That's not entirely so, Chelynne," he said tenderly. "I'm no longer a lad but I think I could love again quite easily. And do so more successfully."

"I would think, having once found it painful you would wish to avoid it again."

How reasonable, he thought. And that was exactly what he had done. He had feared his own capacity to feel. "It's part of growing up, darling. Accepting those things when they come."

"Can one live in this world without it, I wonder."

He looked at the result of his ardent indifference. There she lay, drifting off into some unreachable world. His answer was heartfelt. "No, I think not, darling."

"And what then keeps you alive?" she asked with a bitter voice. He didn't answer her. "Merchanting? Loyalties you were born to? What?"

"Hate," he answered. "And vengeance."

"Who would you hate so much," she sighed wearily.

"Now? Only myself, Chelynne." He paused and considered the puzzlement that was his life. "And until now . . . I have been the object of my own revenge." As he said it he at once realized the truth to it.

She sighed and closed her eyes. "Chelynne," he beckoned softly. She did not respond. "Chelynne," he said, grabbing her in sudden fear. She opened her eyes and stared at him. She looked so tired, so old. "Do you feel love?"

She stared at him blankly for a long moment. Finally she answered in a voice that didn't sound like her own, a voice that was soured and bitter. "I feel nothing."

Chad, the businessman who never felt confusion overpowering, the warrior who never feared his aggressor, who had not felt the shudder of terror since that first day of battle, was more afraid now than he had been in his life. He was afraid of what his own hand had done. He wanted to cut out his heart and give it to her, mend her and make it right.

She began a gentle sobbing, weak and pitiful. He lifted her a bit and held her firmly against his chest as if he would bleed his own strength into her. He offered his love now and she was too helpless to accept it. Too late, he thought painfully. Always too late.

When the physician arrived Chad was sent from the room. He stood for a long while just outside the door, but the servants coming and going could tell him nothing. He gave a few commands to carry in. "Do not let him cut her," he ordered. "She must not be purged," he commanded. "She hasn't eaten in days, she must not be bled." Finally he left to go to his study out of complete frustration. He ordered that either he be called to the sickroom or the doctor sent to his study whenever there was news.

Chad poured a glass of sack, swirling the liquid in the glass. Before him he saw the sweet, seductive smile and bright eyes. There was a vision of her lifting her nose to Shayburn, besting him with wit and defiance of his own loathesome game. Then he saw her as he remembered her best and most beautifully, floating atop the mare's back and riding joyfully, the freedom of her spirit a grand sight to behold.

He closed his eyes. Behind the lids there was a light in the darkness. It was a lace-garbed beauty bent to the task of carefully sewing a gaping wound on his upper arm, urging him to take more brandy for the pain. He couldn't free himself of her memory. Always she was near, patiently waiting. He had been able to force her out of his thoughts at will, but no more.

"My God," he thought stupidly. "I do love her!" Beyond her beauty, beyond her simple devotion, beyond the desire. He shook his head in confusion. He knew that he wanted her. He never pretended that she wasn't every measure of a man's desire, what he would have chosen himself in a wife. All the qualities she possessed were important in the very practical decision. But love? Love was the foolish fopping way he felt when he pursued Anne. Love was the ache he had for his Anne that was never properly sated, never subdued with passion spent. Love was the pain he felt when he lost her. Love was once. He couldn't credit it. It was taking a stranger, different form from what he had previously known and acknowledged.

Fool! It echoed in his ears. He couldn't believe his own stupidity. Anne was gone! Gone, regardless of his pride, his insistence that her memory not be scarred or defiled. She was his wife, mother to his son and now dead. Never to be brought back. Had he learned nothing from his failure to secure love? He had abused Chelynne for a principle that was hardly worth her life. In his attempt to bring a part of his dead wife to life, his new wife was bent to suffering. He had kept himself from her resolutely and cruelly. His best friend, the only man he could trust completely, had warned him that Chelynne's pain was real and intense, but he would not hear it. What time would it have cost his labors to deliver some kindness? To show some tenderness? Small wonder she hated him now.

He began to pray in earnest to a God he had long ago decided was useless to him. He begged, like any doomed man, for another chance, pleaded for her life, promised to right the wrong. No matter what, he swore. No matter how it all would end.

Chad knew remorse so strong, a sense of failure through his own mismanagement that was so complete, that it exhausted his spirit and he laid his head in his arms, weak with fear.

The physician tending the countess was from the palace, one of the best in London. He was learned and skilled, but when he came to Chad he was shaking his head in bemusement. He attempted a report but finding the words did not come easy, and facing the impatient earl made the topic more difficult to broach. Chad offered a glass of sack and urged the man on.

"I can't understand it, my lord. The tiring woman knows of no recent illness save a bout of ague, yet I fear Her Ladyship is dying."

"What the devil! How can she be dying if she's not ill?"

"I've given her a complete examination, my lord. It almost seems as if she's lost her will to live. There's nothing I can do for her now."

Chad stared at the small man coldly. "There must be something, sir. No matter the cost. Something!"

"If there's a cure for this, my lord, we'll all be rich."

"For what? Come, man, what?"

"She simply wishes to die. That's the best way I can figure it, my lord. She fought my attentions and is now unconscious. We cannot rouse her."

"You've considered everything? She does not bleed? There's no infection you missed?" The earl's expression was earnest, pleading. "What of pregnancy? Is she perhaps miscarrying?"

"Pregnancy?"

"Yes, that! The simplest —"

"My lord, Her Ladyship was examined for that. Futilely. She is intact. Surely you would be aware —" The doctor stopped suddenly, not knowing if he had gone too far or was faced with a strange situation in this household. He had served the nobility for many years, had seen everything there was to see. He would be neither surprised nor offended. It was the strange light in the earl's eyes that held him silent.

"Then you suspect she is wishing this illness? To death?"

"It seems a violent state of grief, my lord. The countess has allowed herself to deteriorate, as best I can explain it. I believe her to be badly neglected and careless with her health. I propose you have her purged, burn incense, and give her ample salt water. Keep her in bed and force small amounts frequently. There are no ulcers or fever and as I can tell she's contracted no disease, but in her weakened condition the onset of any could quickly kill her. As it is . . ." The doctor paused and judged the size of the earl as he slowly rose before him. "As it is, she may not last out the week. You might call in an astronomer."

"The devil," Chad muttered, on his way out the study door and leaving the small, balding man to trail along behind.

"Shall I call tomorrow, my lord?" the physician asked.

"Yes, yes. Come tomorrow," Chad replied without turning around.

"I'll say nothing of Her Ladyship's condition," the doctor offered.

Chad stopped abruptly and whirled around, the physician almost colliding with him. Those piercing silver eyes darted over the little man quickly, coldly. "I don't give a damn what you say." Chad turned away and took the stairs two at a time, cursing under his breath as he mounted them. Damn nobility. Damn court. Damn London.

Stella was bending over Chelynne, patiently trying to coax an egg coddle into her mouth. There was a posset stirred and sitting on the table, the smell of herbs smoldering in a dish, and the windows were closed and the curtains drawn. The room was stifling and close. Chelynne did not stir from her deep slumber but there was a troubled frown on her brow. Chad took the bowl from Stella's hands and urged her away, placing himself in the position of nursemaid to his wife.

Chad kept that vigil through the night, gently spooning tiny bits of nourishment past her unyielding lips. Memories plagued him as he worked, of a different sort now. Now with painful clarity he remembered every day since his wedding to Chelynne. The weather had cooled when he put his father to his final resting. His young bride had attempted to ease the deep ache that accompanied death. She had offered herself for the comfort he would take but he had accepted none. Instead he had gone directly to London and bade her follow, alone.

He had taken her to court because it was expected, but he had gone about his gallivanting and left her to survive as she might. When he had occasionally looked in her direction he had found that she had chosen an out-of-the-way corner to sit and wait, smiling demurely at compliments and blushing lightly at the courtly gestures that embarrassed her.

Christmas. It had been a wild and wonderful celebration in London, with decorations and parties and dinners and singing. Chad had accompanied Chelynne to all the festivities, but had not stayed by her side. He had left a gift in her room and later accepted her thanks for the small piece of jewelry. She had sought him out to personally place a gift in his hands. He had thanked her and taken it with him to his study to work. Three weeks later he had opened it to find a pin for his cravat embedded with rich stones, three monogrammed handkerchiefs, and a lock of hair encased in glass for a keepsake. He had never mentioned the gifts again and had not used them. He wondered now what she had done on Christmas day alone. He had gone to spend that time with Kevin. But he had not been reproached and had not heard her cry.

Lord Mondeloy had sent word to her several times that he would come to London as soon as he could. When that noble gentleman had arrived he was in no condition to help his niece. How long ago was that? Chad couldn't even remember when his wife lost her kin.

He crooned to her as the mother of a sick child might. If she stirred restlessly, he lifted her and carried her to the pot. If he wasn't forewarned of her need he changed the bedding himself, not wishing to have any servants near her now.

Thus he bore it through another night. By morning's light he had loosened his shirt and the periwig rested on her bureau. His beard was itching and irritating and he wouldn't take the time to shave it. He stubbornly blinked away the need for rest and kept at Chelynne to nibble and take small draughts.

Stella's offer to relieve him was refused. He ate of meals brought quickly and went on with his duties. He dozed through parts of the afternoon close by her side. Another night and still she was helpless, weak and barely conscious.

He threw open the windows to admit the morning light and air that was none too pure. He was restless and impatient for some kind of improvement. Bestel brought him a message bearing the royal seal and he read it quickly. A summons would have ordinarily sent him hurrying off to his sovereign. Today he answered it without due concern. If the matter was not urgent he begged to be excused because his wife was in a state of illness that was most severe. He was well aware that he could be brought away by royal guards and gave little regard to the possibility. There was nothing of much importance to him now, save his wife's well-being. The same words floated from his tongue wearily, habit to him now. "Come, darling, just one swallow more."

Afternoon brought an answer from King Charles. Chad was to report to Whitehall at his earliest availability, excused from this appointment. Charles was most concerned about the condition of the countess and inquired personally after her. He had also, Bestel explained, interrogated the physician attending them to be sure there was no foul play. Chad reasoned the information. Without Charles's interest in his wife he would likely have been severely reprimanded for not charging to the palace at the first call. A man was not excused lightly for problems with his women.

He carried on, hot and tired and frustrated. He was near the end of his endurance. She was not going to live. "By damn!" he swore at his young wife. "Are you so weak that you cannot rise above some slight misfortune?" He pressed his face close to hers and whispered low. "Will you slip away and never try to better your circumstance? For the love of Christ, Chelynne! Won't you save yourself?"

Her eyes blinked open sleepily with no sign that she heard and understood him. They drifted closed again. "Is there no reason left to live, Chelynne?" he whispered in agony. His head fell to her breast and he uttered, "No reason at all?"

She stirred slightly and her eyes opened again. There was something there, some communication. No further words were spoken. He urged the spoon close to her mouth and she ate obediently. She drank from the cup he held. The amounts were slight and she was not eager, but there was some response. Reason enough to hope.

The next day she took more and her waking periods were longer. The day after she was better still, and she asked him to help her to sit up. One more day dawned and she awoke alert, aware of her surroundings and him.

"I hurt all over," she murmured, grimacing as she moved in the bed. "Every bone in my body."

Chad beamed. She would mend. She could find the strength to complain of her discomforts and that was a sure sign that recovery was on its way. He was flooded with relief. His arms went around her and his lips touched her brow.

He left her that night for the first time to sleep in his own bed. The rest was sorely needed but was not nearly what was required. He, too, had suffered through this illness. His weight had dropped and his face bore the signs of worry. A bath and grooming helped the insult to his good looks and then he went to her quickly.

In the healing process the recovery is swift when there is desire. He found her sitting up with a tray of food before her. It would be a long while before she would regain that vitality and healthy appearance she had had before, but there was tremendous improvement already. He had a great many phrases on his tongue, a grand number of regrets and hopes to speak of, but he simply took her hand in both of his and spoke softly.

"You've been so foolish to let this happen to you. You have so much to live for."

"You're right, of course," she replied softly. "But sometimes that is hard to see. I think God looks unkindly on those who wish to die."

"That's behind you now. You'll get better now."

"I'm a burden to you," she sighed.

"You have been that," he laughed. "You've a most determined nature, madam."

"There's nothing there you know," she whispered.

"Where, love?"

"Death. I thought it would be gardens, perhaps. Beautiful countryside with cool streams. It's only blackness. Nervous and dark. There is no rest there."

"Is that what you sought? Rest?"

"My lord," she said in that strange voice that didn't seem to belong to her. "It would bear considerable preference to what I have had. But no matter, I know now why there was nothing there."

"Why?"

"That is for the soul that has nothing left to believe in. Eternal life is only for the soul that in strength can endure living."

"Chelynne, don't ponder this so deeply. Think only about recovery now. Rest and eat."

"I'm not much good at being a countess. In truth, I don't much want to be."

"That's no fault of yours," he said sternly. "From now it will be made easier for you."

"I don't like London much," she told him.

"Then as soon as you can travel we'll go to the country. Will that help?"

Not entirely, she thought. But she smiled and nodded her head.

"Chelynne, things will be better than they have been, I promise you. Just get well."

How simple the matter of making a man cringe with guilt, she thought. She nodded and pretended that simple devotion. It kept him at bay better than anything else.

"I was called to Whitehall when you were ill, and begged off. I'm afraid I can't avoid it any longer. Will you be all right if I leave you for a short time?"

Again the smile, the brief nod. She could see that he was most reluctant to leave her. She wondered then if there was some love for her after all. But she quickly put it out of her mind. He would feel obligated, of course, to help her during times of great crisis. He was not a man to take duty lightly. The one thing she had learned was that to be tolerated and endured was less dignified than being hated. And it was infinitely more painful.

He patted her hand, kissed her brow, and left her.

His Majesty King Charles had received a message early in the day from the earl of Bryant. It read that the countess was greatly improved and that he sought the earliest possible audience. Charles gave the messenger an appointment time for the afternoon. He breakfasted with the queen, dined with his mistress at noon, and played tennis in the early afternoon. He walked to his apartments with a trail of courtiers and banked by his friend George Villiers and his brother James, the duke of York.

"So, Bryant can leave the petticoats now, sire?" Buckingham asked.

"It seems Her Ladyship is on the mend," the king replied.

"You've acquired an interest in her, haven't you, sire?" James asked.

"You've acquired an interest in my interests," was the reply.

"Will Bryant be going home or shall he become a guest of Your Majesty?" Buckingham asked.

"What is your wager, George?"

"There seems a full house at the Tower. I wager he goes home, sire."

"Don't put too much money on it," Charles advised.

"There's no proof he's guilty of anything," James put in. "So far as we can see."

Charles was mute. He wasn't saying any more.

"There's no such thing as a guilt-free man," George commented.

"And who would know that better than you, George?"

"Not a soul, sire," he confessed.

"There are those who have the opinion you've not done your share of visiting in the Tower." Charles stopped walking and waited for Buckingham to catch up. "What do you think of that?"

Buckingham bowed. "I think Your Majesty's infinite wisdom and profound sense of justice have many times saved the innocent from unscrupulous slander and character assassination." George smiled into Charles's laughing eyes. The king started walking again.

"You know better, I warrant."

"No one serves you more loyally, sire," George defended himself.

"You serve no one better than yourself, George. It's because I know that better than anyone that you're wearing a head."

"You're most generous, sire."

Charles stopped abruptly and stared at him. This friendship had weathered many a storm. It seemed they were always in the midst of an argument or just recovering from one. His eyes were serious and grave but there was a cynical smile on his lips. He started walking again without further comment.

"You're suspicious of Bryant?" James asked.

"I'm suspicious of everyone," Charles replied.

"I'm most curious about his story, " James ventured.

"Your curiosity will have to suffer. I see Bryant alone."

The king went into his apartments and left the majority of his courtiers outside. While he was helped into his coat and wig, George and James stood a short distance away, murmuring with their heads together. Charles looked in their direction once or twice, understanding the mood of the conversation without hearing a word. How much influence did Bryant have with the king? What part did the countess play? The many possibilities would be carefully analyzed.

Charles knew they wouldn't discover the real reason for his interest here since he was a long way from understanding it himself. Sir John had served the crown loyally and was a man Charles personally liked. Since his father's lands had been sold, John would have to petition the king for permission to buy out Shayburn. Charles's consent would leave one baron angry with the king's favoritism. It occasionally created dissension at court. Had Bollering not guessed that Charles would approve of his appointment to his old family lands? Charles was not a man to easily forget a loyalty.

And he was a man to appreciate being eased of constant petitions from his subjects. If they could settle this without upsetting the realm he would be satisfied.

And the countess of Bryant. Not very much time had passed since Minette's death. His beloved sister. He had allowed her marriage to Philippe, whose constant abuse and mistreatment finally brought on her death. Another virtuous maid lost forever because of the limits of his protection. He knew there was little room for virtue at Whitehall.

Charles was not convinced that Chelynne was his own flesh. He never pondered things of that nature severely. He claimed many of the children of the women he bedded because it would be unchivalrous not to. The fact that she was lovely and sweet interested him more. If there was a way to prevent England and his court from destroying her he would see to it. If there was not, he would accept it.

As to Hawthorne, Charles did not forget his loyalty either. Neither did he forget a mistake, a betrayal, however minor.

When Bryant arrived Charles was glad to see the signs of fatigue and worry. He marked it as a positive sign.

"The countess is improved, I'm told."

"She is, sire, and I thank you for your interest."

"Thank me? That's a new twist."

"I thank you," Chad said simply.

"You've not been out of your walls in a long time, Bryant. I believe you did sit vigil at her bedside."

"You can be certain, sire. She was extremely ill."

"And the cause?"

"We're not certain, sire."

"But I've a mighty good guess, since I made it my business. I made your comings and goings my business, too. I know that you didn't leave your house."

"I was being watched?"

"No. You were being heavily guarded. You were unaware?"

A flicker of surprise registered in Chad's eyes. "Completely, Your Majesty."

"The purpose was to see that you did not flee." Charles watched him closely.

"What reason would have me flee, sire?"

"You had not heard?"

"I've been in touch with nothing, sire. I did in fact sit with my wife through her illness and came here at the first sign she would be safe with just her servants."

"We have new guests in the Tower. A baron from your state, Shayburn, and most surprisingly, a man you've killed."

Chad's eyes widened considerably but he tried to keep his composure. "Arrested?"

"Indeed they were arrested. Lord Shayburn claims that Sir John Bollering has ravaged and destroyed that shire and murdered on his land. Bollering reports he did nothing and that Shayburn, in a fit of anger at being fairly bought out, set fire to anything immovable in that town to keep from passing it along. What do you know of it?"

"Christ," Chad muttered. "That's ruined it, unless —"

"Unless what?"

"I must ask, sire, was the manor house burned?"

"That and village houses, warehouses, barns and carts. Just about everything there." Chad marveled at Charles's ability to remain calm. He seemed not upset at all. But he knew that this tolerance could be a temporary thing. He began a long story of what he and John and a brace of men had done in Bratonshire. Charles listened carefully.

"That old feud was due to Shayburn's treachery. We've been aware for a long time that he mismanaged that land and was guilty of more than a dozen severe crimes. Unfortunately there was no way to prove him guilty, for he kept false records and dealt in secrets. We finally came across a document that would incriminate him, but if it was burned in the house it is useless to us now."

"What do you speak of?"

"Contracts for money given to finance Dutch vessels. The treason would have been a tired charge, years old, but the character is the same in the man. Everything he has attained came through thievery of one sort or another. He aided both sides equally in the wars, securing his one high card in every circumstance."

"A rather expensive habit," Charles drawled.

"The people of Bratonshire have supported that habit for years, sire. I placed my father's old manservant in that house and Sebastian was able to locate the contract with the Dutch. I assume Shayburn held it with the purpose of using it in the future if necessary."

"And that is only one of the affairs in your sorry state. Creditors, I'm told, are lining up at your door."

"Not quite so bad as that, Your Majesty. I've dealt largely in credit to keep my money available for emergencies, such as aiding John Bollering in buying back his lands."

"I don't think I have to ask, but that farce of a duel? Why would that be necessary?"

"John was seen on the baron's lands and they set out in numbers to have him murdered. There would have been no trial, you can be assured."

"And those people who were murdered? Abused?"

"None were by Bollering hands. They were taken safely away and the damage was a farce. Those killed by Shayburn were real."

"Your dealings seem to have been all a farce, my lord, aggravating Shayburn's wrath no small bit."

"I have no proof beyond my word, sire, but Shayburn has been guilty of thievery and murder since before Lord Bollering originally lost his land to him. We have in our household now a lass who was raped and beaten and used for the amusement of that animal for debts of a minimal amount belonging to her father. There are a dozen more stories there, each more gruesome than the next. I would have sought to remove him even without Sir John's aid."

"And you couldn't have done it more reasonably than you have?"

Chad had a great many things he wished to tell his king, to excuse or at least explain the action he had taken. But he was without evidence. "No, sire. I could not."

Charles took in an exasperated breath. "The price of power," he muttered.

"Sire, you are not well acquainted with Lord Shayburn. At least not as I am. I accuse him, but without proof. John Bollering is not only rightful heir to that land but loyal to the crown and a just lord. We thought to buy Shayburn out just as he did John's father.

It is not any more just by law, but by a man's moral code, it is fair."

"And will you stand on this principle before me? Before my ministers? Before the whole of England?"

Chad looked Charles in the eyes, unfaltering. "If it is my only recourse, to my death."

Charles relaxed. "I hadn't thought death in demand here; there's been enough of that. It is true, however, that in defiling my land and my people you defile the crown, and that is treason, however virtuous the cause. It would better suit my mood to see the three of you bend your backs to the chore of putting all you have destroyed right."

Chad smiled. "Should you gift us with the absence of one overfed baron, you would see Sir John and me do ten times the labor there, and happily."

"Had you attempted to settle with Shayburn?"

"Quite generously, sire. He refused my offer of twice the land in Virginia and gold to support him. He would have England or nothing."

"I am faced with a choice between evils and that does not please me. I will reserve judgment while supporting my guests in the Tower. Do you think you would like to join them?"

"You have no need to fear that I would flee your decision, sire. I am caught and prepared to abide by your rule."

"A trifle late," Charles muttered. "I had not worried that you would run. I think you've quite exhausted yourself of that."

"Yes, sire. I've quite exhausted myself of that."

During this brief exchange the two looked at each other. Charles felt a certain kinship with Chad since the days of exile. Both were fleeing something then that they hoped to have restored. Chad's coming home was a lot later than Charles's. Charles remembered this man as a youth, his loyal and determined support of his king. If he had ever met an honest man it was Chadwick Hawthorne. But Charles was cautious. He thought it best to keep his subjects from knowing how much credence he gave their word.

"And I am weary of slaughter and useless fighting. I would see the matter done. I will give you my decision in a few days."

"Thank you, sire. I am at your service."

"I would like to visit the countess. With your permission."

"Of course, sire. She is still weak. Perhaps it would be best to give her a few more days."

"It is my intention to offer her a position as Lady to the Queen's Bedchamber and apartments at Whitehall. I know more of her condition than you might guess."

Chad's eyes darkened. "If I have been negligent in her care, I am deeply repentant, sire."

"Repentance will not cure her," Charles replied.

Chad spoke low, softly. "I hadn't intended that as a cure."

"I am not one to lecture on the treatment of women. I have failed in that enough to lose my credibility. If she suffers unduly in your home, she is welcome to another abode and the pension will come from your own purse. Her decision will be final and there will be no interference from you. Is that understood?"

"I will not interfere, Your Majesty."

"I will tell you this once more, Bryant. The action you have taken does not please me. In conspiring against one of my barons you as much as conspire against me, whether or not you think of it in those terms. Now there is waste where there once was life. I cannot see use in more of the same and this feud must end here. Your grace lies in the fact that little of this unsavory business is known and I am impatient to be finished with it. If you get anything good out of this, it is not what you have duly earned but is thrown on you in a generous fit."

"Thank you, sire." Chad bowed, and left his king and Whitehall.

Moments had passed when York entered and found Charles in his closet playing with his medicines and whistling. Neither spoke. Buckingham followed, joining them.

"Bryant goes home to the countess," Buckingham declared.

"Correct," Charles confirmed. "Did you win your wager?"

"I did."

James scowled, the loser. He had thought his brother much more angry with this business. "I don't suppose I'll learn the reason for losing one hundred pound," James sulked.

"I don't suppose," Charles laughed.

"Would Your Grace like to wager on which lordly guest leaves the Tower first?" Buckingham offered.

"Shayburn," James returned. "For two hundred pound. Gold."

Charles looked to Buckingham and saw his nod. He went back to stirring the posset, amused.

"When must he make his debt good, sire?" George inquired.

"He's safe, as I see it. They'll likely leave together."

"And what of the charge?"

"What charge?"

"Treason, at the very least," York insisted.

"That's a bit harsh, James. Don't you think?"

"I think it's generous," York argued.

"Well, perhaps it is best that you are you and I am I. I am much more generous. Which one of you will send for Bollering for me?"

"Bollering will get it, then?"

"I think he will accept lordship there. My mood is so improved I think raising him to baron too modest."

"Your temper cools quickly," Buckingham observed. He remembered the hard glint to Charles's eyes when he heard the full score of accusations on both sides of that feud.

"Temper? I was not angry, George. This is what I have wanted all along."

EIGHTEEN

S THE ILLNESS FADED for the countess of Bryant so did spring make its presence felt upon the land. Brown yielded to the promise of green and the rains were soft and sweet.

Chad looked in on his young wife frequently, and though he did not usually find her in a conversational mood, he was amazed with the speed of her recovery. He took note that her health became progressively better as small tokens of cheer arrived from the king. The fear vanished that her sickness would touch her beauty just as a violent storm marks the land. She emerged from her misfortune more radiant than he would have believed possible.

Chelynne's manner had greatly changed since her close encounter with death. She seemed to have a new hold on herself, a new determination. She was hardly scampering about, as her condition was still weak, but she was carefully groomed every morning and her silky skin was touched with the rose flush he remembered. He marveled at the slim and seductive curve of her red lips and was still enticed with the fine, mysterious arch of her brows. But in the eyes there was the memory of trials. When he would inquire after her well-being and look into her eyes he did not see that warm adoration that had been there the summer before. Now there was a determined distance. She had not seen even seventeen summers and her eyes held the wisdom and pain of one hundred years. They held him at bay with the merest stare. She was ever as demure, but her gaze only a pace away from daring him to touch her. Chad, with his wealth of worldly knowledge, was completely at odds as to how to win her again.

"There's a defiance there," he thought. "And I cannot break through it. She is no longer mourning her lack of success but despising me wholeheartedly. I admit my foolishness, but cannot think of a single way to hold her, touch her. I've wooed dozens into my bed and this one I dare not court. And she is my own wife!"

But he pursued her daily, regularly entering and trying to find some sense of coming home in her bedchamber. But she was as cool as snow, as distant as some star. For every small remembrance Charles sent to her, Chad bought one lovelier. She was not greatly moved by his carefully chosen baubles and trinkets. He purchased carefully a diamond brooch that set him back two thousand pounds and she thanked him politely, placed an unexcited kiss on his cheek, and put the thing in her coffer. At that turn of events he pouted over a bottle of sack for several hours in his study.

Chelynne, this morning, was bathed and groomed and lying in peaceful repose on her daybed. Brandy lay at her feet, dozing as she did, when the rapid thud of Stella's footfalls roused her. It was not her woman's presence that brought Chelynne's alertness, but the speed with which she was coming. "It's the king, mum! The king's come to call on ye!"

Chelynne barely had time to digest the news when he strode into her room just behind Stella. Long and determined were his strides, his wide smile beaming. He was totally casual in his manner and all that much more majestic because of his ease. He was dressed no more royally than any of his courtiers yet the kingly aura was all about him. He came straight to her side, lowered himself on one knee, and took her hands into his.

"Wonderful," he breathed. "You look wonderful! I don't believe you were ever ill. It was all a sham!"

"Sham indeed," she teased, confident and comfortable with him. "To bring a mighty king to his knees before a common subject."

"There is nothing common about you, madam."

"You're kind to call, sire," she murmured, her voice full of warmth.

He hushed her with a finger to her lips. "Don't let it get out that I'm kind." He chuckled to himself. "I'm trying to have it known that I'm gruesome and cruel."

Chelynne laughed easily. There was a time when she had quaked at the sight of him, so awesome and powerful. Now she could see, happily, that he was as human as any man, and one of the most charming and thoughtful she had ever chanced to know.

"You've received my gifts?" he asked.

"All of them. You are generous, but I won't tell a soul."

She gestured with an arm to the silver sitting out and the bracelet lying on top of her coffer. Charles walked about to inspect his gifts, for though he had had them sent, he had not seen them. Beside the silver was a book of poems and he lifted the cover. It was inscribed, a gift from her husband, and dated. He moved to her coffer and eyed the diamond brooch. "This makes mine look a pauper's gift," he remarked.

"From the earl," she told him.

"He is a most considerate husband," he commented.

"Of late," she murmured, lowering her eyes. Charles was quick to sense the cloud of doubt and watched, though she did nothing visible, as she pushed away that feeling and regained the happy mood.

"Perhaps you so frightened him with your illness he's had a chance to think better of his moods. That would be a nice turn, don't you agree, madam?"

She agreed so quickly that Charles knew there was uncertainty. He walked to her dressing table and admired the tapestry that graced the stone wall. He was not a man to pay such close attention to the furnishings of a room, but he was an expert sleuth. There was a comb and brush and hand mirror on display, articulately fashioned out of silver. "These are lovely," he praised aloud.

"Again the earl, sire."

"Since your illness?"

She nodded and he raised an eyebrow in thought. "I believe he is courting you, madam. Many wives would be envious of that."

"Perhaps they would." She smiled. "I know they envy me now."

"I don't have much time," he apologized. "But there is a matter I would like to discuss with you. I wonder what your plans are now?"

She shrugged, noncommittal. "The weather grows warmer, sire. I thought I might go to the country."

"The court moves to Windsor soon. I shall visit Newmarket for the races. Have you ever been to the races, madam?"

"Never, sire. Is it exciting?"

"Not particularly," he laughed. "But it's not Whitehall, if you follow my meaning."

She followed it very well. She knew the king was not wont to move about and wander. He had had plenty of that in his youth. But he was energetic and liked to make short trips for special diversions such as the races, hunting and yacht racing. And he most usually had the company of a mistress.

"Were you considering the quiet of the country to benefit your health?" he asked.

"I thought it might, sire. And it livens my spirits. I was raised in the country and I love to ride. It's more peaceful than . . ."

He lifted her hand and looked at a ring with a ruby stone of great value. "This is a handsome piece, madam," he observed.

"This belonged to the last countess of Bryant."

Charles frowned. He thought for a moment. "For a man who does not care about you he makes most expensive gifts. I know many women who would like to be ignored thus."

His eyes were not teasing her now. She could read in his expression that he found it hard to believe she was unloved and ignored. Charles did not know all of Chad as she did. She was tempted to give her reasons for doubt, and she felt a closeness to this man that would facilitate complete honesty. For some reason she held silent. And her silence saved her husband from the king's wrath. She tried not to think she was protecting him in any way.

"Some gifts come too late, sire," she said softly.

"Too late," he muttered. "That is my most unfavorite sound. Do you have any idea how many times I have been too late? Believe me this once, madam. Sometimes it is too late because you have willed it so and sometimes because it truly is. There is a great deal of difference." She stared at him and digested the words. She dared not ask how much he knew of her. He gave her a reassuring pat and went on.

"But I haven't come to recount all my foolish philosophies. I have a question for you. If you would like to take the appointment of Lady to the Queen's Bedchamber, I am prepared to make you that offer."

"You would do that for me, sire?"

"You're so surprised? Why not you?"

"I . . . hardly seem worthy . . ."

"Oh, madam, you are worthy of it, but that is not my reasoning. I will be frank, Chelynne. I've told no one of my intention, for my purpose may surprise you. If you are not entirely happy in this household you have but to ask and there will be an appointment and apartments at Whitehall. Of course you will have obligations to the court, so think carefully on the matter. I offer this choice."

"How generous of you, sire," she breathed in wonder. She had never expected this kindness from the king. And it was clear to her. She would be free of being at Chad's mercy, but she could not have the ultimate freedom; she would have other duties she detested.

"I'm not as generous as you might think, Chelynne. It certainly doesn't pain me to be surrounded by beautiful women. You have this one chance to look after your own interests. Do so." He lifted her hand and looked again at the beautiful ring. "Think about what you want for yourself, and if you can get it, take it. It's the only way you'll ever be happy."

"Thank you, sire. I'll think on it heavily."

He was on his feet and plopped his hat again on his head. His time was spent. He was in a hurry now with several appointments, all more important than this young countess. Chelynne could imagine the rumors now. She certainly must be thought to be the king's most recent conquest or at least hotly pursued by His Majesty. She almost laughed at the thought. However it thrilled her to have this much attention from the king, she knew she was far from unique. In comparison to what he had given the many women for whom he felt a fondness, his gifts to her were inexpensive and his time minimal. But it was enough to make Chelynne feel very special. A warmness in her heart was a blessing now.

He brushed a kiss on her cheek and smiled his farewell. He stopped at the door to take one last look in her direction. She was so lovely that he pitied Hawthorne. It was as much a curse to have a beautiful wife as to have one with the face of a mule. His shoulders shook with silent laughter as he gained the foot of the stair and saw the earl watching his hurried descent.

"Your Majesty." Chad bowed stiffly.

"My lord," Charles acknowledged. The earl straightened and they met eyes. Charles was in good spirits. Hawthorne was visibly troubled. "I've made my offer to your lady and await her pleasure."

"You're most gracious, Your Majesty," he said, forcing the words out. Damned if it wasn't the greatest curse to have a lusty king. He could hardly fight his own king. Chad was locked into the most precarious position.

"She was surprised with my proposal. I don't believe you did mention it to her."

"Sire, I gave you my word."

"I advised her to think on it carefully," Charles added, amused.

"I thank you for that, sire."

Charles clapped a hand on the younger man's shoulder. He looked with much mirth into those gray eyes. They were stones, smoldering with anger and frustration. But Charles was not concerned. Not at all.

"I think you've always been a man to fight for what you hold dear, Bryant," he said shrewdly.

"When the force of arms is equal, sire," he returned.

Charles fought the urge to laugh outright. "I, too, am a man to go after what I desire. You know that of me, don't you?"

"I've known it for a very long time, sire."

"We're alike in a great many ways, Bryant. If you want something badly enough I believe you'll find a way to have it. You may even win this one."

"And if I do, sire?" he asked boldly.

Charles's eyes twinkled with delight. Games intrigued him, and intrigue was a game to him. "Then I shall find a graceful way to lose."

For only a fragment of an hour Charles gained a fair amount of pleasure. With his usual speed he climbed into his coach and was greeted by Louise with a pretty pout on her face. She did not fancy being left to wait while her royal lover paid a visit to another woman. Charles chuckled and pulled her into his violent and heated embrace, treating himself and his mistress to a prelude of what was to come.

The afternoon sun was high in the sky before Chad had the opportunity to look in on Chelynne. From the door he could watch her, lying so peacefully on her daybed, her honey locks streaming over the velvet cushions. One slender arm escaped the lace dressing gown and rested on Brandy's head. She absently stroked the puppy.

"I thought you were asleep," he said from the doorway.

She jumped, slightly startled, and looked at him. "No, my lord. Just resting."

He strode toward her. He wondered what picture he might strike in her mind. Would he appear the cool and self-confident aristocrat? Would she know that even now he was nervous, quaking inside from being near her?

"If you're tired I'll come back later."

"No need, my lord, I'm —"

"My lord! My lord! Chelynne, have you some aversion to using my name? Do you think I've not noticed how seldom you do? And I've noticed too that the only time is when the hostility between us is gone for some emergency."

"I'm sorry, Chad. I didn't think it much mattered to you."

He paced about a bit nervously, rubbing a hand along the back of his neck where the periwig chafed and annoyed him in the warmer weather. "You know, you've made not a little trouble for me lately. I've admitted my mistake in treating you as I did. I don't know what more you would have of me. I wish to God you'd tell me what you expect of me now!"

"Come sit, Chad." She smiled tolerantly. "Tell me about business."

"About His Majesty's proposal?" he asked, pulling a chair near.

Her eyes widened. "He told you of it?"

"Yes, though he confessed he mentioned it to no one else. He would have the decision be yours alone."

"What is your opinion of it?"

"I didn't think you would have to ask," he replied sullenly.

"I see. So you would like me to accept."

Chad's head shot up in surprise. "You think that? My God, Chelynne, I —" He stopped and drew in his breath. "I gave my word I would not try to persuade you in any way."

"But I wish to know. Please, I wouldn't betray you to the king."

"Truth, madam, I don't give a damn if you do. I've grown quite weary of the secrets and pretending at Whitehall. I don't care if I never have to go back. To be honest, you are my wife and it would suit me if you would act like one, not like a polished whore to the king."

She smiled at his displeasure. "So you think that is his purpose in offering me that post?"

"I can think of no other. Remember, Chelynne, I've been around a bit longer than you. I give you this advice freely. If you accept that appointment thinking you can remain virtuous you will be sadly disappointed. If he's of a mind to have you, he will, despite your token refusal."

Again she smiled, a wise and superior smile that lent him no more comfort. "You act as if it would chafe you sorely to have to share me with another man."

"And that would surprise you? You honestly think me so different from other men?"

"It amuses me. Finally, after so long, you wish to become possessive. And you, a member in good standing of this group of adulterers. With how many, pray, have I shared you?"

His brows drew together in a fierce scowl. "Damn fewer than you might be prepared to believe."

She raised a questioning brow. She was looking down on him, intimidating him with those deep, wise eyes. He ruffled visibly, shifting. It was no easy thing for him to sit still while a mere wisp of a woman judged him.

"Not that it matters," she told him. "It's a little late to be worried about that now."

Chad looked away. He would not be able to convince her otherwise with his oaths. "I would give a king's ransom to start over," he muttered.

"Where would you start, Chad? America?"

"Why would you ask that?"

"It seems to hold that promise of a fresh start. You do have land there, do you not?"

"I have, but I will not have the option to go there. The challenges are enough in England."

"But you could go anywhere, the moment you chose."

He sighed. "I don't think I can make you feel this, Chelynne. I would have to walk away from everything my family has entrusted to me through their deaths. I can hold that land, I can manage the plantation through my overseer and leave something to my heirs, but I cannot build in America and hold what I have here." He reached out and touched her hair, openly desiring her, his eyes clouding over with warmth. "I can want, but I cannot have it all. I have the responsibility of this estate and England has me. That's the way it is."

She looked away from him. "You kill your own dreams. It's no wonder you're not happy."

He turned her face back toward his with a finger. "I don't kill dreams, Chelynne. I live with them. There are some more important than others. To survive here I must live with reality, take what I can and understand what I cannot have. Be practical."

"That's one thing I've known about you from the first," she sighed. "You're a very practical man. I remember the first time . . ." Her voice dropped off and she lowered her eyes.

"The first time what?" he urged.

"I remember the morning after our wedding," she blurted. "I remember your practical solution to the situation you found yourself in. You said that if I was not happy you would set me free."

His face darkened. It was a memory he didn't want to be reminded of. "Yes, I told you that. I wonder why you bring it up now."

"I'm curious. Would you let me go now, if that was my desire?"

Doubt and regret were plain on his face. He closed himself off for a moment of thought. She was expecting a practical answer, one more logical conclusion from the businessman. The arms going around her and drawing her near were a complete surprise. His lips came very close to hers. It was in her mind to put her hands against him and push him away, but she could do nothing. She was passive to his advance. Lightly, caressingly he kissed her. Her eyelids dropped and her head fell back. She trembled and her lips quivered beneath his. Gently, so gently she barely noticed, she was pressed more firmly against him. When after a moment he released her, their eyes locked.

"And now, because of all that has passed between us, you think you would like to give up? Leave me altogether?"

"I only asked 'if,' " she murmured softly.

His lips touched hers again, light and teasing, tempting her. She was amazed at her own lack of control in this lovers' game, for her arms were casually pressed to his and she made no effort to pull away or push at him.

"If you decide you do not want me, I will not hold you against your will. If you cannot live with me as my wife, I cannot force you. But . . . before you make any decisions so final consult your heart. And be sure you haven't left anything untried behind you."

Her lips followed where his led. Lightly, touching and parting, pressing, massaging. It was the most delightful experience, tender yet heated. She couldn't resist the urge to softly stroke his face, tracing the line from his brow to his jaw with trembling fingers.

"Then nothing has changed," she whispered.

"A great deal has changed. I'm in love with you now. I wasn't then." This time when his lips came down on hers the doubts and fears rose within her immediately. She knew too much. She struggled against him weakly and he released his hold on her at once.

"Very well, Chelynne," he said somewhat shakily. "I will not force my affections on you." He took a moment to calm himself, steady his broken will and patch together some restraint. He leaned back in the chair and stared away from her, there being no respite in looking at her. Those ripe, swelling breasts alone were enough to make an animal of him. When he thought it safe, and not a moment before, he looked back at her. "You know where I am and I am at your service, madam, day or night. I hold no stock in whether you come or go and I give you my word, I will not have you unwillingly. I suggest, for both our sakes, that you not have any doubts in your mind when you decide whether you stay or go."

"That sounds like an invitation to your bed, sir. No promises attached?"

"It is exactly that," he said coolly. "You've invested a considerable amount of time in this marriage. You should have all the facts. That," he said emphatically, "happens to be one of the most important."

As he rose to leave he looked as commanding as ever, not upset, not confused. Chelynne was still tremulous. She dropped one hand to her stomach as if the activity within would burst out. He had stirred her to a dangerous level. It was with every fiber of her self that she clung to composure.

"I have business, Chelynne. I'll call on you later." He bowed shortly and was gone.

The pattern followed the same course. He looked in on her daily, keeping close personal guard on her state of health. She wished to be shrewish, to lash out at him and hurt him. Faced with his warmth, she could find no will to fight him. He was devoted and gentle. There was no pressure, no fuel for her hate. Her confusion mounted. Her heart and mind were torn to shreds.

There was no reason to be excused from the affairs at the palace once her illness faded. The dinner honoring the king and queen would be attended by many and Chad confessed he would have to be there with or without her company. He asked her so kindly that she accepted.

As on all the other occasions he did not compliment her appearance. She was forced to decide from the shade of gray his eyes bore whether or not she had pleased him with her choice of gown.

She took up his rote, aping his indifferent manner, and refused to praise his handsomeness. But thoughts of him brought the thumping in her heart and a deepness to her eyes. He was such a fine figure, so bold and hard were his good looks. He could be as richly garbed as all the young gallants and never give off that foppish air. It was no wonder so many women watched him, desired him. No wonder he had had so many previous loves. She knew she would have fallen helplessly in love with him whether or not he had married her.

This night, perhaps because she had been so ill, he stayed close by her side. He hovered there, guarding her as if she were his ward, not his wife. He made no comment or gesture as they heard the gossip together. And what they heard was not complimentary to her. The rumors suggested poison and miscarriage and she was certain there were other things even worse floating around. But she smiled and shook her head, blaming a rather frightening attack of the ague.

The comments were hard to stop. "We're anxious for the news of your first heir." "Isn't it nice that you've time to adjust yourself to marriage before suffering the ills of pregnancy." "I have a friend whose astronomer found the exact day, coming only once in the year." "My tiring woman has the recipe for a draught that makes one terribly fertile."

Through this Chelynne held her composure. She wished Chad were not so near. He discreetly looked away during this women's drivel, but she knew he had heard. He couldn't possibly know how it affected her.

When she saw the king approaching them, she felt a surge of relief. She beamed her smile across the room to him. He floated his back to her and quickened his step.

"You've recovered very well, madam. You're as lovely as ever."

"Thank you, sire," she replied demurely.

"Have you anything you wish to speak to me about?"

She glanced at Chad, patiently waiting and trying not to scowl. "I'm afraid not, Your Majesty. This is in fact my first outing."

"There's no hurry, my dear. I'm a patient fellow." He looked around him. "I have to be."

"I'll be speaking to you soon . . ." she began.

"I told you, didn't I, to take all the time you need?"

She nodded, pleased.

"Will you be offended if I steal the earl away from you for a time? He doesn't seem eager to leave your side tonight."

"She's been weak, sire," Chad defended himself. He didn't like looking like a doting husband to his king, especially when that same one was an amused opponent.

"I'll be only a moment, madam," Charles said, giving her a slight bow. "I much prefer my diversions, but affairs of state do arise to interrupt me from time to time." He gave her a most obvious wink and she couldn't help giggling lightly. Chad did not think the situation amusing at all.

"Could I persuade you to escort me in the direction of the dressing room? I think I would be more content to wait there."

Both were eager to comply. Charles loved a game and was playing this one to his supreme amusement. The lines on Bryant's face were so obvious, so passionate. He fully expected to lose his wife to the king.

And Chad took her arm to prevent Charles from escorting her alone. He was not eager to leave her in a room full of lusty gallants, no matter how careful they were these days.

Chelynne relaxed on a couch after pressing a cool cloth to her face. It seemed as if she had been on her feet for hours, but it had been only a short time. Her exhaustion came from smiling away all the tactless remarks that had been made to her. She closed her eyes and let Whitehall fade away for a time.

Behind her eyes she envisioned herself facing the king, shouting, "I'm sorry, sire, I could never be a Lady to the Queen's Bedchamber. I hate this place! Hate it!"

She knew she would never do that, because she loved him; because she was grateful for his alliance and she wouldn't weaken the bond. Whatever the rest of the court thought, whatever all of England thought, she was afraid to breathe lest she destroy that caring.

"Resting, my lady? Tired already from your affairs?"

She opened her eyes to see the face she hated. Gwen stared down at her with that amused and victorious smile.

"I've been ill, madam. I'm sure you've heard more of it than I have."

She laughed wickedly. "I've heard some nasty tales, to tell you truly. I'm sure you don't want to hear them now."

"Are you sure you weren't responsible for most of them?"

"I?" She raised a dubious brow. "Of course not, madam. I wouldn't dare."

Chelynne was expressionless. She looked away from Gwen. She wanted nothing to do with this baiting game. She was far too weary.

"For a time I thought perhaps Chad had had enough of your games, but now I see that can't be true. He wouldn't be panting after you like a faithful pup."

Chelynne slowly rose and went to sit before the mirror. She dabbed a little powder on her cheeks, steeling her mind against Gwen.

"You had us all mighty fooled, I admit that much. Your innocent act. Not daring to trouble yourself by taking up with the king! You've had a grand time, I doubt not, playing the virtuous maid. Is that what you've been after all along? Royal traffic?"

Chelynne slowly turned and looked at the woman. "Madam, you cannot be blamed for assuming others would take the same road you have traveled. I understand the reason you cannot recognize virtue."

Gwen laughed loudly at that, not offended at all. "Virtue, is it? My, my, whoring goes by some mighty splendid names in your circle."

Chelynne sighed. "I cannot believe you are real, madam," she returned dispassionately.

"Real enough," Gwen sneered. "Real enough to have had enough of your simple game. I am amazed. So sweetly you pull it together. Tell me, how did you convince Chad into such a willing cuckold? You must be mighty tired."

"Gwen!" she snapped. "Have done with this vulgarity. I'm in no humor for it."

"Oh, you're in no humor for it! I protest, madam. You seem to be in grand humor, clinging to your earl like a twisting vine and playing all the while with the king. The sweet little countess! The one virtuous woman at court! I was as fooled as the rest. I thought you nothing of an adventuress. Now I see your schemings! To have them both!"

"So, that's what it is," Chelynne breathed in wonder. "You love him still!"

Gwen only laughed. "Love him?" She moved near the mirror and touched a tight curl at the base of her neck. She saw her age, the tired, listless look about the eyes. It was difficult for her to control the urge to scratch and claw Chelynne's lovely young face. "No, I don't love him! Do you think I would be chasing a man with not one wife, but two? Little countess," she sneered. "They're all laughing at you! All of them! You're nothing! If I wanted him I could have him like that!"

She raised her hand to give a quick snap of her fingers but never completed the action.

"Madam!"

She turned slowly, sick in the pit of her stomach, to face the earl of Bryant, his face twisted with rage. She had no idea how long he had been standing there in the doorway, how much he had heard. Inside she trembled almost uncontrollably, outside she was cool as ice.

He took two steps into the room and faced Gwen. She was a large woman, nearly as tall as he, but faced with his anger she seemed meek and small. It was obvious; the rage that filled him was eager to be spent.

"Two wives," he said. "And who do you make my other wife to be, Lady Graystone?"

Gwen lifted her chin fearlessly. She could either betray her own plots or play the innocent to the end. Inwardly she retreated. "Anne —" she started.

He grabbed her by the arms and brought her face close to his. "Anne has been dead for six years! What game do you play now?"

Gwen trembled in his relentless grasp. "Mondeloy," she breathed. "He told me your wife lives. He showed me where you keep her and I've seen you there. 'Tis your son abiding there rightly enough, you could not deny that. And the woman there is heavy with child."

"Mondeloy? Doubtless you invented the story and plotted with him. Were Anne living, there would be no need to steal the marriage contract that proves my son is my legitimate heir!" He cast her away, wiping his hands on his coat sleeves as if the touch of her had sullied him. He went straight to Chelynne and drew her to her feet.

Once again he faced Gwen. "The boy is my son and the woman is the wife of a friend. She is in my care and under my protection."

He looked down at Chelynne and saw the confused eyes staring back at him. He touched her cheek. "Are you all right, my love?"

Dumbly, her heart pounding within her breast, she simply nodded. Though she could not speak she questioned him with her eyes. Chad looked at her with confusion of his own for a moment. Then his mouth formed a rigid line and he snapped his head back to Gwen. "So that's what you've been about. You had your sport with Chelynne, hoping to convince her that ours was not a marriage true . . . but that I was wed to another?"

Gwen was beaten at one game but held out for a possible advantage in another. She turned her head toward the mirror and smoothed her hair, trying to seem bored with his accusation. "The possibility seemed real enough to me. How would I know Mondeloy lied?" She turned back to Chad and smiled lazily. "I've seen you with the woman. You seemed more to her than her husband's acquaintance."

Chad spoke slowly and clearly. "Do not hope to intimidate me as you would other personages of breeding who would not understand your disgusting methods. I've warned you more often than I care to remember, Gwen. It is only in deference to my wife's distaste for violence that I leave you untouched now."

It was some instinct for survival that prompted Gwen to speak hastily, defending herself. "You play the lover scorned, darling. Speaking up to me in the presence of your wife is most chivalrous, I'm sure, but does the little lamb know what we've been to each other?"

Chad struggled for control. He let his eyes move over Gwen with one long glance before returning to her face. Disgust and utter contempt glittered in his eyes. "I believe she can well enough guess what you've been to me, and to a score of others."

He moved to take Chelynne's arm and lead her from the room, not daring to look back in Gwen's direction. His hands trembled with the desire to find her throat and squeeze the life out of her.

Gwen felt something inside of her collapse when he walked away. She knew it was for the last time; there would never again be a method to have him back, even temporarily. She fought the urge to cry tears of rage and pain. In a sudden fit of temper she whirled, intending to chase after them. She froze in her tracks. There, in the frame of the door that had just seen the earl's departure with his wife, stood the king, a faint, cynical smile twisting his lips.

"Your Majesty, I —"

"Never mind your excuses, madam. I have long prided myself in being surrounded by the most beautiful women. Women of quality, with breeding and grace. I am most disappointed in my own poor judgment this time."

"Your Majesty, I beg your forgiveness, I was —"

"Of course I forgive you, my dear. I know how jealousy smarts and I know the pain of final defeat."

"I'm most grate—"

"The court moves to Windsor soon. You may go where you will. Your company is no longer desired."

"Your Majesty!"

"My mind is made. There is nothing more to say."

Gwen stiffened. Chelynne was all to blame. She never once considered her outburst wrong and certainly not deserving of this punishment. "She's an army to protect her now," she murmured.

Charles shook his head in exasperation. Gwen had had her place with Charles in his more frivolous moments, as many others had. She simply couldn't bind him in any way, as no one could. Her beauty was admirable, but she was as expendable as any.

"Women never cease to amaze me. Instead of loathing her for her success, why not take a lesson from her?"

Gwen died a little at his every word. She was dismissed from Chad, rejected by the king and his court. Everything that held any importance for her was gone.

"It's a little late for that, Your Majesty," she said with harsh resentment.

"Yes, madam. It is."

Chelynne was not put through any more that night. The confrontation with Gwen had been the final straw and Chad took her directly to their coach.

"Now I see what has happened," Chad said. "Gwen compounded your doubts tenfold with her story . . . and you never came to me. Why?"

Chelynne shuddered inside. She turned her eyes up to him and spoke quietly, still shaken by the turn of events. Relief was something she wasn't feeling yet. "I intended to. I went to your study straightaway, the moment I left the coach. She took me there to see the woman she said was your wife." Chelynne laughed ruefully. "I believed her . . . and how I hated you! I would have faced you then, but I heard you screaming that you would do away with 'her' once and for all." Tears collected in Chelynne's eyes and her voice caught. "I thought you meant me," she fairly whispered.

Chad's arms went around her. "My God, what you've been through because of me! If only I had had the sense to tell —"

"But you are not all to blame, Chad. I am at fault. I found the paper you spoke of. It was hidden among my aunt's letters at Welby Manor. I knew Harry had stolen it."

"You have it?"

"I had it taken safely away and stored in my coffer at Hawthorne House." She laughed nervously. "I wouldn't have found it at all, but that I was indeed searching for something of my parents in that house. What I told you was never a lie."

"Even then you didn't come to me." He looked into her eyes. "Did you fear me so much?"

"Fear you? I feared losing you." She sniffed and fought the urge to crumble into sobs. "If there was any chance that you could love me, however slight, I would wait upon that day."

"Even when you thought I hated you!" Chad held her closely, kissing her brow, her hair. "And I have loved you! From the first I loved you! For all the months that I turned on you, 'twas my own heart I held in exile." He lifted her chin to look into her eyes. "The woman I spoke of that day was Gwen. Bestel told me she had come to call on you. She had seduced me with a plan to retrieve that record of marriage from Harry. She has been in his close company for months. Together they've played us for fools and sought to tear us apart."

"And that was Harry's intention? Only to hurt me?" She shook her head in frustration. "I will never understand why he hates me so."

"He is not simply mischievous, Chelynne. In gaining that paper he took part in the murder of the priest and the burning of that church. A young laundry girl was raped, beaten, and left for dead. She names Harry as her attacker. But she will not swear to it again. She is too frightened."

Chelynne's eyes were wide and stunned. She had never suspected Harry capable of such crimes. "And you were silent!"

"I had no proof. Possession of that record would have sent him to the Tower, but it was too well hidden. Even now he could deny having a hand in stealing it."

Chelynne was quiet for a moment, digesting this news. Finally she spoke, not daring to look at him. "You suspected me." Chad started to speak but she cut him off. "If you believed me innocent you would have brought your son home to me."

"In the beginning, perhaps. Early in our marriage I wondered if you were involved, but later it was only because I had held the secret for too long. I looked for a way to tell you."

"And the woman?" she asked quietly.

He sighed. "The wife of John Bollering. He lives. We staged the duel and pretended him dead to protect him from Lord Shayburn. Even now we await the king's decision. He sits with Shayburn in the Tower."

"And you could not tell me that he lives?" she asked with a strong hint of anger in her voice.

His arms tightened around her. "It agonized me to see you suffer with guilt because you thought him dead, but I knew that if you even unwittingly let it slip that he was alive, it could cost him his life. What John has done in Bratonshire could still have violent repercussions. Shayburn literally stole those lands from John's father, and John has turned Shayburn's game back on him. He was the thief who saved you from Captain Alex."

Chelynne gasped. "He sent the knife to me!" Chad nodded.

"Chad, he pitied my state! He hoped I would guess that he lived!"

"I think perhaps that was his intent."

"What will you do now? Could John be hurt for this?"

"I think he will come out of it better than either of us dared hope. My work is done. I cannot hurt Gwen any more than she has hurt herself with her deception. I cannot help John anymore; that is left to the king. And Harry . . . I leave to you. He is your kin. If it is in your mind to forgive him, I will do my best to understand. If you will bring charges against him I will support you."

Chelynne was quiet for a moment. "My work is done, Chelynne," Chad said. "I know I've had a poor way of showing you how I feel. Even with all that has passed between us I believe there has always been love. Long ago I should have seen it and acted, but I was a fool. Even the strongest men are weak in some things."

Just when she would have answered him the door to their coach opened and the footman looked within. Neither of them had even realized they were already home. Reluctantly Chelynne drew herself out of his arms and let the footman help her down.

Wordlessly they climbed the stairs. Chad held her arm, and when they came to his chamber door he paused and looked down into her eyes. His were aglow with warmth and sincerity. "We have allowed time to deal with family and friends, even with those who would tear us apart, but we have taken no time for ourselves. Our time has finally come, love, and I will hold you to me. Let me be your arm, for I would give you strength. And you . . . be my heart, for I need you to teach me the gentle art of loving."

Chelynne looked toward her chamber door. There was a light from within that told her Stella waited patiently to help her make ready for bed. She wondered what words she could use to invite him to join her there. Then she realized no words were necessary. She turned in his arms and told him with her lips. Her arms held him fiercely and she kissed him with a passion even she did not know existed within her. He lifted her into his arms and carried her through the door to his bedroom. With his foot the door was slammed behind them and no servant would dare touch that portal until morning's light.

NINETEEN

UMMER IN THE COUNTRY was flooded with green, with the sweet smell of flowers and the melody of birds. Chelynne came awake slowly and watched the curtains dance in the morning breeze. She moved closer to the warmth of her husband's body and let herself feel the full joy of her contentment. Here, in the lord's chamber at Hawthorne House, she spent many mornings like this one in remembering the beautiful moments that had led to her comfortable place beside Chad.

Her mind voluntarily blotted out the troubles and recaptured the night she had surrendered the full sum of her love to him. She would never forget the love words whispered against her ear when Chad spoke of months given to foolish exile, the long nights alone when he would have had her at his side, and the pain of longing.

That night he was the very image of the warrior in her mind. He was in control. He knew everything there was to know about love-making and she was innocent of it. He was unhurried and methodical, as if leading her down a path in which every curve and turn must be carefully measured or the destination would be altered.

Her transition from acquiescence to need was a gradual magic, her abandon spontaneous and her response natural. When she arched against him in impatience she heard his voice, thick and muffled against her ear.

"This once it will hurt and never again."

He knew the way, even in that first coupling, to possess her body and soul. She gave herself entirely into his care, silently praying he would soon deliver her. Their gentle lovemaking became a wild and frenzied union that exploded within her, blurring and bursting into a wonder she had never before known. He had never doubted he was the first. It could not have been more beautiful in her mind if it had taken place on her wedding night.

At Chelynne's insistence Chad's son was brought to them that very next morning. Chelynne was charmed by Kevin and loved him at once. She found happiness in his presence and vowed he would never be sent to live in another woman's house again. She let herself be consumed by the duties of wife and of mother to her husband's son.

When she thought it impossible to find more joy in her life, yet another blessing came to them. John Bollering was given full title to the lands that had belonged to his father. The king did not wish to appear too kind and levied a heavy fine for the destruction that had occurred in Bratonshire. John willingly promised the sum would be delivered to the court at Windsor.

They all went to the country then, where there was a feeling of rebirth on the land. Newly sown seeds took life and a rich harvest was promised. When summer was full upon the land Chelynne watched the birth of an heir to the Bollering lands. Chelynne learned firsthand how carefully and dutifully Chad managed his holdings. The people grew to love him easily, and she grew to love his people. She found the immenseness of Hawthorne House could fit into the palm of her hand as the servants worked to please her.

Chad's great energy for his duties had not vanished and if anything it was increased. But Chelynne did not despair when he rode off now, for she knew he would return to her for his ease. She would knead the tenseness out of his tired muscles while he discussed with her the needs of his people. She would warm his bath and keep his meals and mind his needs as carefully as a mother tends a newborn babe.

But it was here, in this great lord's chamber, that she learned what it meant to be the wife of the earl of Bryant. When the door to this chamber was closed she was assured of adventure, tenderness and fulfillment. His methods were varied and unpredictable and he brought to life the most deeply hidden spark of her passion. His hunger for her was matched only by her eagerness for him.

Just the thought of feeling his arms around her stirred the embers and she reached for him. His response was automatic as his arms drew her near and he buried his face in her breasts.

"Ah, wench," he mumbled. "In all my days I cannot remember such joy in waking."

She laughed softly, knowingly. "I hadn't expected such eagerness this morn. I thought I had satisfied your lust at last."

"Aha! And you are so weary of my demands that I wake to find you fondling me!" He kissed her cheeks and brought his lips close to her ear. "Do you know what I do to a woman who teases me thus?"

His lips touching her brought the most delicious sensations. "The hour is early," she whispered. "We needn't hurry to break the fast."

His lips found hers and she melted into his heated embrace. Just as they would have been lost in this early morning bliss, the door to their chamber crashed open and they bolted apart, covering themselves as best they could.

"Good morning, sir." Kevin bowed. "And madam." They stared at him in wonder. It was scarcely past dawn and he was fully dressed, sporting his miniature sword at his belt and wearing a very adult-looking plumed hat. "You promised you would rise early this morn, sir. Today is the day I will learn to hold a spear so I can ride with you in the hunt."

Chad cocked a brow. "Am I allowed to dress and eat first?"

"But sir, Sir John will arrive early and I would show him what I've learned. There's not so much time if —"

"All right. I'll be down directly."

"Thank you, sir." He beamed.

"Kevin?"

"Yes, sir?"

"Go first to Mrs. Connolly and ask her to school you on the proper way to enter a room. It shouldn't take long."

Kevin broke into a broad smile. He was very much like Chad in his looks, except when he smiled. That bright and wild smile must have belonged to his mother. It touched a place in Chelynne's heart and she knew why Chad had loved Anne so deeply.

Kevin swept off his hat and bowed before them. "Yes, sir." With a straight back and long strides that greatly resembled his father's, Kevin left the room.

"I must be up and about my son's business," Chad muttered with exasperation.

Chelynne giggled softly and tickled the hair on his chest. "He speaks true. John and Tess will be here early in the day. There is a great deal to do."

Chad threw his legs over the bed and stood. "And it will no doubt be days before we are allowed rest."

"I do think him too young to ride in the hunt," Chelynne told him.

"And so do I," he grunted, reaching for his breeches. "But I am too old to withstand his begging." He found his shirt and stockings and sat on the bed to finish dressing. "I will give him a small horse and personally keep him well behind the action. He will only think he's joined the hunt." He pulled on his boots and dropped a kiss on her brow before leaving. "If you have any love for me you will give me only daughters. They don't require the energy sons do."

Chelynne stayed in her bed for a long while, contemplating the chores that would command them now. John and Chad must oversee the harvest and with that came the celebrations within the farming villages. The people would expect their lord and lady to be present for the fairs and games. The earl of Bryant would begin the festivities with the christening of John's son. Hawthorne House would be opened to all those who would bring gifts and pay their respects. Great quantities of food and drink would be set out and boar and mutton would be roasted over open pits. As soon as the christening and party were past, Chelynne would have to accompany Chad on a tour of the smaller farming villages on his lands and view their celebrations.

It was for this long week of celebrating that Chelynne and Tess together would plan. John and Chad rode with their men to hunt and prepare for the feasts and spend an equal amount of time in looking over the land. Each of them worked long days in making sure every detail was set. They were convinced at last that everything was ready on the eve before the christening.

The two couples settled in the sitting room to relax after long days of preparation. It seemed that only moments had passed when a guard wearing the livery of Chad's house interrupted them. Chelynne had become accustomed to this now that she understood his many responsibilities, but she hoped he would not have to ride out tonight when the hour was so late and the days ahead promised to be so taxing.

After speaking with his man for a few moments Chad returned to face her uneasily. "Chelynne, Harry has been found and brought here to me, as I requested."

Harry had successfully eluded Chad's men since Chelynne came to possess the stolen record of marriage. She had had hopes he would disappear forever, but those hopes were dashed tonight.

"It could wait," Chad offered.

"No," she said quickly. "It's waited long enough. I won't have the coming days spoiled. We'll have it done tonight."

John stood as if he would take Tess and leave Chelynne and Chad alone to deal with Harry, but Chelynne quickly stopped him. "No, John. Stay and stand witness to what he says. You were the first to find him guilty of his crimes."

Chelynne sat looking at her hands, her mind sorting out what must be done. Chad came to stand before her and dropped to one knee. "Tell me what you would have done. I will do it in your stead."

Her eyes lifted to his and she smiled her thanks. "You were right, my lord. This is mine to do." She reached for his hand. "Stand by me, Chad, and be my arm," she whispered.

When Harry came into the room it was several moments before Chelynne could look at him. It had been only a few months since she had seen him, but she hardly recognized him. He was thin and gaunt and his clothes ill cared for. His way of life had not helped his looks.

"I've learned that in stealing the record of the earl of Bryant's first marriage, you burned a church and killed a priest. Harry, what say you to this charge?"

He bowed mockingly and grinned. "I say I had nothing to do with either, dear cousin."

"I am not your dear cousin now. Please answer to your claim of innocence."

"Cousin," he sneered, pressing his face closer. "Dear." Chad moved to stand behind the chair Chelynne occupied. He stared coldly at Harry. Harry did not tremble in fear, but he did straighten his spine and take on a more serious look. He knew the earl of Bryant would love to break his neck, and would, given the smallest excuse. "I claim innocence on the grounds that Captain Alex, whose company I was in, committed those crimes."

"I name you responsible, being it was by your order."

"My order?" he asked, laughing. "I was ordered by another, as was Alex." Chad's shocked expression led him on. "Aye, 'twas my lady Graystone commissioned me to get my hands on the thing and hide it away. I had no idea murder would be done."

"And how did she know about the marriage?" Chad asked anxiously.

Harry shrugged insolently. "She overheard you and your father speak of the place you were wed. She set me to the task on the morning after you were wed."

Chelynne looked up at Chad and then back to Harry. "What was Lady Graystone's intention?" she asked.

Harry laughed. "For a long while she was uncertain . . . until I told her you could be convinced that His Lordship was married twice. Then it was in her mind to draw you away from your husband and she would step in to console him." He scratched his chin thoughtfully. "She nearly succeeded, didn't she?"

Chelynne was neither amused nor relieved. "For the part you've played in this, Harry, you should be severely punished. You've caused countless problems with your own lust for vengeance. Many have been hurt because you would —"

"You will not sit judgment on me!" he shouted. "You're no one to sit judgment on me!"

"I would see the money drawn from your own purse to rebuild that church but I fear you would bleed Welbering dry for the sum. My lady Graystone could afford —"

"Lady Graystone took ship when she was excused from the court. I doubt you'll ever see that good lady again. And I will not answer to your judgments. You take a grave chance with me, princess. Aren't you just a little afraid I'll tell the truth about you?"

Chelynne drew in her breath for courage. "You see me surrounded by my friends and loved ones," she said, gesturing with her eyes to Chad, John and Tess. "You are the one without allies in this room, Harry. Perhaps I should warn you."

"Then your husband knows he's married one of the king's many bastards?"

John's feet hit the floor as he rose furiously, but too late, for Chad had already come around his wife's chair and seized Harry by the front of his shirt. Chad was ready to beat the insolent young lord soundly but Chelynne's voice came through loudly, stopping him before he could do Harry any real injury. "Chad!" Then more calmly, "Chad, it is truth."

"Chelynne," he pleaded. "There's no truth to that. I have long been aware of the rumor."

Chelynne shook her head dejectedly. It was just as well out. "The king admitted the possibility, my lord. It could be so. And there was a letter . . . from my mother . . ."

Chad turned angrily on Harry. "And you, no doubt, nurtured that fantasy," he growled. "Tell her what you know."

Harry looked at the earl in confusion and held silent.

Chad shook him soundly and the earl's greater size and power rattled Harry's thinking considerably. "Tell her what you know! I know you hold the truth to that lie!"

Finally Harry's yelps and pleas indicated he had decided to cooperate and Chad set him on his feet.

"There was never any doubt," Harry said bleakly. "We share a common sire. Madelynne only took to the king's bed to protect my father." He hung his head and muttered, "Likely she knew she was with child."

Chelynne rose a little with every word and stood trembling and staring at Harry with wide eyes.

"How is this known," she breathed.

"My mother has always known. And she has always hated you for the importance you've had in my father's life."

Chelynne sank into her chair, the life drawn out of her. She barely heard Chad's words.

"You will be dealt with, Harry, in good time. For now there is too much astir in my house and on my lands to take the time with you. But you will remain as my guest and if you take that to mean you are a prisoner here, you are right. Your treachery will not be easily forgotten and I will work hard and long to find a way to force you to labor honestly for your retribution."

Chad opened the doors to the sitting room and motioned his men to take Harry away. Still Chelynne could not look up. She felt the wetness on her cheeks before she realized she was weeping. It was not until Chad came to stand before her that she was able to look at him.

"How did you know?" she asked quietly.

Chad knelt and spoke softly. "Sheldon meant to warn me in the event a slander was brought against your name. I'm sure he never underestimated Harry's actions. In his attempt to assure me it was not so he spoke too fondly of Madelynne. Even in my hardened state it was apparent he loved your mother . . . and he cared for you with a fatherly pride." He gently touched her cheek. "You bear some resemblance to the Mondeloys, cherie. It was not hard to guess. But in his eagerness to convince me, Sheldon did not think to mention that you were aware of this rumor that followed your mother. For that reason I never mentioned it."

"I cannot feel shame, my lord," she sighed. "I knew only love for Sheldon." She looked at her hands again and murmured, "But you have been dealt with dishonestly, my lord."

He lifted her chin to look into her eyes. "It was here, in Hawthorne House, that your uncle begged a moment of my time. He opened his chest to let me see his heart, his life. In that moment of honesty I nearly told him of Anne, of my reluctance to marry. Had I been as honest as Sheldon was, the problems we faced this year past would have been minor. We have learned, I think, that there is nothing to fear from the truth."

He drew her to her feet and placed a light kiss on her lips. "If you would cast me away now I would fight for you," she murmured.

He chuckled deep in his throat and lifted her into his arms. She gasped in surprise at being handled so in front of guests, but Chad only laughed roguishly and carried her from the room and toward the stair. He did not pause to bid his guests a proper good night and Tess tugged at her husband's sleeve.

"Did he answer to you, John? Will he stand as godfather to our son?"

John's attention was drawn reluctantly away from the earl's departure. It was not the earl's actions that brought the smile to John's lips, but the contentment that had shown on his friend's face in recent weeks. He patted Tess's hand fondly. "He will." His eyes indicated the sitting room door. "And he will be asking me to return the favor before the next harvest, mark my word."

Robyn Carr was born in 1951 in St. Paul, Minnesota, and lives with her husband and two children in Sacramento, California. *Chelynne* is her first book.